HERALD
OF THE
STORM

Book One in the STEELHAVEN series

HERALD
OF THE
STORM

RICHARD FORD

headline

First published in 2013
by HEADLINE PUBLISHING GROUP

1

Cataloguing in Publication Data is available from the British Library

ISBN 978 1 4722 0392 2 (Hardback)
ISBN 978 0 7553 9403 6 (Trade paperback)

Typeset in Minion by Palimpsest Book Production Limited,
Falkirk, Stirlingshire

Printed and bound in Great Britain by
Clays Ltd, St Ives plc

Headline's policy is to use papers that are natural, renewable
and recyclable products and made from wood grown in sustainable
forests. The logging and manufacturing processes are expected
to conform to the environmental regulations of the
country of origin.

HEADLINE PUBLISHING GROUP
An Hachette UK Company
338 Euston Road
London NW1 3BH

www.headline.co.uk
www.hodderheadline.com

For Wendy

PROLOGUE

Massoum Abbasi hated the sea. The sickly salt smell and the incessant noise bothered him more than he could ever express. He was a Dravhistan nomad, a man of the desert, used to the silence of sand, a parched and arid landscape, and endless blue sky. Roiling cloud, clashing wave and screeching gull were alien to his experience, but Massoum was willing to endure this, for the reward was great indeed.

The fastest route from the Dravhistan port of Aluk Vadir to the cityport of Steelhaven was by ship, and so reluctantly Massoum had paid for his passage and embarked on his voyage. A man could suffer much for riches, they said, and Massoum had believed them, right up until the first storm hit. The *Reigning Sceptre* was almost entirely crewed by brash westerners who could laugh in the face of the lashing winds and the rumbling skies. Though the caravel was picked up and tossed from wave to towering wave, its crew went about their duties unaffected, as though it were routine.

For Massoum it felt as if the world was ending.

He had clung to the rigging for grim death, his fingers white from the fearsomeness of his grip and the chill of the storm winds. The robes he wore to pass himself off as a merchant were covered in vomit and his headscarf had blown away in the gale, exposing his long hair to the elements, but he cared little. Survival was all that mattered. And, of course, despite the raging torrent that threatened to fling him from the deck at any moment, he had survived.

But then, Massoum Abbasi was a born survivor – a man used to taking risks and claiming the consequent rewards. In the past his skills had been much sought after, his benefactors generous with their payments.

1

Abbasi had been trained in the differing philosophies of war by the Shadir of Gul Rasa and been military adviser to three desert princes. He had brokered peace between the warring sultanates of Jal Nassan, acted as diplomat to Kali Ustman Al Talib in the court of the Han-Shar Sunlords and been herald for the Egrit of Rashamen. Over the years his reputation had grown so that the mere rumour of his arrival was enough to spur the richest sultan's court to greet him with a flower-strewn path and a sumptuous banquet. Times had indeed been good, and Massoum had lived the noble's life, lauded as the wisest of counsellors and surrounded by men of influence and opulence who called themselves his friends.

But all that had changed.

Such a trivial act had brought him low: the slightest of smiles towards the Kali's twelfth wife – not even his favourite – but it had been enough to spark rumour in court, enough to have the viziers whispering and the eunuchs chortling in their high-pitched voices, and that was that. Banished. Cast out to the four winds. At least he had been spared the executioner's blade; that was one thing he could thank the Kali for.

The last few years had been hard for Massoum. There was little use for his talents on the filthy streets of Dravhistan's cities. Where before his honeyed words and impartial wisdom had been much sought after, now they were of little use. Hunger and fear were his constant companions and he had almost become desperate enough to consider manual labour; but just when it looked as if the light of Asta'Dovashu had abandoned him completely, the god of the Desert Wind had suddenly smiled down.

Massoum Abbasi thought back to that night – the night he had been offered riches beyond imagining for the simple loaning of his talents. Acceptance had brought him here, to this place, to this city far from his homeland, and he was suddenly wondering if even all the riches of the eastern kingdoms would have been worth the journey.

From the deck he could just see the city of Steelhaven in the distance, squatting on the coastline like a giant ants' nest. Unpleasant though Massoum's journey had been, he knew that worse was to come once he set foot in that foul metropolis. Its reputation was infamous, even in far-off Dravhistan – the danger of its narrow twisting streets, the lack of culture, the savage manners and foul breath of its inhabitants. Not to mention their tasteless food and their insistence on heaving ale down their necks until it made them vomit.

Massoum would have to adjust his usual stringent adherence to etiquette when dealing with these ignorant westerners. His name must be short and sweet – none of them would be able, or even care, to address him properly by his given title of Massoum Am Kalhed Las Fahir Am Jadar Abbasi.

As orders were barked across deck in the gruff Teutonian language, Massoum gripped the embroidered leather bag he carried across one shoulder more tightly, pulling it across the front of his body in a protective gesture. The bag was his lifeline, containing the tools of his trade, and he instinctively wanted to protect them. Though its contents might seem mundane, worthless even, the bag was of more value than anyone could have guessed. And that was the whole point. If stopped and questioned Massoum could easily pass himself off as a merchant here to broker trade. The city guard or inquisition would be hard pressed to prove him complicit in any crime, for should they suspect his intentions only one crime would fit the bill – treason. The last thing he wanted was his head spiked atop Steelhaven's front gate, ready to greet Amon Tugha's army as it arrived to raze the city to ash.

'Almost there, my eastern friend.'

It was a deep voice that nudged him from his thoughts, the words spoken in a rare northern dialect of Teutonian, but Massoum recognised the language and inflection as though it were his own. His mastery of the many western tongues was second to none. That was, after all, one of the reasons he had been chosen for this task.

'Indeed,' he replied, turning with a smile to face the first mate, whose bald head gleamed in the afternoon sun. 'As pleasant as this journey has been, it must unfortunately come to an end all too soon.'

The first mate gave him a knowing wink – it was clear to all the crew that Massoum had loathed the voyage from start to finish.

'You have business in Steelhaven, easterner?'

Massoum felt the skin prickle at the nape of his neck, though he kept his warm smile firmly affixed to his face. Though most likely an innocent question, simple small talk, it would be foolish to take risks and reveal the truth, especially when he was so close to shore where he could become lost in the labyrinthine streets and leave anyone taking too much of an interest far behind.

'Yes,' he replied. 'I am a merchant brokering trade. A seller of spices. I understand Steelhaven is a great market and its traders are willing to pay a fair price.'

This brought a wide grin to the first mate's lips. 'Fair price, eh? Well, just be careful where you tread, traveller. You might find yourself with something you didn't bargain for. Steelhaven takes no prisoners, especially not the foreign sort. Watch your back and your purse at all times, y'hear?'

3

Massoum merely bowed his thanks for the needless advice, touching a finger to his brow then his lips in the traditional manner of the Dravhistan nomad. The first mate nodded before making himself busy elsewhere on deck.

Turning back towards the prow, Massoum watched the city looming ever larger. The ship became a hive of activity as burly seamen cut the sails, barking at one another above the cry of seagulls. Steelhaven, which before had appeared from the distant sea as a massive stone monolith, slowly revealed itself in all its glory. Towers rose from beyond the vast battlements of the curtain wall – not the domed spires he was so used to in his homeland, but square, robust affairs, looming and oppressive. If such was the architectural preference of the city's tallest and most opulent minarets he could only imagine what kind of squat monstrosities had been built within their shadow. Above them all rose two great statues depicting warriors, a man and a woman; he carrying a vast hammer, she a spear and shield. Arlor and Vorena, the ancient heroes revered as gods by the Teutonians. Seeing these monoliths for the first time, peering across the city with ancient stone eyes, Massoum couldn't help but be impressed.

The ship cruised in towards port, and Massoum took yet more solace from the huge harbour, constructed in a crescent shape and forming a bay filled with an array of different boats flying sails of every colour. The *Reigning Sceptre* wove expertly between them, heading for an empty mooring that sat in the apex of the bay, directly below the shadow of Steelhaven's vast harbour gate.

Ropes flung ashore were deftly caught by diligent dockworkers and hastily secured to mooring plinths. Before the *Reigning Sceptre* had even come to rest against a wooden pier, a gangplank was thrust out from the bow and a dozen sailors began to loose ropes and nets constraining several piles of cargo secured on deck.

Massoum moved forward, not waiting to be told to disembark. He had paid his passage in full, and was not about to ask permission to rid himself of the ship that had been so troublesome to his faculties.

The gangplank wobbled beneath his feet as he carefully traversed it, causing his heart to thunder in his chest for a second before the stark sweat of relief washed over him as he set foot on the wooden pier. He breathed deeply, filling his lungs with the stench of stale fish, but he cared little; it was the first breath he had taken on dry land for days.

Massoum began the long walk uphill towards the harbour gate, but immediately tottered as though the very ground beneath his feet were

4

moving. He had heard the seamen of the *Reigning Sceptre* talk about 'sea legs' but he thought it was only a malady that would afflict experienced sailor-types. Clearly he was wrong, as a wave of nausea joined in the dizziness and he had to clench his teeth lest he retch all over the harbour.

Suddenly all Massoum wanted was a glass of anise tea, to feel its warmth soothe his stomach and the sweetness of the cinnamon and honey take away the stinging bile that threatened to rise from his gullet. Reluctantly he reached into his shoulder bag, that precious bag, and fished within, rifling through the random contents until his hand closed around a small pewter flask. Frantically he pulled it out, unscrewing the cap and pressing the spout to his lips. The thick spirit burned his throat as it went down, but it stifled the taste of vomit and within moments the nausea passed.

Feeling a little more himself, Massoum proceeded up the cobbled ramp towards that huge gate, hemmed in by merchants and sailors making their way to and from the city with heavy bales, crates, and various beasts of burden laden with their wares. Drawing closer he could see over the gate's threshold into the city proper, as the thronging crowd moved off like a vast swarm into the myriad streets beyond. Massoum had to pass the gate guards who scrutinised those that might enter, sporadically pulling a merchant or sailor from the crowd to question them and check their possessions for contraband. What was considered contraband in this pit of iniquity Massoum did not know, but he was well aware that with invading forces at the country's border the city's custodians would be on the lookout for any kind of spy or infiltrator.

Keeping his head down, Massoum moved with the crowd. His best chance was to avoid eye contact, not draw attention to himself, though he realised that might be impossible. His dress alone marked him out as a foreigner, and he instantly regretted not adopting a more drab attire that would have allowed him to fit in with these filthy western masses.

Regret turned to dread as the two merchants on his left-hand side were roughly bundled out of the way and a thick hairy hand planted itself on his shoulder.

'Where do you think you're going?' said an amused voice as he was pulled from the crowd and quickly surrounded by burly looking militiamen. There were three of them, wearing identical green jackets, and Massoum could barely tell them apart. Each had a flat broken nose, missing teeth and piercing, porcine eyes. One of them pulled the bag from his shoulder and Massoum felt panic suddenly grip him. Nevertheless he adopted his usual easy smile; a smile that had helped secure peace in five nations and charmed sultans and warlords across all the eastern lands.

'My lords,' he said, touching a finger to forehead and then lips, 'I am merely a merchant brokering trade – a seller of spices. I understand Steelhaven has great need of such—'

'Shut it, camel shagger,' said one of the guards, using an insult Massoum had been told to expect from these uncouth westerners. 'What's in the bag?'

'Meaningless trinkets. Keepsakes from my homeland,' he replied, but the burly guard was already rummaging through its contents. He pulled out a small rag doll, the lifelike horsehair on its head flopping back and forth pathetically before it was dropped back in the bag. The guard dipped his hand in again and this time pulled out a small leather wallet and a smile crossed his face. He dropped the bag to the floor, the rest of its worthless contents now forgotten.

'What's this then?' he said, opening the wallet and looking eagerly inside. His face dropped as he saw what it contained. 'What the fuck is this load of shit?'

Massoum opened his mouth to frame some answer, but he didn't have a chance to speak before the guardsman dropped the wallet to the floor and reached forward, grasping him by the front of his robe and lifting him from his feet. From the delicate silk hem came a painful ripping sound and Massoum prepared himself for the worst.

'Enough!'

At the command the guard froze in mid strike. He looked left, and Massoum followed his gaze to see a tall, fine-looking figure standing just inside the gate, flanked by two towering knights in armour, thorn branches of etched brass entwined around the crimson plates. They were Knights of the Blood, the personal retinue of King Cael Mastragall himself.

'We'll take it from here, serjeant,' said the handsome westerner, but the guardsman had already released Massoum's robe and taken a step back. Massoum quickly stooped and picked up the wallet, stuffing it into his bag of precious trinkets and protectively pulling it close to his chest.

With an authoritative gesture, the man beckoned Massoum forward. He was only too glad to accept, moving past the guards who now stood back, staring warily either out of respect or fear, Massoum didn't care which.

'This way,' said the man, moving off, and Massoum followed obediently. He had been told his contact would be waiting, but a member of the King's Guard of Honour? That was something he hadn't foreseen.

But if this man wasn't his contact? Perhaps . . . no, that didn't bear thinking about. He couldn't have been discovered – not so quickly.

He was led through the streets, the tall man in front, his fitted uniform neat and rigid, its collar high and severe, with the two knights at the rear, their armour clanking quietly as they walked behind, not too close, not too distant.

It was when he was marched into a dark alleyway, far from the thronging crowd, that Massoum suddenly began to fear the worst. His instinct for self-preservation took over. It was time to do some talking.

'Although I am grateful for your aid, and you have my undying thanks for pulling me from the jaws of a certain beating, I can assure you I am able to proceed through the streets of your city without such a . . . sturdy escort.'

The man stopped ahead of him, the knights behind. Slowly he turned, and in the shadows of the alleyway his face became grave, the square cut of his uniform giving him a dark and ominous bearing.

'Massoum Abbasi,' he said. *Curses – he knows my name*, thought Massoum. *I am dead.* 'Did you think that King Cael would not have agents of his own? You were tracked all the way from Dravhistan. We have been expecting your arrival for days.'

With a nod, the man signalled to the knights behind, and Massoum heard them draw their broadswords.

'Wait,' he said, panic rising within him. 'I have information. You should interrogate me at least.'

'Oh, we will. And we will find out everything the Elharim prince has planned, even if we have to flay the flesh from your bones.'

'I can assure you that won't be necessary,' said Massoum, his voice growing shriller. 'You'll find I can be most compliant.'

'But where would be the fun in that?' replied the handsome soldier, the corner of his mouth rising in a sadistic sneer.

Massoum spun around to stare at the two knights, his eyes wide and fearful. The first of them stepped forward, reaching out with one massive gauntleted hand, his well-oiled armour barely making a sound as he did so.

It was then the shadows moved.

Something shone for the briefest instant despite the dimness of the alley and the knight's arm, even encased as it was in sturdy plate, suddenly fell to the ground. He grunted, staggering back and gripping at the stump, which spurted dark blood in an arterial spray. A figure, black as shadow and fast as the sea wind, shot forward. Another flash, and Massoum could see a sword, thin as a sabre but straight as an arrow. It sliced forth with precision, above the knight's gorget but beneath the lip of his full helm, cutting a red line across his throat. As he fell back gurgling, the second knight raced forward, growling in rage, the sound amplified from behind his helm; but the shadow moved faster. Massoum heard that flashing blade cut the air twice in quick succession and the knight fell silently, his head still in the full helm rolling to the left, his arm lopped off at the shoulder sliding to the right.

All this happened in a blink, and still the shadow moved in a fluid motion, spinning and flinging something past Massoum's head. He felt the air whistle close to his ear, then heard a sickening thud as the missile embedded itself in the uniformed man behind him.

Massoum saw him drop, his face slack, a sliver of silver skewering his eye. He collapsed in a heap, his hand still on the hilt of his duelling blade, still only halfway out of its scabbard.

There was silence in the alley. Massoum dared not turn back towards the deadly shadow, even though it had saved him from certain death. He trembled as the figure slid silently past him, its tread not making a sound in the soft earth. It knelt, pulling the metal sliver from the eye of the corpse.

'Amon Tugha sends his greetings,' came a silken voice as the shadow turned to regard Massoum. The face was half hidden behind a cloth mask but the eyes were two golden pools, unmistakably Elharim. 'I was sent here to watch over you, Massoum Am Kalhed Las Fahir Am Jadar Abbasi. To make sure you complete your task in one piece.'

'Thank you,' Massoum replied. 'And my thanks to Amon Tugha.'

'My lord and master does not require your thanks, but for the reward he has agreed he does demand your loyalty. An offer to betray him so quickly at the first sign of adversity might be seen as treacherous – might be rewarded with certain death. But luckily for you, my master is merciful.'

Massoum was about to speak, to protest his innocence, to try to say he would have revealed nothing, even if tortured by the most merciless of King Cael's inquisitors, but he knew the words would be worthless. This Elharim could see right through him and into his heart, that much was clear, so he merely bowed low, touching his finger to brow then lips.

When he stood upright once more the Elharim assassin was gone, but Massoum knew he would not be very far away. Without a further glance at the corpses, Massoum made his way down the alley, eager to carry out his task.

ONE

Standing on top of the stool, she could see out of her open window, out across the city almost as far as Northgate. The sky was darkening outside, but the coming of night didn't bring any relief from the unseasonable heat. The air was still and muggy, and enclosed as she was in so heavy and uncomfortable a gown her flesh was getting clammier with every laboured breath.

'You're fidgeting again,' said Dore in his heavy Stelmornian accent.

Janessa breathed in deeply, sucking in her waist just as he had ordered when this current bout of torture began, and went back to standing like a statue. Dore Tegue might well have been the best dressmaker in the Free States but surely she was the one suffering for his art.

'How much longer?' Janessa asked through gritted teeth.

Dore stopped ministering to the silk brocade that adorned the front of the gown and took a step back, looking at her with an arrogantly raised eyebrow. 'These things cannot be rushed. It takes as long as it takes. Would you like to be announced at the Feast in a threadbare gown or would you prefer to be the talk of the evening?'

'Right now I'd settle for something that didn't cut me in two,' she muttered under her breath, but it was clear Dore heard. It was with a sharp exhalation through his wide nostrils that he went back to attacking the dress with needle and thread.

Janessa glanced over to Graye, who was sitting on the sill next to the enormous window that looked out onto the city – a city of wonders, secrets and adventure that she had been forbidden to ever enter. Her lady-in-waiting had a sly smile on her face, maybe deriving some sadistic pleasure from Janessa's discomfort, but that wouldn't last long. Janessa was determined that her friend would suffer similar torment in her turn.

A sudden sharp prick of pain in her thigh made Janessa flinch, squeal and almost fall from the stool.

'Dore, what are you trying to do, fix the dress or cover me in pinholes?'

'I'm sorry, my lady,' Dore replied, holding up the offending needle innocently. 'But you keep moving. How am I expected to work under these conditions?'

He looked as forlorn as an artist forced to paint without easel or brush.

'Oh, I've had enough of this for now.' Janessa gathered up the heavy dress as she stepped from the stool, then wrenched out the band holding her long, red hair in a knot on her head, allowing it to fall about her shoulders in curling rivulets.

'But my lady, I still have to fix the hem, gather in the bodice and finish the shirring on the sleeves.'

'It can wait, Dore. If I have to spend one more second on that stool I'll explode.'

Petulantly Dore began to throw his scissors, bobbins, thimbles, yarn and needles into the various compartments of his small wooden tailor's box. 'I was treated like a lord in Stelmorn,' he mumbled. 'Ladies of refinement used to beat at my door, begging for the benefit of my skills, and here I am, reduced to little more than manservant. Prey to the whims of the ungrateful aristocracy. Whatever was I thinking?'

With that he slammed his box shut, lifted his nose in the air and stormed towards the door.

'You were most likely thinking about the money in my father's coffers,' said Janessa, before he could slam the door behind him.

Graye began to laugh.

'How many dressmakers does that make now?' she said, smiling at Janessa who was still struggling within the confines of the huge, maroon-coloured gown.

'Three . . . this month. Now will you stop grinning and help me out of this thing.'

Graye giggled as she walked across the chamber and began to unlace the bodice.

'You're going to have to suffer through a fitting sooner or later,' she said as she struggled with the lace bows. 'The Feast is in less than a week.'

'I know. But it's just so tiresome, and see what I have to wear.' She wriggled out of the dress and let it fall to the floor. 'I look like a cake. I should at least be able to choose the colour.'

'And what would you pick? Something blood red or jet black, I'd wager.'

Janessa smiled. 'Wouldn't that be something? Imagine their faces when I walked in.'

'Yes, and imagine your father's when he found out.'

Janessa turned to Graye with a frown. 'Must you pour water on every flame of an idea?'

'One of us has to be sensible. The king has enough to concern him without you causing a stir whenever you get the chance. Sooner or later you'll have to face up to your responsibilities.'

Janessa turned towards the window, fighting back a sudden stab of sadness. Graye hadn't meant any harm, she knew, but reminders of her obligations grew ever more insistent and sometimes she just wanted to forget. It was not a responsibility she had been born to, and certainly not one she desired. She was simply not meant to be queen. Janessa had been last in line to the throne after her brother and sister, before the plague had sent them to an early grave along with her mother. Now she alone bore the burden of succession, and that responsibility weighed all too heavily on her shoulders.

'I'm sorry,' said Graye, placing a hand on her arm, 'I didn't mean to upset you.'

'I know,' Janessa replied, turning to her friend and trying to smile. 'It just wasn't supposed to be this way. Drake and Lisbette were the ones brought up to this, the ones who were taught the airs and graces. The ones born to rule.'

'And you were always the wild one. I was there, remember.'

This brought a smile to Janessa's lips. Graye had always been there, her constant companion, and could share her pain, for she too had lost her family to the plague. Her parents had fallen victim early and, with the death of Lord and Lady Daldarrion, Graye had come to live at Skyhelm, the palace of King Cael Mastragall. Having her as a close friend had been the only thing that helped Janessa through that terrible time, when the Sweet Canker had claimed almost a quarter of the Free States.

Sweet Canker. It sounded like a flower or one of the exotic foreign perfumes her mother had liked so much, but it was a name that struck fear into the hearts of every man, woman and child, not caring whom it took from beggar to king. Coming from nowhere, it had descended upon the Free States like a killer in the night. There was nothing 'sweet' about it. Once afflicted, death came in a feverish nightmare, with the phantom odour of cinnamon and clove assailing the nostrils. That was where the name came from – someone's idea of a joke perhaps. No one was laughing.

'Well I'm not wild any more,' said Janessa, trying to shake herself from her malaise. 'Now I am a lady at court, heir to the throne, the woman who would be queen.' She began to prance around the room mocking the graceful gait of the sycophantic courtiers she had so recently been forced to mix with.

Graye laughed again. 'You've hardly changed, have you? You're still more suited to riding like a man and climbing trees than refinement and public engagements. How will your father ever marry you off?'

Janessa looked pointedly at Graye. Her lady in waiting realised her mistake and the easy smile fell from her face.

'You'll have to come to terms with it sooner or later,' Graye said. 'It's not going to go away.'

'No,' Janessa replied, glancing towards the window, a sudden mad plan coming to mind. 'But maybe *we* could go away. Perhaps we could run, far from here, far from this prison.'

'And go where? We couldn't go anywhere in the Free States; we'd be found by the Wardens in no time. Would you rather we crossed the seas to Dravhistan where they treat their women like servants, or perhaps head north to the steppes where the Khurtas would use us as whores.'

'Graye!'

'It's true. You do say the silliest things sometimes. If your father were here—'

'He's not here, is he, Graye.'

'No, he's not. He's with the army on our northern borders, ready to defend our country from invaders. He's carrying out his duty to his people. Perhaps it's time you did the same.'

'Sometimes you can be such a bore,' Janessa said, but deep down she knew her friend was right. Graye was so often the voice of sanity, but sometimes it was the hardest voice to hear.

The most northerly of the Free States, Dreldun, had been invaded by a massive warhost of Khurtas; savages from the northern steppes. Dreldun was in ruins; its populace, only recently recovered from the horrors of the Sweet Canker, had been put to the sword and flame. The city of Steelhaven was filling with refugees from Dreldun and other provinces, desperate to escape the invasion. In response to the atrocity, King Cael had taken the massed armies of the Free States north to meet the enemy.

They called her father the Uniter: he had brought together the disparate kingdoms of the Free States under one banner when they were facing an invasion force of Aeslanti beast-men from the south. That incursion had ended in their victory, but now King Cael faced a greater threat: the tribes of the Khurtas were said to be allied under their own warlord, a warrior from the Riverlands of the far north. Amon Tughà, an immortal Elharim, cast out by his own people, had now come south to claim a kingdom for himself, and Steelhaven would be his ultimate prize. Only the king and his united armies stood in the way.

And there was the cause of all her problems. Despite King Cael's power and the loyalty he demanded, the alliance of the Free States was still a fragile one. The king was not a young man, and he always led from the front in battle, contrary to the advice of his generals. If he were killed, the treaties binding the Free States might well collapse, which would be disastrous. Janessa had to be married off as soon as possible, to a noble of one of the major provinces. Their alliance would seal the union of Free States for decades, the legacy perpetuated by their children. It was something that Janessa was only slowly coming to terms with.

There was a heavy knock at the door. Before Janessa could answer – or even cover her modesty, standing as she was in her white cotton petticoat – the door opened.

Odaka Du'ur was so tall that to enter he needed to stoop beneath the lintel. His purple robe was patterned with yellow and gold thread depicting stylised birds and intersecting swirls and branches. Astrological symbols surrounded the hem and cuffs and circled the base of the small round hat that adorned his head, adding inches to his already towering frame. But his outlandish attire was not the most striking feature of this man, for his skin was a gleaming black, marking him as native to the continent of Equ'un, far beyond the southern borders of the Free States. It was rare indeed to find any such foreigners in the Teutonian Free States, but this man was known to everyone at the court of King Cael Mastragall, for this was his most trusted counsellor, and in the king's absence the current regent.

Odaka bowed his head. 'My lady,' he said, his deep voice rumbling like a bass horn. He ignored Graye, as ever choosing not to acknowledge those he considered beneath him.

'To what do I owe this intrusion?' Janessa responded, not even trying to conceal herself further. If Odaka had the temerity to enter her chamber unannounced she would not grant him the satisfaction of showing that it bothered her.

'I've just passed your dressmaker on his way out. He looked quite consternated. Has there been any kind of . . . problem?'

'No. No problem at all,' Janessa lied, but she saw Odaka's eyes flit to the dress left in a pile on the floor. He walked forward, stooping and picking up the garment.

'I see there clearly has.' He tried vainly to shake the creases from the fabric. 'How many dressmakers does that make now?'

'Is it three?' said Graye, as though her answer might win her some sort of prize.

Janessa stifled a laugh. Odaka ignored her.

'My lady, I do not think I have to remind you of the importance of the coming Feast of Arlor and your presence at it. I cannot stress enough how essential it is that you look your best. It will mean much to your father, not to mention the future of the kingdom.'

'If you're referring to my being ogled and prodded like a mare in season before being gifted to the prize stallion, then yes, I am well aware of my role, Odaka. I don't need reminding of the sacrifices I am making for my country.'

Odaka narrowed his eyes, and Janessa could see a sudden flash of anger there. She had to admit it frightened her, but it was gone as quickly as it had come.

'We are all servants of the Crown, my lady, and some of us must make greater sacrifices than others.'

'Yes, I'm sure.' *And what have your sacrifices been, Odaka?* she thought, trying to disguise her disdain. *What have you given up in service to my father, other than the savage plains of the southern continent and the dangers of the wild? You seem to have done pretty well for yourself, all things considered.*

'You need not worry, my lady; they say Duke Logar's heir is a very handsome young man. Broad shouldered and well educated. I am sure he would make a very fine husband.'

'Why don't you marry him then, Odaka. You're free to take the dress too.' She gestured to the maroon monstrosity the regent still held in his big hands.

Odaka took a deep breath, this time not showing any anger, but rather disappointment. Janessa realised she was being petulant and demanding, behaviour she had seen in other nobles over the years and hated, but she simply couldn't help the way she felt. Arranged marriages might be fine for the nobility in general, but not for her. Lisbette, her older sister, had always been paraded in front of visiting nobles while Janessa could fade into the background unnoticed. She was the errant younger sister, the flame-haired wolf of the family, allowed to run rampant and play rough. Now all that was changed and she felt flung centre stage like the star turn in a travelling show. It didn't suit her, and she was determined to tell anyone who would listen how much she hated it.

'I will arrange for another dressmaker to visit you tomorrow,' Odaka said, laying the dress across his forearm.

'As you wish,' she replied, feeling defeated by his calmness. Her attempts to provoke him appeared to have failed, and she couldn't help but admire him a little for that.

'My lady,' Odaka said with a final bow before leaving the chamber.

'That could have been worse,' said Graye once the large oak door had shut behind him.

'I'm not afraid of Odaka Du'ur,' Janessa replied, though she wasn't sure whether she believed her own words. 'The only thing I'm looking forward to when I'm queen is ridding Skyhelm of his influence. I have no idea why my father keeps him around. A foreigner as regent? Why did he even consider such a thing?'

'Your father trusts him, and he hasn't been wrong so far.'

'My father trusts anyone who's loyal to him, and Odaka certainly makes all the right noises in that department. He saved my father's life when they fought the Aeslanti, or so Garret says, but there's still something I don't like about him.'

'The fact that he's a foreigner? Or the fact that he has your father's ear?'

'That has nothing to do with it. My father can have any advisers he wants, but if he thinks they can order me around when he's not here, he has another think coming.'

'So you won't be meeting with Duke Logar's son then?'

'I will do as I please and speak to whom I wish.'

Despite Janessa's protestation Graye couldn't wipe a wicked smile off her face.

'I'm sure you will – but they do say he's very handsome.' Graye jutted out her jaw and crossed her eyes, giving her pretty face a ridiculously thuggish appearance. 'And he's broad shouldered, remember.' She began

15

to stride around the chamber like a bowlegged ape, which provoked peals of laughter from Janessa.

'When Duke Logar's son comes to court I will be the perfect lady,' said Janessa, finally composing herself. 'And I'm sure he will be the perfect noble; talking about swords and hunting and war, and I'll be bored but shan't show it and then he'll kiss my hand and that will be that.'

'What will be what?'

'Then I'll be betrothed.' As soon as she spoke the words, she realised that despite all their joking, it was the only conclusion there could ever be.

'You'd better let me carry the wedding train,' said Graye.

'You and Odaka can do it together,' Janessa replied.

They both laughed at that.

But all Janessa could think was that her future had been mapped, the ship set sail, and no matter what she did to steer there was nothing she could ever do to influence its course.

TWO

The Temple of Autumn stood on the second highest promontory in Steelhaven, only eclipsed in majesty by the royal palace of Skyhelm and in height by the Tower of Magisters. It rose like a stone monolith from the bare rock, its yellow granite walls as stark and forbidding as any great citadel. On its northern bastion stood the massive statue of Arlor, the Windhammer, the Wild One, Great Protector of all the Teutonian Tribes, on whose shoulders it was said the Free States had been built. Rising from its southern bastion, guarding Arlor's back and watching for danger from the Midral Sea, was the statue of Vorena. She stood tall and proud, grasping spear and shield, her plumed helm rising towards the blue sky.

Some scholars of ancient history stated it was she, and not the Windhammer, who had first established the Teutonian Free States and that it was Arlor who had followed *her* into battle against the daemons that threatened to annihilate the tribes of men. True or not it mattered little, for both were now venerated across the Free States. Temples dedicated to the seasons were in each of the four city-states, but the Temple of Autumn was by far the largest. It was a place of devout worship, a fortress monastery where the wisdom and philosophies of the gods were taught alongside strict martial traditions. Where priestesses were inaugurated and warriors tempered.

It was also the place Kaira Stormfall called home.

She stood in the central courtyard, a training square for the Shieldmaidens of Vorena, but also consecrated ground and a place of devout worship. On clear days the Matron Mother would often lead the

Daughters of Arlor in prayer here, while the Shieldmaidens watched from the sidelines, guarding their territory, ever vigilant. Now though, the square was being put to its primary use – a practice yard – and nothing but the sounds of battle permeated the air.

Under Kaira's watchful eye young acolytes of Vorena were being trained in all manner of weapons. The youngest girls, some barely more than five winters, used wooden swords, their bodies covered in layers of light cloth armour lest they became overzealous. Older girls, almost ready to become full Shieldmaidens, trained with real weapons, their blades razor sharp, their spear tips easily able to penetrate the most well crafted plate.

At Kaira's side stood Samina, her sister in all but blood, and a warrior equal to her in rank. They called her the Coldeye, for her ability to stare down the most ferocious opponent; her aim with spear and bow was almost matchless.

Almost.

Kaira was more than her sister's match, as she had proved a number of times, and the rivalry still burned between them.

'No!' Kaira barked suddenly, striding forward to grasp the haft of a javelin about to be thrown by one of her students. The girl, maybe thirteen, was a square-jawed acolyte called Reham, gifted to the Temple years before by her pious parents. She had not yet graduated sufficiently through the ranks to be granted her maiden's name, and Kaira guessed if she carried on like this she never would.

Kaira took the javelin. 'You're still throwing the tip forward like a ball. This is a javelin.' Reham stared back at her sheepishly. 'You must thrust the haft through the tip, otherwise you might as well throw a stick at your enemy.' Kaira hefted the weapon to her shoulder. 'Throw *with* the javelin, not against it. This weapon is not dependent solely on brawn – technique will always beat strength.' With that she flung the javelin effortlessly at the target board thirty yards away. It hit dead centre, spearing the wood and echoing around the noisy courtyard.

Reham and the rest of the trainees stared in awe.

'Wise words you should all heed,' said Samina, coming to stand beside Kaira. 'But do not disregard the importance of power in combat. Sometimes there is simply no answer to brute strength.'

Kaira raised an eyebrow at her sister's intervention. It was not the first time the Coldeye had publicly expressed a differing philosophy of warfare. As was so often the case, her seemingly straightforward statement was a challenge in disguise.

'You can't abide just observing and teaching, can you?' said Kaira under her breath. She knew what was coming.

'A javelin,' said Samina, to one of the acolytes. Instantly a weapon was placed in her waiting palm. She tested the balance for a second, took a quick sidestep and let fly. The javelin soared across the courtyard, over the heads of the trainees. It embedded itself in one of the mannequins used for practising the placement of critical blows. The wooden statue wobbled, transfixed by the javelin, then came to rest, like a taunt to Kaira from fifty yards away.

Kaira saw her students standing agog. For the briefest moment she considered taking up another javelin, clearing the courtyard and demonstrating her superior skills, but what had she to prove? Let Samina have her moment. The Coldeye so rarely had opportunities to prove her worth these days. With the armies gone north and the Shieldmaidens left behind as little more than temple guards, it seemed they never would.

'Carry on,' Kaira said. Instantly her students went back to their routines.

'Most impressive.'

Kaira turned to see Daedla standing behind her. The Daughter of Arlor was short, diminutive even, and had a habit of turning up unexpectedly. Her amiable smile masked a keen and calculating nature; Kaira knew to be always on her guard around her. Not that Daedla had ever done her harm but, as a Shieldmaiden of Vorena, Kaira had always been taught to keep her counsel around the Daughters of Arlor. Two different factions of the same religion, they were discouraged from mixing, lest the violent nature of one taint the benevolence of the other.

Samina and Kaira towered over the stooped Daedla, who, despite her only middling years, was hunched like a crone.

'Your new recruits look a keen batch,' said Daedla, as they watched the youngsters begin their drill once more. 'It seems the students get better every year. Where do they keep coming from?'

'Most are orphans of the plague,' Kaira explained. 'Even so young they understand they must prove themselves or face being cast out from the safety of our walls.'

'That is surely not necessary. Arlor's Daughters would take care of them,' said Daedla proudly, but Kaira knew different.

'More refugees are flocking to Steelhaven every day, and there is only so much the Temple can do. Our armies need supplies to the north: crops, livestock, weapons. There will be few resources for those of us left in the city once the king begins his campaign. With more mouths to feed than ever before it will be a long winter for those who do not prove themselves worthy to remain within our walls.'

'You make it sound so bleak, sister. We Daughters of Arlor take a very different view.'

Kaira frowned. As compassionate as Daedla's words were, Kaira knew they were impractical. However good the intentions, pride and benevolence would always, ultimately, be subordinated to survival. The plague had certainly taught that. The Temple of Autumn and its Shieldmaidens had been quarantined during the scourge of the Sweet Canker, to avoid the sickness that would leave the place defenceless. Some of Arlor's Daughters had been allowed through the gates to minister to the sick, but none had been allowed to return in case they contaminated the Temple. When the plague was over, most of them were dead.

Despite her expressed compassion, Daedla had not been one of those who had gladly sacrificed herself to bring solace to the sick.

'What brings you to the courtyard, Daedla?' asked Samina, impatiently. 'We would not want to see you tainted by our martial display.'

'Oh, I am long past the fear of taint,' Daedla replied with her enigmatic smile, which only served to annoy Kaira even more. 'But the Matron Mother has summoned you.'

'The Matron Mother?' Kaira asked. 'What does she want us for?'

Daedla shrugged. 'I am simply the messenger.'

Kaira glanced at Samina, who only shot back a confused look. Quickly they made their way from the courtyard to change into their ceremonial regalia. It irked Kaira a little that they were being so hasty; Daedla was probably relishing this eagerness to respond to the Matron Mother's call, but there was really no alternative. Though Kaira's superior, the Exarch, was the highest ranking Shieldmaiden, and the sisters obeyed her implicitly, the Matron Mother held ultimate sway within the Temple of Autumn, and a personal summons from her was a great honour . . . or, on occasions, the ultimate disgrace.

'What do you think this is about?' Samina asked whilst placing her breastplate over the tight, silver brigandine beneath and securing the buckles.

'I have no idea,' Kaira replied, but the possibilities were rushing though her mind. Some kind of mission? Might they be required to leave the Temple and head to the front – to fight beside the king? Such a prospect excited her. Though defending the Temple and its inhabitants was her main duty, she relished the thought of real combat, instead of endlessly patrolling the walls of their impenetrable bastion.

Having donned their armour they strode though the Temple's vast corridors towards the inner chapel, carrying their ceremonial helms, with their golden swords at their sides. In uniform they both intentionally mirrored the statue of Vorena. Only Samina's dark, cropped hair and Kaira's blonde distinguished them. Seeing their approach in full regalia, the Daughters of Arlor and the Shieldmaidens all moved aside, bowing their heads in respect.

As the two warriors reached the antechamber to the Matron Mother's sanctum, Daedla was ready for them, two white-veiled handmaids at her side.

'The Matron Mother awaits,' said Daedla, beckoning towards the door. As Kaira took a step forward Daedla said, 'If you please, sisters. Your weapons.'

It was a foolish and annoying protocol, but the Matron Mother frowned upon weapons being carried in her presence, and forbade them within her sanctum. Reluctantly Kaira and Samina unbuckled their sword belts and handed the weapons to the waiting handmaids, and with her sickly smile still plastered to her face Daedla heaved the door open, bowing her head as the Shieldmaidens strode past her and into the sanctum.

The Matron Mother sat at a massive oak desk covered in parchments. She scribbled on a piece of vellum with a long elaborate quill, whose feather danced in time to the scratching sounds. Kaira and Samina stopped before the desk as the vast lead-lined door closed behind them with a resounding thud. Moments passed and Kaira could hear her own heart beating. She stared straight ahead, standing at attention, a sentinel of discipline awaiting the Matron Mother's notice; but still the old woman continued her incessant scribbling.

Finally, she placed the quill in its well and looked up, her rheumy eyes regarding them from beneath heavy wrinkled lids. The Matron Mother wore the plain white smock of the Daughters, but not the usual veil, and her dry, silver hair was tied back in a simple clasp.

'Thank you for coming,' she said with a smile that creased her entire face. She looked like a kindly old woman, one who might spend her latter years gifting alms to the poor or knitting shawls for street urchins. Kaira knew otherwise; the Matron Mother was a stone hard and powerful icon, whose words must be obeyed, whose example revered. 'You are probably wondering why I have summoned you here.' She paused, but neither Kaira nor Samina spoke. 'The fact is, I have called for you both because you are the finest warriors of this temple, perhaps even all the temples in the Free States. As such you are to receive an honour.'

For the briefest moment Kaira felt her heart leap. This was a mission, perhaps an opportunity for them both to leave the city and act in defence of the country.

'Word has reached us from the Temple of Winter in Ironhold. The High Abbot is making his way to Steelhaven to visit us and attend the Feast of Arlor at the royal palace. He will require a bodyguard while he is here – the finest warriors we have to offer.'

As quickly as it had soared, Kaira's heart sank. Though guarding the High Abbot *was* a great honour, fighting at the front with the armies of the Free States was all she had ever trained for. She wanted to protest, but knew the decision had been made. Nothing she could say would change it. Samina, however, was not above complaining.

'Surely the High Abbot has his own guard of honour, the Sons of Malleus?' she said, her voice doing nothing to mask her disappointment. 'Why does he need us? We have duties within the temple. Our recruits are at a crucial stage of their training.'

'Your students will still be waiting once this duty has been fulfilled. It is unlikely the High Abbot will be staying long.'

'But surely the Exarch would rather we concentrated on our training than guarding visitors?'

If the Matron Mother was shocked by Samina's petulant question she didn't show it. 'The Exarch agrees with me, that the High Abbot must be protected by our best. It is a great honour, one you should both relish.'

'We shall, Matron Mother,' Kaira said, before Samina could say anything further. The Matron Mother's placid mood could change without warning, and the last thing Kaira needed was Samina landing them in trouble.

The Matron Mother smiled. 'I realise this must come as something of a disappointment to you both. Menial duties within the Temple are beneath the pair of you. You want nothing more than to head north with our armies, that much is clear, and so you should. You are warriors born. To fight in defence of your nation and religion is what you were raised for.'

'We live to serve,' Kaira answered, though she agreed with everything the Matron Mother said.

'I know you do. And we are grateful. It is how I know I can trust you with this duty. And fear not – when it is fulfilled there will be more for you to do. Things more suited to your skills. If King Cael's army cannot stem the flood from the north you may well be called upon to aid his forces.'

'We only wish to fight in defence of the Free States,' Samina said. 'To do what we were trained for.'

The Matron Mother nodded wryly. 'You should be careful what you wish for, Shieldmaiden. The High Abbot will be here within three days. I expect you to be ready and waiting for his every command.'

'We shall, Matron Mother,' Kaira said. She bowed, as did Samina.

'Very good,' the Matron Mother replied, before turning back to her parchments. The Shieldmaidens took this as their signal to leave.

As the two warriors retraced their steps through the corridors of the temple it was clear the Coldeye could keep her peace no longer.

'Guard duty?' she said furiously, scattering a group of Arlor's Daughters who had been unlucky enough to cross her path. 'Guard duty? What is the Exarch thinking, allowing this? The High Abbot has his own warriors—'

'Enough,' said Kaira, glancing up and down the corridor. 'This is not the place.'

Samina was angry, but gritted her teeth. The pair of them remained silent as they made their way back to the chamber of arms. Once inside, Samina flung her gilded helmet at the wall where it bounced with a clang.

'I'm as annoyed as you are,' said Kaira. 'But it is our duty.'

'It is our duty to defend the temple. Not act as handmaids.'

'It is a great honour, sister. That is why we were chosen.'

This seemed to calm Samina slightly, though her annoyance was still obvious. 'We'd better be richly rewarded for this. We should at least be allowed to take the Shieldmaidens north to aid the king. That's all I can say.'

'I'm sure it's not,' replied Kaira with a grin.

There was silence for a moment, before the two of them began laughing. But, as they unbuckled their ceremonial armour, the words of the Matron Mother seemed to nag at Kaira – *be careful what you wish for.*

THREE

I t was a sad unwanted building in the shoddier part of the city, an old disused chapel, a remnant to the Old Gods that just hadn't got around to collapsing yet. Birds had taken to nesting in the rafters, rats under the floorboards and termites in the walls. In a city long past its best, this was one more relic of bygone days, evidence of a golden age now all but rotted and dead. It was perfect for Merrick Ryder's needs.

He checked his attire one last time, self-consciously adjusting collar and cuffs. Merrick was going for a particular look; as if he'd come from money but fallen on hard times. This was crucial to his act and explained the silken shirt, masterfully tailored jacket and britches, not brand new, but not moth-eaten either. Like a master angler, he could select just the right bait and present it in just the right spot. All he needed now was the old trout.

And in she came.

Lady Elina Humburg glanced around the chapel, eyes wide and fearful. In her fine frock and with her painted face and her glittering jewels, she was clearly unused to being in this part of the city.

Merrick could have shown himself straight away, could have spared her the fear, but where was the fun in that? Besides, he wanted her nervous, afraid. It would make this subterfuge that much easier to pull off.

He watched her for several moments, letting the tension build, and just when she looked as if she might flee in fright, he stepped out of the shadows.

'My lady,' he breathed, 'I cannot thank you enough for coming.'

24

She turned with a jangle of jewellery – a sound that never failed to fill Merrick with excitement – and rushed into his arms. 'Oh, my Lord Franco, how could I ever stay away?'

He embraced her, holding her close, making her feel safe, feel wanted. An easy act, at which he was well practised. Hells, he'd done this more than a dozen times, but Merrick Ryder was nothing if not proficient.

'It's like a dagger to my heart to think you might put yourself in danger,' he whispered into her ear. She shuddered at the nearness of his lips and he felt her grip him all the tighter. 'The Sultan's spies could even now be watching us, waiting to strike.'

'The danger is worth it, Lord Franco,' she answered, gazing at him. 'And I know there is nothing to fear when you are close.'

He paused for a second, his lips hovering near hers, letting the expectation build. Then he kissed her. She responded vigorously; a truly passionate kiss – he had to give her that – but then Lady Elina was a passionate woman. Just a shame such passion was wrapped in a body so clearly partial to sweetcakes and honey wine. Luckily, Merrick wasn't courting the woman for her looks – but rather for her seemingly endless riches.

When he looked down her eyes were still closed, her body still reeling in delight. Merrick held her close, feeling her trembling in his grasp. She had fallen for him like a suicide off a cliff and perhaps he should have felt guilty for that. Then again, he was providing a service; he was giving her everything she wanted – passion, excitement. And what did he ask in return? A coin purse here, a spot of jewellery there. Was that too much to ask?

It wasn't as if she couldn't afford it, and plainly his need was the greater.

A penchant for the gambling tables had left Merrick Ryder with rather large debts, owed, unfortunately, to Shanka the Lender. It didn't do to owe Shanka for too long. Not if he wanted to keep his various appendages intact. Consequently he needed coin and fast, and that was where Lady Elina came in.

So what if he'd told her his name was Lord Franco of Riverbeach, a noble from Ankavern cast out by his evil uncle? So what if he'd made up some shit about having a brother who had been helping the brave rebels of Mekkala overthrow the despotic Raj Al'Fazal, Divine Sultan of Kajrapur? So what if he'd told her his brother had been captured by the Sultan and a substantial ransom was needed to secure his release? And

25

that they needed to meet in secret? That the agents of the Sultan were everywhere, watching, waiting? That at any minute they could be waylaid by assassins and slaughtered?

Lady Elina was a widow – a filthy rich widow, past her prime and in need of excitement. If it wasn't for Merrick she'd be stuck on her estate: bored and fat and lonely. If you looked at it that way, he was doing her a favour.

'You are so brave, my lady,' he said, pulling away. 'So selfless. I am not worthy of you.' He turned as though to leave.

When she grabbed hold of him once more he could barely contain his grin. It was just like landing a fish – let out the line, wait for the bite, then reel it in.

'Never say that, Lord Franco. I am honoured to help in any way I can.'

He turned to her, his eyes projecting just the right degree of concern and gratitude. 'Oh, my lady. I am not worthy of such devotion.'

'Oh, but you are, my lord.'

She leaned in then, grasping the lapel of his jacket and planting her lips firmly against his. Merrick barely had time to open his mouth before she'd stuffed it with her probing tongue. Her breath smelled faintly of wine and figs but this was mostly overpowered by the liberal dousing of sickly sweet perfume she had used. Despite the harshness of it on his nose and throat, Merrick grasped her firmly, pressing back against her lips, making a satisfied groan as though this was all he wanted and yearned for.

When the kissing was done and Lady Elina had gathered herself, Merrick looked at her expectantly, glancing at the myriad jewelled chains that hung about her neck. 'Though it pains me to even say it, my love, might I beg for a further contribution to our cause?'

She smiled back at him, as she had done a dozen times before. A dozen times when she had taken one of those chains from her neck and pressed it into his hands with a kiss.

This time, however, she didn't move.

'This has been most pleasant, Lord Franco – if that's even your real name – but I am afraid, as with most pleasurable things, it has come to an end.'

Merrick's brow furrowed. This wasn't how things were supposed to go. She was supposed to hand over the goods and send him off on his merry way. What the fuck was—

'I am afraid, my lady, that your suspicions were correct. His name is not Lord Franco.' It was a shrill voice that echoed through the derelict chapel.

Merrick turned, his hand instinctively straying to the sword at his side, but there was no sword there. He'd needed money for his new clothes – for how was he to impress a real noblewoman if he kept turning up in the same attire – and had to pawn his blade for the money to pay for them.

In hindsight a bloody stupid move.

Three men strolled into the light that beamed down through the collapsed roof. The first two wore plain black coats, nicely stitched. They looked as if they could handle themselves in a fight. Behind them was a skinny bloke, well past middling years, in a frilly shirt and frock coat and, obviously, a wig on his big, wide head.

Merrick was already looking for the quickest exit but there was only one way out and that was blocked. He was about to try talking, the next best thing, when Lady Elina piped up, 'Why, Ortes. How good of you to join us.'

Ortes, the one at the back, raised his head but didn't bother to step in front of his men. 'It's my pleasure, Lady Elina.'

Merrick had no idea what was going on, but didn't like it one little bit. It was time to start talking . . . just until he could start running.

'I'm afraid I am at a loss,' he said, taking a step away from the man Ortes and his dangerous-looking companions. 'The lady and I were just conducting—'

'I know what you were conducting. And I know you're no nobleman,' said Ortes. 'You're a back street chancer. A swindler, thief and gambler . . . Merrick Ryder!'

'Preposterous! I have no idea what this man's talking about,' Merrick said to Elina quickly, desperate to salvage the situation, even though it was obvious he'd been rumbled. 'Who is this man, anyway?'

Before she could answer, Ortes finally found the courage to step out from behind his men, raising his chin and clamping his hands on his hips as though some hero of legend.

'I am Ortes Ban Hallan, Duke of Valecroft, and that,' he pointed to Elina, 'is my beloved aunt!'

'Ah,' said Merrick. 'Well . . . I can assure you, this is not what it looks like.'

'Shut it,' said one of the black-coated henchmen, taking a threatening step forward. Merrick had never regretted pawning a sword so much in his life, but he did as he was told.

'You see, my dear,' said Elina, all smiles and sarcasm. 'I've had my doubts about you for some time. That's why I had you followed. That's why my nephew has been checking up on you for the past few days.'

Merrick turned to her, at his most solemn and sincere. 'I can assure you, my lady, this is all an unfortunate misunderstand*oooff*—'

The closest henchman punched him in the gut. It was like being hit with a hammer: all the air in his lungs escaped in a violent rush.

'No more of your lies,' spat Ortes as Merrick dropped to his knees, gasping for breath. 'Get him out of here – make sure he never bothers Lady Elina again.'

Before Merrick could move the eager thugs grabbed hold of him and dragged him across the crumbling floorboards.

This couldn't be happening. How could that old trout have rumbled him so easily? How could he have been found out by a pompous, over-dressed sow? Curious though he was to know, this wasn't quite as pressing as getting himself out of his current and worsening predicament.

The interior of the chapel lurched past as Ortes' henchmen dragged him along. Merrick's head slammed against the threshold step as they pulled him into a back street. As he floundered in mud, his head pounding, one of them got in an opportunistic kick to his ribs.

This was getting serious. If he didn't think of something soon these morons could do some permanent damage, perhaps even to his face. And he was happy with his face just the way it was.

As though on cue, one of his assailants pulled a knife from his black coat.

'Now I'm gonna fucking slice your guts. It'll be the last time you take advantage of kindly old ladies.'

Merrick held up his hands instinctively as the knife came down to slash his flesh. He cried out in anticipation of the pain and blood; but they never came. Hearing a sharp thud, he opened his eyes in time to see the knife man collapsing sideways, blade falling from limp hand. Beside him was a hulking brute Merrick didn't recognise, carrying a wooden cosh that he'd just used to good effect.

The remaining henchman stumbled back, raising his hands in surrender as a second brutish thug emerged from the shadows.

One of the new thugs seized Merrick and hauled him up. Merrick was groggy, his legs unsteady, but he still had wit enough to grasp an opportunity when he saw it – even if presented by a bull of a man who looked like he might eat Merrick's liver as soon as look at him.

The two thugs dragged him off as Ortes' henchman looked on in silence, in total fear of these two behemoths. They were easily a full head taller than Merrick and twice as wide at the shoulders. A sudden 'out of the frying pan' feeling crept up on him. How much of a *rescue* was this?

'Look, gents,' Merrick said as they led him around a corner and down a dark alley. 'If Shanka's sent you, I've got his money. At least . . . in theory. There's just a couple of arrangements I have to make to release the equity.'

'Stop talking,' said one of the brutes. Merrick wasn't going to argue.

They walked in silence along the back alleys, through slurry and shit, past rats and garbage. Merrick guessed that if they'd wanted him dead they would have killed him already, or just left him to Ortes' men, so there was no point trying to escape – at least not yet.

Eventually, and without warning, the two brutes bundled Merrick through an open doorway into a dimly lit warehouse. It seemed to contain only two large crates, which could easily have been used as man-sized cages. Some paraphernalia on the walls, difficult to recognise in the gloom, looked like farming tools, but in Merrick's head could quite easily have been implements of torture.

'Sit down,' said one of the thugs.

'But there's no chair,' Merrick replied, glancing around.

He screeched suddenly as the other brute kicked him in the back of the knees and sent him sprawling.

Before he could ask what all this was about, two figures walked from the shadows.

The first was tall and bald, his face long and gaunt. He had something of the undertaker about him, a demeanour that was mirthless, as though he had never smiled in his life. The second was shorter and much fuller about the waist. His curly hair was receding and framed an open and strangely jovial face. This man's welcoming smile seemed at odds with his partner's skull-faced stare, and it did nothing to reassure Merrick. He recognised these two men instantly, and knew there was nothing to smile about.

'Hello, Ryder,' said the shorter figure.

'Hello, Friedrik,' Merrick replied, then turned quickly to his silent friend. 'Bastian. How are you both?'

'We're very well,' Friedrik replied. 'Clearly much better than you.' He glanced towards the hulking goons behind Merrick. 'You were told to bring him here unharmed.'

'That wasn't us,' said one of the thugs, pointing at Merrick's torn shirt and bruised face. 'We found him like that.' Despite his size, he was clearly intimidated by the little man, and with good reason. Friedrik and Bastian controlled the Guild – the organisation that ran every illicit racket in Steelhaven. Nothing happened in the city without their say so. No one was mugged, extorted, pickpocketed, burgled, swindled, brutalised or murdered unless it was on their explicit orders. Working within the boundaries of Steelhaven outside the purview of the Guild carried very harsh penalties indeed.

'Making friends as usual, Ryder,' Friedrik said with a grin. 'That's good to see.'

'I'm popular. What can I say?'

'Yes, very popular. Or so we hear. Apparently Shanka the Lender wants your balls on a skewer.'

'That's just a slight misunderstanding I'm currently trying to resolve.'

'Of course you are. You'll be pleased to hear I may just have a solution to your problem.'

Merrick felt cold panic begin to rise in his guts. Being in debt to Shanka the Lender was one thing. Being in debt to the Guild was quite another. At least without his balls he'd still be half a man – what the Guild might do was much worse.

'Honestly, Shanka and I are just ironing out some teething problems. There's absolutely no need for you to get involved.'

'Oh, but I insist, Ryder. For old times' sake.'

Fuck.

'Okay. I'm all ears.' Merrick tried a casual smile, but he knew it wasn't very convincing.

'We have a job which will utilise your truly unique skills.' *Thieving? Gambling? Drinking? Surely they didn't want to borrow his skills in the bedroom?* 'We want you to broker a deal with some foreigners. To see it through from start to finish, using your usual charm and finesse.'

'Really? There's no one in the whole city better suited to this than me?'

Bastian suddenly stepped forward, his piercing eyes staring down with barely masked hatred. 'It's your particular pedigree we're interested in, Ryder. You have contacts. Friends in high places who will come in very handy. Bribes will have to be paid, blind eyes turned to certain actions. You will make this happen, Ryder, and in return your debts to Shanka the Lender will be paid off.'

'Sounds fair,' Merrick replied, though it actually sounded shit. 'Exactly what deal do I need to broker?'

Bastian looked towards the diminutive Friedrik, who gave a long sigh before he spoke. 'A slave ship will reach port in two days. When it arrives it will be empty. By the time it leaves, you will ensure it is full. Will this be a problem?'

Shit right it'll be a fucking problem. Slavery had been outlawed in the Free States for over two centuries. The penalty for slave trading was public castration and execution by hanging.

Merrick looked first at Friedrik, then at the cold, calculating eyes of Bastian.

'No. No problem at all,' he replied

'Excellent.' Friedrik smiled. 'You'll be given the details of when, where and how. All you need do is be yourself and turn on that famous Ryder charm. It's unlikely you'll see us again; from now on you'll be dealing with Palien, so if there's anything you need before you go, best speak up now.'

Merrick thought for a moment and then gingerly rose to his feet. 'Just one thing.' Bastian scowled as though Merrick had just left a shit on the floor behind him. 'Any chance you can lend me a sword?'

FOUR

Eastgate Market was the oldest in the city. Not the largest, certainly not the cleanest and it definitely didn't display the richest wares; but it had a long history. It dated back to the Age of the Sword Kings, when the river barons had brought their goods down the Storway from the foot of the Kriega Mountains.

How Rag knew this she couldn't remember – it was just one of those useless pieces of information you picked up. She did know other things, however, that weren't quite so useless. Things like where Harol the Fishmonger kept his stash of crowns and when it would be at its fullest. Things like which hand Carser the Butcher wielded his cleaver with so she could avoid it if he got too close. Things like what the fastest routes out of the market were for when things got too hot. Things like when the lads in the Greencoats would be patrolling and what time they took a break for dice and a swift jar of ale.

The Greencoats were the least of her worries. Well, maybe not the least, but they were way down the list. They didn't bother much about a lone street urchin. Some of them were even fairly sympathetic at times and turned a blind eye, either too lazy or too preoccupied to pay attention to young wastrels stealing morsels from the market stalls.

No, it was the Guild that was the worst.

They'd have someone wandering around now, sizing up the best punters for the catch, signalling to their pickers, pinchers and cutters so they knew which marks to go for. It was organised, disciplined, and so they took the richest pickings. If Rag got in the way, distracted a picker or drew undue attention, she'd get more than a hiding; she'd be lucky if she'd be left with her eyes. Then it'd be a life on the corners of Dockside or worse, the Rafts, and she'd have no choice but to beg with the rest of the cripples, *if* she were lucky. If she weren't lucky she'd be whored out for scraps, a freak, treated like an animal until someone ended her short life for her. Rag had seen it happen, and she was determined it weren't a fate she'd share. Yes, the Guild controlled this market, and thieving here without their say so was dangerous indeed.

Nevertheless, a gal had to eat, and Rag was mighty hungry.

The smell of Gunta's bread stall was wafting her way, almost as though the fat baker was just asking her to take one of his plump, brown loaves. She'd robbed him before, more than once, and it was likely he'd be looking out for her, but Rag had a knack for going unnoticed. For some children, normal children with parents who bought them food and clothes and kept a roof over them, lack of attention might have been a problem. Not so for Rag. Her talent for being ignored suited her just fine.

Across the market the Guild lookout was busy marking a punter for his pincher, so there'd be no trouble there. The three lads in the Greencoats were laughing and joking with two well-dressed girls who looked well out of their league, so no trouble there neither.

Fat Gunta was busy chatting to two equally fat women, who by the looks of them needed to skip a few meals. It was almost as if the baker was begging her to help rid him of his wares.

Rag walked up all casual. She matched the pace of a passing merchant, allowing his bulk to shield her, and for a split second thought of cutting his purse, but she knew it wasn't worth it. Loaves was of no interest to the Guild. Purses was quite different.

As the merchant passed the end of Gunta's stall, Rag stopped walking and let him move on, never looking up, never locking her eyes on the mark lest he glance round and see her, or those fat ladies spot her and give the game away. Most times if you didn't look at someone they wouldn't look at you, wouldn't even notice you were there. She was right next to the stall now, within arm's reach of a nice crusty loaf. It weren't nothing just to take one, and it was in her hand before anyone noticed; not so fast as to attract attention, not so slow as to take all day. In less time than it took to suck up a breath, her coat was open and the loaf aiming for the inside of it, when someone banged into her. Rag stumbled, the bread spilling from her grip and cracking on the cobbles right in front of the stall, crust breaking to bits like a shattered mirror, and making not much less noise.

'Oi!' screamed Gunta, ladies forgotten and his face all twisted in rage. 'You little bastard! Come here!'

Rag didn't need further encouragement to head off through the crowd, but before she could take a step someone had grabbed her coat by the collar. She struggled in vain – he had her. She glanced back to see who it was, hoping it weren't a Greencoat, terrified it might be someone from the Guild, but it was just an ordinary bloke, going about his business.

She struggled and squirmed her best, even trying to stamp on the wanker's foot, but he was immovable, and Gunta was coming from behind that bread counter, his face all puffy and red. She was going to get a right beating for this and no mistake.

Rag let her body go slack, bending her knees and dropping out of her coat, just before Gunta was able to grab her. Then she was off and running, through the crowd and all the hubbub. She'd had that coat for years, and it pained her to leave it behind, but better a coat gone than maybe some fingers, she reckoned.

Gunta was coming on behind, screaming his head off and stirring up the whole marketplace, but Rag, concentrating on escape, only thought to get to the nearest alley and disappear.

Before she could make it, she caught sight of a figure moving fast and purposeful towards her through the crowd. A Greencoat – young and eager, unlike most of the others, and definitely in better shape than Gunta. He had the determined look of a man with something to prove, and catching Rag was his way of doing it.

Ducking a swipe of his arm, she dodged sideways into one of the narrow streets that led from the market. Her bare feet mashed the shit of the alley as she increased her pace, but the Greencoat continued his pursuit, helmet rattling and crossbow slapping against his back. Rag sped through the tight labyrinthine alleyways with practised ease, but her pursuer was matching her pace with sheer power. For a brief second she considered her knife – pulling it on her pursuer might make him wonder whether catching her was worth being cut – though she hadn't used a blade in anger for years. Truth was she'd never been convincing with a shiv. She remembered how Gus the Puller had just taken it off her once and put a stripe down her cheek for her trouble. After that she never bothered again.

Rag realised she wasn't going to outrun the lad so she would just have to disappear. As she turned another corner she jumped, planting her bare foot against a narrow windowsill and propelling herself upwards, catching hold of the lintel and dragging her body up above head height. Within two breaths the Greencoat turned the corner, splashing through the puddles and heaving air into his lungs. Thinking Rag had gone, he stopped, cursing loudly and slapping his thigh in anger. All the while she watched from above him, holding her breath, but this Greencoat obviously wasn't a clever one; he never even bothered to look up.

When he was gone Rag climbed down from the sill, with neither food nor coat. All in all it hadn't been a good day's work, but the day wasn't over yet – something else might come along.

With the market too hot to return to, she headed for Slip Street where she usually bedded down. Slip Street was on the edge of Dockside, not the worst place in that district, but certainly worse than anywhere in Eastgate. It was generally filled with drunks looking for a good time, and expecting to find it there. Aside from the alehouses that lined the street, almost every spare doorway housed a whore of one type or another. Rag would have felt uncomfortable here, vulnerable even, but this was where she'd grown up; her face was known to most of the girls and boys who plied their trade, but for the most part she was ignored. But then that had always been her talent.

She climbed the rickety stairs at the side of the Silent Bull inn, her filthy feet padding lithely across the cracked and broken wood. Her weight made the whole staircase creak violently, but it held beneath her. A full grown man using those stairs might have made them collapse; he'd certainly have made a hell of a racket climbing them. It was the kind of early warning that kept Rag alive in the foul and dangerous streets. Rag and her fellas.

As she made her way up, past the third storey and onto the roof, Tidge was there waiting for her as usual. His big sad eyes stared hopefully from his dirty, podgy face.

'Didn't get nothing, mate,' Rag said, walking past him towards the rickety shack that sat on the flat roof of the inn.

'Where's your coat?' Tidge asked.

'I had to lose it, but don't you worry, I'll find another before the cold nights come.'

She stooped below the broken lintel of the makeshift shack that sat in the centre of the roof and climbed inside. The previous night's fire had burned down to embers, which smoked feebly in the bottom of the rusted old shield that made do as a fire pit. On the bench opposite were Migs and Chirpy, sitting close enough to be hugging, as they usually were.

'All right, Rag?' Chirpy asked with his usual smile. Migs was silent as ever, looking out from beneath the long fringe that fell down almost to his nose.

'Yeah,' Rag answered, but she knew she wasn't. Another failed day in the market meant they had another night with nothing to eat. She could only hope that Fender would bring them something later – if he decided to come back at all.

Tidge climbed into the shack and sat beside her, resting his head on her arm. She hugged him close, looking through the cracks in the wall of the shack and out across the city.

Below, from the streets surrounding the inn, came the sound of the corner girls plying their trade, their sweet voices full of promise and allure. Rag felt both disgust and envy. She resented them for giving their bodies away so easily, degrading themselves for a few coins, but deep down she knew they only did it to survive; if they had an alternative they'd take it. She was jealous too – jealous that she'd been born so pig ugly, so awkward and unsightly. There was no way she'd make any money on the street corner even if she could lower herself enough to try. Not that she ever would.

Back in the dim past, Rag's mother had been a corner whore – and a beautiful one too. They had lived in a room back then. Not a big room, and it was none too clean, but they had a roof and walls and it was warm. There'd been food on the table and all Rag had to do was make herself scarce while her mother did the business. She'd been called Morag then, Morag Rounsey; a real name for a real girl. That had all changed after her mother met the man from Silverwall. He wore fancy clothes, had a sweet smell about him and flashed his pennies around like he was someone that mattered. Rag's mother had told her she was going off with the man, back to Silverwall to be with him, but she'd return soon enough to take Morag with her. Then they'd both move to Silverwall to live with the fancy bloke in his fancy house.

Rag had stayed in that room for days – she couldn't remember how many. After a while the landlord come to turf her out; she didn't have any coin and where her mother was weren't none of his problem, any road. She'd hung round the building for weeks after, always waiting, begging for scraps, selling what little she had left for food. It was a while before she realised her mother weren't ever coming back.

And so she'd become Rag, a thief and a beggar. She'd learned harsh lessons – who were your friends and who weren't, where to go and where not, who to thieve from and who to avoid – and now here she was with a crew of her own, for what they were worth. Orphans all, and none of them any good at stealing, apart from Fender of course, but they were her crew, and they loved each other in their own way. She felt like they were family and she'd do what she could to look after them for as long as she was able.

A sudden noise made her jump up. Tidge gave a squeal as he fell sideways, and Chirpy and Migs grabbed each other even tighter.

Rag moved to the doorway and peered out. Relief washed over her as she saw Markus walking across the roof. He gave a wave and a smile.

Markus entered their shack with a jolly 'hello', sitting on the little woodpile and looking round as if he was one of them, as if he belonged. It was obvious to anyone with half an eye that he didn't. The boy was clean for a start . . . well certainly cleaner than any of the street kids he was sitting with. His clothes had no holes and had been washed within the past week and his hands weren't grimed with filth, the nails white, not black from scrabbling through garbage for food. He'd been hanging round with them for weeks, and Rag hadn't seen the harm in it. He wasn't an orphan; he lived with his father in the Trades Quarter, but Rag had found him wandering the streets, sad and alone like a lost puppy. Of course she'd taken him under her wing – that's what she did – but he didn't thieve and he didn't beg. No use but no harm, so what was the danger?

'You all right?' Rag asked, when Markus didn't speak.

He shrugged back. 'Good as ever,' he said.

Rag hadn't asked, and Markus hadn't told, but she reckoned on the boy's father being a bit of a bastard, which was why he had taken to wandering the streets so far from home and hanging round with the urchins. It weren't none of her affair so she didn't pry. Everyone had their own private business, she reckoned.

'Might be cold tonight,' said Chirpy. 'We should maybe think about getting the fire going again.'

'Don't talk wet,' Tidge replied. 'Ain't been cold for ages. I reckons we should save the wood for another night.'

Rag smiled at his good sense. For his age he had a solid head on his shoulders. He might even be clever enough to leave this shit life when he was old enough.

'We'll wait and see,' said Rag. 'Could be a storm coming.' She nodded through the missing slats in the shack towards the north. A dark

37

cloudbank was gathering on the horizon, an ominous blackness that threatened to consume the clear blue.

'What the fuck's this, a mothers' meeting?'

Rag started at the voice, but as soon as she saw the tall figure framed in the doorway she relaxed.

Fender climbed inside, his lithe muscular limbs moving with feline grace within the confines of the makeshift shelter.

'What's the matter? You've a face as long as a donkey's cock.' He sat down in the middle of the group, with Migs and Chirpy shuffling up to give him room. 'Looks like you've had a shit day at work, Rag? Where's your coat?'

'I gave it to your mum,' she replied. 'She said she was cold sucking cock at night time.'

Fender smiled back. He'd never known his mother or father, so it weren't any insult. 'It's a good job one of us has been busy, ain't it?' He reached in the pocket of his coat and pulled out a tiny bronze vase. The younger boys looked at it with awe, their little faces lighting up at such a flagrant display of wealth.

Fender tossed the item to Tidge. 'Go deal this to Boris downstairs. And don't let the fat bastard sell you short.'

Tidge didn't need telling twice and ran out of the shack faster than Rag had ever seen him move. This was good – they might eat tonight. Boris, innkeeper of the Silent Bull, didn't mind them making a home on the roof as long as they kept providing him with the odd trinket. He'd even give them food and a little grog if the items were valuable enough.

'What the fuck's he doing here?' Fender said suddenly, looking daggers at Markus.

'He ain't doing nothing,' Rag replied defensively, but she knew it wouldn't placate Fender – he hated Markus. It was jealousy, pure and simple, and Fender could be a nasty bastard sometimes. Nevertheless, Markus had always taken every slap and insult Fender dished out, and kept coming back for more.

'I've had enough of it.' Fender stood, ducking beneath the low roof of the shack but still towering over the rest of them. 'If he stays, he pays, like the rest.'

'Sit down, Fen—'

'Fuck off, Rag, I mean it. Get out, rich boy, and don't fucking come back until you bring something worthwhile. We all gives a bit for the pot. Time you did the same.'

Markus had already moved to the door, clearly fearful of Fender and his cold challenge, but he raised his chin defiantly. Rag had to admit she was a bit proud of him for that.

'All right, I will,' he said in a small voice. Then he ran off across the roof.

'You didn't have to do that. He's one of us,' said Rag.

'Like fuck he is. He's got family. He don't need us. Let's wait for winter, shall we, wait for the biting cold and the hunger to set in? Then we'll see how many times he comes to stay.'

Rag didn't answer. She wanted to tell Fender where to go, wanted to tell him that Markus was a member of her crew and she trusted him, but she couldn't – because, deep down, she couldn't help but think that Fender was right, and when the going got tough they would never see Markus again.

FIVE

The song of steel was not a pretty tune. It rang out, discordant and loud, hammered in with muscle and sweat and dirt. Nobul Jacks performed the song like an artist, working his anvil as well as any fiddler at his bow, his powerful strokes expert in their precision. His formidable frame struck out the rhythm; hammer smashing white-hot steel, which sparked in quick quick time, filling the smithy with a dirge to rival any orchestra.

In the darkness of the forge a fierce fire burned, blades protruding like the spokes of a wheel, ready to be struck flat or quenched in water, ready to sing like the strings of a harp. Nearby stood the grinding stone whose voice called out as it sharpened and honed in a perfect falsetto.

For Nobul this was more than mere craft, more than a living. When working the forge he could forget what his life had become – all that existed was the song, the music of his labours, and it swept him from the world, his nightmares and his grief. Once he had closed the door behind him, he felt safe, deep in the sanctuary of his noisy, dirty, honest work.

But the door could not stay shut forever.

It opened, letting the sunlight from outside wash the interior of the forge and breach its sanctity. Nobul paused, hammer raised, as, with the opening of the door, the magic of the song was lost.

Two men entered; big men, burly men. Both taller than Nobul, with thick necks and shaved heads, but they were not lean like him, not hard, not wrought of iron sinew as he was. Nevertheless, Nobul placed his hammer down gently, and with a leather-gloved hand shoved the glowing steel back into the coals of the fire.

One man walked forward as the other closed the door behind them, shutting out the noise of the street. The first smiled, confident, his head slightly cocked to one side.

'Hello again, Nobul,' he said, in a deep, arrogant voice. 'You know the drill.'

Nobul did not speak; he did not have to. Instead he moved to the back of the forge to the worktable that sat against the wall. It was scattered with cross-guards and pommel heads, some ornate and made from bronze or silver, others simpler, crafted from polished iron or other base metals. Whatever the material, they were all of the highest quality; Nobul never made second-rate gear. He was a craftsman: though his wares varied in price they were all finished with meticulous care.

A layman might have considered the table a mess, but Nobul knew where everything was, everything kept in its proper place. He reached for a small leather pouch secured by a drawstring. Still silent, he walked back across the forge and placed the pouch in the big man's upturned palm. The brute smiled, weighing it in his hand and jingling the contents before untying the drawstring and glancing within.

'Feels a little light. Do I have to count it?'

'It's all there,' Nobul replied. There was no fear in his voice. These men didn't inspire fear in him as they did in others. Nobul was too proud to be scared. He'd gone through too much to be afraid of men such as these, despite their size. Despite their reputation.

'I'm sure it is,' said the man, smiling again as he secured the drawstring and secreted the pouch within his jacket. 'How's business anyway? Good, I'll bet. You must have more work than you can manage, what with the war coming.'

'Business is fine,' Nobul answered.

'Come now, Nobul. It's more than fine, we both know that. The Guild keeps abreast of these things. We're always watching, even if you can't see us. Weapons and armour for the soldiers at the front are in high demand, especially from a smith of your . . . talent. And a man of your talent needs protecting, needs looking after. You never know when an agent of the Khurtas might come knocking, might want to do you harm to sabotage the war effort. That's why we'll be taking extra special care of you over the coming months. And consequently this extra care will cost a premium.'

Nobul didn't answer; there was little point. He paid his protection money to be left alone, not to be looked after.

With a nod, the big man turned. His burly friend opened the door, allowing the clangour in once more. 'Be seeing you,' said the brute, with a smile; then they were gone, letting the door slam shut behind them.

Nobul clenched his fists, feeling helpless, full of rage. Truth was he *had* received a big commission from the Crown, but he was only one man and he couldn't afford an apprentice. His son was too young to work the forge, and this backbreaking work wasn't something he wanted for the boy anyway. It was hard, dirty work, for hard, dirty men, and Markus was not suited to it. Though Nobul had raised him as best he could, their relationship was far from ideal. The last thing Nobul wanted was to *make* him work the forge and drive an even deeper wedge between them.

Yet what choice did he have? If he hadn't got to pay back his loan for the forge, together with his stipend to the Guild for their 'services', he might have been able to get ahead. But if he now had to pay out even more, how could he keep a roof over his head and feed himself, let alone Markus?

Standing around lamenting wasn't going to solve the problem. Nobul pulled the glove back onto his hand and picked up his hammer.

It was dark when he finally left the forge and ventured out into the cool of the street. Several people were busying themselves hanging banners and bunting for the Feast of Arlor, but Nobul wasn't interested in any of that. What was the point?

He closed the heavy door behind him, turning the large iron keys in their mortise locks at the top and bottom of the door before taking the short walk to the small house he and Markus called home. Though the tiny space was cramped with the furniture they owned, it still felt empty without her there. He looked towards the hearth where she would have been . . . should have been sitting, but the chair was empty. The fire was lit though, and above it bubbled a pot of broth which filled the room with a rich smell that made his stomach rumble with approval.

'Markus?' Nobul called. He was answered by a clattering upstairs from their shared bedchamber, followed by his son's muffled answer. The boy came down the stairs as quick as he could at his father's call, stumbling halfway down. He was a clumsy child, gangly, thin, weak at the shoulders. Something inside Nobul resented him for that. If Nobul had been able to forge his son as he could forge weapons and armour, Markus would indeed have been a formidable child. It hadn't worked out that way.

'Father,' Markus said, reaching the bottom of the stairs, and attempting to compose himself.

'Asleep again?' Nobul said, not expecting an answer. Markus only ever seemed happy when he was napping, only seemed to smile in his sleep.

It was a laziness that Nobul should have beaten out of him. It was time Markus learned some of his father's hard work ethic, but beating him never seemed to work. It certainly hadn't toughened him up, and Nobul was loath to continue on that path. It might eventually drive his son away altogether, and Nobul had lost enough.

'Lay the table,' Nobul ordered as he kicked off his boots and sat by the fire.

'I made the broth,' Markus said, placing wooden trenchers on the table and laying out the spoons.

'Yes, I can see that.'

'And I went and got the bread like you asked. Baker said he was doing a deal on the soft kind, the stuff with no grainy bits in, so I got that.'

Nobul frowned. 'Markus, how many times? The soft kind doesn't last; it'll be stale in a day. We need a loaf to last the week. I'm not made of—' He stopped himself. It would do no good. Markus didn't seem to pay heed to any chastisement; he just retreated further into himself.

Nobul lifted the lid of the stew pot, and picked up the wooden spoon that sat by the hearth. Then he stopped – the pot was filled to the brim. It looked like Markus had used their entire stock of meat and vegetables for the month.

'What's this?' he demanded. Markus froze by the dinner table, trans-fixed. 'When will you think, boy? Our food has to last. If you cook it all in one stew it'll be bad in a few days.'

His son's eyes began to well with tears, and Nobul suddenly found himself twisting the wooden spoon in his hands like a damp dishcloth. He must keep his temper, stay ahead, not let the daemons within rise up.

'Never mind. We'll just have to make do.'

They sat down to eat in silence, as always. No grace was said, no thanks to the gods. Why bother? It wasn't them had paid for the food, it wasn't them had cooked it.

Nobul was ravenous but he took his time, savouring the meat and the taste of the fresh bread. He had to give his son something – he could certainly cook a decent broth. Markus, however, gobbled his stew down faster than Nobul had ever seen him. Steam was coming from his mouth, and his cheeks were reddening with the heat; it was obviously burning as it went down, but the boy seemed heedless of the pain.

'You in a rush?' Nobul asked.

Markus looked up. It was a guilty look if ever Nobul had seen one, but his son shook his head nonetheless. He slowed his eating somewhat, but still finished well before Nobul, quickly getting up and taking his trencher and spoon to the bucket that stood in the corner. Nobul watched his son clean his plate, stack it by the windowsill to dry, then turn, anxiously.

'Am I keeping you?' Nobul asked.

Markus shook his head, but his leg was twitching, quivering like the hind end of a rutting stallion; it was obvious he wanted to be somewhere, anywhere, else.

'It's getting late. Sun's gone down. You know I don't like it when you—'

'I'll be careful,' Markus said. 'And I won't be out later than last bell.'

Nobul nodded, then bent his head towards the door in a *go on then, get out* gesture.

Markus gave a half smile, and was rushing towards the door when Nobul suddenly reached out to stop him. He had only wanted to tell him to keep a lookout, and not stray too far, but when he grabbed his son's arm he felt something hard beneath the sleeve.

Whatever he was going to say was forgotten as he pulled Markus towards him, dragging up the sleeve of his cotton shirt and seeing the tiny pouch tied to his forearm. He didn't speak but pulled the pouch free and wrenched it open. He could already tell what was inside. Four tiny coins sat at the bottom: three coppers and one silver piece. Enough to feed them for a week.

Nobul stood up slowly as he poured the coins into his open hand.

'Where did you get these?' Rage was building, and it wasn't helped by the fact that Markus looked so guilty, like someone caught red-handed. There was no answer, and his anger bubbled up like that thick broth, in the stew pot. Nobul towered over the slight form of his son. 'Tell me!' he shouted. 'Did you steal it? Who did you—'

Then he froze. It wasn't possible, it couldn't be, but deep down he already knew it was.

'Did you get this from under my bed? For what? To give to those urchins you've taken up with? What have I told you about that street scum?'

The tear that suddenly ran down Markus' cheek spoke the confession his lips didn't dare.

The slap was loud as Nobul's meaty palm struck his son's cheek. It was hard enough to knock Markus off his feet and send him sprawling, his gangly limbs flailing. It had been instinctive, a result of the rage, and as Nobul watched his son fall he instantly regretted it.

He took a step forward, reaching out to pick the boy up, his mouth open to speak a word of regret, perhaps even to say he was sorry, but

44

Markus was immediately up on his feet and at the door. Nobul didn't even have time to call out before Markus had wrenched open the door and run out into the night.

Nobul could only watch him leave.

The coins were still in his hand. They seemed to burn in his palm like he was holding a searing brand, reminding him of his guilt. With a feral growl he flung the coins across the room where they bounced and scattered.

Slowly, with each breath, he calmed, the rage cooling, his eyes tightly shut. For another man, a weaker man, they might have been shut to quell the tears of his regret, but Nobul had done all his crying twelve years ago. He had no tears left.

He closed the door and went to the hearth to sit in the chair. Her chair.

Rona had been young when they met. Too young for Nobul, or so everyone had told him. At first he'd ignored them, just happy that she had shown him any attention, happy that they were together. He'd never met anyone like her before, anyone so innocent and sweet and kind. Eventually though he had listened to the voices: his old friends, or what Nobul had in the way of friends, and also her parents, though they had never spoken ill of him to his face. He'd responded by trying to put her off, tried to explain he was no good and she should find someone better, someone younger. It hadn't worked at first, not until he got drunk one night and into a bar fight. Then she had seen the real Nobul Jacks, the fast Nobul Jacks, tough and ruthless. Yet two days after, when all the dust had settled, she'd come back to him. He hadn't been able to turn her away, and he had promised, as she asked, not to fight any more.

They were married north of the city, just the two of them under an old elm tree. Just them and the druid, a wedding looked over by the Old Gods just as she'd wanted. They returned to the city and hadn't been back more than a day before Nobul got the call up. There had been rumblings in the south for months. The Wardens of the South had come back with reports that there were Lion Men abroad, beating the drums of war with their eye on the Free States. As an ex-mercenary Nobul was expected to fight, expected to offer his sword arm to the cause, despite the promise he had made to Rona. He had no choice.

Before he travelled south with the armies, he promised Rona he would come back, promised he would return with everything he went with still intact. Nobul had asked nothing of her. How could he? She was young, and if he died she would have to move on, find someone new to take care of her.

War against the Aeslanti had been worse than any of them could have thought. They'd heard the tales that the beast warriors of Equ'un were giants who lived on the flesh of men. The truth had been much worse.

The Battle of Bakhaus Gate was legendary now; a thousand brave men holding the pass against a horde of roaring monsters. Fighting valiantly with the flags of the Free States held aloft with pride.

Reality was somewhat less glorious – it always was.

They had been closer to ten thousand, every one of them pissing in fear. No one gave a fuck about flags or pride or glory, they just wanted to run, and they would have if they hadn't been more afraid of their commanding officers than the enemy. The vast host they faced had been enough to make them question that fear though, and their loyalty to officers or even the king. An armoured sea of bestial daemons, waving massive blades and roaring louder than a thunderstorm, had swept towards Bakhaus Gate.

But somehow they had won.

Nobul kept his promise to Rona, and brought himself back with all parts still working, but what he had seen down in the south, the slaughter and the cruelty, had deadened him inside. Deadened him to her joy at having a baby and deadened him to watching that child grow. Instead he had learned a trade, a hard punishing trade – and busied himself with it heart and soul. What heart and soul he had left.

When Rona fell ill with the Sweet Canker, Nobul only flung himself into his work still further.

Only when he found her corpse lying in bed, her blue eyes staring at the ceiling, her body eaten away by sickness, did he realise just what he had missed . . . what he had lost.

All he had left was Markus, and now it seemed he had managed to drive the boy away. He needed Rona, needed her sweet touch, her careful words and her kindness, but she was gone.

Now he had nothing.

Nobul picked himself up from the chair, pulled on his boots and walked the short distance to the forge. He was pleased to find the embers of the fire still burned.

With a heavy heart he picked up his hammer and began the song of steel anew. Perhaps, with luck, he might lose himself in it once more.

SIX

The chamber was on the north side of the Tower of Magisters, its single window looking out onto the Storway and the Old Stone Road where they both began their long journeys. It was far from the highest room, only at the mid point of the vast citadel, but the view from its window still rivalled that from any other spire in the city of Steelhaven.

At one end of the chamber stood a pitch-blackened chalkboard covered in sigils, ciphers and runes, arranged in a web-like pattern of equations. To any man literate enough to read it would have seemed like a random scrawl, a pretty pattern of outlandish characters that might represent some ancient and forbidden language. To the members of the Caste, those within the Free States who were given licence to practise the arts of magick, it represented the source of their power, the meaning behind the Veil, a way to tap sorceries from the diabolical storms that raged unseen throughout the lands of men.

To Waylian Grimm it was all nonsense.

He had been such a promising student back in his home province of Ankavern. The college he had attended in the town of Groffham had lauded him as their best scholar, heaping praise on him, apparently delighted that his intellect was far in excess of any of his peers. Waylian had even been considered more able than some of his tutors, and it was only natural that he be recommended to the Tower of Magisters for advanced study. His parents had been eager too, even his mother, who had treated Waylian like a helpless infant until he was well into his teenage years. They were only too happy for him to travel the road west to

Steelhaven – the promise that their son might one day become a magister clearly outweighing their need to protect him.

Unfortunately, since his arrival, Waylian had found that the vast intellect and excellence at study which had made him so remarkable back in Ankavern seemed quite ordinary amongst his new peers. He was beginning to feel like something of a failure. That was not to say he hadn't learned much since starting his apprenticeship. Indeed, he had consumed knowledge voraciously.

In the few months since his schooling began he had learned the basics of seven different languages, from the distinct clicks and sighs of the differing Equ'un tribes to the lilting singsong dialects of the Elharim. He had mastered histories both ancient and modern, from the many campaigns of the Kaer'Vahari Dragon Wars to the military strategies of the Sword Kings, and the migratory routes of the early Teutonian tribes. He had studied the origins of the Old Gods and their eventual demise before the rising veneration of Arlor and Vorena. Waylian had become an accomplished theologian with expert knowledge in the pantheons of a dozen polytheistic cultures, from the various Khurtic death cults to the Aeslanti sky gods and their relevant constellations. His knowledge of eastern manners, rituals and customs was second to none, and had he so desired Waylian could easily have become a valuable envoy to the East in the court of King Cael.

All of no use though, if he couldn't even grasp the basics of magick.

The Magistra stood beside the board, speaking in her rapid monotone. She was the only other person in the room, her focus solely on teaching Waylian the intricacies of the art. She might as well have been speaking in tongues for all he understood.

Waylian *had* studied the books – one of them was open before him even now, the relevant page taunting him with almost indecipherable language. He had learned all he could by rote: the relevant sigils, gestures, equations, components, incantations, meditations and means of execution; but he simply couldn't understand any of it.

Of course he had retained some things. He knew that the conjuration of fire required coal dust, soot or some other carbon based ingredient, spread on the skin in the correct manner whilst evoking the requisite incantation. He knew that the weather could be harnessed and manipulated to the magicker's will through the tapping of simple elemental conduits. He knew that non-sentient creatures could be influenced into carrying out the will of any man who knew the relevant language and the particular words to speak. But when asked to recall any of the details, when he had to remember the specific incantations or the components that went with a particular conjuration, his mind was a blank.

Without this secret knowledge, without being able to put all these things together instinctively, it was impossible for a magister to tap into the storm, to break the Veil and become a true caster.

Waylian's only consolation was that, for now, he wouldn't have to. He was only an apprentice, a journeyman, a neophyte, and consequently forbidden to perform magick until he was inducted as a member of the Caste. For now his studies were purely theoretical, and as long as they stayed like that, Waylian would be able to disguise the fact that he was struggling. More than struggling – he was failing, drowning in a sea of knowledge he could neither comprehend nor control.

'Am I keeping you awake?'

It was the Magistra.

At her words, Waylian suddenly realised he had been staring at the hard wood of his desk, rather than hanging on her every word. She gazed at him, her white hair swept back, pulled tight and severe, her mature features, her piercing blue eyes, glaring with contempt.

'No, Magistra,' Waylian replied. He swallowed hard.

Waylian was fearful of his teacher – more fearful of her than he had been of any other human being in his short life. She was his mentor, his tutor, but above all his mistress. Gelredida . . . the Red Witch as she was called by the other apprentices, though Waylian only ever called her Magistra. She stood tall and erect, though the lines of her face showed an age and experience far beyond mortal years. Waylian had often wondered if she used her magicks to keep herself youthful. Perhaps she was centuries old?

Not that he would ever dare ask.

She was well respected and feared within the Tower, treated with reverence even by the other magisters. Trust his damned luck to end up apprenticed to such a formidable tutor.

It was not just her commanding air and reputation that fuelled Waylian's fear. It was her aura of power, the self-assurance that emanated from her, as though she could snatch the life from anyone who crossed her – not that she had ever demonstrated such power. Indeed, since Waylian had arrived in Steelhaven he had not seen so much as a minor invocation being uttered. He had learned quickly that magick was a powerful tool, never to be used lightly. Its use came with a price that was paid by every magister, one way or another. This was demonstrated in some of the older magickers who wandered the halls of the Tower – some muttering to themselves in dementia-fuelled rants, others stooped, toothless and horribly scarred, their bodies withered or maimed; by what fell magicks Waylian dare not imagine.

'I'd hate to think I was talking to myself.' She gripped the piece of white chalk in her slender hand and motioned to the blackboard. 'So, just for my edification, remind me what is the basic principle of elemental conjuration.'

Waylian felt panic grip him. He glanced towards the chalkboard for a second, hoping the random scrawl upon it might suddenly offer some kind of answer, but no – it was still utterly meaningless.

Elemental conjuration – now that was a tough one.

Or was it? Was that actually one he knew?

Conjuration referred to summoning – that was easy enough – but was it elemental beings, like giant fire daemons, or was it elemental phenomena, like lightning storms and tidal waves?

He had no idea.

For a second he considered trying to bluff it, perhaps making something up that might sound convincing, but he knew that was stupid. Gelredida accepted nothing tentative, tolerated no guessing. She wanted the answer and she wanted it as it was written in one of her dusty tomes, spoken verbatim and with confidence. A wrong answer would have been just as bad as no answer at all.

Waylian gave a shrug of his shoulders, trying to go for the brave kind of shrug, the one that demonstrates valour and overarching confidence. He knew deep down he just looked pathetic.

'What a surprise,' said the Magistra, clearly unsurprised that her student didn't have a clue. Well, she must have been getting used to it by now. 'Just in case you choose to remember it next time, the basic principle is harmony. All life is, at its most fundamental, made up of the same elements. Components for elemental conjuration do not determine the results; that is for the magister to decide. A component will simply translate the form to a specific task. Understand?'

Waylian nodded.

'Somehow I doubt it,' said the Magistra. 'But essentially it means even by using water, with enough practice, you could conjure and harness the element of fire to your will. Though why I'm bothering to elucidate is beyond me.'

She closed her eyes. Waylian didn't know whether she was quelling her anger or merely showing frustration. Either way it made him nervous.

'From now on, my non-conversant student, we will call you *Pultra*. I believe you are now familiar with our arrangement, Pultra?'

He nodded despondently.

Waylian was all too familiar with the 'arrangement'. The Magistra would pick a name, an insulting, demeaning or otherwise unpleasant name, from some foreign and obscure dialect. Until Waylian could identify the origin and meaning of the name, he would continue to be known by it. This in itself might not have been so bad, but until he found the answer to his mistress's little quandary he was also given the most menial of menial tasks to perform, like clearing the swill after mealtimes and wiping clean every blackboard in the tutorial chambers.

'Excellent, Pultra. Then I believe you have some studying to do.'

'Yes, Magistra,' Waylian replied, closing the book on his desk. He stuffed the book, his quill, ink and some loose parchments into his battered leather satchel and shuffled past the empty rows of desks towards the door. He didn't dare look at the Magistra; he didn't want to meet her withering stare.

In the corridor outside, Waylian felt relief wash over him. Without the twin swords of *expectation* and *disappointment* dangling over his head, he could breathe again. It was all he could do to stop himself from running to the Grand Library.

The *Liber Conflagrantia* took up an entire floor of the Tower of Magisters. It truly was the grandest of libraries – the repository of five thousand years of history. It held tomes on cultures and religions long dead and maps and parchments showing borders and boundaries trampled into obscurity under the feet of ancient conquerors and kings.

Whenever Waylian entered its hallowed confines he was struck dumb.

Two Raven Knights, standing like black armoured statues, guarded the doorway to the library, their spears reaching almost to the ceiling. Waylian kept his head bowed as he passed them – though he couldn't see their eyes within the beaked full-helms he wasn't going to chance drawing undue attention to himself. The Raven Knights were the guardians of the Tower of Magisters, an order dedicated to the protection of the vast citadel and those housed within it. They had no magickal abilities, but their martial prowess was unrivalled – even by the Knights of the Blood. They lived only for one purpose – to carry out the will of the Crucible of Magisters, and this they did with a fanatical zeal. Even though he knew each one would lay down his life to protect him, Waylian could not help but be fearful of them.

Inside the library, the overwhelming smell of parchment, dust and old wood assailed his nostrils. In one corner stood the huge skeleton of an Aeslanti warrior – over seven feet tall, the bones twice as thick as a man's, the fangs of its skull as long as Waylian's middle finger. Even in death the beast was a fearsome thing to behold, a grisly reminder of the courage shown by the armies of the Free States and their king.

The vast chamber was eerily quiet for a room of such size. Two old magisters sat at the far end, silently poring over antiquated codices, but otherwise the place was empty.

Waylian's heart sank as he began to understand the size of the task ahead of him. The place housed thousands of tomes, and he was charged with finding a single piece of information.

He had never been one to admit defeat; he would just have to begin somewhere and carry on until he found it.

Magistra Gelredida had registered her displeasure this way before. She had always selected the most obscure languages from the least known cultures to test Waylian to the limit. Previously she had called him the ancient Sword King name for cow dung, a word used by the monks of Han-Shar for the ring they inserted through a bull's nose; then he had borne the Khurtic slave word for goats' testicles. *Pultra* sounded Teutonian in origin, but there was no chance it would be that simple. Perhaps it was Golgarthan or from the Ice Holds of Morath further north – though it didn't sound guttural and savage enough.

'The Red Witch given you another one of those tedious names to work out, Grimm?'

Waylian almost leapt out of his skin at the whispered question, but when he saw the speaker he let out an audible sigh.

Rembram Thule sat at a small wooden desk, squirrelled away between two extremely large bookshelves. He was smiling, as usual, his dark hair flopping down over his handsome face. He was charismatic, self-assured, attractive – everything Waylian wasn't.

'How did you guess, Bram?' said Waylian in lowered tones, moving to sit in a chair opposite. 'And stop calling her that out loud. If one of the magisters hears, you'll be doing menials all through the Feast of Arlor.'

'Those two old goats are deaf as posts.' He motioned casually over a line of study desks towards the magisters sitting deep in thought.

'I'm sure. But she has . . . ways, you know. I'm sure she hears everything that goes on within these walls. I wouldn't be surprised if she can hear this conversation.'

'You sound paranoid, Grimm.'

'Well wouldn't you be? I feel cursed; it's like nothing I ever do is right – nothing I say, no answers I give. I'm sure she's just waiting to expel me from the Tower, or worse.'

'What, turn you into a frog?' Bram smiled slyly.

'It's no laughing matter. You don't know how good you've got it.'

'Oh yeah, I've got it easy, apprenticed to a senile old bat. Why do you think I'm here stuck in the library when everyone else is relaxing in the apprentices' lounge? Because nothing Magister Arfax teaches me is of any bloody use, that's why. I may as well be tutoring myself.'

Waylian suddenly felt jealous. Bram was an exemplary student, breezing through the theoretical tests of magick all first year students were given, and it seemed he did it all off his own back. Even with the stern ministrations of Magistra Gelredida, Waylian hadn't even managed to master the basics.

'Trust me,' Waylian said. 'You've got it much easier. Besides, you seem to be doing fine. The way I'm going I won't be here for much longer, anyway.'

'Don't give in so easily, Grimm. Trust me, you'll get it eventually; it'll be like turning a corner and the whole thing's just laid out before you. Everything will be clear. I promise: you'll wonder what all the fuss was about.'

'I hope so,' Waylian replied, thinking of life back in a provincial town, a dull life inescapably mapped out. He would make any deal, any pact to avoid returning to it.

'I know so.' Bram closed his book and stuffed it into his satchel. He stood up and squeezed Waylian's shoulder. 'Anyway, what's the name you've got this time?'

'She's started calling me *Pultra*.'

'Sounds nice. Got a bit of an Eastern ring to it, but the morphology's a bit too archaic. How did she say it?'

'She said, *Pultra*.' Waylian repeated the word as best he could remember, but there were no stresses on any of the syllables.

'Yeah, that's no help. What was she teaching you when she decided you needed a new name?'

'Something about elemental conjuration. I can't remember exactly what.'

'Then I suggest you start there.' And with a wink, Bram walked across the library towards the exit, sandals clicking rhythmically on the wooden floorboards, leaving Waylian alone in that vast repository of knowledge.

He gave a sigh, glancing round the massive library, then began searching for the section on conjuration.

It took him three hours, but eventually Waylian found what he was looking for. It was in a little used tome regarding elemental definitions entitled *The Way of the Five Sages*. There was a small section on materialising golems from the earth itself, all theoretical and very confusing, but Waylian kind of got the gist. Right at the bottom of the section it explained that if these conjurations were cast incorrectly, the golem would fail, becoming nothing more than globules of earth and tar. These failed abortions were known as *pultra*.

Waylian wanted to feel happy that he'd managed to discover the answer to his quandary, but somehow it seemed a hollow achievement. Magistra Gelredida was obviously sending him a message loud and clear – he was a failure of the worst kind, lingering around the place like a leprous old dog.

As he watched the moon shining through the grand window of the *Liber Conflagrantia*, Waylian hoped she would have the grace to put him out of his misery sooner rather than later.

SEVEN

The smell of the streets was repugnant, the sound clamorous, the view dazzling. Northgate was lit up, a thousand fires twinkling from windows or glowing from street braziers, the dots of light mirroring the constellations that burned in the clear night sky above.

For River it was the perfect setting in which to ply his trade.

He wore the shadows like a cloak, the light slipping off his shoulders like blood from a blade. With noiseless tread he moved across the dark rooftops, his every sense heightened to sights and sounds that both repulsed and thrilled him. He yearned to be back within the sanctum, safe from the din, but also relished the freedom of being out in the open, moving across the rooftops like an animal, testing his mind and body to their limits.

The warehouse lay up ahead, shadowy against the surrounding illumination. To River it stood like a beacon in the middle of the city, a dark target towards which he was drawn *like a shark to a cornered fish*.

He homed in on his prey, eager to reach the warehouse, to reach his mark and carry out his task, padding across the rooftops with unparalleled surety. His clothes were dark rather than black, able to reflect the light and better hide his movement. A hood drawn over his head disguised his scarred features, not that anyone would see his face – not see it and live, anyway.

River reached the edge of the roof. Between him and the warehouse was almost twenty feet of empty air. With a lunge he was across the gap, grasping the edge of the warehouse roof within a steel grip, the sound of his landing muffled by the crowds of revellers below. River pulled himself up easily, crouching low to reduce any silhouette against the dark sky. He searched the roof for an entry point. A single window sat in the centre of the crooked pattern of tiles and carefully River tested its edge. He let out a long breath as it moved in his grip, and he willed it to be silent and not let out a noisy creak alerting those inside to his entry. The gap was less than a foot wide, but River easily slid through it. He hung in the darkness for a moment, allowing his eyes to adjust to the black, then dropped to wooden floorboards, more gently than a pattering of raindrops, but deadly in the dark.

Muffled voices echoed from the floor below – one raised in anger, others making the placatory noises of assent. The angry voice bore a hint of desperation, as though some man were in a rush, and to tarry here made him fearful. River knew this was the right place.

He moved to a rickety wooden staircase leading down from the loft, careful to distribute his weight evenly lest he cause one of the ageing timbers to creak. This was second nature to him, to move silently, to be aware of his surroundings, keeping his eyes and ears open, to recognise smells and even tastes that might aid his silent passage through unfamiliar terrain.

Peering ahead he could make out a lone figure standing at the top of a second staircase – a single guard . . . not enough. River moved, flowed through the shadows, *like the water in a stream*, creeping up on the bulky figure to within an arm's length. Even in the gloom he could see him picking at his fat nose, his finger probing deep for something in that vast cavity. He hadn't washed for at least five days – River could smell him – the faecal matter in his trews, the musk of sweat from his armpits, the stale smell of sex in his crotch.

River darted from the dark, his short blade silently slipping from its sheath to embed itself in the back of the guard's head. The man trembled in River's grip, his finger still stuck way up in that big gaping nostril until his body realised it was cut off from the brain . . . dead. River removed the blade, helped the corpse to the floorboards with almost reverential care, then moved on without remorse.

These men were not innocents – they were robbers and larcenists, deviants and kidnappers, the lowest scum of the city . . . not that it mattered. Fact was they were employed by his mark, and they were in his way. They could not be allowed to live.

The voices were louder from his vantage point at the top of the staircase and River paused, assessing the battlefield. The warehouse was wide and scantly lit, with men moving purposefully in its midst.

'Fucking move it!' A voice loud and desperate. 'I don't have all night. The longer we stay here the more chance they have of finding us.'

The speaker moved into the light, a short man, his clothes made of satin, probably silk lined, his boots fastened with shiny golden buckles. The other men were larger, their clothes less fashionable, more functional. Six of them: four moving with haste to stack barrels into a cart; two standing guard, their crossbows loaded in clenched hands, edgy, afraid.

Good.

Fear was as potent a weapon as any blade; sometimes it could prove even deadlier. It was clear who the mark was, but first River had to down the six guards, fast and efficiently, *engulfing them like the rising tide. Washing them away in the flood.*

River drew his second blade. He began to descend the stairs two at a time, fluid, silent, never taking his eyes off his first target, but also keeping the rest in his periphery lest they spot him as he moved. The man saw him at the last second, only time to widen his eyes in surprise before River slashed a gaping wound in his throat. Quick and silent, but enough to leave the man clutching at his neck, desperate to stem the tide of lifeblood flowing out and down his chest as he gasped his last. He was no longer a threat.

River was almost on his second target before someone saw him – a tall thin man at the opposite side of the warehouse – but his warning came too late. The blade slid in easily, between the third and fourth ribs, stabbing into the lungs, which then flooded with the gush of blood.

'Look out!' cried the thin mercenary even as his comrade fell, clutching at his side. No longer a threat.

The two guards with crossbows would have heard now, would be finding their aim. He had perhaps the space of two breaths.

More time than he would ever need.

Another man dropped the crate he was carrying. River was on him before it hit the ground, twin blades lashing at neck and groin simultaneously. He opened his mouth to scream but fell dead, his weapon untouched in its sheath.

River could hear the shrill and desperate voice of the mark. The words came fast and garbled; meaningless, unimportant, *he was riding the water now, pulled along by the undertow, silent beneath the surface.*

The tall thin bodyguard was moving in, his tread practised, his blade held low and ready. As he faced off against this challenger, River heard the telltale thrum of a crossbow string. He had been anticipating it, patient as an angler on the shore. He rolled forward, allowing it to shoot well overhead before springing to his feet in front of the swordsman, his left blade parrying the incoming attack, the right slipping into his opponent's gut, angled upwards towards the heart.

The man retched out a breath as though gagging on his own entrails, then went limp. River grabbed his shirt and swung him sharply to the left as he heard the second crossbow being loosed. The bolt thudded into the dying man's back, but with no air left in him to expel, he uttered no sound.

River whipped his blade free of the man's gut, spun round and flung it towards the second crossbowman. The knife thudded into his throat, propelling him backwards to land against the wall of the warehouse. With a hideous grimace he slowly slipped down it, leaving a trail of crimson on the stone. No longer a threat.

River could hear the last of the mercenaries, huffing desperately as he tried to pull the string of his crossbow back over the nut, his foot in the stirrup, the stave bending – but not far enough. Hired thugs just weren't what they used to be.

The man squealed in his desperation, not daring to look up, fearful of seeing his dead comrades. Almost a comical sight, but River could have no remorse, no mercy . . . not even for jesters.

He moved quick, there was no need to draw this out. Reaching the man as he struggled with his bow, River pushed his head up and clamped a hand over his mouth. He saw a tear in the man's eye, and watched it roll down his cheek as the blade pierced through to the heart, stopping the blood, *cutting the flow*. No longer a threat.

The mark was standing alone now, staring wide-eyed at the corpses of the men who, only moments before, had stood ready to defend him with their lives.

They had done that all right.

'Wait!' he said, holding up a hand.

How many times had River heard that word? How many times had it been the last plea of a condemned man?

River stared at him from beneath his hood.

'Do you know who I am?' said the mark, his voice growing shriller with every word. 'I'm Constantin Deredko, one of the richest men in Steelhaven. I can get you anything you want; money, jewels . . . girls . . . boys . . . whatever you want.'

River moved towards him, slowly now; there was no longer any urgency. He had been told to draw this part out, to make the mark suffer. Though River was no sadist, he was nothing if not obedient.

'Do you know why I have come for you, Constantin Deredko?' River said, pulling the hood back from his face, revealing those striking features, marred on one side by a crosshatch of scars.

The mark paused, then nodded, as though finally accepting his fate, as though seeing in River's face that there would be no mercy this day. 'Yes, you were sent by the Guild. You were sent because I owe them money and I didn't pay. Well, it's *my* fucking money, and they can go—'

River's raised hand halted Constantin's rant. The man fell silent, realising it would do him no good now.

'You have a choice,' said River, reaching into his jerkin and producing a small glass vial. 'You can take this, or I can use *this*.' He held out the vial in one hand, and showed Constantin the blade he held in his other, still slick with blood.

'What's in that?' asked Constantin, gesturing towards the vial.

'I don't know.' It was true – River had no idea of the contents, but he had been told to give his mark this choice, and that was what he would do.

Constantin glanced from vial to blade, weighing up his options. It wasn't a great choice. 'Will it be quick?' he said finally, pointing again to the vial.

'I don't know,' River repeated.

Constantin gave one final, remorseful gaze towards the red blade in River's fist, then held his hand out for the vial.

River handed it over and Constantin held it for several seconds, staring defiantly, steeling himself to make one last gesture of hopeless bravery. River couldn't help but admire him as he wrenched out the stopper and chugged the clear liquid down his throat, swallowing with an exaggerated grimace.

They stared at one another for several moments as nothing happened. River simply standing and waiting, Constantin trembling but trying his best to show a smattering of courage.

'Nothing's happening,' said Constantin, a flicker of a smile crossing his face. 'Was this some kind of tes—'

Suddenly he doubled over, groaning in agony and clutching at his stomach. He fell to his knees and began to retch, but nothing came out but a thin line of red bile. River could only watch as his mark writhed on the ground, screeching in pain and torment. Constantin looked up, red tears streaming down his cheeks from the burst blood vessels in his eyes. The look was accusatorial, and if the man could have spoken River was sure he would have cursed him to the hells. River could have spared him this torment if only he had chosen to die by the blade. He would have made it fast and painless.

With a last agonising gasp, Constantin died. River paused for just a second, just a heartbeat's length to look down at the man, his eyes pooling with red, the black bile oozing from his mouth. Then there was nothing else to see.

He walked to one of the dead crossbowmen, his blade still embedded in the man's neck. After pulling it free he knelt, pausing for a second to clean the blood from his weapons on the man's tunic.

A sudden panicked scrabbling noise from the opposite end of the warehouse made River start, and the blades were in his hands in an instant as he adopted a defensive stance. In the shadows at the other end of the building he saw movement, but it was no attack . . . it was an escape.

A door burst open, allowing in the street noise as a figure ran out.

Stupid.

Foolish.

River had been seen at his work – been seen with his hood thrown back. And the witness had fled. How could he have let his focus on the kill make him so careless?

In a blur of movement he was across the warehouse and in full pursuit. The noise and light of the street were unsettling, but River had only one thing on his mind – catching his prey; there must be no witnesses.

He glimpsed a figure moving at speed into a passing crowd of revellers. Concealed by stylised masks in the shape of grinning daemons, they held aloft gaudy banners and flags.

River pulled up his hood while weaving through them, keeping his blades low and hidden lest he slash one of the crowd by mistake. It was a dense throng, with revellers moving like a great wave, laughing and oblivious of the drama in their midst. For anyone else the sea of bodies might have been overwhelming, but River was no ordinary man, *he could follow the ebb and flow.*

He passed smoothly through the crowd, moving inexorably towards his target whom he could see pushing past the wall of people in desperate panic. River's grip tightened on his blades as he moved in. He would strike quickly then disappear, leaving his final victim to bleed out on the packed street.

Before he could reach him however, his quarry, with a final desperate burst of strength, broke from the crowd. River emerged to see him turn down an alleyway. They both splashed through the filth of the back street. It was never really a contest: River was on him well short of the bustling avenue at the end.

The man must have sensed that death was on him, because he turned, hands held up in surrender.

'Please don't kill me. They only hired me for one night. I knew it was wrong. I just needed the money.'

River had been expecting a plea for clemency, the same as he had heard a hundred times before, but it was not the words that stayed his hand. Looking back at him was not a man, but a boy, maybe five winters younger than River himself. His eyes were wide and blue – innocent, even childlike, not the hawkish, brutal eyes of a seasoned thug.

For several beats of his heart, River simply stared, his blade still poised to deal the killing blow – but he couldn't.

It simply wasn't right.

Surely he could have done nothing in his short life to be deserving of a blade across the throat, just for being in the wrong place at the wrong time.

Roused by a sudden scream, River darted a glance towards the bustling street.

'Robber! Murderer!' screamed a woman, staring down the alleyway at River with his blades drawn and ready to kill.

Damn it!

Before he could flee, the woman gained two companions, open-faced bascinets on their heads. Weapons in their hands.

Greencoats.

Without giving the boy another thought he turned tail and fled.

He could hear the Greencoats ordering him to stop, wasting their breath on calling out instead of chasing him. Let them – by the time they started in pursuit he would be gone.

River leapt atop an abandoned cart then vaulted upwards, planting his foot against the side of the alleyway and boosting himself to the rooftop above. Glancing back he saw the Greencoats setting off, splashing down the alley behind him. One put something to his lips, blowing hard, and a shrill whistle rose high above the sounds of the crowd.

Not giving it a second thought, River moved off, but heard another whistle, as though in answer to the first. It was quickly followed by a third.

'Oi! Bastard!' cried a voice to his left, and River looked up in time to see another Greencoat taking aim with a crossbow.

He could so easily have taken the man down – flung one of his blades and silenced him – but this was not the mark or one of his thugs. This was a Greencoat; one of the city's custodians, and River was not a simple murderer.

No, as he ran from his Greencoat pursuers, some of whom had already made it to the rooftops, he vowed that tonight he would do no more killing.

He just hoped that his pursuers would return the favour.

EIGHT

Rag stood on the roof of the Silent Bull, arms round Tidge's shoulders. All of them looked out towards Eastgate, from where there still came the sound of celebration.

It had been a good night. Everyone had eaten well, Fender's bronze trinket paying for a large pot of broth and fresh bread, courtesy of Boris the Innkeeper. Migs was lying on his back, caressing his swollen belly, whilst Chirpy sat cross-legged beside him gazing over the rooftops at the bright lights. Where Fender was, Rag had no idea – he'd left before sundown and not come back. Not that she gave a shit. She'd not spoken to him since he'd bullied Markus away earlier. The longer Fender was gone the better.

But she couldn't stand here enjoying the show all evening. Down in the streets below were thronging crowds, vendors selling ale and food, live entertainment and carny stalls. People had full purses and couldn't wait to part with their money. Rag could certainly help.

Before she could drag herself away from her boys, the rickety staircase at the side of the building give off a whiny creak. Tidge and Chirpy jumped, but Migs just continued rubbing his bare tummy as if polishing it to a shine. When they saw it was Markus coming up the stairs, the boys let out a sigh. Rag's welcoming smile dropped when she saw the look on his face. His eyes looked red from crying, and the streetlight showed up a livid bruise on his cheek.

'You okay, Markus?' Rag asked, gently.

He shrugged in reply. Rag put an arm round his shoulder and they turned to watch the endless procession of revellers. She was concerned for sure, but she wasn't going to pry – it was none of her business. If Markus wanted to tell her he would, in his own time.

They watched the show until Rag decided it was time to go to work.

'Right, you stinkers, I've got to go. I'll try and be back before sun up, so the lot of you had best stay out of trouble.'

There were faint noises of acknowledgement from the younger boys, who were still captivated by the display. Markus, however, looked at her questioningly.

'What is it?' she asked.

'I think I should come with you,' he stated, uncertainly.

'What? On the rob?' She couldn't help but grin at the suggestion. 'You must be joking.'

'I've got to learn some time. I need to start paying my way. Fender said—'

'Fender says a lot of things and most of it's horseshit. You're fine to come and stay with us any time you want.' She glanced at his discoloured cheek, wanting more than ever to know what had happened. 'It's safe here for you, there's no need to fret. You leave that long streak of piss, Fender, to me. I'll soon change his mind.'

'No.' Markus raised his chin determinedly. He had never been so forceful before – Rag was impressed. 'If I stay I'm going to learn what you know. You can teach me, Rag. You and Fender are the best purse pinchers in the city.'

Rag was flattered – she couldn't help it, even though she knew Markus was wrong. If she had been one of the best in the city the Guild would have grabbed her up for sure by now and she'd be sleeping under a roof rather than on top of one. Markus had a point though – he could do with learning the trade. An extra pair of hands bringing in the steal would benefit them all. Besides, persuading Fender that Markus could stay would be much easier if he was earning his cut.

She stared deep into his eyes, looking for any doubt there, any weakness, and it pleased her to see only cold determination. If Markus was going to walk this road with her he had to be damn sure it was what he wanted to do.

'All right then,' she said. 'Best follow me, hadn't you.'

Markus smiled, a wide naïve smile, as though this was going to be some kind of laugh. It gave Rag second thoughts. This was no laugh – it was deadly serious.

'You do *what* I say, *when* I say it,' she made clear as they went down the rickety stairs from the roof. 'Keep your eyes open and your mouth shut. Tonight you'll just be watching and learning and staying out of the way. And if the Greencoats spot me, you just run. Run home and don't look back.'

Markus nodded obediently, a trace of a smile still on his face.

They made their way from Dockside up towards Eastgate, sticking to the shadows like the rats they were. Markus was with her every step of the way and it didn't take long for Rag's doubts to leave her. He was doing well, keeping silent and close and out of view. If she hadn't known better she'd have called him a *natural*, but it was obvious he weren't. Rag was a natural – had a sixth sense for this kind of thing, Fender said. Saw trouble coming before it hit and knew when a mark was ripe for the picking. Anyone could see that Markus was keen and young, and stealthy. Whether a natural thief, only time would tell.

Glancing over her shoulder she gave Markus a reassuring nod and he smiled back. In that smile she saw his innocence, his inexperience. Again she had second thoughts, but then they came out on the Promenade of Kings and she became totally focused on the seething array of targets milling around before her.

The Prom was a major street that ran all the way from the Stone Gate to the Sepulchre of Crowns. It split Northgate from neighbouring Eastgate, an impressive street lined with timeworn statues depicting historic kings from the most ancient of the Sword Kings – whose names Rag had no idea of – right up to King Cael himself, standing looking towards the palace, his armour shining even in the night, his face proud and handsome. Rag had never seen the king close enough to make out his features, but if the statue was even half realistic, he must be a man to be reckoned with. These were his streets, governed by his laws, and in any other life Rag could well have been happy to abide by them. But times was difficult, and King Cael's laws put no food in her mouth, so she guessed she'd just have to ignore them.

With Markus at her shoulder, Rag made her way amongst the press of bodies. A band somewhere was playing music – strings and pipes working together to rise above the din of the crowd. The perfect opportunity for a couple of quick pinches. By the time they'd crossed the Prom and reached the cobbled pavement opposite she had two purses inside her shirt. Once in the relative safety of the shadows she looked back at Markus, still following like a faithful puppy.

'See that?' she asked.

'See what?' he replied, then noticed the purses bulging in her shirt. 'Oh, no, I missed it.'

She shook her head. 'I thought I told you to keep your eyes open. We're not here for a good time; we're here to work. If you're not up to it, just go back to the Bull.'

'Sorry. I'll do better next time.'

Rag looked at him sternly, but couldn't hold it for long – his expression was too pitiful. Shaking her head wryly she cuffed him playfully around the head.

Safe in a side street she secured the purses in her trews, tying their drawstrings tight to the loops inside her waistband.

'Right, let's go. And this time, *concentrate*.'

Markus nodded, composing his features sharply . . . perhaps a little too sharply.

'And try to look relaxed. You don't want to look like you're desperate for a shit. That's only going to draw attention to us.'

Another nod, and his features slackened into a vacant stare.

It would have to do.

Rag led the way once more onto the Prom and this time went with the flow of traffic, taking them south towards the Crown District, where the richer punters were. Normally Rag never got anywhere near the Crown before being spotted by one of the Greencoats and chased away. Pinching there could be more trouble than it was worth. Tonight though would be different. With so large a crowd they were unlikely to be noticed.

The stream of folks moved at a merry pace, and they were soon at the big old gates that led into the Crown District. As Rag hovered outside, trying to spy a perfect mark, her attention was drawn to a pair of Greencoats standing watch over the gate. She cursed silently – did they never have a bloody night off? It was the Feast of Arlor after all!

'We'll never get inside,' she said to Markus, 'those two look keen as mustard.' She was turning back when she spied something that brought a smile.

The young woman was beautiful, her gown billowing out from a tight waist in a pastel harlequin pattern. Her hair was tied up in a gravity-defying bouffant and a gold mask covered her eyes. The fat man on her arm was equally well dressed. A merchant and his wife, maybe, and rich – there was no way a beauty like her would be married to such a fat bastard if he weren't swimming in gold.

The couple walked through the gate from the Crown District bold as brass, swanning past the Greencoats. Rag guessed the Feast celebrations must have been pretty tame in the Crown if these two fancied seeing how the scum were faring on the Prom.

Slumming it with the yokels, eh? Rag would show them how they did things out here.

'Stick close, and get ready to bolt,' she instructed Markus, moving aside to let the couple to walk by.

She followed her mark closely, watching as the couple breezed through the crowd. The fat merchant's purse was at his waist, fastened to a double leather loop over his belt. This wouldn't be easy, and Rag realised she'd need a distraction if she was going to pull it off. She saw that Markus was alert this time, focused and watching – just as she'd told him. For a second she was conflicted, caught between putting Markus in harm's way and stealing that big juicy purse, but the need to eat triumphed, as always.

Putting an arm around Markus' shoulder she leaned in close.

'Move in front and bump into the woman. Just for a second, just enough to take their attention, then move north and I'll meet you at Shoulders.'

Markus listened to her simple instructions and moved off as he was told.

Rag moved in behind the fat merchant, keeping her eye on the prize. The purse was attached by drawstrings. She had little time to pull it, but little time was all she'd need.

Markus suddenly came out of the crowd ahead, walking straight into the woman. He bounced off her, looking up all surprised, and Rag was so taken with his performance skills she almost forgot to do her bit.

'Watch where you're going,' barked the merchant, as Markus disappeared into the crowd. Before he could say more Rag had cut the purse strings with her knife, and was off in the other direction.

When she got to the headless statue of the king they aptly called 'Shoulders', Markus was waiting patiently, an assured grin on his face.

'Well? How did I do?' he asked.

'You did okay,' Rag replied, giving him a playful nudge with her elbow. 'How much have we got?'

'Dunno, but we ain't gonna count it here. If two pups like us are seen looking through a full purse, someone's bound to guess we're up to no good.'

Markus nodded at the sage advice.

She was about to say they needed to find a quiet spot, lift the coins, ditch the purse then spend some of the pennies on hot pies when she heard the noise cutting through the music and the laughter of the crowd.

Whistles!

Cold fear ran down her back and instantly she regretted having brought Markus. The Greencoats were signalling something was afoot! How could she have brought him to lift a purse from someone in the Crown District? Stupid! Stupid!

Well, now wasn't the time for wallowing . . . now was the time for running.

'Come on,' she said, grasping Markus by the collar and pulling him to the side of the street out of plain view. Markus clearly had no idea what was going on, but he followed her anyway.

The pair ran down an alley, into the dark and out of sight. Rag paused, listening, hoping on hope that the whistles would grow quieter, that the Greencoats would be heading off in the wrong direction, looking vainly for the two thieves stupid enough to rob a couple of rich gits from the Crown.

But the sound only got louder, joined by more and more whistles, rising in a chorus that seemed to be drawing closer.

The alley was dark but empty – there was nowhere to hide. It was only a matter of time before one of the Greencoats came this way, and found them skulking there.

'We have to go up,' Rag said, pointing towards the eaves of the building they hunkered beneath.

Markus nodded, needing no further encouragement as he grasped one of the cornerstones and began to pull himself upwards. Impressed, Rag followed him towards the roof. Without growing up on the streets as she had he almost matched her for agility, and within moments they were scrabbling onto the sloping tiles, well above the alley, the crowds and the searching Greencoats.

With the whistles still blowing Rag felt keenly the need to escape. She led Markus north, towards the Bull, dodging the chimneys and skirting the edge of the rooftops. But the sound of the whistles carried on, now seeming to surround them.

At the corner of a high, sloping roof Rag suddenly swallowed a sharp breath. A Greencoat was coming at her; she could hear his heavy footfalls over the noise of the street below. In his mouth was a whistle that squealed with his every laboured breath and in his hands was the biggest crossbow she had ever seen.

Rag froze, instinctively raising an arm to warn Markus, but he, oblivious to the danger, ran straight into the back of her. They both stared as the Greencoat loped towards them. Then he spat the whistle from his mouth to dangle around his neck on its chain.

'Out of the bloody way,' he snapped and trotted straight past them. Rag heaved a sigh of relief. 'You shouldn't even be up here,' the Greencoat cast over his shoulder as he rounded the edge of the building and disappeared into the night.

Rag saw that Markus was grinning like an idiot.

'Something's going on,' he said. 'Maybe something good.' And before she could stop him he was off in the Greencoat's wake.

Before Rag could shout him back he disappeared into the shadows.

'Bloody bollocks,' she breathed, as she made after him along the rooftops.

They were both following the whistles now, padding across the top of the city, lifted by the excitement of the chase. Every instinct told her this was foolish but she did it anyway. She couldn't just have Markus running straight into harm's way, could she? He had disobeyed one of her express instructions, but she still felt responsible for him. And besides, part of her wanted to know what was going on too.

There was a commotion ahead; by the ambient light from the revelling crowds below Rag could see there was a stand-off on the rooftops.

Craning for a better view, she found herself at Markus' shoulder. His eyes were locked intently on the action and they both peered through the dark, scarcely daring to breathe.

A single figure stood at the centre of a flat roof surrounded by Greencoats. Two had crossbows trained on him, three more had blades clear of their sheaths and were approaching slowly.

Markus edged closer, keen to hear what was being said, and rather than pull him back into the shadows Rag found herself moving up beside him. Something inside was screaming at her to flee, yet it was trumped by her boundless curiosity. Things like this didn't happen every night.

'Don't move,' said a Greencoat, moving forward with tentative steps and fumbling a pair of manacles from his belt. 'Don't you fucking move.'

The lone figure stood, awaiting the Greencoat's approach, his face hidden in the shadow of his hood, his dark, plain garb making him almost invisible in the night.

As the Greencoat reached forward with the manacles, there was a blur of motion. The figure burst into action, his movements too fast to follow in the dark. The Greencoats began shouting, the one with the manacles loudest. Rag could see that somehow the Greencoat's wrist had been clapped into one of his own manacles, and the man he had been trying to cuff had him around the neck. A blade in his free hand was pointed at the Greencoat's throat.

'Shoot him!' cried the Greencoat. 'For fuck's sake shoot him!'

The rest of the Greencoats tried to move into better positions, their voices a confused cacophony of bellowed orders and curses. Meanwhile the hooded figure held his victim fast, his blade winking in the moonlight. One of the Greencoats suddenly ran in from the flank, his sword aloft. Still holding his victim, the dark figure dodged the other's blade and struck out with his foot. The second Greencoat went down screaming and clutching his snapped knee as the rest of his fellows stormed forward.

Rag couldn't really see what happened next, it was all too fast, too dark. A slashing of blades, grunting, cries of pain, the telltale thrum of a crossbow being fired off wildly. Then it went quiet.

Creeping forward she could just see the Greencoats on the roof – all five of them were down, some not moving, others rolling around in agony. Of the hooded man there was no sign.

Rag suddenly realised that Markus was no longer at her shoulder. Spinning around she saw him lying there, and her mouth dropped open in a silent scream.

Markus was spluttering, choking and spitting blood into the air. In his neck was lodged the shaft of a bolt, a stray shot fired from a Greencoat's crossbow, a thousand to one chance that had struck him in the throat, straight and true.

She kneeled by his side, gripping his hand, watching his eyes begin to glaze.

'Help me!' she screamed into the night. 'Somebody please help me!'

But there was no one there to help.

NINE

Samina tapped her finger on the inside of her shield, drumming away as though she was trying to leave a dent. It made a tinny sound – the only sound on the tree-lined Avenue of Spears, the great thoroughfare that led to the gates of the Temple of Autumn.

'Must you make that noise?' Kaira asked, frowning from beneath her plumed helm.

'I hate this,' Samina said, carrying on with her incessant tune.

They both stood in full regalia, guarding the gate as though the Khurtic horde was about to charge down the street and assault it. Lining the road in the shadows cast by the rows of great elms were twenty Shieldmaidens, similarly garbed in their armour, with shields and spears presented in formal salute.

'It is what it is,' Kaira replied, squinting up the long straight road, hoping that the High Abbot and his entourage would get a move on so that there could be an end to this nonsense. 'We've been over this already.'

In fact they had been over it several times, but Samina seemed determined to make her annoyance clear for all to see.

'It's still ridiculous – standing here like a palace guard waiting for the High Abbot when we should be—'

'That's enough! We are Shieldmaidens of Vorena. We will perform our duties. This is an honour granted us by the Matron Mother and we will carry it out until told to do otherwise.'

She could tell Samina wanted to complain further but was thinking better of it. Mercifully, they didn't have to wait much longer before the procession came round the corner of the Avenue of Spears. The Shieldmaidens quickly stood to attention, readying themselves for the High Abbot's arrival.

The column proceeded down the road towards them, the Sons of Malleus – the Sons of the Hammer – bedecked in black armour, warrior priests of Ironhold, each as dedicated to the service of their god Arlor and the defence of their temple as their female counterparts.

Halfway down the column, Kaira could see a carriage being pulled by several tired-looking horses. Clearly the High Abbot did not march alongside his men.

The head of the column reached the end of the avenue and the warriors spread out, allowing the carriage to get as close to the gate as possible. Arlor forbid the High Abbot should walk a step further than was necessary.

One of the Sons pulled open the door to the carriage, while another grabbed a small set of stairs, extending them to the ground. The High Abbot descended heavily, holding up the hem of his black and white robe so as not to trip himself.

Kaira stepped forward. 'High Abbot,' she began, regarding the man with as respectful a look as she could muster, 'greetings from the Temple of Autumn. I am Kaira Stormfall, and this is Samina Coldeye, First Maidens of Vorena. We will be your guards of the body inside the temple grounds.'

A smile spread over the High Abbot's shiny swollen cheeks. His eyes roamed over Kaira's body, then back up to her face after lingering for a second over the ceremonial breastplate that accentuated her athletic figure.

'Excellent,' he said, his fat palm wiping sweat from his balding pate. 'Do lead on, Sister Stormfall.'

Kaira gripped her spear tightly and signalled to the Shieldmaidens at the top of the staircase to open the gate. As she and Samina led the High Abbot up the stone stairs and over the threshold, the Sons of Malleus stood and waited. They were not permitted within the Temple of Autumn – the High Abbot was the only man allowed within those hallowed grounds – and they would lodge instead in the almshouse of the Daughters of Arlor, located just outside.

In the temple courtyard the priestesses stood waiting, heads bowed, faces hidden beneath white veils. At the centre of the square was the Matron Mother, with Daedla standing at her shoulder. To her left was the Exarch, the highest ranking of the Shieldmaidens. Though she carried no shield or spear she still struck a formidable figure, her tall powerful frame dwarfing that of the Matron Mother.

As they approached, the Matron Mother bowed. 'Greetings, High

Abbot. It is truly an honour to receive your gracious visit. I trust things are well at the Temple of Winter?'

'All is well. But it has been a long journey. I trust I might be able to bathe and rest before the formalities begin.'

'Of course, please come this way.'

With that, Daedla and the Matron Mother led the High Abbot towards the Temple. Kaira and Samina followed in their wake as the High Abbot was conveyed to his chambers.

Later, as the Shieldmaidens stood guarding his door, it was clear Samina was not coming to terms with their appointed task.

'Is this how it's going to be?' she whispered, though she might as well have shouted such was the anger in her voice.

'It is what it is,' Kaira replied quietly. It was a phrase she had found herself repeating a lot over the past few days.

He was inside now, bathing his fat, sweaty body. Unusually, he had demanded there be one of the Daughters present to aid him in his ablutions. This did nothing to endear him to Samina, nor Kaira.

There was a sudden splash from within the room, and what could only be a man laughing. To Kaira's ear it sounded debauched, as if he was deriving some illicit pleasure. What could he possibly be doing that would cause him such mirth?

'What's he up to in there?' said Samina.

'He's bathing.'

'He's sloshing around like a cow stuck in a river.'

Kaira wanted to laugh at that one, but the solemnity their duty demanded was not lost on her. This was a great honour, and it was not her place to belittle it.

They could suddenly hear the High Abbot speaking from within the room. His voice was muffled, the words indistinct, but he was clearly amused by something.

'Poor girl,' said Samina. 'Being bored to tears with tales of far-off Ironwall.'

The High Abbot laughed again. More muffled words. Then they could hear the priestess's voice, high and timid.

'Don't encourage him,' said Samina, as though she were whispering advice in the young girl's ear. 'It's the worst thing you can do.'

'Will you be quiet? We're supposed to be vigilantly guarding our honoured guest, not censuring him behind his back.'

'We need to do something to pass the time.'

'We have our duties. That is all we should need.'

Samina for once didn't come back at that.

They heard the High Abbot talking again, heard him sloshing. The priestess began to talk too, her voice rising in pitch, her words coming in faster more urgent sentences. There was an almighty splash of water and the girl let out a squeal.

Kaira and Samina glanced at one another just as the door to the chamber was wrenched open. The young priestess came running out, sobbing as she rushed past, her head bowed, face not visible.

'I only asked for a towel,' came an amused voice.

Kaira peered reluctantly into the room, her eyes widening as she saw the High Abbot standing there, naked, the dark hair that covered his body slick with wet, his flaccid penis dangling between fat thighs.

'Is there any chance one of you could get me some wine?'

It took several moments before Kaira could compose herself enough to do as she was bidden. She went off like an obedient little serving wench and got the High Abbot his wine. There was no chance that Samina would have done it – more likely she'd have skewered him with her spear.

Once the High Abbot had dressed, the Matron Mother came to admonish him gently for his behaviour. Kaira had expected more, but then the High Abbot was the most powerful of Arlor's representatives.

Later when he and the Matron Mother sat down to dine together in her chambers, Kaira and Samina gained some well-earned respite. At first they sat in silence, eating dried meat and bread. Kaira could only wait for the torrent to begin.

'What in the hells is going on?' Samina spat half-chewed bread onto her lap so violently that Kaira moved her own cup of water to a safe distance. 'The High Abbot is supposed to be a pious man. He should be flogged out of the Temple, not be dining with the Matron Mother. How has such a man risen to head our religion?' Kaira didn't have an answer. 'Why is he even here? Most likely come to avoid the war, when he should be on the front, giving holy succour to our troops. But no, he's here, hiding behind our walls, eating our bread, abusing our—'

'Hospitality?'

Samina raised an eyebrow. 'Something like that. Well, not any more, I say. If he lays a finger on another of these girls I'll cut it off and make him eat it.'

'And what good would that do you? What good would it do us? We're assigned to protect him.'

'Protect him from what?' She took a bite out of her hunk of bread, then began to speak with a full mouth. 'The only thing he should be scared of around here is me.'

'Yes, I'm sure.'

Samina grinned.

Later, as Kaira reflected on the day, she could only hope the next one would go much quicker. And smoother.

The High Abbot was tucked up in bed and she was back to guarding the door. Samina was getting some rest – it didn't take two of them to keep watch over the High Abbot's chamber in their own temple. And, though it pained her to admit it, Kaira much preferred carrying out this duty on her own. She loved Samina as much as any of her sisters, but that constant griping was starting to grate on her nerves.

With any luck, the High Abbot's business in Steelhaven would be concluded quickly. Then they could pack him off with a wave and a smile and things would get back to normal.

Normal.

With the Khurtas at their border – no, over their border, treading their lands, burning their crops – it was doubtful anything would be normal for quite some time. And here she was: First Shieldmaiden of Vorena, standing watch over a fat, licentious old man. It pained Kaira. She should have been at the front, should have been standing shoulder to shoulder with her sisters, facing down Amon Tugha's hordes.

But it was what it was.

Someone approached along the corridor and Kaira snapped to full attention, hands gripping shield and spear, muscles tensed and ready to adopt a defensive stance if she had to. When she saw the white-robed figure of a priestess walking towards her she relaxed somewhat.

The girl carried a bronze platter on which sat a crystal carafe of red wine and a bowl of grapes. She stopped before Kaira but didn't glance up from beneath her white hood.

'The High Abbot requested some wine, sister. I have brought it for him.'

No one had told Kaira about this. She regarded the girl for a moment, wondering whether she should taste the wine for poison, or at least check the story with one of the more senior priestesses, when the door opened a crack behind her.

'My wine?' keened the High Abbot. 'Do bring it in, there's a good girl.'

Kaira stepped aside, resisting the temptation to glance back at the man she was here to protect lest he be standing there in all his hirsute, tiny-cocked glory.

The Daughter of Arlor stepped into the room and the door slammed shut behind her.

Once again Kaira could hear the muffled voice of the High Abbot – amused clearly, but with no warmth in his simpering voice. And again, she heard the priestess answering in low tones . . . innocent . . . naïve.

The High Abbot laughed and Kaira suddenly heard a squeal. He laughed again, then said something more loudly. This time his words had harsh tones, the aggressive tones of admonition . . . or punishment.

Then the girl screamed.

That was enough. Kaira had done her duty, stood guard at the behest of the Matron Mother and acted with honour. She could keep her peace no longer.

Kaira left her shield and spear against the wall lest she do something with them she might regret, then threw open the door and stepped inside, brow furrowed as though she were about to meet an enemy on the field rather than a bullying, perverted old fool.

The High Abbot looked around suddenly. In one hand he had the girl by her robe as though trying to pull it from her shoulder, in the other he grasped her upper arm, squeezing it tight. The girl's face was visible now, her cowl thrown back. She couldn't have been more than seventeen summers.

'Enough!' said Kaira, coming to stand beside the Abbot, staring at him, as though goading him into a fight. He merely smiled.

'Come now,' he said, releasing the girl, who quickly adjusted the robe at her shoulder and pulled her hood back over her face. 'We were only having some fun.'

'That's not what it looks like to me.' Kaira turned to the young priestess. 'What's your name, girl?'

'Claudya,' she said, her voice tiny, mouse-like.

'I suggest you go back to your sisters.'

Claudya needed no further urging, walking from the room with quick, staccato steps.

The High Abbot was still smiling.

'Come now, that was just a misunderstanding.' He walked to a table where the carafe sat on its bronze tray, and poured two goblets of wine. 'A silly girl, heady with the bloom of youth. Giving off those signals – you know the ones? But of course you do. I can see you are a woman of experience.' He picked up the goblets, offering one to Kaira. When all he got in return was a contemptuous stare he put it back down with a shrug.

'Look.' He moved closer, too close, until he was standing right next to her, looking up towards her face as she towered over his diminutive frame. 'There's a hierarchy here. I happen to be at its peak . . . and I can help those that are, shall we say, *beneath* me.' He reached out with a podgy hand and ran a finger down Kaira's bare forearm. She felt her skin crawling as if with a line of maggots beneath his touch. 'If we all just get along, there's benefit in it for everyone.' His finger moved up to her shoulder, then, to her horror, began to trace a line towards her breast. 'There's no reason we can't be friends, is there? Because, trust me when I say: *you wouldn't want me as an enemy.*'

Something snapped inside her, like a bowstring pulled taut until it could be pulled no more. Kaira took hold of the High Abbot's finger before it could move any further. His mouth opened, eyes widening in shock as she bent it back. She knew she should have stopped there – she had done enough to teach him a lesson – but she didn't. Later she would see it as a culmination of things that had brought her to this – the girls he had abused, Samina's constant griping, her need to fight at the front, to feel worthy – all this had caused her to carry on, to move beyond the point of no return.

The High Abbot screamed as Kaira snapped his finger back, breaking the bone. Simultaneously, her free hand shot up as though with a will of its own, slamming into his nose, flattening it to his face in a spray of snot and blood.

He collapsed to the ground, knocking the bronze tray from the table and shattering the carafe on the floor in an explosion of red wine. Above the noise of smashing glass rose his high-pitched scream. He screamed as though his guts were hanging out, calling bloody murder, calling for help, for guards, for Arlor to protect him.

And Kaira merely looked down at him, that pitiful mess of a man. Though she knew that the consequences of her lack of control, her moment of madness, would be grave, she couldn't bring herself to regret it.

TEN

fter the Temple of Autumn had been built, all pagan burials had been forbidden within the walls of Steelhaven. Worship of the Old Gods had previously been common throughout the Free States, and so to appease those who still followed the ancient pantheon King Murlock had granted them Dancer's Hill, and the consecrated ground that surrounded it, to carry out their various rites of birth, death, marriage and seasonal sacrifice. From the massive oak tree at the crest of the hill, it had been the practice to set criminals swinging, to dance their last twitching dance, before being buried in the ground that surrounded it. But since King Murlock had started executing ne'er-do-wells within the city walls, Dancer's Hill had become redundant – no reason not to grant it to those who still worshipped the Old Gods.

Nobul stood now, under the shadow of that big old tree, just him and the grey-bearded druid. He wasn't watching proceedings though; his attention was held by the branches rocking in the breeze. He listened to them creaking, thinking about the ropes that used to swing off them and the hanged beneath, bodies all swollen and purple, just dangling there. It was a gruesome thing to recall, but better than thinking of the alternative – his boy Markus lying there in the dirt, waiting to be covered over and left in the dark for the worms.

Nobul didn't put much store by the gods, didn't really care for being told what to do in general, especially by priests, but this wasn't for him. It's what Rona would have wanted. If there was an afterlife, and Nobul wasn't convinced there was, then Rona would want Markus buried the same way she had been, so they could be together. Even though Nobul didn't think it would make much difference, didn't think there was anything waiting after you were put in the ground, he did it anyway.

The druid had been going on for longer than Nobul would have liked, but he didn't complain. He was talking in a language Nobul barely understood, every now and then saying a name of one of the Old Gods Nobul recognised, but they were all irrelevant really. The only god that would be making an appearance now was the Lord of Crows. He'd come up through the ground, or so the old tales told, and he'd grant you a boon. You'd get one last request before he took you, get to finish one last task or say goodbye to your kin or have one last moment under the sun.

In the end everyone had to face the Lord of Crows.

Nobul found himself grinning at that. If the Lord of Crows came for him he'd want one last request all right – he'd want to find the bastard that did this, find the bastard and be let loose on him.

Stray shot they said it was – couldn't be helped. The Greencoats couldn't be held responsible as they were trying to catch some killer in the night. For that reason Nobul wasn't eligible for 'monetary redress' as they'd called it. Not that he wanted money, even though it would have come in damned handy. No, he just wanted justice. But there was no justice in Steelhaven, not unless you had money and friends and power to begin with. The rest just had to lump it.

He glanced over at the druid and saw him looking, hands clenched in front of his green robe. The old man just stared, finished talking to the trees and the earth and the Lord of Crows. That was that, Nobul reckoned. He pointed to the short shovel he'd dug the grave with and the druid nodded. With a sigh he picked it up and began to fill in the hole, covering his son's hemp-wrapped body with dirt.

When he finished he didn't pause, didn't stand around to say any words of his own. He just headed straight back towards the Stone Gate. On his way, he was sure he caught sight of someone watching from the side of the road, some child maybe a little older than Markus was . . . had been. But by the time he looked closer they were gone.

The house would be empty – a shell full of memories Nobul was none too keen to remember, so he went straight to the forge. He shut the door to block out the world, looking around at the embers in the fire, the anvil standing cold and silent, the little table he did his crafting on.

Nobul stood at that table and looked down; looked down at the mess that only he could make a sense of. He picked up a half-finished pommel, feeling the weight of it in his hand, running his thumb over the rough finish.

Some men whittled, hacking away for hours at pieces of wood, scraping bits off, sanding them down, smoothing them into small animals to give to their children. Nobul whittled with iron and steel, carved gilding into pommels, hammered rivets into hilts, wrapped handles in the finest leather, and even set gems into the steel when asked. He was a craftsman: he made things of beauty from the basest materials, but he suddenly realised he had never made anything for his son. Even the scum off the streets made toys for their children to play with, but not Nobul Jacks – he had always been too busy for such things, always too preoccupied with his work. All he had given Markus were harsh words and anger. The last thing he had ever given him was a slap to the face. He reckoned he had to be some sweet kind of bastard for that.

Nobul gripped the pommel tight, gritting his teeth, biting back the pain, biting back the tears. He turned, ready to fling the worthless hunk of metal across the room, when he saw the door was open. Two men walked in, burly, hard looking men. Men Nobul recognised.

The first was bald, the smile on his face friendly, as if he was expected. The second was taller, grimmer than the first . . . a right evil-looking bastard.

Nobul gently placed the pommel back on his table as the second man closed the door behind him.

'Hello, Nobul, my old mate.'

Nobul didn't answer, merely stood and looked at them.

The bald man looked to his friend and shrugged. The other one made no move in reply, merely staring at Nobul as though he wanted to do him harm. Nobul just stared at the ground. He didn't care any more, didn't have the energy to face them down. They could have what they wanted, take anything he had – it didn't really matter any more.

'I know this is an unexpected visit, and you've already paid this month, but you know how things are. That premium we were talking about before . . . it seems our boss wants it now.'

Nobul merely nodded. He glanced around the forge, trying to think if he had any coin here or if he'd left it back at the house. Then he remembered he'd spent the last of what he had to pay the druid for the ceremony. There was nothing left.

'I don't have it,' he said. There was no emotion in his voice; he wasn't scared, not of these two. They could do what they had to.

Baldy nodded. 'That's a problem then.' He glanced to his companion again. Still no reaction. 'But, you know, we can probably come to some arrangement.' He strolled slowly to a barrel with bars of untempered steel poking out, picking one out and feeling its weight in his hand. 'We're not unreasonable men. It's not like we're going to damage you . . . not yet anyway. How are you going to earn any coin if you're all beaten up to a *fucking pulp*?' The last words were screamed at the top of his voice as he slammed the steel down on the anvil. The echo rang through the forge.

Nobul just nodded.

'You've got until tomorrow,' the thug said, casually throwing the steel back into its barrel. 'Fifty coppers or five silvers. Makes no difference to us. You know . . . now that we're friends and all.' He turned, signalling to his companion, who seemed to have to drag his eyes away from Nobul before heading towards the door.

'Oh, and by the way.' Baldy turned, smiling, all self-satisfied as if he'd just won a hand at cards. 'Sorry about the boy.'

There was silence, a moment that seemed to linger as Nobul slowly acknowledged the glib statement.

Looking up, he fixed the man with a glare, feeling his fists clench involuntarily. 'What?' he said.

'Your boy. Nasty business that. But I suppose you've got one less mouth to feed now. Should be no problem making the monthly payment, eh?'

Baldy turned, smiling conspiratorially at the second thug. This time his companion cracked a smile in return.

A joke. A fucking joke about Markus. His son, who was lying dead in the dirt, dead and couldn't speak up for himself. Wouldn't ever speak again.

'Wait,' Nobul said, before they could open the door. The two men stopped, turning expectantly, Baldy cocking an ear as if he were waiting for something to be said in reply – as if he wanted Nobul to start trading insults, to rise to the provocation and give him an excuse to dish out a beating.

'What?'

'I don't know your name,' Nobul said. 'Since we're friends now and we'll be seeing more of one another. I should know your name, shouldn't I?'

Baldy smirked, glancing at his companion, then back at Nobul. 'My name? You can call me "Sir". How's that for starters?'

'Call you what?'

'*Sir*. You fucking deaf?'

'Sorry, I didn't catch that.'

Baldy's grin spread across his face, then he swaggered closer, so close that

Nobul could have reached out and touched him. He leaned in, giving a hard stare. Nobul had seen that stare a hundred times in the mercenary companies and in the levy regiment. Seen officers give it to subordinates, seen big men give it to small. Now it seemed he was the one on the end of it.

'I said, you can call—'

Nobul's hand snapped forward, twisted in a claw shape as he grabbed hold of Baldy's face like an eagle would grasp a rabbit in its talons.

'*Fucking cunt!*' he screamed, digging in his thumb, ploughing it into Baldy's socket and beneath his eyeball to gouge out the eye with a faint popping sound.

Baldy fell, yelping like a dog with its balls slashed, but Nobul was already moving on. The second thug was coming forward, an evil grin on his face like he'd been expecting this, like he wanted it. The man was big but lumbering. Muscular but under a thick layer of fat.

Not hard like iron. Not tempered like steel.

Nobul grabbed the man's head before he could take two steps, slamming it down onto his waiting knee, while spitting a grunt of rage through gritted teeth. He felt the head hit his knee and a biting pain ran up his thigh. Sharp pain. Good pain. As he dragged the man's head back up he felt him going limp, floppy in his hands. But Nobul wasn't finished yet, dragging him back towards the anvil and slamming his head down again, this time on the hard metal block. His skull rang out, not melodically like hammer on steel, but dull like an axe on a wooden stump. Again he slammed it, this time seeing blood spreading over the block. Then one last time before letting him drop. He lay there not moving as Baldy screamed in the background. Could have been unconscious . . . could have been dead, hard to tell. Nobul raised a foot and slammed it down on the man's throat. It gave way beneath his boot, and blood and spit burst from the open mouth. Nobul stared down at the head, now lolling from those big shoulders. If he had still been alive after having his head slammed into an anvil, he was definitely dead now.

'My fucking eye! Bastard! Bastard!'

Nobul turned to see Baldy still writhing on the floor. His hand was clasped to his face and the eyeball was poking out between his fingers on a meaty stalk.

'Shush now, son,' Nobul said, taking up his hammer. 'This'll be over soon.'

He stood over the screaming man, raised the hammer and went to work . . .

When it was over, when he had cleaned up the shit and gore, Nobul pushed his barrow through the dusk-darkened streets, his arms straining under the weight as it went over the cobbles. Usually he would be carrying a batch of weapons or armour in it, covered over with a sheet of canvas, taking it straight to the market stallholder where he'd get a good price or, if he'd been given a commission, straight to the wholesaler where he'd get a better price. It was doubtful he'd get anything for the two dead pieces of shit he had in his barrow right now.

He wasn't worried about being discovered. The Greencoats in this part of town knew who Nobul was, had seen him on more than one occasion carting his wares through the streets. They might think it a bit curious he was pushing his barrow at nightfall, but even if they asked him to stop and took a look inside, Nobul didn't care. Let them have a peek under the canvas, let them see the bodies he was carrying, let them reel backwards in horror, pressing those stupid fucking whistles to their mouths, raising their crossbows, ordering him to get on the ground while they clapped him in irons.

Let them.

But they didn't.

He reached the Storway where it ran past the Trades Quarter, and pushed his barrow down to the little towpath. There were three canal boats moored nearby, ready to take the long journey upriver to Silverwall. Nobul paused for a second, standing stock still, barrow still held upright, waiting to see if anyone would come. Nobody did.

It took him only moments to ease the two corpses gently into the river. They floated there, bobbing on the waves like apples in a barrel, before the current caught them and dragged them off. He watched as they slowly sank below the surface on their way out to the Midral Sea. The tide might wash them up later, but it would be far away from here.

Without giving them a second thought, he made his way home.

When Nobul got back to the forge he paused just long enough to fill up the barrow with wood from his shed. He'd always kept a well-stocked woodshed – a forge was useless without one. Once inside he filled the fire pit, watching as the old embers worked at lighting the wood. Then he went to his table and pulled out the long chest that lay underneath. It was made of plain hardwood bound with iron, four foot long and a foot wide, made even heavier by what he kept inside. He paused with his hand on the top, wondering whether to open it up and take a look.

There was no real need for that, he knew what was inside. No need to drag up more old memories.

After he leaned the chest next to the door he took his spade and began shovelling burning wood into each corner of the forge, then stacked kindling on top of that. It didn't take long before there were several fires burning, filling the forge with smoke, burning up to the rafters above and setting light to the walls.

With a last look back, Nobul picked up the chest, walked out into the street and locked the door.

There was only one place he could go after that. Old Fernella was probably the last friend Nobul had. He knew her from the old days, when he'd been a boy up to no good, fighting anything that looked at him twice. It was a bit of a walk to her house, but Nobul still remembered the way. When she opened her door to his knock he saw her look of recognition. It wasn't quite as warm as he'd been expecting.

'Nobul Jacks at my door, after how many years?' said the old woman. 'Must want something.'

He glanced down at his feet, then shrugged. 'Just a small favour. Don't have to if you don't want.'

'I know that. You don't scare me, lad.'

No, of course he didn't scare her. She'd scared him a long time ago though, back before he wasn't scared of anything.

'I need you to look after this for a while.' He passed over the wooden case and, despite her age and her withered frame, she took it from his hands as though it weighed nothing.

'Why can't you look after it?'

No mention of Markus. Maybe she didn't know.

'Got nowhere to put it any more.'

She nodded, then cocked her head towards the inside of her house. 'Want to come in for a bit? I'll read to you like the old days.'

Maybe she did know. Maybe this was her way of saying she was sorry for his loss.

For a moment he considered it. For a moment sitting in Fernella's parlour, listening to her old tales, seemed like just the best idea he'd ever heard. But then he remembered. Remembered that slap he'd given his son. Remembered that last painful look in the boy's eyes. Remembered he didn't deserve any respite from his own pain. Didn't deserve anything.

'No, I've got to be off.' And with that, he turned and left her at the door.

He hadn't walked long before he could smell the smoke from his forge and heard the sound of people milling around frantically, not knowing how to deal with it. Nobul was turning away when a young lad ran around the corner. He recognised the boy, but didn't know his name. Only a little younger than Markus was . . . had been.

'Nobul,' the boy said, breathless and panicky. 'Your forge is on fire.' He pointed back the way he'd come.

'I know,' said Nobul, just standing there.

'Quick then. If it's not put out you'll have nothing left.'

Nobul smiled at that. Smiled because he already had nothing left . . . nothing worth a shit anyway.

He turned his back on the boy and the smoke and the raised voices, and walked away.

ELEVEN

River waited in the dark chamber, blood rushing in his ears. *Raging like a torrent towards the sea.* It had been two days since he had completed his task – two days since his return, since he had started his vigil, waiting for the Father of Killers to appear. In that time he had neither eaten nor drunk – *the cool waters* – but it mattered little to him. He was here to obey, to serve, and that was what he would do.

The sanctum was located far beneath the streets of the city, hidden deep in the arterial maze of ancient sewer tunnels just east of the Storway. *The river from the mountains, flowing fast, giving life . . . and taking it.* River knew the secret ways better than anyone, could walk the dark tunnels without need of a torch, could circumvent the ancient flooded rooms that would bar the way of anyone else wandering beneath Steelhaven. This knowledge served him well in his work, and he was able to move quickly across the city at will via the rooftops or the subterranean passages. *Flowing and crossing like myriad tributaries.*

Despite the damp and the cold, River felt comfortable here. It was home, it was where he had grown up, grown strong and learned his craft. It was a place like no other, both prison and shelter. He was bound to this place, drawn to it. *Like a stream to the ocean.*

He heard them approaching from down the tunnels, recognising their quiet footfalls and knowing they were not intruders. Their steps were too unhurried, too surefooted in the night-dark tunnels to be those of interlopers. They could only be led by one man.

The door to River's cell opened and there he stood, tall and rake thin, his hair and beard greying, his face lined and showing the weight of his years. But his eyes – those eyes of ice blue – they were young, and showed not a fleck of kindness within their lambent depths. The Father of Killers looked down, his smile bereft of warmth or greeting.

Behind him were River's brothers – Mountain, standing tall and powerful, his dark brow creased by a perpetual furrow; Forest, lean and furious even in repose. They too looked on impassively, greeting him without compassion.

'You have returned to us,' said the Father, his voice ancient yet filled with strength. A voice to be both feared and loved. 'Word was you had trouble, that the militia almost had you. Are you hurt?'

'No, Father,' River replied, bowing his head.

'That is good. Come, we shall talk.'

River stood for the first time in two days. His legs were numb from his vigil but he still moved with grace and speed, standing quickly to follow his Father as ordered. Outside the cell was their vast training room, lit by bright torches and glowing braziers. Lining the walls was an array of weapons, wooden mannequins for target practice, beams and ropes for climbing and leaping. It was River's home, a room in which he had lived and learned and mastered his art for as long as he could remember.

'You have done well, River,' said the Father as he led his sons out of the training room and through a dark tunnel. 'I am pleased with the result of your work.' They came out into a massive subterranean cavern, carved from the bare rock centuries before for a purpose River had never learned. 'Our crusade to rid these streets of their wanton lechery, the disease of the wicked, is progressing well.' He turned to face River, towering over him as he always did. 'But you were seen. The streets have been in uproar, the militia searching for you, when Constantin Deredko's killer should have remained a secret – a mystery for the inquisitors of this city to solve.'

'I know, Father, and for that I am sorry.'

The Father of Killers laid a hand on River's shoulder. 'I know you are, my son.' His words were suddenly warming, soothing, and River glanced up to see his Father looking down with a smile. 'But with every mistake we are a step nearer being discovered. Every mistake puts us in ever greater danger, and our crusade cannot be allowed to fail.'

'I understand.'

'Yes, my son. You do understand.'

The Father held out his hand, and Forest stepped forward, placing a dark leather scourge into his outstretched palm. River was already taking off his tunic.

He dropped it to the ground and fell to his knees, bowing his head.

'What is pain, my son?' asked the Father, as he whipped the cat's-tailed lash across River's exposed back, leaving a trail of red across the taut muscular flesh.

'Pain is my strength,' River replied. 'Making me powerful, like the waves of the sea against which all will break and fall.'

'And what is avarice?' said the Father with another vicious swipe of the scourge.

'Avarice is the purview of weaker men. The flotsam to which they cling in the storm of the world.'

'And what is wrath?' Another swing of the arm, another sting of the whip.

'Wrath is my tool, my armour and my sword. It is with wrath that I will slaughter my enemies, welling up like a flood to drown them in their own iniquity.'

'Good,' said the Father, taking River's chin in one gnarled and calloused hand. River looked up into those deep eyes, seeing tears welling there. 'You are my son, River, and the lessons I must teach are as painful to me as they are to you.'

'I know, Father,' he replied.

The Father smiled, and as a tear rolled down his cheek he beckoned River to stand. Despite the searing fire in his back he obeyed, showing no sign he was in pain, showing no weakness in front of his Father.

'Mountain, bring our guest to us. Forest, attend your brother.'

With that the Father of Killers shrank back into the dark of the great underground hall.

Forest saw to River's back in silence. Though River wanted to ask his brother who this 'guest' was, he knew better than to speak unless given permission by the Father. The sting of the liniment made his back burn as though being branded with hot irons, but still River made no sound as his brother cleaned and dressed his wounds. When he had finished they both waited in silence, listening to the constant drip drip of the damp cave and the distant scuttling of rats in the blackness.

River heard Mountain's approach well before he reached the hall. Though his brother came in silence, the guest he brought with him seemed to speak constantly, complaining of the blindfold he had been forced to don, the smell of the dank tunnels, the slippery floor beneath his feet, the constant cold encroaching on his bones. He spoke in a thick accent River struggled to recognise. It was similar to those he had heard at the city's docks, when foreign sailors would arrive speaking in broken dialects he could scarcely understand.

Mountain appeared, his huge fist grasping the man's arm. River saw that the newcomer was dressed in strange garb, a flowing robe of blue tied at the waist with a red sash, his head wrapped in a scarf. Over his shoulder he carried a bag of velvet which he clutched to his side in a white-knuckled fist. His eyes were covered with a blindfold, beneath which poked a prominent nose. His mouth was open, constantly babbling through teeth of bright white and gold.

'Is there really such a need to grip me so hard?' the stranger asked pleadingly, clearly at the end of his rope. 'And I can assure you, for the thousandth time, this blindfold is not necessary. I am a man of the utmost discretion and the secrecy of my purpose here is well understood by me.'

Mountain stood him in the centre of the hall and removed his blindfold. The man blinked in the winking torchlight, then glanced around, his eyes wide. He regarded Mountain, together with River and Forest who were now standing, surrounding him, watching him in silence.

'Is one of you the man I am to see?' said the weirdly dressed stranger. 'Is one of you the Father of . . . the Father of Killers?' His question was met with silence. 'I am Massoum Am Kalhed Las Fahir Am Jadar Abbasi, former envoy to Kali Ustman Al Talib of Dravhistan. My current employer is—'

'I am well aware of who your current employer is,' spoke a voice from the darkness. Out of the black towered the Father of Killers, descending on the little man like an eagle on its prey. River saw Massoum take a stumbling step back before composing himself once more.

He forced a smile onto his face before bowing his head and touching a finger to forehead and lips. 'It is an honour to meet the fabled Father. Prince Amon Tugha sends his deepest regards.'

'Does he?' said the Father, staring down with his sparkling blue eyes. 'Does he indeed?'

'Yes, he does. And, as a token of his esteem, he sends you this.' Massoum delved into his shoulder bag. River and his brothers tensed for a moment, always on guard, always wary of danger, but Massoum merely produced a battered leather wallet. He held it out with an amiable smile.

The Father of Killers surveyed the little man, then the wallet, before reaching out a weathered hand and taking the proffered item. He opened it slowly, as though something might leap out at him if he did not use caution, and looked inside. The Father stared for several moments.

Silence pervaded the hall; not even the sound of the dripping damp encroached on the moment, as though the cave itself were holding its breath in anticipation. There was no sign on the Father's face of what he thought of this gift, even when he looked back at Massoum.

'What would he have of me?' he asked, closing the wallet and holding it tight in his fist.

The messenger looked uncertainly at River and his brothers. 'Perhaps we should conduct this in private?'

'There is nothing you could say that I would not have my sons hear, herald. Now speak.'

Massoum smiled the wider. If he was intimidated by the Father he did not show it. 'Amon Tugha asks that you complete a single task for him. King Cael's heir is to be removed from the game. The warlord has eyes and ears in the palace – an agent with whom you may consort for the planning of this task. The details are contained within this.' He held out a small folded piece of parchment. 'Once the task is done, Amon Tugha will restore—'

'I know what has been promised, herald,' said the Father, snatching the parchment from Massoum's hand. 'I have waited for this day longer than you could know. Very well, your task is done.'

The Father signalled once more to Mountain, who grasped Massoum by the arm, holding out the blindfold. Massoum looked disconsolately at the dark sash, before tying it around his head.

This time, as Mountain led him from the chamber, Massoum made no sound of complaint.

The Father of Killers regarded River and Forest carefully. 'This is a subtle task that has been asked of us,' he said, moving slowly towards them. 'One that is beyond the skills of Mountain. He is a blunt instrument, devastating yet brutish. This task will call for a gentleness of step. Which one of you will serve? Which one of you could enter Skyhelm and take the life of a princess?'

River dropped to his knee immediately. His back still stung but he ignored the pain, pushed it to the back of his mind as an ephemeral thing, fleeting and unimportant. 'I will serve, Father. Allow me to atone for my recent mistake. I only ask the chance.'

Forest was down by his side in an instant. 'No Father, please allow me to fulfil your desires. My brother has proved he is not yet ready for such a task.'

When River looked up the Father was smiling. 'You please me, my sons. You please me well.' He regarded them carefully; River only hoped he would pick Forest for this task. River was never reluctant to kill at his Father's behest, but to kill a woman, a princess no less? What crime could she have possibly committed to deserve such a fate? Despite his eagerness to atone for his failures he was not ready to take the life of an innocent.

The Father laid a hand on Forest's head and River felt relief wash over him.

'You have always pleased me,' he said. 'You have always proved your abilities, never shirking your duty, never giving me a moment's doubt.' He turned to River. 'That is why it must be *you*, not your brother, who carries out this gravest of tasks.'

Forest did not flinch at the rejection, and neither did River react, even though he felt his heart sink.

'Thank you, Father,' was all he could say.

'You are welcome, my son. Now, prepare yourself for what is to come. You must be fit and strong, for the task ahead will not be an easy one.'

And with that, he was gone into the dark once more.

River stood, feeling his brother's eyes upon him.

'Do not fail him again,' said Forest. River could hear the disdain in his voice. His brother's rejection by their Father had hurt him to the quick, River could feel it. They had always been companions, though never friends, and this would not help to bring them closer.

'I will not fail,' River replied, as he walked back towards the training room.

But inside, he could not feel the conviction of his words. Somewhere a girl had been marked for death. And whether he liked it or not, River had been chosen to carry out the task.

He trained hard for hours, honing his body and fortifying his mind. The wounds in his back stung worse than when his Father had first used the lash, but he pushed the pain away, defeating it as easily as any flesh and blood enemy.

When he was done, when his brother had left him alone, he wiped himself down with a cloth and donned his dark tunic. By now it would be light outside, his chance to see the sunrise.

He crept from the sanctum and made his way through the subterranean tunnels, unhindered by the blackness, coming out onto the city streets to be greeted by the crisp morning air and a bright sun shining down from a cloudless sky. The sight made him smile and he would have loved to bask in its glory, but he did not tarry, did not pause to appreciate the morning.

She might be waiting for him, and he would not risk missing her.

The sense of freedom got the better of him; the shackles were off, his duties momentarily forgotten. River quickly scaled a nearby building, climbing in silence, keeping to the shadows, unseen. The rooftops of this city were his domain, though he shared them on occasion with the birds and alley cats. It was a vantage point few were privy to; the city was rarely seen from such heights, and River occasionally felt sorrow for those who never got to experience it.

As he raced from rooftop to rooftop, leaping over and between them, *as the salmon swims upstream*, he felt suddenly alive . . . felt free. This was life, to be unburdened by the sanctum, to be free of his obligations. Though he loved his Father dearly, the tasks given him often played on his mind.

Yes, he was ridding this city of its filth, saving it from itself, but River couldn't stop the occasional feelings of remorse that crept into his mind. Had Constantin Deredko deserved to die in so gruesome a manner? To choke out his last sickly breath alone? Had he chosen River's blade his death would have been quick, and who was to say he hadn't deserved such a grim end for the pain he had inflicted on others?

But what could this princess have done to deserve to be marked?

River knew it was not his place to question the will of the Father. He did not know who this Amon Tugha was, or why his Father would so eagerly carry out a task given by him, but he dare not question it. He could not question it.

Before River could bring any more doubt to his mind, he had reached his destination.

The small square was paved and tree-lined – a haven within the bustle of the city. He looked down from his vantage point high up on a nearby roof, seeing the place empty, as it almost always was. It often surprised him that the square was so seldom visited. It was clear the people of this city favoured din and bustle over peace and solace. Not that River cared.

For she might soon be here.

She was his one secret. His one betrayal. Were the Father to know that he came to such a place in daylight to unburden himself, there would have been a grave price to pay. But River was careful – he always had been.

Some days he would find her here, sitting patiently, and they would talk until dark. Others, he would wait until the sun had crossed the sky and there would still be no sign of her. It was a vigil he often kept, her company the reward he granted himself for the grim work he had to do. It was his one concession to normality, his one pretence at being one of the ordinary thousands he moved amongst, unseen, unknown, unwanted. She was his confessional, even though he never told her of the men he had killed or the real life he led.

And so he sat and waited.

TWELVE

She'd cried until she couldn't cry no longer; hard tears, racking sobs, until she could hardly breathe. Rag had never felt anything like this before.

When she'd started thieving it had been there, that guilt, a constant weight on her innards, as if she had always known what she was doing was wrong, that other people would have to live with the consequences of her actions – but nothing had ever felt like this.

She was scum off the streets; she weren't supposed to have no responsibilities. Weren't supposed to care about nothing but herself.

But she *had* cared about Markus.

He might have been older than the other boys, than Migs and Tidge and Chirpy, but he was more innocent than any of them. He didn't have half the street smarts of Tidge, nor the skills of Chirpy. He shouldn't have even been with her that night. And he wouldn't have been, would he, if it hadn't been for Rag? It was her that took him along, her that said yes to his eager talk of joining their crew.

Crew? Who was she kidding, they weren't a crew, they were just a band of street filth, robbing what they could and staying out of sight.

The feeling in her guts had been so bad she'd even gone to see poor Markus buried on Dancer's Hill. She'd seen his father too, or at least the man that took him and put him beneath the ground. He'd looked sorry enough, standing by that grave, though she didn't see him shed a single tear.

She'd wanted to say something, wanted to give him some kind of condolence, but when she saw the look on his face, that look of loss in those steel features, she thought better of it. What would she have said anyway? *I was the one that took him up on the roofs, mister. So you could say it was me that got him killed. Anyway, sorry for your loss, and all. By the way can you spare us a few coppers?*

Yeah, she was sure that would have gone down real well. She might even have felt less guilty as he was twisting her head off her shoulders.

And it was all this . . . all this shit, that had got her to thinking about herself.

It was only a cruel twist of the gods that had seen Markus take that quarrel and not her. It was only by a hair's breadth and a bit of luck that it hadn't been her gasping her last on a rooftop, blood pumping through her fingers, waiting for the Lord of Crows. And after all that thinking she'd come to a decision . . .

It was time for all this to end.

She'd talked to Fender about it. Explained to him that she'd had enough, that she didn't want to end up just another dead urchin on the streets. Talked to him about how she couldn't go on like this, couldn't keep living this way and she needed something more.

At first he'd been his usual angry self, calling her an idiot for wanting to break out, saying she was foolish to have ambition above being more than she was. But in the end, despite all his angry words and trying to persuade her otherwise, he'd agreed to help her.

He agreed to help her get into the Guild.

Of course Fender'd had the chance to join himself a while back but he'd bottled out. He said the Guild was a nasty bunch, bastards all, just out for themselves, but he still had connections and he could get Rag an introduction if she wanted it.

Maybe he thought that if she was in the Guild it was as good as them all being in – a licence to thieve, connections in all the right places, on to the big time. Maybe he just wanted rid of her after all this time, with them both being at odds over who was leader of their crew. Whatever Fender's reasons, he said he knew someone who could have a word with someone, and that was that.

So now she just had to wait for him, standing on the roof of the Bull, trying her best not to look Migs and Chirpy and Tidge in the eye. If this was going to happen she would be leaving them behind, moving on to better things. Course she'd be able to see them again, maybe even see them right for food and a few coppers, but things would never be like they was. She was moving up, moving on, and it didn't pay to keep looking back over your shoulder when you did. You had to keep looking straight ahead, keep your wits, keep strong and fuck everything else.

'Sure you want to do this?'

Rag turned to see Fender standing there at the roof edge. She hadn't even heard him arrive. He was getting far too good at sneaking around and she had to admit it made her a bit nervous. Maybe another reason it was time to move on.

'You don't have to, you know,' he said, sounding almost sympathetic, but not quite. 'There's no need to take things so hard. He was a—'

'Don't talk about him, Fender.' She didn't want him even mentioning Markus' name. It would only make her angry. 'And yes I do have to. The thing with Markus just made my mind up quicker. I was always going to do this sooner or later.'

Fender smiled and gave a little nod. 'Yeah, I suppose you were. Not like you was gonna play mother forever.' He glanced towards the rickety shelter in which Chirpy, Tidge and Migs were sitting.

Suddenly she felt guiltier than ever, and not because of Markus. Try as she might to convince herself she had no responsibilities, she knew there were three little lads that relied on her. Three little lads she was turning her back on.

As though he could read her thoughts Fender said, 'Don't worry about them. I'll see them right.'

As Rag looked into Fender's eyes she actually felt he was telling the truth. First fucking time for everything.

'You gonna say goodbye?'

She looked again to the little shack, hearing a giggle, probably Chirpy, from within its confines. 'Nah,' she replied. 'No point ruining their day. They'll find out soon enough. Did you speak to your man?'

Fender nodded. 'Course I did. He says "yes". In fact he knows someone looking right now. If you want the intro we can go straight away.'

'Right then, let's go.'

Fender didn't say any more, just led her down the rickety stairs off the roof of the Bull. Rag followed, head bowed, resigned to it now, knowing there was no turning back. And she didn't turn back, didn't try to snatch a last look at her boys. It might have stopped her doing what she had to do.

When she got down to the filth of Slip Street she didn't look around. She was hoping to leave all this behind, to move on to a better life, so she just kept her head down and followed Fender's lead.

They walked quite a way through the city until they got to Northgate. This was a massive sprawling part of Steelhaven, a warren of rickety houses, easy to get lost in. Quite soon Fender stopped, pointing to the building where his contact was.

'In there,' he said. 'Ask for Krupps.'

Rag felt a knot tighten in her throat. Even down in Dockside she'd heard of this place. The Black Hart was one of those alehouses you avoided. Even the Greencoats gave it a wide berth. She'd never been in there. Had she tried plying her trade and lifting a purse from anyone in The Black Hart she'd likely not have lived long afterwards . . . certainly not with all her fingers.

But there was no way but forward.

'Thanks, Fender,' she said. 'Guess I'll see you later.'

'Just watch your fucking back, Rag.'

When she turned to nod her thanks, he was gone.

No one but her now. Her and a bar full of scumbags and cutthroats. And she had a chance to get into the Guild. Into a better life.

Well, it couldn't get any worse, could it?

The door to The Black Hart was almost hanging off its hinges, wood rotted, black paint chipped and peeling. She swung it inwards and stepped into the gloom, expecting everyone inside to immediately put their drinks down and look her way with dark, furious eyes. But no one so much as glanced in her direction.

There was a hum of hushed conversation and a pipe-smoke haze hung in the air like the breath of some ancient firedrake. Rag took it all in, careful not to catch anyone's eye, mindful she shouldn't stand too long just gawping. She didn't want to attract undue attention by looking like she didn't belong.

Her best bet was to move to the bar and do it with some bloody purpose – don't draw attention, don't be seen. So she moved, head bowed, keeping focused, staying wary. It wouldn't do to let her guard down now.

She strode boldly across the creaky floorboards, past hunched men playing games of cards, until something screeched in her ear.

She jumped almost out of her skin and gave off a girly squeal. There was an ugly bastard monkey, one of those hairy foreign things, on one of the hunched men's shoulders. The old fella himself was untroubled by the noise, but laughed, in an old phlegmy voice, at Rag.

Well done, Rag. How to make yourself look like a horse's cock. Great first impression.

Rag made it to the bar, all pretence at looking natural thrown to the gutter. The barman had a bald head and a big greasy moustache and was running a filthy rag around the rim of a tankard. He was smirking, most probably at that stupid fucking noise she'd made.

She expected him to ask what she wanted but he just stood there, with that idiot grin. She guessed she'd best do the talking.

'I'm looking for Krupps.' She tried to sound as tough as possible, all gruff and emotionless, but it just came out in her same old voice.

Still staring, the barman nodded towards a corner. Rag turned to see a man looking at her from the shadows. In the scant light from one grimy window she saw two other men with him.

Not wanting to show any reticence lest it be mistaken for fear, Rag strode straight up to the trio of men, her chin as high as it would go.

'You Krupps?' she asked, again trying to talk tough but failing miserably.

'Indeed, I am,' he replied with a surprisingly amiable smile. 'You must be this Rag I've heard about. Take a seat.'

One of the other men shifted a wooden chair from beneath the table with his foot. Rag gave it a cursory glance before grabbing another empty chair behind her and pulling it up to the table. None of the men reacted to her feigned attempt at bravado. They could probably hear her heart fluttering like a pennant on a windy day.

She took in the features of the three men. Krupps didn't look bad, she had to admit. In fact, all things considered, he looked extremely out of place in The Black Hart. He was handsome, probably in his early twenties, with a floppy mop of dark hair more befitting a Crown District dandy than some underworld criminal. Nevertheless, Rag knew better than to let his easy smile lull her into lowering her guard. No danger of that with the other two. As much as Krupps looked out of place, these two fit right in.

The one who had slid the chair with his foot was bald and burly, what little hair he had slicked back in greasy knots over his ears. He was chewing on something, and Rag really didn't want to know what.

In the corner, seemingly clinging to the darkness, was the last of the trio. He was stick thin, with hollow cheeks perched beneath two piercing eyes. His dark hair was pulled back in a tight topknot and his body shrouded in a tatty, ill-fitting coat that failed to hide how skinny he was.

'This is Burney,' said Krupps, motioning towards the thickset man who acknowledged her with a wink. 'And that's Steraglio.' The thin man in the corner merely scowled. 'We hear you're quite the purse-cutter, young Rag,' Krupps continued.

She shrugged her answer, trying to look casual about his comment. Probably just made her look more scared.

'Because we've got a job coming up and we might need someone with your skills. Someone stealthy. Someone lithe.'

Again she didn't answer, still trying to size up exactly what she had got herself into.

'This is horseshit,' Steraglio suddenly said from the corner. His voice was reedy and thin, but it still filled Rag with an unsettling sense of dread. 'Look at her: she's a fucking child. And just because she can cut purses don't mean she can break houses.'

Krupps gave him a look – a *shut the fuck up* look. Steraglio took the hint.

'As my friend just mentioned, we don't necessarily just want you to steal someone's coin. But I've a feeling you've broke a house before.'

No, she fucking hadn't. 'Course I fucking have,' Rag said with a confidence that surprised her.

Krupps smiled. 'Excellent. We've got just the job for you. And it's an even four-way split if you're in, Rag.'

A four-way split sounded damn good, but coin wasn't the main reason she was here.

'What about the Guild?' she asked. 'Will this get me entry to the Guild?'

Krupps' smile widened. 'That's why you're here, ain't it? Entry to the Guild? Do this job right and you're in. Write your own ticket, Rag – the only way is up.'

She suddenly felt at ease, felt safe. This mob needed her, and needed her so bad they were prepared to give her exactly what she wanted. This was turning out easier than she'd expected.

'So what's the job? Whose house we breaking?' she asked, feeling her confidence rising.

'All you need worry about is breaking in and opening a door for the rest of us. After that we'll handle things.'

Open a door? For this crowd to just walk into someone's house? Glancing around the table she wasn't sure this was such a good idea after all. If she ever owned a house she was damn sure she wouldn't want the likes of Steraglio and Burney slipping into it in the middle of the night.

'Handle things how? I'm not gonna be part of no murder or nothing.'

Krupps laughed, joined soon after by Burney, but Rag noted Steraglio hadn't even cracked a smile.

'Oh, Rag. We're not in the *murder* business – we're in the taking-what's-not-ours business. Do we look like assassins? Do I look like the kind of bloke who steals into someone's house in the middle of the night and slits their throat?' In all honesty, Rag wasn't reassured. 'The house we're breaking into . . . sorry, *you're* breaking into, is owned by a rich merchant – a greedy fucking merchant – but he won't even be home. So, empty house, easy pickings. Sound good?'

Rag had to admit it was sounding better and better. Her nod of assent was greeted by a big smile from Krupps and a firm slap on the shoulder from Burney.

'Varson! Break out the good stuff,' Krupps called across to the bar. Within moments, the greasy barman had placed a dusty bottle on the table with four relatively clean glasses. Krupps filled them – and Rag picked hers up, staring at the murky-looking liquid inside.

'Here's to other people's money,' said Krupps, raising his glass with a wide grin. Rag couldn't help but be charmed by that smile, raising her own glass with the rest and swigging its contents in a single slug before slamming it back to the table. The taste was hot and sour, burning her throat and making her nose sting. It was all she could do to hold it down, but to Rag's dismay, Krupps was already filling her glass up again.

'To our new friend,' said Burney, his baritone voice resonating through the interior of The Black Hart.

'To Rag!' said Krupps, lifting the second glass to his lips.

In for a penny, Rag thought, taking a swig. But this time the thick alcohol made her snort and, without warning, she was spewing the stinging liquid out of her nose and all over Krupps' lap.

A sudden silence. Then the rest of them, Steraglio included, began to laugh hysterically.

Wiping sour-tasting snot from her nose, Rag had to admit that, despite just having ruined a man's britches, things were looking up.

THIRTEEN

Another day, another book filled with indecipherable nonsense. This one apparently detailed the metaphysical aspects of healing through the Primary Art of Divination; but all Waylian could appreciate was the weave of the book's binding and the craftsmanship of its embossed cover. He'd always admired the work of skilled artisans, their attention to detail and the years of practice it took to produce a work of supreme artistry. Writers of complex treatises on the ins and outs of the magickal arts, however, he did not appreciate so much.

He was losing patience with the whole thing. What was the point? The frustration at his lack of understanding was manifesting as a distinctly short attention span, and he often found himself daydreaming both in and out of Gelredida's lessons. At least here in the Grand Library he wouldn't be reprimanded for his inattention.

Waylian glanced out across the rows of desks, flanked by the seemingly endless line of bookshelves. They seemed to taunt him with their mystery, looming over him like impassable mountains, laughing at his ignorance and jealously guarding the knowledge they would never impart to him. He guessed he wouldn't have to suffer this indignity for much longer. The Red Witch would doubtless see him expelled quite soon.

Casually glancing across the room his eyes settled on one of the other students. That girl, with blonde hair falling in curly locks about her face. She smiled at him, but before Waylian had a chance to smile back she turned back to her studies.

What *was* her bloody name? Gael? Glorie? Balls, what was wrong with his memory these days! Whatever her name was she was the prettiest thing he had seen in a while . . . and she'd just smiled at him.

Not that it would have meant anything, just a friendly smile across the library – nothing to get excited about, Waylian. You won't be here long enough to do anything about it anyway.

Then again, it wouldn't hurt to have something nice to focus on while he was here.

He glanced towards her again, hoping she might look up, but before that had any chance of happening a cold shadow fell over him.

'Hard at work again I see, Jotun?'

Waylian jumped at the voice. He didn't know if he was more annoyed or scared – *Jotun* was her new name for him . . . and he was nowhere close to working out what it meant.

'Erm, yes, Magistra,' Waylian replied, looking up sheepishly to see Gelredida staring down at him with her usual haughty disdain. 'I was just . . . er . . .'

'Yes, I can see what you were doing.' The Red Witch raised an eyebrow and peered over to where the blonde girl was sitting. Waylian could see her watching as he was humiliated by his stern tutor.

Great first impression, Waylian. Just great.

'Jotun, you'll be pleased to know I require your assistance.'

'My . . . ?'

'Assistance, yes. I'm sure it comes as a surprise considering your uselessness in all other matters, but I'm heading out into the city and it wouldn't do for me to be seen traipsing the streets without my faithful apprentice, now would it.'

'Well, I . . .'

'Yes, I'm sure you are, Jotun. Now take your books back to your chambers and meet me in the entrance hall as soon as you're done.'

With that she stalked from the library.

Waylian gathered up his books as quickly as he could, not daring to glance over towards the blonde girl lest she be laughing at his humiliation, and rushed from the library.

Gelredida was standing in wait for him, and it was clear she was less than amused. He had only been a few moments, rushing to his chamber, then straight back down the long winding staircase to the entry hall, but she looked as though he'd kept her waiting an age. She didn't speak as he appeared, merely set off through the massive double doors as they were pulled open by four towering Raven Knights.

On first arriving in Steelhaven, Waylian had come through Eastgate, a relatively affluent area of the city, and been ushered straight to the Tower of Magisters. Since then he had seen little of the city, beyond what could be spied through one of the Tower's many windows. As Gelredida led him out through the Tower's grounds it was clear they were not heading towards an area of affluence.

He followed his mistress north, through streets that became gradually more filthy. Houses of stone and timber soon gave way to twisted shacks of rotting wood and chipped slate; polished cobbles to mud pits swimming with effluent. If Waylian hadn't been so frightened of the Red Witch he might have asked why they weren't being accompanied by a Raven Knight or maybe *five*. However, the ever more insalubrious characters wandering the streets seemed to be giving them a wide berth – as though they knew who Gelredida was and what it would mean to confront her. The pair went ever northward, as if with an aura – an aura that said *we are of the Caste, and if you try it on you'll regret it.*

They continued in silence. Waylian was beginning to wonder if they were lost, when he saw something of a commotion up ahead. A crowd had gathered: a mob of bedraggled-looking peasants all barracking one another for a look at something. As they drew closer Waylian could see that two Greencoats were standing vigil at the door of a ramshackle three-storey house, occasionally pushing back anyone getting too close or peering too far through the partially open door.

Gelredida walked up to the back of the crowd, and as Waylian was wondering how they might make their way through, one of the peasants suddenly sensed the Red Witch bearing down on him. He blanched and moved from her path. Like a whisper on the wind, the knowledge of her arrival seemed to sweep through the mob, heads turning, eyes suddenly widening as each caught sight of the stern visage of Waylian's mistress. A gap big enough for a horse and cart appeared in the crowd and she strode through, Waylian stumbling to keep up with her as he slopped through the muddy thoroughfare.

One of the Greencoats bowed his head in respect as she approached; the other pushed the door fully open to allow her entry to the house, which seemed to be listing dangerously and at risk of imminent collapse. She entered without acknowledging the men; Waylian offered them a limp smile of thanks. His nicety was not returned.

The interior of the house was decrepit, with plaster peeling from the walls and furniture not fit for firewood slung about the place. More

Greencoats stood inside, their faces pale, their shoulders slumped. It was then that the smell suddenly hit Waylian. He lifted a hand to his face to block the stench – it was like rotten eggs and dead badger – but to no avail. The stink was in his nose, in his head. No amount of lavender or mint would clear it any time soon.

They took the stairs, which creaked ominously, but somehow managed to bear their weight. The higher they went the worse the smell became. Something was definitely dead in here, and Waylian felt a growing sense of foreboding.

At the top of the landing stood a grim figure, waiting as though expecting the Red Witch. His grey hair was cropped short, a leather patch covering one eye, adjacent a nose that had been broken more than once. His lantern jaw and grim visage gave Waylian pause for a second. As Gelredida reached the top of the stairs the stern Greencoat gave her a nod. It was a gesture of familiarity, which the Red Witch returned in kind.

'Ben Kilgar, as I live and breathe.' Though Gelredida's words were warm, her expression did not soften.

'It's Serjeant Kilgar now, Magistra,' he replied in a deep rumbling brogue. 'Good to see you. It's been . . .'

'A long time. I'd say too long, but perhaps I'd be wrong about that.'

He nodded in agreement. It was then Waylian noticed he only had one arm, his left one missing at the elbow.

'If only we were meeting under better circumstances,' she said. 'Shall we proceed?'

Serjeant Kilgar didn't speak, merely leading them along the corridor. Two pale-looking Greencoats at another doorway stood to quick attention as their serjeant approached. He pushed the door open and stepped inside. As he did so, the smell that was plaguing Waylian's nostrils suddenly intensified, though neither the stern Greencoat serjeant nor Gelredida seemed to notice.

She walked in, and Waylian dutifully followed, though with every step his stomach churned, as much with dread at what he would find as with the increasingly nauseating aroma. Having stepped over the room's threshold he regretted it immediately.

The room was lit by dim candlelight, the single window having been covered with neatly arranged boarding. In the flickering light he could see strange sigils had been daubed on the walls, though in the dimness it was difficult to tell what with. The symbols seemed to exude a strange

103

miasma that numbed his head and made his eyes water. Indeed, the whole place seemed filled with a thick pall, like strong pollen – only with a sicklier sweetness.

But it was not this that made Waylian baulk. It was not this that made him retch, clamping a hand to his mouth to hold in a stinging uprush of bile. It was not this that made him rush into the corridor to evacuate his stomach contents on the dirty floorboards.

It was the disembowelled corpse nailed down in the centre of the room.

Waylian heaved. He heaved until he could heave no more, evacuating his breakfast of fried bread and black pudding. Nowhere near as nice coming out as it had been going in.

And it wasn't even the entrails strewn across the floor that got him, but rather the staring blank eyes of the corpse. He couldn't seem to get that image out of his head, no matter how much he puked.

Eventually he managed to swallow back what was left in his throat and leaned against the wall, gasping for air. As he wiped his moist nose on his sleeve, Gelredida marched from the room with Kilgar behind.

'I can assure you, serjeant, it is a hoax.'

'But the symbols, the murder, it's—'

'Your problem, I'm afraid. The symbols are gibberish, the manner of death made to look like some infernal rite, more than likely to divert attention from the real culprit to a member of the Caste. No, Ben, you're not looking for any warlock. Just a run of the mill sadist.'

'I'm sorry to have wasted your time.'

'Not at all. You were right to send for me. One can never be too careful. The last thing we need right now is a rogue magicker wandering loose in the city.'

'Indeed. Thank you for your time, Magistra. It was good to see you again.'

'And you, serjeant.'

With that she turned and regarded Waylian like shit on her shoe. 'Do pull yourself together, Jotun. It won't be the last corpse you ever see. Better get used to it.'

She strode past him, and Waylian could only follow in her wake. As they traversed the filthy streets in silence, he dared not ask any questions about the murder, and she, clearly, would volunteer no information. When they reached the Tower, Gelredida abandoned him without a word, stalking away into the bowels of the massive building.

Waylian was not sorry to see her go.

Later, lying in his bedchamber, Waylian could think of only one way to erase the image of that blank-eyed corpse from his mind. Squeezing his eyes shut he began to picture Glorie.

Or was it Gael?

Anyway, whatever she was called she was firmly implanted in his psyche, and lying there alone and in the dark he could think of nothing else. Slowly his hand crept down beneath the covers. At first he felt a pang of guilt – what would she think of him if she knew what he was about to do, *and* while he was thinking of her – thinking of her naked, in his bed, touching him, running her lips up and down his . . .

Then the guilt was gone. He bit his lower lip, tightening his grip on himself, his head filled with her, imagining what she would look like after he'd had his way with her. That smile, which in the library had been friendly and open, in his dark chamber would be coquettish, filled with promise. Her hair, which fell about her shoulders in those red-gold locks, would be tousled and unkempt. Her complexion, usually pale and smooth, would be rosy red about the cheeks and glowing with the sweat of lovemaking.

Waylian felt himself grow harder as he imagined taking her breast in his hand, drawing it closer to his mouth, taking the nipple between his teeth and . . .

'Leave that thing alone, Jotun.'

He almost leapt out of his bed, but had the presence of mind to pull his blanket up to his neck as he saw Gelredida standing over him. She looked even less amused than usual.

'Get dressed,' she ordered, raising an eyebrow in displeasure. 'We have work to do.'

With that she turned and left his chamber, closing the door behind her and leaving him in darkness once more.

Waylian stared at the door for several moments after she'd gone, wishing fervently that he hadn't just been caught cock in hand, but no amount of staring would turn back time.

He dressed quickly, his cock rapidly growing flaccid as his vision of the girl was shattered and replaced by the memory of Gelredida leering down at him as he frantically abused himself.

The Magistra was waiting for him in the entrance hall, the vast double doors already opened. Waylian couldn't bear to look her in the eyes as he approached. He was thankful when she turned and walked out into the night without acknowledging his arrival. Thank the gods she hadn't questioned him further. What excuse would he have dreamt up? *I'm sorry, Magistra – it wasn't what you thought. I was actually just scratching vigorously at a troublesome itch on my thigh.*

They made their way through the streets once more, heading from brightly lit, cobbled avenues to filth-strewn alleyways. Waylian would have felt more intimidated at night, walking in the troubled quarters of the city, but he knew from his earlier experience that there would be nothing to fear . . . at least not while his mistress was present. He didn't ask where they were going, but even at night, with his limited knowledge of the city's geography, he could tell they were repeating their previous journey. His suspicions were confirmed as they came again upon the ramshackle house with its eviscerated occupant.

There was only a single Greencoat now, the street mob having clearly lost interest and wandered off to find some other misfortune to ogle at. Gelredida approached the guard, her head hidden beneath the hood of her robe. At first the Greencoat stayed at attention, clearly obeying his orders to allow no one in the house. The Red Witch spoke a few words Waylian couldn't hear. The Greencoat's stern features softened – he even managed a smile – and he moved aside, beckoning her in. Waylian suddenly felt a wave of calm wash over him, along with a strange feeling of goodwill towards his mistress. He followed her inside, glancing briefly towards the Greencoat and seeing the idiot grin on his face. Whatever glamour his mistress had used was potent indeed.

As they made their way up the rickety stairs, Waylian couldn't hold it back any more. He had to know what they were doing – especially if he was going to have to view that hideous corpse again.

'Why have we come back here, Magistra?'

No answer.

It was probably wishful thinking that she might deign to let him in on why they'd returned.

As she entered the room Waylian paused just outside. He felt his stomach churning in anticipation, the mushroom soup and hard bread he'd eaten for dinner threatening to broil up to the surface, but by a titanic effort of will he managed to keep it down. Clenching his fists to his sides he followed her in.

The body was still there. Waylian could see it was a man in his thirties, a detail he'd failed to notice previously. The guts were still strewn randomly but the blood that surrounded him like a black halo had dried and darkened.

Gelredida held up a single candle as she knelt by the body.

'What do you notice, Jotun?'

What, other than there's an eviscerated man on the floor? That he doesn't look like he'll be up and about any time soon? 'Erm . . . I don't know what you mean, Magistra.'

'There's been a murder. This body has been lying here all day and most of the night. It's unseasonably warm for this time of year. What is odd?'

'Erm? There are no flies?'

'Very good.'

Waylian almost fell over – those were the first words of praise she'd ever granted him.

'So this isn't just a murder?'

She stood up, staring at him from beneath her hood, her face eerily framed in the light of the single candle.

'No, Jotun, this is not just a murder.'

'But you told the serjeant—'

'I told the serjeant what he needed to hear. He would not benefit from knowing the source of this killing. He can do nothing for this poor soul, nor the ones to come. It will take a hunter of equal cunning and skill to catch the quarry we seek.' She glanced down at the body, and a look of sorrow passing over her features disappeared as quickly as it came. 'A ritual has been enacted here. A rite of such despicable evil it will need to be purged. A dark sacrament so blasphemous it has sucked the life from everything around it.'

'So we are looking for a member of the Caste?'

Slowly the Red Witch nodded, her face looking haunted beneath the hood. 'And unless we find him quickly, there will be more like this . . . many, many more.'

FOURTEEN

It was a yard of steel, an inch and a half wide at the hilt, straight in the blade and tapering to a point an inch from the tip. The crossguard had been worked in bronze, the grip wrapped in leather and the pommel wrought from iron. It was also a pile of shit. But then, Merrick hadn't really been expecting anything better.

The sword he'd been given by the Guild rattled in its scabbard, rust flaking off the metalwork. He hadn't dared try to swing it with any impetus lest some part of it fall off, but at least it had cost him nothing.

Almost nothing.

Whether he liked it or not he was about to start earning it, and no mistake.

He stood down at the edge of the wharf just east of the Rafts, looking and feeling like a spare part, but those had been his instructions. There wasn't much he could do about it. If the stink of dead fish and sweaty sailors wasn't bad enough he was downwind of the Rafts, and the stench coming from the scum and filth that dwelt there was appalling.

Drunken mariners stumbled along the esplanade, weaving expertly in and out of the whores and pickpockets. Some hung in groups, singing shanties, blowing their rum breath all over each other. Merrick did his best not to catch anyone's eye, leaning against the corner of a massive warehouse, trying his best to blend in. He had to admit, that wasn't hard: he looked like shit – just like everyone else in this part of the city.

'You Ryder?'

A voice from behind him. He'd been told to expect a contact, but would it be a friendly kind of contact, or a 'stab you in the back soon as look at you' kind of contact?

Only one way to find out.

'Who wants to know?' Might as well come across as careful. Better than coming across like an arsehole.

'*I* do, and I'm the one standing behind you with a knife.'

Ah, well that puts a different complexion on things.

'Yes, I'm Ryder. But you knew that already. So there's really no need for all this rudeness, is there?'

A figure moved out of the shadows, swarthy and foreign. He was small, with a pointy rat's face, massive nose, big teeth, squinty eyes. He hadn't been lying either: he had the wickedest curved shank Merrick had ever seen.

'You can never be too careful,' the man said. 'But they told me you spoke like a noble and looked like shit. Now I know I have the right man.'

Charming.

He spoke in a Kajrapur accent but his grasp of Teutonian was impressive, particularly for a ratty little cutthroat.

'Yes,' Merrick replied, pushing himself off the wall and doing his best to look impressive. Maybe not succeeding. 'My reputation clearly precedes me. I assume you're here to guide me to Bolo?'

Without another word, the cutthroat sheathed his weapon and led the way from the wharf into the labyrinthine alleyways of the Warehouse District.

Bathed in gloom, Merrick immediately began to feel nervous. He hadn't often had to entrust himself to strangers, especially when they looked as if they might stick him full of curved blade and steal his boots at any minute, but what choice did he have? It was this or go against the Guild, and doing that was as good as chopping his own fruits off.

They moved through the contradiction of architecture that was the Warehouse District. Ancient stone storehouses stood beside crumbling timber granaries, with basalt gargoyles leering over rooftops, flanked by loose slates and rotting wooden eaves. In the days of the Sword Kings, when Steelhaven had been a hub of commerce throughout the Midral Sea, traders from across five provinces had used the district to store grain, livestock and slaves before bartering them off to merchant barons from three continents. Since those golden days had ended, treaties had been forgotten and friendships between kingdoms soured, and most of the warehouses stood empty. Nowadays the lion's share of trade involved the stink of fish or whores down the docks. Merrick knew it wouldn't be long, though, before one of those ancient traditions would be revived. Some time soon, in one of these dilapidated buildings, cold, shivering and scared half to death, a group of men, women and children would be bound for distant shores and the horrors of enslavement to savage foreigners.

And Merrick Ryder was the one who got to arrange it all.

Oh, how his mother would be proud, Arlor rest her soul.

Eventually Rat Face stopped outside one of the crumbling old buildings, looking left and right as though they might be being followed. Merrick did likewise, at any moment expecting an angry detachment of Greencoats to jump out and arrest them – but there was nobody there.

Rat Face knocked against a small studded iron door: three quick raps and two slow ones. Then he waited.

Merrick could feel his heart beating faster as he stared at the back of Rat Face's head, wondering what might happen if he just turned tail and ran. If he managed to get to the docks he could probably board a ship for Equ'un or Dravhistan, maybe even to Han-Shar, paying for his passage with hard work on a long haul freighter. He'd be leaner by the time he got there, and have a tan. Those rich merchants' wives at Tarr Vanau would go wild for a handsome westerner.

Before thought could turn to action, the iron door opened. Rat Face stepped over the threshold, disappearing into the dark within.

Merrick thought about it one last time. If he followed, that would be it; he would be tied into this endeavour, tied to the man it would make him – an evil, slaver bastard. If he ran, he would always be running, never safe, and eventually the Guild would find him, no matter how far he went.

There was nothing to think on, was there.

Clenching his fists, he followed his guide inside.

The iron door closed behind him, and he stood there for a spell, waiting for his eyes to adjust, all the while expecting a club or a blade to come swinging in from the shadows. Nothing came at him, but by the time he could see through the gloom he noted that he was surrounded by big burly bastards.

Rat Face stood to one side of the room, waiting patiently. Merrick moved forward, squeezing past the towering bodyguards, as his guide led him towards the only source of light which was down an adjoining passageway.

Merrick moved as quick as he could without looking as if he was running, finding it hard to ignore the scary individuals that were following him. He also had a hard time ignoring the stink of this place – stale, damp, with an insistent odour of the great unwashed.

The corridor came out into a dimly lit room. Lanterns lined the walls, their red-tinted glass giving off an eerie glow. More hulking figures stood waiting, the lantern light playing off their faces making them look almost daemonic.

In their midst stood a giant, his skin black in the red light, his head topped with a huge headscarf and his hand resting on the pommel of a massive falchion. Scars criss-crossed his arms and bare chest, and his top lip had been sliced to the nose and crudely stitched back together.

This must be the man Merrick had come to see – Bolo the Slaver.

He stepped forward, planting his feet, raising his chin and staring the giant right in his furious eyes. It wouldn't do to look weak, even though this beast could most likely snap his neck without thinking.

'I'm Merrick Ryder. I assume you're the man I'm here to see?'

The giant simply stared back at him, but some of the other pirates sniggered behind him, one of them guffawing like a donkey.

Not a great start.

'I believe *I* am the man you're here to see,' said one of the pirates, walking to the front of the group. He was tall and swarthy, his skin washed dark by the sun and sea spray, his eyes a piercing blue, his hair falling about his handsome face in shiny black curls. The silken shirt he wore hung open to the navel, revealing a well-defined chest; his right hand rested easy on the jewelled pommel of his cutlass.

If Merrick had been expecting some monster who preyed on children and babies this man certainly wasn't it. Bolo appeared every inch the pirate lord of legend.

'Kneel before the great Bolo Pavitas,' said the giant in a voice as deep as Merrick had ever heard. 'Slavelord of the Four Seas. Prince of Keidro Bay. High Admiral of the Silken Fleet and Seventh Lord of the Serpent Road.'

Now here was a conundrum. It wouldn't do to start these proceedings from a position of weakness, and bending the knee like a lapdog would certainly accomplish that. Merrick tried to think quickly, but surrounded as he was by hulking brutes, no ideas were readily presenting themselves. If he showed a lack of strength he'd command no respect. If he showed impertinence he might leave in several pieces.

Luckily Bolo, stepping forward past his enormous bodyguard, made the decision for him.

'Enough, Lago. This man is our guest,' he said, and the huge scarred man bowed his head and moved aside obediently. 'I must apologise. Lago takes the responsibilities of his position most seriously.'

'Think nothing of it,' Merrick replied.

'So you're the man Bastian and Friedrik sent to smooth our arrangement and see the deal done aright?'

Well, I'm not the local cockle-seller. 'I am.'

'Excellent.' Bolo smiled and his eyes shone. Merrick recognised that smile – it was a smile he'd flashed a thousand times to win the confidence of a thousand rich fools.

He didn't know whether to hate this Bolo or invite him out for a drink.

'I trust your credentials are all in order?' said the pirate.

Merrick frowned. 'If you mean have I done this kind of thing before, then yes; I've brokered one or two deals in my time. If you mean have I sold people to foreign slavers, then no; this would be my first time.'

He realised he'd said too much as soon as the words were out but he hadn't been able to stop himself, and he certainly couldn't take them back now. This was a shit deal for all involved – the slaves particularly, him especially – but he had to get over it. Showing remorse in front of this callous bastard was likely to get him killed.

Bolo merely smiled and took Merrick by the arm, guiding him towards the rear of the chamber where a passage led deeper into the gloomy interior of the building.

'You should not concern yourself, Ryder. It's only natural that you should harbour pangs of doubt. Do you think I am not without regret at what I do?' *I think you sleep like a fucking baby.* 'But I have come to realise I am merely part of a commercial enterprise, just one link in a larger network, and if not me, someone else would be carrying out this task – perhaps someone with less compassion, someone who might treat his charges with cruelty and malice. Besides, if you look at it closely, the only alternative for the poor souls we will be transporting is a life of misery.'

They had come out into a huge, dark storehouse. Merrick could smell the stale odour he had experienced on first entering through the iron door. It was the musk of unwashed bodies mixed with the stink of stale piss.

'The Elharim warlord has already crossed your northern borders. Thousands flee before his wrath and where do you think they'll be headed?' Merrick could make a pretty good guess but he held his tongue; it wouldn't do to interrupt Bolo while he was in full flow. 'They'll be headed right here. Thousands of souls crammed within these walls, no food, no shelter, spreading their disease, rioting in the streets. I am merely . . . relieving the congestion. These lost souls won't suffer; they'll be well cared for. The Dravhistani treat their slaves very well – almost like they're part of the family. And what's the alternative for them? Do you think

112

the Khurtas will offer them anything better?' Merrick doubted it. 'Of course not. So you see, if you look at it in practical terms, we're saving lives . . . and making a pretty penny into the bargain.' Bolo accentuated his sentence by rubbing the fingers of one hand against his thumb.

Merrick almost bought into his explanation. Almost convinced himself that Bolo was making sense; that somehow he was helping the people they would be transporting on their slave ships. Keeping them safe from the horrors of war and beyond the reach of the Khurtas.

It wasn't until he saw what awaited him in the gloom that he realised it had been nothing but foolish whimsy.

Row after row of steel cages filled the storehouse. In each one sat a barely human figure, dead eyes staring at nothing, faces wan from lack of food, what clothes they had hanging from shoulders barely broad enough to keep them on. Everything Bolo had just told him faded into insignificance to be replaced by a rising anger.

Who was this bastard trying to kid? They weren't helping these people; they were condemning them to a life of misery and bondage. And what kind of businessman was this cunt anyway? How was he going to get a decent price at market if his 'goods' were half dead?

'Now,' Bolo said, with a toothy grin, 'let's talk about price.'

Merrick suddenly had to ball his fists. 'The price has been negotiated and finalised already,' he replied, barely able to speak through a clenched jaw.

'Yes, of course you're right. But as you can see, the livestock is not all it could be . . .'

If there hadn't been so many of Bolo's men standing around with their curved swords and the muscle to use them, Merrick might have strangled him then and there.

'That's not my problem!' His voice echoed within the storehouse. 'The price is fucking fixed!' Bolo's smile slid from his handsome face. 'If you want to make more money on your livestock, fucking feed them!'

Bolo's eyes shifted to his men. Merrick knew he had overstepped the mark, berating Bolo in front of his subordinates, but there was little he could do now. He had to follow through, had to show his mettle or he would more than likely end up in a steel cage of his own.

'Don't look at them!' Merrick said, and Bolo's eyes shifted back to him. But Merrick could still hear the brutes shuffling uncomfortably behind him. One word from Bolo and he was done for. 'Don't think they'll help you. If anything happens to me, the Guild will have a hundred men here cutting you to slop before you can wipe your backside. You do know who I mean by the Guild, don't you? The organisation that's been running this city for two hundred years. That has eyes and ears in a score of ports. That has more money than any of you and your pirate friends. The organisation that, should you dick with this deal, will follow you all across your Four fucking Seas and back to Keidro Bay where they'll fuck you in your arse while your men watch!'

Bolo looked on impassively, and for a moment Merrick thought he'd finally spoken his last words.

Then the pirate smiled.

'Of course,' he said, patting Merrick on the arm as if they were old friends. 'No hard feelings – the price is the price – I get it.'

Merrick nodded, feeling relief wash over him. 'The price is the price.'

'And just to show there's no hard feelings, how about sampling some of the merchandise?'

Before Merrick could answer, Bolo's thugs had ushered forward three gaunt figures. The girls looked young, the youngest barely old enough to have had her blood yet. Each had a face that might have been pretty once, but was now marred by dirt, eyes haunted as though having seen horrors no one so young should have to look upon . . . or experience. Their hair was lank, their dresses soiled, but still they stood with chins raised, still brave, still with a seam of hope . . . of defiance.

Merrick felt the rage rising once more, but he had danced on the edge of his luck enough for one day and managed to bite his tongue, unable to tell Bolo exactly what he thought of his offer.

'I have boys if you'd prefer?' said the slaver after several moments of silence.

'Not interested,' Merrick managed to say, dragging his eyes from the girls and moving back to the red-lit chamber and away from the store-house and its pitiful inhabitants.

'I am led to believe you can facilitate my needs,' said Bolo as he followed Merrick from the storehouse.

'I can. You won't have a problem with the Greencoats or any of the harbour workers. Just tell me how much more . . . *livestock* you need and we'll see it's brought to you. I trust you have enough room for them?'

'Of course. I am having more cages brought as we speak.'

Merrick felt a little bile rise in his throat. 'Then I think we're done here, for now.'

'Not quite.' Bolo gestured to one of the men standing behind Merrick, and he turned, half expecting to be set upon by a knife-wielding maniac.

Instead, the giant henchman Lago stepped forward with something in his hands. At first Merrick thought it was a rope until it suddenly moved of its own accord, one end whipping and curling and casting weird shadows on the wall. It was a serpent, and by the careful way the dark-skinned henchman held it, Merrick could only assume it was venomous.

Lago stretched it between his muscular arms as another man walked forward and slashed the creature across the belly. Blood poured out in slimy rivulets and the henchman filled two goblets, offering one to Merrick, who took it before he could even think to refuse, and the other to Bolo, who grasped it with a gleeful smile.

'*Ka'i dellan*,' Bolo toasted in his native tongue, raising his goblet to Merrick before swallowing the liquid down with gusto.

Merrick watched some of the sticky red goo run from Bolo's lips and down his chin.

There would be no getting out of this.

'Here's to making coin.' *And living long enough to fucking spend it.*

Merrick swallowed down the blood as quick as he could. It went down like a gob of someone else's warm snot.

'Indeed,' said Bolo. 'This has been a pleasure.' *I'm sure it fucking has.* 'My men will escort you back.'

'No need, I can make my own way. Until the next time.' With that Merrick handed his goblet back to the henchman, turned and walked back into the dark, feeling his stomach churning, trying his best not to run like fuck.

As the iron door opened ahead of him, seemingly of its own accord, he could hear Bolo laughing in his chamber, quickly joined by the gruff braying of his sycophantic henchmen.

When Merrick was sure he was far enough away from the warehouse not to be seen or heard, he bent over, grasped his knees and heaved red snake's blood onto the cobbled path.

That went well, he thought, moving off as quickly as his trembling legs would allow.

But no matter how he tried to make light of it, to tell himself he had done all right, he still couldn't get the image of three sickly-looking girls out of his head, or what might happen to them as he left them to their fate.

FIFTEEN

In the end she had gone for something modest. In fact the only thing that could have been considered daring about her dress was the lacing in the bodice. It was in the Valdoran style – long billowing sleeves, high and tight in the neck, cut from a thick slab of blue floral velvet that was already beginning to chafe at the waist and armpits. How did those northerners stand it?

Right now though, the cut of her dress was the least of Janessa's problems. Right now she was fighting the urge to vomit, waiting in the vestibule, about to be announced to the crowd and paraded like the prize heifer.

At her side was Odaka, her ever-present shadow. He stood in silence, his stern, lean features fixed on the archway ahead from which flooded the sound of music and merriment. There was a big crowd, that much was obvious. All the great and good of the Free States come to Skyhelm to gawp and preen and fawn, while their nation was under threat of invasion, its king far to the north facing who knew what kind of danger.

The Feast of Arlor was traditionally held at the Autumn Equinox, and the streets of Steelhaven had already been filled with revellers celebrating the victory of their ancient hero of legend. For the great and good of the Free States, though, it was different: Arlor forbid that they observe their rites on the same day as the peasants. Consequently, a banquet was held at Skyhelm several days after the rest of the Free States, where the nobility could gather without having to feel they were on a level with the thronging masses. The arrogance of it sickened Janessa. She would much rather have been celebrating in the streets with everyone else.

Nevertheless, she had her duty to perform. She would have to walk out and smile and greet them all with the proper airs and graces. She could do with a friend by her side right now, but she had no idea where in the hells Graye was.

An old stentor, ready to announce her to the world, approached from beyond the archway. He was an ancient man, his thinning white hair swept to one side of his head, his back crooked, but still he looked impressive in his official regalia of red and gold. The old man gave a nod to Odaka.

'It's time,' said the regent, not deigning to look at her.

Janessa felt her stomach churning, the blood draining from her face. Odaka took a step forward but she was rooted to the spot. When the regent had reached the edge of the archway and realised she was not at his shoulder he turned to glare at her. The old stentor glanced towards her too.

The crowd would be expecting her. All ready to look and judge, to snigger and laugh in their little conspiratorial factions. It was as though she was condemned to the gallows and the crowd was waiting with rotting cabbages, their mouths full of phlegm to spit on her as she passed. Who would help her? Who would come and save her from this?

Then the old stentor smiled.

It was a smile of reassurance that wrinkled up the old man's entire face. She'd never met him before, didn't even know his name, but there was something in that smile that reassured her – that made her realise everything *might* be all right. It reminded her of the smile her father used to give when she was hurt or lonely. That one gesture alone made her realise she had a duty to perform; a duty as important as that of any soldier on the front.

With a deep breath, she walked forward.

As she reached the arch she saw what awaited her. The nine flags of the Free States had been draped from the ceiling, hanging down in all their heraldic glory. To the right hung the flags of the five provinces: the mountain leopard of Valdor; the rose of Braega; the red dragon of Dreldun; the black warship of Ankavern; and the hunting hawk of Stelmorn. On the left were the flags of the four city states: the gauntleted fist of Ironhold; the portcullis of Coppergate; the mountains of Silverwall; and at their centre, the largest and most prominent, the crown and swords of Steelhaven.

Below these, their faces covered in an array of brightly coloured and bejewelled masks, were the nobles and their courtiers. The crowd milled about, winding around and through itself like a seething mass of snakes, locked in a seemingly endless dance of pomposity, insincere flattery and snide calumny.

It sickened Janessa. All she wanted to do was turn and run, but it was too late now. At a signal from the stentor the orchestra, positioned high on a gallery overlooking the crowd, fell silent. In turn, once the music had ended with the clumsy parp of a bass horn, the masked throng slowly ceased its squalling and looked to see what was happening.

'Her royal majesty, the Princess Janessa Mastragall,' bellowed the old man in a voice deep and rich. How he managed to conjure such a sound from his frail and withered body Janessa had no idea, but it was not the time to ask.

Odaka paused at the top of the marble staircase, glancing down sternly at those below him. She waited with him, following his example, standing stock-still and regarding the crowd with all the hauteur she could muster. It really was like she was being paraded at market – all eyes were on her, assessing her, judging her suitability. It didn't help that she was practically the only person present without a mask. But it wouldn't do for the future queen to hide her beauty from the masses, would it?

Janessa almost laughed at the thought. Beauty indeed!

She'd been plucked and primped and perfumed before the Feast. Bathed in oils, her red curls washed and combed and bound, but she still felt like an urchin inside. Still felt wild. Only now it was as if the wolf inside her had been caged. Locked behind bars to be leered at and prodded with sticks until it performed – until it bit back.

'Shall we?' said Odaka, taking the first step down towards the waiting throng.

It wasn't a request she could refuse.

Janessa followed Odaka down the staircase, her hand on his arm. For that, at least, she was thankful. She wasn't used to navigating staircases in such formal attire, and had he not been there to support her she was sure she would have tripped over her hem or toppled over in the impractical shoes she'd been forced to wear, then gone tumbling down into the crowd. It would certainly have made an impression.

The crowd parted as she reached the bottom of the stairs, all eyes on her as Odaka led her across the carved stone floor of the dining hall. Janessa suddenly felt unable to breathe in the stifling air, but managed to hide her discomfort. Everywhere she looked people were staring, whispering behind their hands. In moments she was surrounded, hemmed within a tightly packed mass of heaving, seething bodies. All she could smell was a rich mix of perfume, all she could hear was the low hum of voices interspersed with the shrill giggles of ladies of the court.

Then the orchestra began to play.

It was like the first rush of rainfall in a storm, and it relieved the black cloud that had been hanging over her head. Suddenly the crowd was diverted, its attention taken. Yes, some still stared, but most went back to their previous conversations, as though they'd lost interest in a brief distraction. Janessa felt relief wash over her, but she knew this was just the start; she had an entire evening of preening sycophants to endure.

As though on cue, the fat waddling form of Chancellor Durket huffed its way through the crowd, eager to be the first to greet her. He was easy to spot, despite his full face mask. It was a bejewelled face of a fawn, but a pig would have been more appropriate. Durket had been her father's Master of Coin for as long as she could remember. During that time his waistband had swollen as the Crown's coffers had shrunk. With the many wars and the plague which the Free States had been forced to endure it had been difficult for the chancellor to keep his accounts balanced. But Durket had always managed to find enough coppers to fill his beak, even when the king had little to spend on his subjects.

'Your majesty,' said Durket, bowing as low as could be managed over his barrel-sized gut. 'May I say how stunning you look this evening? Your dressmaker has clearly worked wonders.'

Nice! Backhanded compliments about her dress, and superb that they were coming from a boar wrapped in ribbons.

'Thank you, Chancellor,' Janessa replied, trying to sound regal. She was pretty sure she didn't. 'And might I say you look somewhat resplendent yourself, this evening.' Janessa tagged the last on as an afterthought, but it sounded quite genuine as she said it. She couldn't help but be pleased with how well she was settling into the fawning insincerity of it all.

'Your majesty is gracious with her praise.' Durket smiled, but she could see his eyes behind the mask, and they most definitely weren't smiling. 'Now, if I might have a word with the regent, there is a matter of state to discuss which I'm sure would not interest your majesty.'

'Of course,' she replied, her hands balling into fists, though she resisted the temptation to punch Durket's condescending face.

The chancellor took Odaka by the arm. The tall regent gave her a glance, which Janessa couldn't quite read. It was a curious mix of concern and threat, as if he was both ordering her not to make a fool of herself, whilst at the same time wanting to stay there to protect her. Nevertheless, Odaka allowed himself to be ushered away by the portly chancellor to discuss whatever grave matters of state they considered beyond her understanding.

Once alone, she barely had enough time to accept a goblet of wine from a passing serf before she felt a presence at her shoulder.

'Your majesty.'

It was a female voice, one that Janessa didn't recognise, and its honeyed tone made her skin crawl slightly. A small, middle-aged woman stood beside her, a half smile on her weathered face which, just as Janessa's, was not covered by a mask. Her dress was immaculate, purple satin with silver filigree, the sleeves night black.

'In the absence of your chaperone, please allow me to introduce myself. I am Baroness Isabelle Magrida of Dreldun, and this is my son, Leon.' She gestured to a youth beside her. His fox mask was pushed up far enough to expose a mouth, currently being stuffed with a goose leg. He couldn't have looked more uninterested.

Seeing the ill manners of her son, the baroness frowned. Young Leon dutifully concealed the goose leg behind his back and bowed with surprising grace.

'It is an honour to meet you,' Janessa replied, inclining her head, not too much, not too little, as she had been shown by her governess. 'And please accept my condolences for the loss of your husband. I know my father thought very highly of him.'

In fact he had considered Baron Harlan Magrida a devious snake whom he was well rid of, but even Janessa knew that at court many truths were best left unsaid.

Isabelle's mouth twitched slightly as though she were about to smile her thanks but thought better of it. 'Yes, we are all deeply aggrieved at his loss, not least his subjects who loved him with a vigour, and are now forced to bear the brunt of the Khurtic hordes.'

By all accounts Baron Harlan's subjects had considered him an ogre, and would probably thank the Khurtas given the chance.

'And I am sure my father will do all he can to see the invaders driven from our lands and your people restored to their rightful place.'

'Indeed. And on that day, my son Leon stands to inherit a powerful kingdom. He will be Baron of all Dreldun and Steward of the High Forest.'

Actually it was a province rather than a kingdom, since the establishment of the Free States, but Janessa was prepared to let that go.

'And a fine lord he'll make too, I'm sure.' She glanced at Leon, who had by now restored his mask, but still looked as though he would rather be anywhere else.

'We would love for you to come visit us, when finally this conflict is ended.' *Oh no, here it comes.* 'I'm sure the Dreldunese air would suit you.' Almost on cue, Leon slipped his mask up, raising an eyebrow and smiling.

Janessa had to admit he was handsome, though his manner smacked of arrogance – the way he stood, his disdainful insouciance, even his lacquered hair. She found herself lost for words. What was she supposed to say to such an invitation? What was the proper response? To refuse would be seen as an insult but to accept might be tantamount to betrothal.

Janessa felt the oppressive air pervading the dining hall once more. The massive chamber began to spin at the edges, the music seeming to grow louder and discordant.

Where in the hells was Odaka? Wasn't it his job to ensure this kind of thing didn't happen?

'Please excuse the interruption, your majesty, but the Lord Governor of Coppergate wishes an audience.'

Janessa turned away feeling relief wash over her as she recognised Graye's delicate features beneath the slight gold mask she wore over her eyes. About to accept gratefully, she checked herself.

Don't seem too eager. This is all a game. Neither offend nor flatter; that is the way of kings and queens.

'As you can see, I am speaking with the baroness.'

'I'm afraid the Lord Governor was most insistent,' Graye quickly replied. 'There are grave matters in Coppergate which, in the absence of the king, require your royal attention. And he is unable to remain for long at the Feast.'

'Very well,' said Janessa, trying to affect the suitable level of disappointment. 'If you would excuse me, Baroness. Leon.' She inclined her head to each, and was rewarded with a curtsy and a bow, though Isabelle looked as though she had just sipped from a wine glass and tasted horse pissle.

Graye led them both off through the crowd, with Janessa nodding graciously to everyone she passed, until they found a shadowy alcove at the edge of the hall.

'Where have you been?' Janessa said admonishingly, though she couldn't help but feel grateful.

'You're not the only one who needs to find a husband,' Graye replied with a grin, her perfect teeth almost dazzling in the torchlight.

'Young Leon Magrida's evidently free. Soon to be Baron of all Dreldun.'

'No thanks,' said Graye, her mouth twisting in disgust. 'I've heard he's a nasty little toad, just like his mother. And you're welcome, by the way. I could have just left you in their clutches.'

Janessa smiled her thanks. 'Where would I be without you to come and rescue me?'

'Betrothed to some northern weasel, no doubt. And you'll get no more help from me until you admit how indispensable I am.'

'Well . . . you're fairly good for picking out shoes. Although the heels on these did turn out to be too high, as I predicted.' She hiked up her skirt to exhibit her impractical footwear.

A shadow fell over them both, and Graye looked up with a guilty expression.

'Lower your dress, majesty,' came Odaka Du'ur's deep whisper.

Janessa quickly released her skirts and composed herself before turning to face the regent.

'I was merely—'

'Never mind what you were "merely" about to do. There are people you must meet. Gossiping with your lady in waiting is not the reason you are here.'

Clearly not – being sold at market is the reason I am here. 'Then let us proceed,' Janessa replied, lifting her chin and stepping from the privacy of the alcove and into the crowd.

She couldn't tell for how long she was exhibited before the various nobles of the Free States as Odaka made introductions and she smiled dutifully, doing her best with the mindless small talk. Most of the governing dukes and barons of the Free States were away north with her father, but they had sent their envoys. Magistrates, stewards and ministers were paraded in front of her, as well as the High Abbot of Ironhold, who, she noted, had yellow bruises about what could be seen of his face and a bandage covering one hand. If a lord should be absent, his wife or one of their offspring was present in his stead. Janessa tried to remember all their names, but there were simply too many. Only those with particularly offensive breath or unpleasant facial features made a lasting impression; like Judge Burtleby's black teeth, or Lady Morgana Hirch's enormous nostrils.

Just when Janessa thought she could take no more, Odaka guided her towards a tall, haughty, but handsome-looking man in his early twenties, and made his introduction. 'Lord Raelan Logar, son of Bannon Logar, Duke of Valdor and Protector of the North.'

Janessa inclined her head as she had so many times already, smiling the necessary smile and hoping this would be the last.

'Lord Raelan. It is a pleasure. I know our fathers think very highly of one another.' Unlike most of the platitudes she'd uttered tonight, at least this one was true.

'Indeed,' Raelan replied. 'I only hope they return to us safe and victorious.'

Janessa tensed at the sudden reminder that her father was in mortal danger. 'We can but hope.'

'I only wish I could be by his side – but here I am.' Though his expression was composed his tone spoke accusation. Did he think her responsible for his presence at court? That she'd requested he abandon his father to the front that they might be forced together like stallion and mare in the rutting season?

'I can assure you, Lord Raelan, that I feel the same.'

'I'm sure.' He glanced around the dining hall as though seeking a more interesting companion.

She was leaning in closer, shame and anger rising within her, desperate to tell him she hated this mummers' farce as much as he did, when the orchestra unleashed a raucous tune. Whatever she *might* have said was drowned in a blaring torrent of music. Odaka leaned towards them.

'The dance begins, my lord,' he said to Raelan. 'Perhaps you might offer her majesty your hand?'

Raelan inclined his head very slightly and offered his hand, as was tradition.

Janessa glanced around in panic. She wanted to refuse, but her conversation with Raelan had already turned heads and they were being watched by a score of courtiers. To refuse him now would only make her look scornful.

Reluctantly, she accepted his proffered hand.

He led her to the centre of the room where perhaps a dozen courtiers had assumed their positions: men on one side, ladies on the other. Someone in the surrounding crowd clapped as a gleeful audience gathered and Janessa could only look around in panic at the prospect of making a spectacle of herself.

Desperately she tried to recall the steps. She had been trained in courtly manners, and dance was one of the many things she'd been forced to learn, but she had completely forgotten the type of dance that went with this tune; even what the first step was.

The row of men bowed as one to the ladies before them. The ladies bowed in their turn, and Janessa managed to join them. With that one simple gesture it all seemed to come back to her.

Both rows advanced, touching their raised right hands and turning in unison, weaving in and out in time to the rhythmic beat of the music. Occasionally partners would switch, and she'd find herself with another of the young dancers who would invariably look at her in wide-eyed fear. But she always came back to Raelan. It didn't take her long to relax into the repetitive steps and she was even starting to enjoy herself.

'You dance well,' she managed to say to Raelan on one of their passes.

'Yes. We do have feasts in the north, your majesty,' came his gruff reply.

She was going to get nothing from him. It was clear he hated this as much as she did. Possibly more.

With a blare of pipes the dance came to a halt, with both rows of dancers bowing to each other as they had at the start. When Janessa looked up she saw Raelan was pushing his way through the crowd to disappear amongst a press of bodies.

She immediately felt alone and vulnerable. It didn't help to see Baroness Isabelle Magrida scowling at her, clearly enraged that it was someone else's son who had managed to poach a dance from the heir to the throne.

Janessa turned, summoning as haughty and proud a manner as she could, and the crowd parted before her. She would not hang around for someone else to take her hand and lead her out for another dance. She'd had more than enough. Let them stare, let them gawp – she wouldn't play this game any longer.

Two of Skyhelm's Sentinel Guard moved aside as she left the banquet hall, desperate to find some place of solitude. Nowhere in that massive palace was empty; every corner she turned concealed a gossiping courtier or vigilant guard. Eventually she reached a mezzanine overlooking the palace gardens where she paused for breath, looking out into the dark, fighting back the tears.

Where was her father? Why couldn't he be here to take care of her? To fight off all the unworthy suitors, the gossiping prigs and toadies.

But she knew why he wasn't here. She knew why he had been forced to leave her to her fate.

'Your majesty, I was worried.'

Odaka – her shadow. Deep down she'd known he would be watching her, following her, anticipating her every move. She should have been grateful that there was someone so concerned for her, but all she felt was resentment.

'Was that a good enough performance for you, regent?'

A pause. She could almost hear him calculating the proper response.

'I do not understand, my lady.'

'I've played my part. I've met your preferred suitor and made all the right noises. I even danced with him. Is the deal done? Is the covenant sealed?'

Odaka conjured up a smile. Even in the dark she was aware of it.

'My lady, apologies if I have led you to believe otherwise, but the choice to marry is yours. Your father has made that most explicit. Should you find Lord Raelan wanting we will find another, more suitable, match.'

Janessa stared in disbelief as his words sank in. She had flogged herself over this for days, weeks, and now it seemed as though she had done all that for nothing.

'You mean I have the choice to marry whom I wish?'

'Of course. Your father and I discussed this at length. He knows how . . . wilful you are. He realises there could never be a match with anyone you yourself had not approved.'

Janessa felt foolish. Of course she should have trusted her father – he would never have condemned her to a loveless marriage.

'Very well,' she replied. 'Thank you, Odaka.' And she meant those words of thanks. Odaka was showing a side she had never seen before. Perhaps that deep, powerful chest of his housed a heart after all.

'Your majesty.' He bowed. 'I am here to serve.'

'Really?' A wicked thought began to form in her mind. 'You could start by ridding the palace of a few gossiping courtiers. How about the Magridas, for a start?'

'I'm afraid that won't be possible, my lady. Your father has offered them refuge within the palace until his return. With the loss of Dreldun to the Khurtas they have nowhere else to go.'

Oh well – you can't have everything.

'Very well, Odaka. I will retire now. Could you make my excuses to our guests?'

'Of course.' And with a bow he was gone.

She looked out again into the night, knowing that far to the north her father might be fighting for his very survival as well as that of the Free States. But here she had to face battles of her own, though from what Odaka had told her, she knew her father was doing his utmost to help her fight those too. For that she could only thank him.

And, despite the chance he had given her – to choose her own suitor – she knew there would never be one suitable, not even the handsome Raelan Logar. There would never be one who could capture her heart . . . because her heart already belonged to someone else.

SIXTEEN

It had been years since Nobul had experienced the discipline of the drill yard. Even after all that time the memory of it still left a strange feeling in the pit of his stomach. Waiting for the serjeant-at-arms, standing alongside your fellows, unsure of what was to come while fully expecting pain and humiliation. And the times when you were forced to march and run for hours, when the serjeant would single someone out for 'special treatment' and all you could do was pray it wouldn't be you . . .

Now though, he stood in the courtyard, feeling the chill of the coming winter creeping into his old bones, and all he felt was boredom.

He stood there alone, surrounded on all sides by barrack buildings. The insistent tweeting of a single bird from a rooftop behind him was the only sound. Had any other men come forward to volunteer? Most likely no one wanted to join up. With the possibility of war and maybe even siege, the city's last line of defence would be the Greencoats. They were the ones best trained for the job. King Cael had already taken northwards half the standing Greencoats, Knights of the Blood and Sentinel Guard, leaving a skeleton crew to safeguard the city.

Nobul wasn't sure why he'd decided to join up with the Greencoats, especially when it was one of them who had been responsible for Markus being laid in the ground. Was it the possibility of being sent to the front? Was he so eager for death? Or maybe he was just eager for a purpose, just eager for something to fill his days, and what better way than this? He had been a fighting man before, and he guessed a fighting man was what he would always be.

But no matter how he tried to tell himself this was his calling, he also knew that alone, on the streets, with no one to watch his back, it wouldn't be long before the Guild caught up with him. It wasn't as if they were going to forget about the two enforcers he'd killed.

Did that make all his bravado so much horseshit? Was he really scared? Was he just telling himself he was tough? Just telling himself he was iron and steel, and doing this because he was a breaker of heads?

It didn't matter any. There was nowhere else for him to go. Nothing else for him to do. He could have joined a mercenary company, but those days were over for him. He was too old for the sleeping rough, the shitty food and the constant fight against illness, thieves and the biting cold.

Besides, if it didn't go well in the north they would soon have a howling, savage bunch of barbarians battering down the gates of this city.

That would certainly solve all his problems.

Nobul had enquired about recruitment two days before and been told by some mustachioed Greencoat to *come back later; there was no one to help him.* When he'd come back a day later, the same uninterested face greeted him, telling him *come back tomorrow, and wait in the drill yard for the serjeant.* When he'd come back a third time there had been no one to greet him, but as the door was open he'd just walked in. And so here he was, dutifully waiting in the drill yard, even though he was starting to think no one was coming.

Before he could decide to jack in the whole thing, he heard a wooden door slamming somewhere in the distance. More recruits? Would it be raw young meat or some gnarled and bearded veteran – an old man just like he was?

Someone was whistling tunelessly.

Into the courtyard strode a young lad looking as if he hadn't a care in the world. His green arming jacket was slung over one shoulder, his halfhelm clasped casually by his side. He had no weapons.

When he saw Nobul standing there he smiled and nodded, like they were old mates. He seemed unconcerned that a man he'd never seen before was standing in the middle of the courtyard where only Greencoats were supposed to be allowed. So much for the vigilant city militia.

Before the youth passed Nobul he stopped, frowning slightly, as though it was suddenly dawning that something was awry.

'You the new recruit?' he said, pointing his finger. As if Nobul would be standing there waiting if he wasn't.

'I suppose I'm one of them,' Nobul replied, unsure of whether to show some kind of respect. This boy could be one of the serjeants for all Nobul knew, and it wouldn't be a good idea to piss him off before he'd even started.

'One of them? There's no one else coming. You're it, mate,' said the boy with a smile. 'I'm Denny.' He held out a hand to shake.

It seemed a bit inappropriate, but Nobul shook it anyway.

'Where is everybody?' he asked.

'Ah.' Denny looked round as though his fellow Greencoats were hiding and might jump out at any minute. 'It's shift changeover. Last watch probably fucked off ages ago. They're supposed to wait for relief before they do, but to be fair, we're usually late anyway, so they don't hang around.'

Nobul glanced around in disbelief. 'So the place is just abandoned?'

'Yeah. But not to worry, they lock the weapons store after them. Not that any of the shit in there's worth pinching anyway.'

Maybe this had been a mistake. He should have seen the signs two days ago when he'd first tried to show interest and been welcomed with a total lack of enthusiasm. The Greencoats were clearly an ill-disciplined rabble. But hadn't he known that anyway? No wonder the Guild ran rampant throughout the city. No wonder he'd been preyed upon for so long by scumbag enforcers demanding his hard-earned coin in return for 'protection'.

Nobul suddenly felt angry. These men were supposed to be the city's guardians. They were no more than a bunch of boys playing at soldiers.

'Thanks for letting me know,' said Nobul, turning to leave.

'Denny! Why the fuck are you standing around like a limp cock? Get your uniform on and empty the slops from last night's shift – they won't have cleared up after themselves, will they?'

Nobul was stopped by the authority in the voice. He stood to attention, feeling slightly intimidated and not a little relieved that there was at least someone with a bit of clout around.

A tall grizzled figure stepped out onto the drill yard as Denny ran off to carry out his duties. He wore an eye-patch over his right eye, and his left arm was missing at the elbow. From his weathered face and the easy confidence with which he walked, Nobul could see he was seasoned. At last, a veteran.

The Greencoat walked up to Nobul, standing close. Scrutinising. Assessing. Their noses almost touching. Nobul had been here many times before, many years ago. The memories came flooding back of the mud and pain and shouting. He had to admit: part of him liked it.

'You must be the new recruit. They told me someone had shown an interest. Name?'

Name? Now there was a quandary. Most likely the Guild were still wondering what happened to their two collectors and Nobul was top of the list for knowing where to find them. Probably best not to go around shouting his whereabouts from the rooftops.

'Lincon.' He'd known a lad from the Free Companies called Lincon. It was as good a name as any, and the lad who used to own it wouldn't be needing it any more since he was twenty years in the ground.

'Any experience?'

'Some.' Nobul knew better than to be too elaborate, and definitely not to overstate where you'd been and what you'd done. That was a sure way to mark yourself out as an arsehole.

'Some?' The veteran looked Nobul up and down again. 'You certainly look the part, if nothing else.' *Because he was iron. Because he was steel.* 'Most of the lads we've got left are too young to wipe up their own shit or too old to piss without it stinging. I suppose you're heading towards the old side. Why should we take you on?'

'Because from what I've seen so far you're desperate for men.'

That one eye regarded him for some moments. All Nobul could hear was a single bird singing. He wondered whether he'd said the right thing or just fucked his chances.

'You're right there, Lincon. Desperate for men is something we definitely are. But despite what you might think, we also don't just take on any old shit.' That was good to know. Now all he could hope was this bloke didn't consider him shit. 'So, what exactly is your experience, son?'

Nobul thought about it. He tried not to think about it too long but this was an important question. Did he give him the whole chat or try to underplay it? There was no point fucking about – this guy didn't seem like he suffered any fools.

'Bakhaus Gate,' Nobul replied, trying not to think too much on the memories that saying those words inspired.

The Greencoat raised the one eyebrow that wasn't hidden under a patch.

'Bakhaus Gate, no less? I was at Bakhaus, in the First Battalion. What about you?'

'I was in the levies,' he replied. 'Under Captain Graig.'

'I remember him. He was a good man. It was a shit way for him to go.'

Nobul agreed with that all right, the memory of it almost made him chill, but there was no point dwelling on it now. The way Graig had been torn to pieces by tooth and claw had given him nightmares enough.

The man regarded him again – weighing him up as though for the last time.

'If you served in the levies then you're good enough for the Greencoats. You'll call me Serjeant Kilgar, or just Serjeant, if it please you.'

'Yes, Serjeant.'

'Before you start, you should know that the wages are poor – two crowns a week. And you'll get no thanks from the heaving masses we're obliged to protect. They'll smile at your face then gob on your back, if they don't stab you in it first.'

Nobul had lived amongst the filth and scum of this city all his life and the fact the Greencoats took the brunt of their ire was no surprise to him. And two crowns a week was more than he had a chance of earning now his forge was ashes.

'Sounds fair,' he replied.

Kilgar nodded sagely. 'Easily pleased. You'll fit right in. Go see Denny. He'll sort you with a uniform, give you the proper papers to put your mark on and introduce you to the rest of the lads. They should be here soon, or I'll know the fucking reason why not.'

'Yes, Serjeant,' Nobul said, feeling the old memories flooding back. The 'yes sirs, no sirs' of military life. The running around, being told what to do, what to eat, when to shit.

He had to admit, he was starting to like it. It was clear Kilgar was right – he *would* fit right in.

Denny did as Kilgar had said and found a uniform: green leather jerk with the crossed swords symbol below the king's crown emblazoned on the back. He gave Nobul an open-faced helm: a bit too big, but it would do, especially if someone tried to rap a cosh over his head. It might make a dull tune but at least it would stop his skull cracking open.

When that was done he went to a tiny chamber, fished around in a desk drawer and got the recruitment papers out. Nobul didn't even bother reading them – he could have been signing on for life for all he knew, but he didn't care. He just made his mark and left it at that.

Denny also did the introductions as more of the watch – Amber Watch as they were known – sloped into the barracks one by one. There were eight in the watch in all, including Denny, Nobul and Serjeant Kilgar, and they were tasked with watching Northgate, closest to the outer wall.

They patrolled in twos, which wasn't the safest thing to do in Northgate, especially at night, but each man had a tin whistle in case he got into strife he couldn't get out of and needed someone to help.

The rest of the watch consisted of Dustin and Edric, the twins. Each had a gawping expression about him, and Nobul couldn't work out which looked the stupider. It wouldn't do to underestimate them, mind. Nobul had fought alongside dumber-looking fellas and they'd turned out to be brave and loyal all the same.

Anton was a fairly good-looking lad, but young and with a dolorous expression about him like he'd lost his pecker end and had no clue where to find it. He gave up a half smile when Denny introduced him, meek and limp like an old man, and Nobul could only wonder how the lad would react if he got himself in real trouble on the street – most likely run like the Lord of Crows was after him.

Old Hake was next to arrive. Nobul didn't know if that was his real name or if he was named for the fish, but it suited him anyway, and not least because of the smell he gave off. He was amiable, giving a smile and a nod as he chewed on some pipeweed. The old man looked fit enough, but not much use in a fight.

Last to arrive was Bilgot. Denny introduced him, a big lad with a mop of red hair and a burgeoning beer gut beneath his jerk. Nobul could tell he was trouble even before he opened his mouth. He'd seen it a thousand times before – young fella, grows up big, takes advantage of the smaller lads and no one's got the stones to stand up to him. Big fish in a little pond. Nobul wasn't here to put any backs up, so when big Bilgot said 'Who's the new fucking meat?' he didn't say anything; just let Denny do the explaining.

'New recruit,' said Denny. 'His name's Lincon—'

'Lincon?' Bilgot walked up, facing off, a good inch or two above Nobul. 'You look like a tough one. You a tough one?'

Nobul had been in this situation very recently, and two men were dead and floating down the Storway and into the sea for their trouble. It wouldn't do to fly off on one and fuck this up too, so he just stood and said nothing, not looking away but not doing any provoking.

'Let me tell you, I'm top dog round here. What I say fucking go—'

'Right, you set of lazy bastards!'

There was a sudden commotion at the sound of Kilgar's voice.

Bilgot shut his mouth, turning to stand to attention along with the rest of the lads. Nobul was beside them, not needing anyone to tell him what to do – he'd been here enough times before.

'As you can see,' said Kilgar as he walked into the barrack room, 'we have a new body with us today. Denny, you'll show him the ropes. Shouldn't be too hard for you, he's a veteran – Bakhaus Gate no less, served under the king, so he's no stranger to being in a fix and living through it.'

Nobul could feel the atmosphere change at the mention of Bakhaus Gate. Some of the lads would instantly respect him for it, others would think it was horseshit. They could think what they wanted; it didn't change a thing.

'Right! On your ways.'

At that Amber Watch filed out of the barrack room.

On their way out onto the streets they stopped at the armoury, though calling it that was a bit like calling a turd a tiara. Denny explained later that due to lack of funds and the fact most of the lads sent to the front had taken the good stuff with them, they had to share weapons between the watches, and after your shift you had to put them back, safe and sound, in the small locked room they called the armoury. The pickings were slim, and Nobul chose a short sword for himself since it looked the weapon least likely to break after a hefty swing. The other lads went for the stuff more intimidating – Bilgot going for a massive banded cudgel. It only showed what little these lads knew, going for weapons that looked the business despite being useless for the job at hand, but then they didn't have much to choose from.

When they got out on the streets of Northgate, Denny was quiet. At first Nobul took it for vigilance; he was feeling the pressure himself after all. In their helms and green jackets they stood out as easy targets for anyone wanting to cause a bit of bother.

Denny pointed out the dodgy alleys to avoid and the faces that might cause the most trouble, but he seemed unconcerned about investigating them, so Nobul just followed his lead.

They got beaming smiles in some places, but Nobul could tell that behind half of them there was little friendship. He found himself looking round at the slightest noise, keeping his hand close to that short blade, conscious of the whistle hung about his neck in case they needed help. But he was also conscious of the respect they were being shown, just for wearing the uniform . . . or was it fear? People moved out of their way as they approached and if someone looked like they were up to no good they'd disappear as soon as Nobul and Denny approached them.

Nobul had to admit: he was beginning to enjoy himself.

133

As the afternoon wore on and there was no sign of any trouble he even relaxed a little. It was then that the questions began.

'So, Bakhaus Gate. Not many blokes still around from those days. You must have seen some sights?'

'None that I'd wish on anyone else.'

'No . . . course not. Just wish I could have been there is all. Wish I could have done my bit like you lads.'

Nobul didn't answer. There was no point shattering anyone's dreams of glory and battle, even if they were talking shit. Let the lad have his dream. Hopefully he'd never have to experience it, but if the Khurtas swept down across the Free States and he had to face them at the city gates he'd learn soon enough what the reality was like.

'Did you see the Black Helm in action?' said Denny, his eyes widening. 'That was the tale most made me want to sign up for the Greencoats. One of the old boys from Leach Street used to tell us about the Black Helm. Held the Gate single-handed while the king got his wounded out of the breach. They say he took half a dozen beast-man pelts, wielding that hammer of his like it weighed nothing, smashing those lion-faced bastards all over the place.'

'Those kind of stories ain't usually right in the telling,' Nobul replied.

'No,' Denny agreed, obviously feeling foolish for being caught up in an old man's tales of war. 'Six pelts does sound like a load of bollocks. Bloke probably never even existed.'

They walked on in silence as the sun fell beyond the north wall.

All Nobul could think was that six pelts *was* a load of bollocks.

By his reckoning, it had been more like a dozen.

SEVENTEEN

Kaira waited in the anteroom, stripped of arms and armour. It was a silent chamber, built for contemplation. She had meditated here many times, eyes closed or staring at the bare, white plaster. But she was not meditating now.

Her whole world seemed to have crumbled in a few short hours. The High Abbot's screaming had almost brought the roof of the Temple of Autumn tumbling down around their ears. Samina had come running, closely followed by more of her sisters. Then the Exarch herself.

She had said little. Merely ordered Kaira to her chambers. Later she had come, guiding Kaira to the vestibule where she now sat, awaiting her fate.

It had been a grievous act, but one Kaira could not bring herself to regret. That foul pig of a man deserved everything she had given him, and more, but now she was the one who would be punished. She was the one who would suffer for her actions.

The waiting was beginning to grow unbearable. It was as though she had been condemned, as if the gallows awaited her – though she knew the Daughters of Arlor would never see her harmed. The Shieldmaidens, however, were much sterner with their punishments.

Kaira had contemplated running. Though the door to the anteroom was closed, it was not bolted. She could easily escape this place and, should she wish to leave the Temple, there would be no one who could stop her. But Kaira Stormfall had never run from anything before, and despite having dishonoured her vows, she was still loyal to the Temple of Autumn and those within it. She could never run away from her duty to this place.

Footfalls in the corridor outside. It was not the first time she had thought they were coming to take her to judgement. Unseen figures had been passing by the chamber all night and day, some quick with urgency, others measured and slow. These steps approached with a purposeful rhythm, stopping when they reached the door. Kaira watched as the handle turned and the door opened, allowing herself a smile when Samina entered, but her friend did not return the gesture.

'Sister,' said Kaira, standing.

'I am sorry,' Samina replied. 'They've sent me to fetch you.'

Kaira nodded. 'I understand.' She stood tall and proud, ready to meet her fate. 'We should not keep them waiting.'

As the two warriors walked the halls of the Temple, the Daughters of Arlor moved from their path as they always did, only this time Kaira felt no pride. Now, all that surrounded her was shame, and though none of the priestesses showed her any disrespect she still felt she had betrayed them and the tenets by which she had been raised.

The warriors made their way solemnly to the antechamber outside the Matron Mother's sanctum. As Kaira had expected, Daedla stood waiting for her.

'This is where I leave you, sister,' Samina whispered. Kaira offered her a solemn smile before she departed. As much as she wanted Samina by her side, she knew this was one battle she would have to face alone.

Daedla opened the door to the sanctum, saying nothing. Kaira chose not to look at her, not wanting to see her look of condemnation as she walked past, and the door was closed behind her.

At the great oaken desk sat the Matron Mother, and to her right hand stood the Exarch. Both looked serious, but what had Kaira expected? That they would greet her with open arms and easy smiles? That they would treat her like a hero?

'Come closer,' said the Matron Mother. Her voice was calm and measured. Kaira could detect no anger in it. As she walked forward she could see the Exarch looked stern, but that was no great surprise – the greatest of the Shieldmaidens always bore a grim visage.

'Please, sit.'

Kaira was taken aback by the Matron Mother's request. Without thinking she sat in the seat that awaited her. She had not been expecting this. She had been expecting to be admonished, forced to stand to attention while the two heads of the Temple railed at her for her behaviour.

Then the Matron Mother asked the strangest question – 'Are you well?'

Was she well? She had been condemned to a cell and forced to await her fate for savagely beating the High Abbot of Ironhold. It was highly likely he had called for her execution – at best her banishment from the Temple of Autumn. *Was she well?*

'Yes, Matron Mother,' she replied.

'Good. That is good. Of course your sisters are most concerned for you. We are pleased we can put them at their ease.'

'How is the High Abbot?' She asked the question before she could stop herself. It was foolish, she knew. It would have been prudent to wait. If the Matron Mother wanted her to know, she would have told her, but prudence was something that Kaira seemed to have thrown to the four winds recently. Why be any different now?

A flash of a smile crossed the Matron Mother's lips. It was there for only a second, but it was definitely there.

'He will recover,' she replied. 'Though he has demanded to be sheltered elsewhere in the city until he is fit enough to make the journey back to Ironhold. But you must not concern yourself with him.'

A curious thing to say. Why should she not concern herself with him? He was, after all, why she had been summoned here.

The Matron Mother pushed herself up from her chair. Other weaker women might have used a cane to aid them at such an advanced age, but the Matron Mother, despite her years, walked on her frail legs seemingly by the power of her will alone. She moved around the desk, and laid a hand on Kaira's shoulder.

'The Exarch and I have been discussing you at length. Discussing your future.' *So at least she had a future. That was something for which to be thankful.* 'And it is clear your future lies beyond the walls of the temple.'

Kaira felt something tighten in the pit of her stomach. Her teeth clenched and for a moment the room seemed to swim before she forced herself to regain control.

'I am to be banished then,' she replied.

It was to be expected. She should count herself lucky that was to be her only punishment.

The Matron Mother smiled. 'On the contrary. You think we would abandon you to the vagaries of the outside world? You think we would squander the loyalty and skills of such a valuable servant? Rather we should pull the walls of this temple down around our ears than be so wanton in our disregard of you who have served us so well.'

Kaira considered the Matron Mother's words, unsure of her meaning. 'If I am not to be banished then why am I to be sent away?'

'There is a task we wish you to perform. A mission of sorts that will take you into the city. It is a dangerous task, and one we would consider for no one else. Recent events mean you can be sent away without being missed. Everyone will believe you to be banished, but we will know the truth of it.' She patted Kaira's arm conspiratorially.

'What mission?'

The Matron Mother looked to the Exarch. Kaira looked to her too – the woman who was as much a mother to her as anyone ever had been. She was strong featured and handsome. In her prime she had been stronger, faster and deadlier than any Shieldmaiden since Vorena herself. At Bakhaus Gate it was said she had defended the very life of the king and slain a warbeast of the Aeslanti with nothing but a broken spear. Age might have lined her face, but she still commanded total respect.

'The Temple of Autumn has learned of a plot.' The Exarch spoke, as always, in a measured, steady tone. 'Innocents are to be shipped abroad and sold into bondage. We need you to find those responsible and eliminate them before they can succeed.'

Plots? But why would the Temple of Autumn concern itself with such things?

'How do we know of this?' Kaira said, confused. The temple was no clandestine guild; it had no spymasters in its employ.

'We have eyes and ears throughout the city. They learned of this some time ago, but only now are we in a position to act.'

'Eyes and ears? You mean spies? The Daughters do good deeds for the poor and the sick. The Shieldmaidens protect the temples and the city. Why would we need spies?'

The Exarch smiled. 'Our temple has come under threat from many sources over the years. Almost been brought low many times. We have learned that caution and information are as valuable as spears and shields.'

'But if there is such a plot why would we not just alert the Greencoats, or the Inquisition?'

'Because they would merely blunder in. They would make their arrests and punish the guilty, but the real power behind the plot – the true evil – would escape, as it always does. To succeed fully we must be subtle. That is why you must carry out this task for us.'

'But I am no spy. I don't understand what you want of me.'

'Not the role of spy. We already have an informant within the plotters' organisation but they are not in a position to do more for us. We need someone of your unique skill and prowess to enter this organisation and destroy those who seek to enslave our people.'

'But how? I am no mummer. I cannot act a part. The Temple is all I have ever known.'

'You will need to act no part,' said the Exarch. 'You have seen to that already. Having committed sacrilege within the walls of the Temple of Autumn, you will be banished onto the streets of the city. That will be no deception, but the truth. People will not know that it is only temporary. Later you will be contacted by our agent and invited to join the organisation of which we speak. Once inside, you will carry out the tasks they give you until the moment is right to strike. You will simply do as you are bid.'

Kaira felt an unaccustomed anxiety rising within her as the Exarch spoke. She had only ever been in the city on military duty, never alone; how was she to infiltrate some kind of criminal ring and break it up? Must she become a common assassin?

But what choice did she have?

'When must I leave?' she asked.

The Matron Mother placed a consoling arm on her shoulder. 'You must leave now. There is little time to waste. Speak to no one before you go. Though we trust our sisters and daughters, absolute discretion is essential.'

'But what must I do? I don't know where to go or how I might begin.'

'You will have directions to an inn north of the city. There you will be contacted and told what to do next.'

Kaira looked to the Exarch. Tried to make it a look of resolve, but she felt she must have only looked pitiful. The Exarch raised her chin, demanding strength as she always had, and Kaira Stormfall was determined not to disappoint.

'Very well. If that is your will, I am bound to serve it.' And she really had no choice.

'When this is over, you will be welcomed back a hero,' said the Matron Mother. 'It will be as though you never left us. And always remember: Arlor is strength. Vorena is courage.'

Kaira stood and repeated the Matron Mother's words, gaining no real reassurance from the cant. She bowed to them both before turning and leaving the sanctum.

In her chamber a plain woollen cloak and battered leather satchel awaited her. Within the satchel was a set of drab clothing, a purse containing five crowns and a map showing a route to the inn where she would meet her contact. She donned the simple travelling garb and covered her head with the hood of the cloak.

Fortunately, the great courtyard was empty as Kaira crossed it to the main gate. As she went, she dared not look up to the statues of Vorena and Arlor lest they be looking down with judgement in their dead, stone eyes.

It pained her that she could not say goodbye, could not embrace Samina one last time, but it could not be. No one must know the reason for her leaving – one loose word might jeopardise her mission. If Kaira was ever to return to the temple, she knew she had to succeed.

The gate stood open, and, as she walked through, the Shieldmaidens on guard did not even look at her. Kaira took her first step beyond the threshold and felt the pressure of the outside world almost as a physical burden. She was no longer Shieldmaiden, no longer protected by her temple and her sisters. The future was daunting, but she would meet it head on, as she always had. Always would.

Up the Avenue of Spears, a road she had walked along a hundred times before, she felt more lost with every step. At the end of it she opened the satchel and took out the crude map, gripping it tight to stop her hands from shaking.

This was madness. She was a Shieldmaiden of Vorena, a warrior born, now afraid to be left alone in the city. Steeling herself, Kaira followed the scant directions, wending her way north and quickly finding herself in an area she was unfamiliar with.

The closer she got to her destination, the more insalubrious became the sights and smells of the street. Kaira had seen the drunks and wastrels of the city before, but with the advantage of wearing her armour of office, which had naturally commanded respect. The crowds had always cheered, moved aside to allow the Shieldmaidens passage. Now, just another traveller on the street, she had no defence against the gawping looks of the citizenry. As she made her way, she avoided the shady figures that lurked at street corners and in doorways. She was not afraid of what they might do, but of what *she* might have to do should one of them approach her. How would it help her mission to risk trouble with the Greencoats before she had travelled a league from the temple?

More disturbing to her, though, were the whores who seemed everywhere, selling themselves for a few coppers. Kaira had heard of these women, of course, but she had not imagined they would be so brazen, plying their trade openly on the streets. It sickened her. How anyone could fall so low.

Surely they could find sanctuary in the temple? Surely the Daughters could care for these women and save them from a life of degradation?

But as Kaira pushed through the press of human filth, she soon realised that would be impossible for the sheer numbers of these pitiful beings. The Temple of Autumn could not give succour to them all.

By the time she reached the inn it was getting dark. Lamplighters were at work on the lanterns that hung intermittently on their iron stanchions. Kaira saw a sign hanging limply outside a three-storey building, its crudely painted sigil announcing it as the Pony and Fiddle.

She walked in, holding her cloak tight around herself as though to shield her from the denizens within. Once inside she realised she needn't have worried. Through the candlelit gloom she could make out fewer than half a dozen patrons, none seeming concerned with her. Nothing barred her way as she walked to the bar. A thin, greasy figure behind it straightened as she approached, as though he had been expecting her.

'I have come from the Temple of Autumn,' she said, keeping her voice low. It pained her to be skulking so, like just another ruffian off the street.

'Yep,' said the greasy man, turning to pick a dark iron key from where it hung with others on a row of hooks. 'Follow me.'

He led her through the bar and up a creaking set of wooden stairs to the first floor. It was even darker here, and Kaira pulled back the hood of her cloak, the better to see any danger that might be lurking.

The man unlocked a door at the far end of the corridor and ushered her in.

'I'll bring food later,' he said as she entered the room. In the candlelight she could see a small bed and a wooden table sitting beside it. Other than that the room was bare.

'What do I owe?' she asked, reaching for her satchel.

'Taken care of,' he replied, then closed the door.

Kaira stood in the gloom for several moments, listening to his footfalls creaking down the stairs.

Then it was just her in the dark and the silence.

For the first time in her life, she felt truly alone.

EIGHTEEN

Governess Nordaine was an altogether humourless woman and stultifying in her dullness. Why the king had ever chosen to take her into his employ was well beyond Janessa's grasp. She was completely unsuited to be a tutor of either knowledge or manners. The woman wore drab shades of grey, concealing her entire body – from the headscarf on her tiny head to the frayed hem of her skirts. How she could teach style and deportment when her own was so lacking was a mystery Janessa and Graye had mulled over many a time.

The woman's teaching style was also an endless source of amusement. She spoke in a high falsetto and, when quoting from the antiquated texts she used, she would occasionally affect an accent to better mimic the ancient theologians, philosophers and scholars she was citing. Janessa and Graye would be hard pressed to stop themselves giggling out loud when she quoted Pastergan, especially since he was fabled to have had a severe lisp.

But it was Nordaine's manners that were the greatest cause for concern. The Governess, a pious and chaste woman, took things to extremes. The girls were not allowed to wear garments that showed anything below the neck or above the ankle, and most definitely nothing above the wrist. They must at all times remain unsmiling, unless someone of import said something droll, and they must never speak the first words in a conversation, especially if that conversation were with a man. And should they ever be anywhere near a member of the opposite sex, they must at all times be accompanied by the Governess herself, or someone of whom she approved – which usually meant Odaka Du'ur.

This excessive virtuousness had led the girls to come up with their own theories about the background of Governess Nordaine and the reasons for her rigid principles. Janessa had postulated she must have been trussed up until her thirtieth winter by an overprotective father, whereas Graye, as ever, dreamed up a much more exotic background: Nordaine had been a promiscuous harlot, given to nights of wild abandon with foreign sailors – until she saw the error of her ways. Then, in her shame, she had decided it best to teach history to young girls. They had both laughed long and hard at that.

Today though, Governess Nordaine displayed some flexibility in her stringent rules by allowing them, even at the risk of distraction, to have their lessons on the veranda at the north end of the gardens. It had been a hot morning for the time of year, and so all three of them sat with the sun beaming down and the birds singing their last songs before winter flight. Nordaine had insisted on them wearing their shawls though, lest they catch a chill, and Janessa had reluctantly agreed to it.

Not that Nordaine's small concession meant her lessons were any more appealing, and during the course of the morning Janessa had found herself drifting off, staring into space, wishing she could be as free as the birds that chirruped and frolicked nearby.

It was better than thinking the alternative – that soon she would have to choose a husband, one who would rule the Free States beside her and to whom she would have to bear children so the line of kings and queens might continue. It was a thought that both disgusted and angered her, even though she had been given the choice of whom to marry. Surely if she wanted none of her would-be suitors, it was no real choice at all.

Janessa caught herself. She must not dwell on such things. Must not blame everyone around her for her predicament. She was strong and she would survive this. And so she turned her thoughts to other things: those singing birds, the sun shining on the first falling leaves. It was her inattentiveness to Nordaine's relentless monologue that allowed her to notice the messenger across the gardens. He was moving with some urgency, and even from a distance Janessa could see his garb was travel-stained, his face wan under its filth, as though he had ridden for many days. He was accompanied by one of Skyhelm's Sentinels who was struggling to keep up with him. When Janessa saw Odaka advancing to greet the messenger, she could hold herself back no longer.

Ignoring the cries of her governess, Janessa hurried across the gardens to where the men were exchanging quick words. Her stomach was

143

churning, a rising sense of dread worming its way up from inside her belly as she speculated on the news the messenger had brought.

Was it about her father? Had he been killed in battle? Had the Khurtas smashed the armies of the Free States and were even now rampaging across the provinces?

By the time she had crossed the garden Odaka and the messenger were finishing their conversation.

'What is it?' Janessa demanded, in no mood to stand on ceremony.

Odaka turned at her words, regarding her first with surprise, then with thoughtfulness.

'Tell me! I demand to know. Is the message from my father?'

'I am sorry, regent,' said Nordaine, arriving behind her, breathless from an ungainly pursuit across the gardens.

Odaka continued to regard Janessa curiously, as though weighing her up. Janessa had seen that look many times before, and never been sure what he was thinking. But now it was obvious he was musing whether she was mature enough to be entrusted with this latest news.

'Come along, young lady,' said Nordaine. 'Whatever news has arrived, you need not concern yourself with it. It is a matter for the regent and your father's council.'

'No,' said Janessa, shrugging off her governess's hand. 'If one day I am to be queen I must learn about matters of state. What better time than now, when our lands are threatened. Odaka, what does the message say?'

He looked from the parchment to Janessa. 'I will be discussing this message with all the council members still in the city. We convene shortly in the war chamber. Meet us there, your majesty.' With a respectful bow of his head he withdrew.

Janessa turned to Governess Nordaine, whose face by now was quite flushed.

'That will be all for today, Governess,' she said. She tried for the first time to sound commanding in the manner of her father. It seemed effective, for the governess lowered her eyes and backed away.

Behind her stood Graye, looking on with a half smile. Oh, how Janessa would have loved to just take her by the hand and run away like they had planned so many nights ago, but her life had moved on. She was no longer just a callow girl. She had grave responsibilities; she was part of her father's council.

She needed time to dress appropriately before greeting the council and chose a plain brown dress with little adornment. It seemed proper

144

for such a sober occasion. Consequently, by the time she reached the war chamber the rest of the council were already convened.

Janessa had been in the war chamber many times before, but today it appeared different. It bore banners and trophies from a hundred battles, some of which her father had won. As a child, playing at her father's feet, she had taken little notice of them, but now they seemed in sharp focus, screaming out their history, impressing on her their proud legacy.

Three tattered pennants of the ancient Sword Kings took pride of place on the northernmost wall, flanked by axes and spears won by the Duke of Valdor in the border wars with Golgartha. The black iron crown of the Mad King Xekotak, taken in the ancient Dragon Wars of the Kaer'Vahari, stood on a plinth to the east, and to the west was the twisted, hideous skull of Groë Magnon, the reiver lord of the Blood Isles.

There were scores of others, both ancient and new, but Janessa had no time to regard them all as she walked towards the table of oak and iron that sat in the chamber's centre. At the head of that table was Odaka Du'ur, looking as stern and resolute as she had ever seen him. To his right hand was Captain Garret of the Sentinels. Janessa had known him all her life, and he was a constant feature of the palace; always there, watching over her vigilantly from the shadows. The years had turned his brown beard to grey and made his smiling eyes more careworn and dark. She trusted Garret more than any other man, and it comforted her to know he was there.

To Odaka's left sat Chancellor Durket, smiling his pig-faced smile even as she entered. Durket had been as much a feature in her life as Garret, but never as welcome.

And that was it: what remained of the King's Council. There were other seats around the black oak table, eleven in all – one for the king, two for his generals of foot and horse, two for the lord governors of the city states, five for the nobles of the provinces and one for the Master of the Wardens. They each sat empty now, the men whose places they represented gone north to see off the Khurtas.

Of course there were other men of import who served the king – the Seneschal of Inquisitors and the High Constable of the Greencoats amongst them – but they were men of Steelhaven, men of the city only, and not privy to the machinations of the Free States or sufficiently worthy of a seat at the council table.

As Janessa walked forward the three remaining council members stood. She stopped before the chair opposite Odaka. The one set aside for her father.

'Please sit, your majesty, and we will begin,' said the regent.

Janessa sank into her father's ornate chair with surprising composure. The three waited for her to sit before taking their own places and Odaka made to open proceedings. Janessa could hold back no longer.

'How is my father?' she asked.

All eyes turned to her, Durket's looking perturbed at the break in protocol, Garret's looking sympathetic.

'He lives, your majesty,' Odaka said, unflustered by her interruption. 'The messenger from the front carried his very words.'

Janessa nodded her thanks, now feeling somewhat foolish. If she was going to participate in the war council's meeting she must keep a better control of her impulses.

'The news from the north is not good, though. The king sends sobering words. Dreldun burns, its capital smashed, its people fled.'

Durket looked up, almost fretful. 'But how? The Khurtas are savages. They are no besiegers. How could they have razed Touran?'

'Dreldun's capital is a frontier city,' Garret said, 'and Touran is no fortress. The Khurtas could have conceivably taken it, but my question is: how did they do it so quickly? Clearly their Elharim warlord has taught the Khurtas well. There is no way those savages could have pulled off so audacious an attack without the guidance of a skilled tactician.'

'However it was achieved,' said Odaka, 'the fact remains that the way is now clear to Coppergate. The king has tried all he can to negotiate with Amon Tugha, but it seems his entreaties have been rebuffed. The Elharim prince is happy for now to let his horde rape and plunder our northernmost province, but inevitably they will move south.'

'Maybe they won't,' said Durket, clinging desperately on to what little hope he could. 'Coppergate is a bastion of the north. It will not fall so easily. Amon Tugha would be mad to try and take it.'

'It may not come to that.' Odaka glanced towards Janessa, as though she would not want to hear his next words. 'King Cael intends to face the Khurtic horde on the field before it ever reaches Coppergate. He will smash them in the valley of Kelbur Fenn and send them back to their blasted plains.'

'But that would be madness,' said Garret, putting into words Janessa's own thoughts. 'Why give up a defensible position to face the enemy in the open? Coppergate is almost as impregnable as Steelhaven.'

'The king has twenty thousand foot who would be well placed to defend the city, but his five thousand horse are useless behind Coppergate's defences. He has not laid out his plans to me, but I can only guess he intends to smash the Khurtas with his cavalry in the narrow pass. The enemy will have a single line of approach and even that horde can never stand against the Knights of the Blood. It is the only viable plan.'

'But what if it fails?' Janessa could hear the alarm in Durket's voice. It almost sickened her. He was leagues away from the front, from the danger her father faced, and yet he quailed in fear.

'That is out of our hands,' Odaka replied. 'Our main problem is the refugees from Dreldun headed towards us in their thousands.'

'But what of Ironhold? And Braega?' said Durket. 'Surely they can take in some of them.'

'They have, but the people of Dreldun are fleeing in huge numbers. The Khurtic horde has spread terror throughout the province. There are simply not enough cities secure enough to take in all those displaced so, inevitably, they are heading here.'

'Then we will take them in.'

It was the first thing Janessa felt she could comment on. It silenced the three men.

'Your majesty,' said Durket with a condescending smile. 'We simply have no room. Steelhaven is a hub for trade from the provinces and overseas. Its streets are already overfilled with waifs and strays. We have little room for visitors, let alone thousands of refugees with barely the clothes on their backs. How would we feed them? Where would we house them?'

'We will find a way,' she replied, though admitting to herself she had no idea where the city might accommodate hundreds of starving families.

'That's all very well, majesty, but the details are important. Resources are scarce, what with the war in the north. People are already panicked and scared. There will be unrest on the streets. Hunger . . .'

'Then we will eat less, Chancellor.' Without thinking she had raised her voice, all thoughts of propriety gone, but Durket's obstinacy was too much, and the mention of hunger had been about all she could take from him.

'Your majesty, the Chancellor speaks the truth,' said Odaka. Janessa's heart sank. If she was to have support on this she was hoping it would be Odaka. 'Our resources are scant at best. We must find an alternative.'

'But what about our trade ties with other nations? What about Dravhistan? Han-Shar? Kajrapur? Surely they can help us?'

'You are right, majesty; they have been trading partners for many years.

But they will offer us no charity. In this we must fend for ourselves. Feeding and housing so many refugees is something we can ill afford to do.'

Odaka's words seemed final. It was clear they would receive no aid from overseas.

What would happen if her father failed, and the Khurtas ran rampant throughout the Free States? What would happen, gods be merciful, if they eventually found their way to the city walls? Unless Steelhaven opened its gates for the refugees they would be slaughtered to the last innocent child.

'No,' Janessa said, thinking fast. She could not allow the council to make this decision over her head. There must be a solution. 'What about the Old City? We could house them there. And if we began to ration food now we could keep stores to last until the Khurtas are turned from our borders.'

Durket opened his mouth to speak, obviously with an objection, but he could think of none.

'Garret?' Odaka asked.

Janessa looked to the captain to see his face racked with doubt. Had she assumed wrongly that he, of all of them, might have agreed with her?

'There will be problems,' he said, his face grave, his hands locked together beneath his chin. 'With so many new faces the Greencoats will struggle to keep the city safe, even if we put the refugees in the Old City. And anyway, it's mostly derelict – old ruins, a haven for criminals fleeing the city proper.'

'Then we must clean it out,' said Janessa. Every argument against her was making her more determined. She would not be denied on this. 'We must make it habitable. Food must be retained, requisitioned if need be. And the Old City must be made safe.'

Durket opened his mouth to speak, but Odaka cut him off. 'If that is your wish, majesty, then it shall be done.'

And that was that. There was no further argument. Odaka's next words showed that her wishes would be carried out despite what the others thought.

'Captain Garret, you will inform the High Constable that the Old City is to be cleared to make way for refugees. Durket, you will levy a stipend on all farms and fisheries, and also secure locations in the Warehouse District for the storage of grain.' They both nodded, though Durket looked as though he were trying to swallow a wasp. 'That is all for now. Unless we receive further news beforehand we will reconvene in four days to see what progress we have made.'

148

Janessa stood, as did the other three council members, and Garret and Durket left the room. Odaka stared at her from across the table. Was he back to that old contemplative look – assessing her, looking for weakness?

'You have what you wished for. But what have you learned?' he asked.

It was a curious question, and Janessa could not work out if the regent was annoyed or proud. And what had she learned? That she had power she'd never before known? That Durket was a miserable sot?

'I don't know what you mean.'

Odaka frowned, and she felt she had disappointed him once again.

'You have learned that for every decision you make there will be consequences. That as the future queen of this realm you must weigh every outcome, consider every option. For every refugee who does not starve because we have requisitioned grain, there may be two children to the east who go hungry. Who can be sure their father might not grow desperate, might not take his neighbour's calf to feed them? Who can be sure that the neighbour might not pursue him, for his own family is also hungry, and slaughter the man for his crime?'

'I didn't think—'

'Then you must start,' Odaka said, making no attempt to hide his anger.

'If you disagreed with me then why did you not speak out? Why did you go along with my request?'

He looked deep into her eyes, his anger dissipating. 'You will one day be my queen,' he answered with a bow. 'And I live to obey.'

With that he left the war chamber, leaving Janessa amongst the trinkets and trophies of kings long dead.

NINETEEN

Had it been three days? The amount of vomit on his shirt said it probably had been. Three days since he'd met with Bolo and been offered those pitiful girls. Of course he'd refused – what else could he do? He wasn't an animal, after all.

Was he?

Of course he was a fucking animal, otherwise why would he be doing this in the first place. And he might not have taken his fill of those girls, but it hadn't stopped him running straight to the Verdant Street whorehouse and taking his fill there.

Merrick could barely remember the last two nights of drinking and whoring. He thought to check his purse, but he knew it would be empty.

Now that was a problem. He'd been given a full purse, been told to do his thing. He was pretty sure that meant paying off the Harbourwatch and any Greencoats that might be on patrol around the wharfside, rather than wasting it on whores and wine. Though frankly, whores and wine were never a waste.

He sat up, looking down at his bare legs and his flaccid cock, sitting there beneath the hem of his shirt all useless and stubby, and his head began to swim. A wave of nausea hit him and he lay back down, head sinking into the goose feather pillow. It would have been nice to lie there forever. To forget the world outside, forget the debts he owed, forget the job he had to do. Forget Bastian and Friedrik and Shanka and Bolo the fucking Slaver.

But they would not forget him.

He forced himself to sit up, biting back the sick feeling, swallowing down the bile. Gradually the room stopped spinning and he swung his legs over the side of the bed. Whose room was this anyway? Lilleth's? Meagan's? Not that it mattered – after a while every whore's chamber looked the same.

Merrick pulled on his britches, and fumbled with his sword belt until he finally managed to fasten the buckle. There was no bowl of water to wash with, not even a half-empty glass of wine to wet his parched throat, but then that was the way with whorehouses: they were all smiles on the way in and not even a polite 'fuck off' on the way out.

He stumbled down the stairs, ignoring the prone bodies lying around, trying to avoid looking at the other patrons as they tried to leave without looking at him. Not that he shared their shame. He'd been here too often to feel that sting any more. Nowadays he didn't feel the sting of anything much, which was most likely why Bastian and Friedrik had picked him for this job in the first place.

It was cold out on the street, and busy for so early in the morning. Someone was noisily selling fruit at a foul-smelling stall right outside the brothel, but Merrick had no money for food. Besides, if he didn't get to Palien soon, hunger would be the least of his worries.

He tripped more than once, still feeling the after effects of his revelry. Not that it had been much fun – a couple of drunken fucks and the rest of the time lying in a stupor. Still, it had at least served to kill a couple of days, numb the dread feeling inside him. That kind of service couldn't be counted in gold or silver.

Somehow he managed to make his way to the Northgate slums unhindered. It was as though the scum and footpads knew he was coming, and knew to stay out of his way.

The Guild had a hundred safe houses throughout the city, and Merrick Ryder was in the privileged position of knowing more than a few. The one where he was to meet Palien was hardly one of the nicer ones, though. It stood on a street corner, stretching up three storeys. How far it dug down into the shit and sewers below, Merrick had no idea, and no great desire to find out.

Before he could even knock, the door opened a crack, and a big figure looked out. Merrick recognised him; he was one of the thugs that had rescued him outside the derelict chapel. Merrick had always been good with faces, especially ones that had saved him from a stabbing and then dragged him halfway across the city by the scruff of his neck.

The man said nothing, just opened the door and nodded for Merrick to enter.

It was dark inside, dark enough for someone to be lurking in wait with knife in hand, but Merrick had already done all this back in Bolo's lair; already braved the dark – and lived. Besides, if the Guild wanted him dead he'd already be lying in the street with his head smashed in or floating down the Storway with his throat gaping wide, so there was nothing to fear here. He hoped.

In the dimness he could make out a tiny candlelit room beckoning him on. At the doorway his confidence took a blow to the gut as he saw Palien.

Tall and lithe and athletic, his hair and moustache waxed and coiffured, not a hair out of place, as always. Merrick had met him a few times before, been drawn in by his charm and looks, which was odd, as usually Merrick was the one doing the charming. His past experience had also taught him how dangerous Palien was, and explained why he wasn't looking forward to this one bit.

'Where the fuck have you been for the past three days?' Palien said as Merrick entered.

'I was doing as I was told. Organising the smooth transaction of goods.' It wouldn't do to explain how he'd been pissing up the last of his coins from the Guild on cheap wine and whores.

'So you weren't dipping your wick on Verdant Street?' Palien raised one eyebrow a full inch higher than the other.

'Well . . .'

'I don't really give a fuck what you were doing, Ryder. What I do give a fuck about is whether you met with Bolo and sealed the arrangement. And I've been waiting here three days to fucking find out.'

'I got a little bit waylaid.'

'*I don't give a fuck!*' Palien's voice almost raised the roof. At his yell, the thug at Merrick's shoulder stood a shuffling step back, as though the comment had been directed at him.

Merrick felt his heart beating faster. Time to put Palien at his ease, perhaps.

'Everything is good with Bolo. I finalised the deal. We drank on it.' *And I threw it up outside.* 'He tried to barter on price but I made it clear we're not to be trifled with . . . *you're* not to be trifled with. He already has some merchandise.' *And it looked in a sorry state.* 'I told him it wouldn't be a problem getting more.'

As Merrick spoke, Palien's raised eyebrow slowly lowered until it was level with its fellow.

'It won't be a problem getting more,' Palien confirmed. 'What have you done to square the dock? Have the bribes been paid, or have you pissed all that money away?'

'That's all coming together nicely.' *Kind of.* 'But as a matter of fact, the money you gave me for that side of things may not cover it.' *Because I have indeed pissed all that money away.*

Palien simply stared, giving no indication he had even heard.

Merrick had been here before, staring hard bastards in the face. Usually he would be able to run away or talk his way out, but right now there was nowhere to run and no excuse he could think of, so he just stared back. Palien was waiting for him to crumble, for him to admit either he still had the money or he'd spent it. Fact was, he didn't have the money, and if he told Palien it was gone, there would be unpleasantness.

And Merrick really wanted to avoid any unpleasantness.

Despite the chill of the room a bead of sweat broke from the nape of his neck and ran down the back of his shirt. A bang behind made him jump, and it was with relief that he heard the muffled sound of voices as Palien's attention was redirected to the doorway.

Another henchman walked in, his face sheepish, like he was scared for his life for interrupting. Beside him was a second figure, not as tall as the thug, but very much larger than life.

He was foreign, an easterner, most likely Dravhistani, his clothes woven from bright silks, his hair covered by a headwrap usually worn in the Eastern Kingdoms. A sash held in his generous waist and over one shoulder was an ornate bag which Merrick noticed he clutched to his side protectively.

'Erm . . . he's here,' said the henchman.

Palien began to raise that eyebrow again. 'Yes, thank you. I can fucking see that.'

He turned his attention back to Merrick, reaching behind him, and for a second Merrick felt the bite of panic. He thought about reaching for his sword, but that would have been the dumbest thing to do. If Palien was reaching for a blade killing him wouldn't solve anything.

Luckily he wasn't. He grabbed a coinpurse and threw it to Merrick.

'You'd better make that last,' Palien said. 'If you need any more you'd best sell something, and looking at you it's not likely you'll get much for your arse.'

'Of course. This should do nicely.'

'Fuck off then. As you can see I have a proper guest.'

Merrick didn't wait. He nodded at the three men – only the foreigner deigned to nod back – and left as fast as he could manage.

Back out on the street he began to feel better, his hangover waning. A cup of ale and some kind of unidentifiable meat from a street seller filled the gap in his belly and quenched his thirst. Merrick knew he had a task to finish, though, and that gave him a bellyache that no amount of meat pie could halt.

The coin was in his purse and bribes needed to be paid. It was best for his health if he did the paying before the temptation to spend it all on cheap whores and cheaper wine got too much, and his first stop would be the hardest.

The barracks of the Sentinels stood to the eastern side of Skyhelm. Merrick's face was well enough known to see him into the Crown District – that was, after all, why the Guild had hired him in the first place.

He was ushered into the barrack block. It was late enough for morning reveille to have finished and in the centre of the paved training square was the man he had come to see.

Captain Garret sat at a small table, on an equally small chair. It was almost funny to see his long legs and bulky torso on that fragile-looking seat. Or it would have been funny if Merrick hadn't been there with such a distasteful purpose. He had to size Garret up, to see if the incorruptible captain was quite as pious as he made out. The old man wouldn't need to know exactly what Merrick was up to, but if he could be persuaded to turn a blind eye here or there it would help him no end.

'Been a long time,' said Merrick as he strolled across the drill yard adopting his easy smile.

Garret looked up from his sourbread and ham, and smiled back.

'Too long.' He stood, offering his hand to Merrick, who was glad to shake it. 'Sit down,' he said, gesturing to the second chair opposite his own. 'Are you hungry? There's plenty for both of us.'

'Just tea, if you're still addicted to that Han-Shar brew you insist on.'

Garret grinned, sitting himself down and pouring Merrick a cup from the pot in the centre of the table.

'Sorry I don't have any wine. I know you're partial to that Braegan filth.'

'Tea will do for now.'

'Hah. Rough night? You don't change, do you, lad?'

You've got no idea, Garret. 'You know me. But what about you? Still here after all these years – it's like you enjoy acting the caretaker to the royal palace.'

Garret's smile lost its humour. 'It's a duty. One I'm proud of. Not that I'd expect you to understand that.'

'I understand it well enough. Just don't ask me to join up.'

Garret gave a knowing smirk at that one and the men paused to sip from their cups. They were made of porcelain, imported from the East, and each one had an exotic bird painted in blue on the side, a refinement which looked quite ridiculous in Garret's big hairy hand.

'So how have you been keeping?' asked the captain, leaning back in his chair. 'Because you look like shit.'

'Thanks. It's all the fashion in Northgate.' Merrick thumbed the lapels of his grubby shirt. 'And you're the last person to comment on dress. That uniform's older than I am.'

'It's served me well enough, and I'm proud of it. As proud as when I wore it beside your father.' The mere mention of Merrick's father made the sweet taste of tea suddenly sour in his mouth. Garret knew he'd said something clumsy. 'Sorry, lad. I know how you feel about him, but I'm an old soldier, and I served with your father for a lot of years. It was a shame what happened.'

'A shame, was it? He left us. Left us with nothing. Disappeared without a fucking word, never to be seen again.' Merrick knew he hadn't come to whine about his own problems, but the merest mention of his bastard of a father was guaranteed to get him riled.

'Now that's not fair, lad, and you know it. No one really knows what happened to him, and he left you and your mother wealthy enough. I did my best to look out for you. It was an awful shame the way things ended up.'

An awful shame? That was one way of looking at it. After his mother had died from the Sweet Canker, Merrick had been left with a fortune. It had taken him less than two years to piss and gamble it away.

But then what he had lost in untold riches he had gained in friends from the Guild, so it worked out a sweet deal in the end. Psychotic friends who would sooner cut your balls off than look at you were by far the best kind.

'Anyway, enough of the past,' said Merrick, keen to get back to business. 'How are you? Things must be difficult right now. I don't envy you your lot.'

Garret suddenly looked grave. 'You have no idea, lad. News from the north isn't good. There'll be a battle soon, slaughter we haven't seen since Bakhaus Gate.' Merrick had heard the tales, though he'd only been a boy at the time. Garret would never have made such a comparison lightly. 'The future of the entire Free States hangs in the balance and wicked things are afoot here. Word from the Greencoats is there's a rogue magicker on the loose. The magisters say it's nothing to be concerned about, but those shady bastards tell two lies for every truth. And the Inquisition lost a lieutenant last week – young Petraeus and two Knights of the Blood, hacked up for sport in a back alley. They were on their way to arrest some spy but they never made it back. Petraeus was a champion fencer, and his two knights seasoned campaigners. They wouldn't have gone down easy, but there was no sign of anyone else. Petraeus didn't even get a chance to draw his blade. It's clear we've got some dangerous foreign killer on the loose as well as some murdering caster.'

'Maybe it's the same person,' said Merrick, though he wasn't really interested in Garret's woes.

'Aye, maybe. But we're not even close to catching him, whoever it is. We just don't have the men. All the best are in the north, and whether they'll be back or not is still in the balance. More and more people are coming to the city every day, some from Dreldun, burned out of their homes, others just scared of an invasion and of what that might bring. And if King Cael loses . . .' Garret took another sip from his cup. He had clearly said enough, and was unwilling to contemplate the consequences should the king fail to stem the Khurtic tide.

Merrick suddenly began to feel uncomfortable. He had come here to size up Garret for a bribe, to see if this proud man, one he'd known since he was a child, would take money to allow him to deal in slaves.

It was obvious Garret would never do such a thing.

'It's clear you have much to do, old friend, so I'll be on my way. Thanks for the tea.'

He had to go, had to get away from this place. This had been a stupid mistake. Garret reminded him too much of a past he'd left behind, a past he'd gambled away and would never get back.

Before he could leave, the captain laid a hand on Merrick's and smiled.

'What is it, lad? You wouldn't just come here out of the blue for nothing. If there's a problem, you can tell me. I promised your father and mother—'

'I know,' said Merrick, suddenly feeling panicked. He didn't deserve this. If Garret knew what he was up to he wouldn't just be furious, he'd be deeply ashamed. 'You don't have to feel like you owe me anything. There's been a lot of water under the bridge since then. I'm not a child any more, Garret.'

The old soldier laughed. 'I know that, lad. That's why, if you're ever struggling, you can come to me. If you ever need help, or a job, I'll be here. There's a place for you in the Sentinels. We could always use a man of your talents.'

His fucking talents! Why was everyone always interested in his talents? Why did no one want him just for the pleasure of his company?

'Thanks for the offer.' Merrick stood, desperate to get out, though he managed not to set off like the place was on fire. 'But I've already got a job.'

Wasn't that the truth? A job that might see him dead at any moment.

Without another word they nodded their goodbyes, no long platitudes, no warm embraces.

Merrick found himself out on the street again, breathing heavily, his head swimming, the sick feeling back in his gut.

What a stupid fucking idea. What an idiot he'd been to try to come here, to think he could sway old Garret, make him betray his city and his king. If Merrick Ryder had never thought himself a treacherous bastard before, then now was the time to start.

Clearly it was time for another drink.

TWENTY

It was at its worst when he was left alone with his thoughts. That face seemed to haunt him, taunting him in his dreams at night and sitting behind him during the day, just out of sight.

The *Liber Conflagrantia* was vast, but to Waylian it seemed like a coffin in which he was trapped . . . trapped with a corpse that stared with glassy eyes, reproachful, vengeful, crying out for a justice Waylian could never provide.

Magistra Gelredida had, in recent days, turned her attention solely to the hunt and capture of the killer loose in the city, so much so that Waylian's lessons were seldom and brief. She did spare enough time to allot him a task every day, each of which demanded he spend endless hours in the Grand Library. He had little time for anything else, and as a consequence was becoming more and more reclusive – the last thing he needed right now.

Every time he tried to turn his attention to his studies all he could see was a dead man's face staring back from the page of the dusty tome. Every night he spent in the dark, forcing himself to think of something else, all he could see were those cold, dead eyes. On occasion he would manage to picture the blonde girl he had admired from afar – Gladdis? Gemmy? – but it wouldn't be long before she too paled, her skin turning waxy, the light from her eyes extinguishing to resemble those of a rotting fish.

And it wasn't as though he didn't have other things to worry about. For one, he still had to work out what in the hells *Jotun* meant. Despite all that had happened, despite all she had on her mind, Gelredida still insisted on using that as his name and giving him demeaning, menial tasks to perform until he could decipher it. This time, though, Waylian was convinced he almost had it.

He had rounded it down to Golgarthan origin – the stem *tun* meaning faeces – but from there he was stuck. He had studied most of the clan dialects and only had one more to go – the Kharna Khel – a fierce northern tribe who were perpetually locked in a battle with the reivers of the Blood Isles and the foul beasts of the Morathi Ice Holds. It was only a matter of time before he stumbled on the right word, but his task was made all the more difficult by the shadow of a dead man following him everywhere he went, his face manifesting on the page of every book.

'Bet you even read in your sleep, eh Grimm?'

Waylian turned so sharply he felt a twinge in his neck. Bram was sitting on the desk behind him with that easy smile on his face, hair flopping down over one eye the way the girls liked so much.

'I wish I could,' Waylian replied, glad of the distraction. 'It's not like there are enough hours in the day.'

'Still having problems?'

'Always.'

Rembram Thule laughed, a little too loud. One of the library's scholars looked over with a furrowed brow but Bram ignored him. 'You work too hard, Grimm. Maybe that's your problem. Sometimes it's just best to step away from the work for a bit. Do something to relax. If I've got a problem I just try and think of something else – more often than not the solution will just come to me out of the ether.'

'That's great, I'm so pleased for you.'

Bram patted Waylian on the arm. 'Come on. It's not that bad. Word is the Red Witch has something else taking up her time now. That means you're left alone by all accounts. How can that be a bad thing?'

'It's bad because she's left me with so much work it feels like I'm drowning in a sea of bloody books. If that weren't bad enough, if I can't work out her new pet name for me, I'll soon be drowning in a sea of shit when I have to muck out the latrines.'

'Yes, I can see that being something of a quandary.' Bram's tone was solemn, yet he still couldn't avoid a sly smile. 'So what's she calling you this week?'

'*Jotun.* I've managed to round it down to a few Golgarthan texts, and the end stem means "shit", but I can't get any further.'

Bram's grin widened. 'It's fish roe, Grimm.'

'No, it can't be. *Tun* means shit, it definitely does.'

'Trust me, Grimm. The ancient Golgarthan mariners used to think roe was fish shit and threw it away, long before they decided to dispense with their superstitions and start eating it. You must be growing on the old girl – she's just likened you to a Golgarthan delicacy.'

Waylian was stunned. 'I guess that's an improvement: I'm now as much use as something in a fish's guts, rather than what's dangling between a goat's legs.'

'She'll be proposing marriage before you know it.'

Just the thought appalled Waylian.

'Yes, can't wait to see what she comes up with next.'

'It won't be anything Golgarthan, that's for sure.' Bram idly picked up one of the thick leather-bound histories Waylian had been poring over. 'Which is a shame. For a savage race they have a lot to say that makes sense.'

'You think so?' All Waylian had read about were their endless wars. There were certainly no great thinkers or scholars amongst them – unless you liked reading endless verses about how to disembowel your enemies and set their hill forts ablaze.

'Absolutely. The Golgarthan skarls and wytchworkers were the first in the West to regard magick as an art. The ancient Teutonians stole everything they know from them, making alliances with their disparate tribes, then betraying them in the War of the Red Snows. *They took our words of power with hearts of black stone* the northmen used to say.'

Waylian had heard of that war, though with a slightly different slant. The ancient Sword Kings had fought an invading force from Golgartha, defending their borders against a rampaging horde of bearded savages. There was nothing in the library's texts about betrayal.

'If they hadn't fought that war, we'd all be running around in loincloths smashing each other over the head with stone axes, by all accounts.' At least Waylian had remembered that much from his studies.

'Don't underestimate the Golgarthans. They were from a time when magick was untamed. Before the Archmasters forbade its use outside the Caste. And we're still persecuting rogues today.'

'It just so happens we've got a rogue on the loose in the city.' Waylian knew he shouldn't have mentioned it, but it was only Bram.

'Really? What did they do – turn some farmer's wife into a frog?'

'Not quite. They gutted some poor wretch, after nailing him to the floor.' *And I've been seeing that poor wretch's tormented face ever since.*

'That's no evidence, is it? People get cut up in this city every day.'

'Not like this. There were sigils on the walls, foul things: I felt sick even looking at them. The Magistra had to purge the chamber and she says there'll be more killing before it's over.'

'So, the witch-hunt is on? Wonder how many poor buggers they'll burn at the stake this time, before they find the right culprit.'

'The Magistra knows what she's looking for. She won't make a mistake.'

'Don't be so sure, Grimm. It wouldn't be the first time a magicker's been persecuted for nothing.'

'You'll be telling me rogues aren't dangerous next.'

Bram laughed. 'Of course they're dangerous, Grimm. But we don't have to hang every hedge witch in the countryside who makes tinctures from mushrooms and pimple remedies from cow pat.'

There was a loud shushing from across the library. The old scholar whose job it was to organise the thousands of books and codices looked sternly from behind a pile of scrolls.

Bram only grinned at him. 'Come on, Grimm, let's get out of here. Too much work'll make you go blind anyway.'

'I can't. I've still got—'

'Oh, don't be a slave to it, man.' Bram swept Waylian's books off his desk where they thudded to the wooden floor, the noise echoing up to the library ceiling.

The old scholar looked almost apoplectic with suppressed rage.

Waylian was suddenly gripped with panic as the scholar made his way across the library, weaving clumsily between the rows of desks. Bram was already nearing the massive double doors. If Gelredida found out Waylian had been misbehaving in the *Liber Conflagrantia* instead of studying, he would be on privy duty until the end of days.

Grabbing his satchel he leapt up and ran after Bram. There was incensed grunting behind him, but the old man would never catch up.

Waylian ran out into the corridor, past the ever vigilant Raven Knights, to see Bram disappearing around a corner. The thrill of the chase was invigorating him, and the knowledge he was misbehaving in the austere Tower of Magisters only spurred him on. The risk that he might be seen by one of the stuffy old sorcerers and punished severely only added to his excitement. The stress of the past couple of days was released, expelled in a rush of wanton defiance.

Bram sped through the empty corridors, his lanky legs powering him along, but Waylian was determined not to be left behind. Skidding around corners, he ran up an ancient stone staircase, taking the weathered steps three at a time. When Waylian finally reached the summit, Bram was waiting for him, a wide grin on his face.

They were at the top of the northern bastion of the Tower of Magisters, the highest point in the city, and Bram was looking out over the Free States. On a clear day the southernmost tip of the Kriega Mountains was just visible to the northeast but today a smattering of cloud concealed them. Steelhaven itself, though, was laid out in all its glory – a vast hive of winding streets and tiled rooftops. To the west the city was cut through by the Storway, dividing the old city from the new, and to the southeast, atop a craggy promontory, stood the statues of Arlor and Vorena, watching for invaders from both land and sea.

Waylian knew that there was nothing approaching from the sea they need fear, but from the north . . .

'Look at it, Grimm.' Bram was barely out of breath, so Waylian tried his best not to pant like an old nag pulling a turnip cart. 'Makes you feel small, doesn't it?'

I've not really thought about it. 'Erm, yeah. I suppose it does.'

'Come on, Grimm, look. Look at how vast the place is, full of the teeming masses. And all they do is fuck and fight and pup more souls to do more fucking and more fighting. That's all we are, Grimm – animals. That's why we need to enjoy it while it lasts.'

'I know what you mean.' *Kind of.*

'Do you? That why you spend all your time in the library? There's a world out there, Grimm. A world just waiting for us to take it by the scruff. Some things you just can't learn in books. Some things have to be experienced.'

'But we're not here to experience, Bram. We're here to study. Archmaster Marghil says—'

'Who gives a shit what that dried up old newt thinks? Don't try and tell me you believe all that pious, high and mighty bollocks he spouts. I've seen you looking at Gerdy.' *So that's her bloody name!* 'There's a pleasure you wouldn't mind experiencing, I'll bet.' *You don't know the half of it.* 'Something you can't learn about in a book.'

'Well, you can, but—'

'Exactly! You can, but it's not the same, is it, Grimm?'

'It's irrelevant anyway. Students are forbidden from consorting with one another. So it's best to just put it out of your mind.'

'And have you managed to put it out of your mind?' Bram leaned casually against one of the merlons and grinned.

'Yes, of course I have.' *Liar, liar, cock's on fire. You think about her every night whilst stroking yourself silly.*

'You won't mind if I have a go then?'

'What?' Waylian felt a sudden cold chill.

'If *I* have a go? She's pretty enough. Think she'd go for my charms?' Bram seemed totally confident of the answer. She would most definitely go for his charms – and there was little Waylian could do about it.

'No I bloody don't! She'd think you were being wholly inappropriate.'

'All right, Grimm, keep your hair on. Clearly we have another quandary. The only way to settle it is to ask the girl herself, isn't it?'

'She's not here, is she? So we can't.'

'No. But I've got a pretty good idea where she'll be.'

With that, Bram pushed himself off the parapet and moved towards the stairs. Waylian made a grab for him but, as before, Bram was too fast, dodging aside and breaking into a run.

Again they rushed, down into the body of the vast tower, but this time Waylian was more careful as he navigated the stairs. Though his limbs were almost as long as Bram's, his friend had grace and coordination, whereas Waylian was a gangly clot.

By some miracle they managed to avoid stumbling into any of the magisters before they reached the refectory. Bram, there first, immediately made his way through rows of long trestle tables towards a group of apprentices at the far end. To Waylian's dismay he saw that one of them, apparently laughing at some joke, was Gerdy. His heart fluttered as he saw her blonde hair and bewitching smile, but he felt sick inside as he saw Bram advancing on her: what might he say? Would he be in the mood to humiliate and demean? Waylian liked Bram but knew his friend could be cruel with his japes – he had so often been the target of them.

Waylian almost fell over himself in his haste to cross the hall. He would never make it to Gerdy before Bram, but the quicker he got there the more he could limit any damage.

Bram was already introducing himself, smiling that smile, not a bead of sweat on his brow despite his recent dash to the refectory. The apprentices, and especially Gerdy, laughed as he joined them. Waylian, though hindered by the intervening tables, was almost there. Bram saw him coming, said something and the other students turned. One smirked, as though Bram's remark had been vulgar – well no change there then.

Though Waylian was almost at the table he lost Bram's next words as the group erupted into laughter.

What had he said? Was it about Waylian's hair, his stupid thin limbs, his ridiculous backwater accent? Or, gods be merciful, the fact that he wanked over Gerdy every night?

That was it – Bram had told her all about the secret wanking!

'He's a bloody liar!' Waylian yelled.

The laughing of the apprentices stopped.

Throughout the rest of the refectory the buzz of chatter died. All eyes turned to Waylian, standing there, panting and sweating like an old dog left out too long in the sun.

Bram smiled.

Gerdy looked at him as though he'd just vomited all over her lap.

Waylian turned tail, moving back across the great hall as fast as he could short of breaking into a run, winding his way between the trestle tables, trying not to catch anyone's eye.

He didn't stop until he got back to his chamber.

It was only later that he realised he was no longer plagued by the image of a disembowelled corpse. The image now haunting him was of a score of laughing, mocking faces.

TWENTY-ONE

They called it the Town. It had borne many names in the past, most of which Nobul didn't know, ancient names in old languages long dead. Back then it was most likely a group of fishermen's huts built where the river met the sea; a huddled community fending for itself in the leanest of times. Later it would have been a makeshift fort, with a wooden palisade defending it from the land to the north and with the sea at its back. Over the centuries the wooden buildings had become stone, the palisade of tree trunks a curtain wall. The rickety wooden jetties built by the fishermen of old had been stripped down and rebuilt as a vast harbour, turning an ancient hamlet into a massive port – a hub for trade and commerce with countries from three continents.

With its trade in arms – its artisans crafted the finest weapons and armour in the provinces – and its standing as the most impregnable fortress the Teutonians had ever built, it had taken on the name of Staelhafn in the old tongue – Steelhaven. It was a bright beacon in a time of shadows, a monument to the dawn of a new civilisation.

But times changed.

In the days of Arlor it was an inhuman threat the Teutonians faced, and the Sword Kings had been raised to face it, tribal leaders given powerful weapons hammered and tempered in the forges of Steelhaven. However, in the early years of that conflict they had faced an infernal foe, and could do nothing to save the great port from the daemons that wanted the races of man enslaved or dead. The city had been destroyed: fires burned and the dead screamed from one winter to the next, they said.

The Old City, as it became known, had been abandoned, only its ghosts left to walk the shattered streets. A new Steelhaven was built alongside, greater than the old one had ever been, a testament to the enduring spirit of Arlor and his Sword Kings, but in its shadow the Old City stood, a constant reminder that even the greatest metropolis can fall.

Despite its reputation as a sepulchre of revenants, people still lived amongst the ruins. It was a haven for the desperate and the mad, those who cared little for the spectres, real or imagined, who might stalk the shadowy ruins. The inhabitants called it the Town. A quaint name that hid its sinister nature.

'This place is a right shit hole.'

Denny had a way of summing things up.

Nobul just grunted his assent, keeping a careful look out. Amber Watch was alone here – the other watches were clearing out other sections of the Town. This place made him nervous – too many places to hide, too many blind spots where someone could be waiting with a knife . . . or worse. Dustin had almost been decapitated by some desperate bastard jumping out from the ruins of an old chapel, screaming at the top of his voice and waving a rusty cleaver around like he was trying to chop up the flies swarming round his head. Dustin, Edric and big Bilgot had managed to subdue the man. Then Bilgot had kicked him until he stopped moving. Nobul hadn't liked that, but he knew it was necessary. Not safe to leave someone who might get up and threaten you again. Nobul had kicked enough men like that over the years. He had no room to complain about someone else doing it.

'Right!' Kilgar appeared above them, standing on an old, fallen pillar. 'We've another two streets before sundown. Keep your eyes open. We don't want any casualties.'

'This is a shithouse detail,' Denny complained as they moved after their serjeant. 'What good's it gonna do anyway? We move these fuckers on and they're back again like rats.'

'It's our orders,' Nobul replied. 'Best just get on and do it.' He liked Denny, though the boy could go on a bit. And he had a point.

Amber Watch was the first of a group sent in to 'clear out' the Town. Apparently they were making it habitable for thousands of refugees flooding towards the city. How many, though, would turn tail and head straight back towards the Khurtas, once they caught sight of the digs laid aside for them?

Once the filth and scum had been removed from the streets, labourers were due to come in and make the buildings safe, removing loose masonry and repairing fallen walls. Whether they'd get that chance before the evicted came back to reclaim their hovels was another matter.

Kilgar led the way, moving down the thoroughfare, or at least what remained of it. Almost totally overgrown, the flora that had thrust through the flagstones now smothering the ancient stone buildings in a leafy embrace. Stray dogs hung on every corner, snarling defiance, then slinking off like the curs they were. Human waste lay all around: the place was a stinking open sewer. Even the hovels of Northgate didn't smell this bad; the men of Amber Watch found themselves continually gagging. Anton tied an old scarf across his face, but his retching every ten paces confirmed its uselessness.

Nobul planted his foot against a pile of rotten planks blocking a doorway and shoved. They all but crumbled, leaving the way open. Stupidly, they had neglected to bring any torches with them so he was left to enter the dark interior slowly, hoping his eyes would adjust before anyone still lurking could leap out at him. Denny was at his shoulder, but though he talked bold, it was unclear how much help the lad would be in a fight.

Once inside, he realised there was nothing to fear, apart from rats and spiders. A clutter of broken furniture and a blackened hearth suggested someone might have tried to make a home of it – long years ago. It was like that with many of the hovels – despite the Town's reputation as a hive of the lost and villainous, it was only sparsely populated. Whether it was the dangers of cutthroats and rapers, or of ghouls stalking the Town's moonlit streets, people had kept away, and every empty building they came across gave Nobul some relief.

'Who the fuck's going to want to live in here?' Denny demanded, his nose scrunched up in disgust, though the smell inside was nowhere near as bad as outside.

'People will live anywhere if they're desperate enough. Streets in the city are already filling up.'

'You'd have to be pretty desperate to want to live here. Think I'd rather take my chances on the streets of the city than get a roof in the Town.'

'It's dangerous either way.'

'I'll say. Word is there's refugees going missing. Dozens of them. People have been complaining to the Greencoats all week about it. They've disappeared just like that, grown men and all.'

Nobul had heard the rumours but, with no reliable numbers of how many refugees were entering the city, it was hard to know the truth.

'No point worrying about tales from the streets. Let's just concentrate on what we can do something about.'

'It's all right saying that.' Denny took on a grave look that didn't suit his face. 'What about the bloody murder up Northgate? That witch from the Tower said it was nothing, just some mad bastard, but Kilgar didn't believe her. He says there's something diabolical afoot, and I know who I believe.'

'If there *is* a magicker on the loose, there's not much we can do about that, is there? Let's concentrate on the job at hand. Worrying about shit elsewhere's only going to distract from shit right here. And I need you focused.'

Denny nodded. Though he was more experienced in the Greencoats, Nobul clearly had more experience in general. The boy was willing to accept his orders almost immediately, especially on these dangerous, shitty streets.

Nobul wasn't questioning Kilgar's judgement either, though if one of the wizards from the Tower said there were no rogue casters who was he to argue? As for missing refugees . . . all sorts of rumours were rife at the moment, from tales of dragons or gremlins, to men taking on the shapes of beasts at the full moon. Nobul believed in the things he could see with his own eyes, and let everyone else worry about the rest. He'd seen enough of the horrors men could inflict on other men to worry about the horrors in other folks' heads.

Moving outside, they came on old Hake and the twins dragging someone into the open. The bloke was screaming insults to the sky and gave such a struggle that they lost their grip on him and he was off down the broken streets. Kilgar's raised hand checked any pursuit

'Let him be. There'll be plenty more like that and if we chase every wretch we find we'll be worn out by noon.'

They worked their way up the street, but this particular part of the Town was mostly abandoned but for mangy dogs and mangier rats. Not until they reached what must once have been a main square were there any further signs of life.

Once it might have been a hub of the Old City, where stallholders sold their wares and wealthy merchants came to trade. Now it was a wasteland, covered in detritus, with ragged sheets draped over large fallen statues pinned together to shelter the hunkering masses. So many men, women and children – just sitting there.

Nobul's heart dropped at the task ahead. They would have to be careful here. Though none of these wretches looked in a fit state to put up much of a fight, together, and provoked, they could turn into a dangerous mob.

'All right,' said Kilgar, careful not to raise his voice. 'Stay within sight of one another and let's take this steady. No need to rouse them if we don't have to, but we've got a job to do and we'll bloody well do it.'

They moved forward, cautiously. Kilgar approached the first of the homeless rabble, nudged him with his foot and ordered him firmly but calmly to 'move on'. The man didn't put up much of a protest, gaining his feet unsteadily and moving off with nothing more than a scowl. The rest of the lads followed his lead, and began moving the loitering rabble on. At first it went well, and the square slowly began to clear. Nobul began to think they might well get away with this unscathed – until Bilgot homed in on an old woman sitting by a dead tree.

'Come on, you old bitch,' Bilgot said, quietly as he could, but still far too loud. 'On your way, by order of the king.'

'Fuck off, you fat bastard,' she replied, spitting the words from a toothless mouth.

'I said, fucking *move*.' Bilgot punctuated his words with a harsh kick. The old woman barely registered he'd even struck her.

'Take it easy, Bil,' said Denny, moving closer. 'She's an old woman.'

Nobul looked across the square, seeing other squatters taking an interest. Bilgot needed to calm down.

'Don't tell me what to do, you little arsehole,' Bilgot responded. Denny backed off, anxious not to provoke his hulking comrade. 'I told you to move, you old cow. Do it!'

Bilgot reached forward but Denny stopped him. The big Greencoat rounded on Denny, and Nobul was pleased to see the youngster stand his ground.

'She's an old woman, Bil. Just take it steady.'

Bilgot puffed himself up, readying for a fight.

Nobul had seen enough. If Bilgot wanted a fight it was time he bloody well got one, but before he could intervene, the old woman struck.

Where she'd pulled the blade from Nobul could only guess, but, despite her years, she moved with frightening speed. Denny screamed and clutched his arm, his cry attracting the attention of everyone in the square.

Before Nobul could stop him Bilgot was kicking the old woman in the head. 'Fucking bitch,' he snarled, stamping down with his massive boots.

Nobul pulled Bilgot away. Kilgar was shouting something from behind them but it was too late. A piece of masonry flew right at Denny, as he clutched his arm, blood running red and free through his fist.

'Enough,' Nobul growled. The old woman lay still on the ground, her matted grey hair partially covering the mangled mess Bilgot had made of her face. 'We need to get the fuck out of here,' he urged Denny as another jagged piece of rock from somewhere in the crowd clanged off Denny's halfhelm.

'Fucking hells!' said the lad, staggering back from the escalating barrage.

With sudden jeering the vagabond mob seemed to mobilise. Seeing one of their own, an old woman, being kicked worse than a dog had sent them into an instant frenzy.

'With me,' shouted Kilgar, moving back to the south of the square from where they'd come. Nobul grabbed Denny, who was staring vacantly, and dragged him along.

'*Bastards!*' someone yelled, as a hail of rocks pelted them from all sides. '*Kill the fuckers!*' yelled someone else.

This was turning from bad to worse.

Anton, Dustin and Edric led the way and Nobul shoved Denny after them. 'Keep moving,' he barked, waiting only for Hake as the old man limped along behind. Bilgot could look after his fucking self.

Before they were clear, a scream alerted Nobul to a wild-eyed man leaping at him, wielding a blunt shank. He spun away as the shank tore a strip out of his jerkin. Nobul knew he had to put the fella down fast. He grabbed his attacker's knife hand at the wrist and stabbed viciously with the fingers of his other hand, deep into the desperate bastard's throat – once, twice. The man went down choking, dropping his shank and lifting his hands to his shattered throat, for all the good it would do him.

'Come on,' shouted Kilgar, as though Nobul was hanging around for the laughs. He didn't need encouragement. As the mob began to charge forward he turned tail and ran.

They raced back down the overgrown thoroughfare. Ahead, Nobul could see Kilgar and Bilgot, that fat bastard, huffing as he was forced to heave his bulk down the street, jumping over fallen masonry and squelching through the dog shit.

They were quickly hemmed in by the incensed mass of wild squatters at their heels and there was trouble ahead.

Dustin and Edric were rolling around on the ground, trying to fend off some red-haired youth with a knife. Hake and Anton were nowhere to be seen. Kilgar and Bilgot waded into the fight. Denny screamed as he struggled with some wild-haired ruffian and Nobul could see he was going to lose: his slashed arm was useless, and his free arm only just warding off a vicious piece of sharpened slate from his throat.

Forgetting the others, Nobul shot forward, pulled out his short sword and stabbed in, taking the guy below the ribs before he could stick his own makeshift blade in Denny. The man squealed, falling back a pace. He glowered hatred at Nobul, standing there with dripping blade, then staggered off trying to cover the bloody gash in his side.

Nobul spun to face the oncoming crowd, pulling Denny behind him. The lads had subdued the red-headed fella and also turned to face the mob.

The crowd closed in slowly on Amber Watch, hungrily baying for blood, keen to vent their anger.

'Steady, lads,' Kilgar said, gripping a sword in his one remaining hand. 'Looks like we're scrapping after all.'

'There's too fucking many of them,' said Denny, fear in his voice.

'Then we'll go down fighting,' Kilgar replied.

Nobul nearly laughed.

He'd survived Bakhaus Gate. Survived the Guild. Now he was going to die at the hands of a load of homeless bastards from the Town.

Then again, he reckoned one death was just as good as another.

As the first murderous bastard made ready to charge, he suddenly screamed, hand shooting to his chest to grip the quarrel shaft that had appeared there. As he fell, a volley of bolts flew overhead, some hitting their targets, others bouncing off the surrounding ruins. That was all it took to send the mob scuttling away through the foliage, only too keen to escape before a second volley was fired at them.

Nobul turned to see half a dozen crossbowmen on a crumbling rooftop – Greencoats!

'That you, Kilgar?' one of them shouted.

'Aye. Just in bloody time, Serjeant Bodlin. We were about to dispense the King's Justice on those bastards.'

'Course you were, Kilgar,' replied Bodlin. 'Even so, I reckon that's still one Amber Watch owes us.'

'If you like, Bodlin,' said Kilgar, his face almost cracking a smile. 'Right, I think we've had enough for one day, lads. Let's get the fuck out of here.'

None of the lads complained.

TWENTY-TWO

In days long gone she and Graye had played in this garden, giggling as little girls, laughing raucously as young ladies. Now Janessa was a woman grown it seemed all the mirth had been stripped from the place. Autumn was setting in, and the leaves had faded through yellow to brown and fallen to the damp grass, leaving the trees bare and forlorn. The ornamental statues of frolicking maids and their handsome suitors seemed as cold as the stone they were hewn from, in stark contrast to the spirited quality they seemed to take on in the long, bright days of summer.

'I hear renovation of the Old City is well under way,' Graye said as they strolled along a gravelled path between two hedgerows of lavender.

'Yes,' Janessa answered, rebuffing another attempt by Graye to strike up conversation. She knew she was being impolite. She didn't mean to be, but she couldn't seem to shake off her bad humour. Her responsibilities weighed on her now more than ever. She simply couldn't dislodge Odaka's words from her mind; *for every decision you make there will be consequences.*

For all her attempts to lighten the mood Graye knew her friend was troubled, and she did not impose. If Janessa had wanted to unburden herself she knew Graye would listen.

The smell of the lavender was faint but still there, clinging to the faded flowers. Behind them, Governess Nordaine hummed a tuneless dirge, clearly bored with her duties – not that she would ever have complained.

'I'm sorry, I'm not much company today,' Janessa said. She mustn't wallow in self-pity, especially when others had situations so much worse than hers.

'You never have to say sorry to me.' Graye smiled, linking arms with Janessa and giving her hand a squeeze.

It was a simple gesture but meant the world.

'No, I rarely ever do, do I?' said Janessa. 'Remember when I found that frog?'

'Yes, I do: you chased me around the garden from noon till sunset with it. When your mother told you to apologise you blankly refused.'

'It was only a frog.'

'They're slimy disgusting creatures that should be killed on sight.'

'Not like hedgehogs then?'

They both laughed. Graye had found a hedgehog in the gardens when they'd been no more than nine winters. She'd been determined to keep it as a pet, right up until the creature's fleas infested her hair and attacked her so mercilessly that she'd begged the Governess to hack her waist-length locks off. Janessa hadn't remembered laughing at the time, but the memory was funnier than anything she could recall.

Their laughing stopped when they saw Odaka approaching.

'Here he comes,' said Graye. 'Happy as ever. I think if that one ever smiled his teeth would fall out from the shock of exposure.'

Janessa shushed her friend, but had to fight back a giggle.

'My lady,' said Odaka, with his customary bow. He was dressed in a red robe, lined with black silk, and wore a matching hat. 'I trust you are well. It is cooler today, but still pleasant, do you not think?'

Janessa couldn't think how to reply. It wasn't like Odaka to make idle conversation about the weather. Immediately she was on her guard.

'Yes, very pleasant,' she said, though she really wanted to ask what in the hells he wanted.

'Lady Daldarrion, Governess Nordaine, I trust you too are well?'

For Odaka to even acknowledge the existence of Janessa's companions was unusual, but to ask them how they were . . . Consequently, both women merely mumbled their reply, as surprised as Janessa at the regent's behaviour.

Janessa was impatient and about to ask what was wrong when Odaka announced, 'One of your guests awaits in the vestibule, my lady.'

He extended an arm, signifying she shouldn't keep the guest waiting – whoever it was.

'Thank you, Odaka,' Janessa said, moving towards the palace. 'Come along,' she encouraged her entourage, but Odaka had other ideas.

'Er, I think your majesty may want this to be a private audience.'

'But I am her majesty's chaperone,' Nordaine replied. 'I should be by her side at all times. Especially when she speaks with her guests.'

'That won't be necessary on this occasion,' said Janessa, not entirely sure. *One of her guests* could mean anything. Might she risk being alone with Baroness Isabelle or her foul son Leon?

She followed Odaka into Skyhelm, only a little reassured by the heavy presence of the Sentinels. Before she reached the vestibule, she could not stop herself from asking, 'Who is this guest, Odaka?'

'Someone who has requested an audience, my lady.'

'I might have assumed that,' she said, on the edge of irritation. 'Which of our guests?'

Odaka stopped before her, bowed and ushered her forward. To her surprise she realised they had already reached the vestibule, and within, waiting for her, was Raelan Logar.

'What is the meaning of this?' she said quietly, hoping Odaka would answer before Raelan even noticed she had arrived.

'Lord Raelan wishes to speak with you, my lady. I am merely carrying out the wishes of our guest.'

'I don't understand. At the Feast the man was gruff and rude, and you said I could choose my own suitor.'

'And nothing has changed. But if you do not speak to him, you will never know why he has requested to see you.'

All this Odaka said while still locked in a bow, his arm still gesturing into the vestibule. By now Raelan had turned and could see them both standing there. Janessa could only imagine how ridiculous they looked – her whispering from the side of her mouth and Odaka bent at the waist like a cripple.

'My lord,' she said, greeting Raelan with a smile. 'What a pleasant surprise.'

Raelan's mouth twitched at one side, into a half smile. 'My lady, the pleasure is all mine.'

I'm sure it is. 'I understand you have been with us since the Feast, but I have had little time to spend with guests of the palace.' *Because I've been avoiding you like scurvy.* 'Please accept my apologies.'

'None are necessary, my lady.'

'How are you enjoying your stay at Skyhelm?' *Would you rather be having your legs sawn off, perhaps?*

'The rooms are adequate. Though in Valdor we prefer a little less ostentation.'

I'm sure you flog yourselves to sleep at night too, after washing in snow. 'I find them somewhat gaudy myself. Not to everyone's taste.'

Raelan nodded, his mouth twitching once more. Janessa noticed his fists were clenched, his knuckles white.

He smiled faintly, as did she.

What was she supposed to say now? She looked to Odaka, but he had moved from sight, leaving her alone with Raelan. Her sense of unease increased as the silence wore on. Surely it was time for him to say what was on his mind. Why had he requested an audience if he wasn't going to speak?

She glanced to left and right, desperate for something else to say. It was clear Raelan had something he wanted to get out but was tongue-tied. Janessa felt her heart thumping as the awkwardness of the moment dragged on.

She looked at him, and he at her. His eyes were doleful, as though at any moment he might burst into tears.

'You know our houses have been allied for many years?' he said, finally.

'I do,' she replied, knowing full well the lines of the Mastragalls and Logars had been close for centuries.

'And that even now our fathers stand shoulder to shoulder against enemies of the Free States?'

'Yes, Lord Raelan, of course I do.'

'Then you know our duty is clear.'

'Our duty, Lord Raelan?'

'To join our houses and strengthen the union of the Free States.'

She paused, taking in his words, unsure if she had heard him correctly. 'Was that a proposal of marriage, Lord Raelan?'

He cleared his throat. 'I know this is not ideal for either of us, but there is no alternative. The Mastragalls will have the strength and support of the Logars and all Valdor. The Free States will remain secure.'

How romantic. 'Yes . . . erm . . . but . . .'

'I know this must come as a surprise. But we must remain rational.'

Yes, rational. Just how I'd always dreamed. 'I understand, Lord Raelan, but . . .'

'We cannot tarry on this matter. It is a good match for you, and a practical one for me.'

Please, stop. My heart flutters and I'm feeling faint from the praise. 'I must send word to my father first. He must approve the proposal.' *Or rather, I must tell him I'm refusing it . . . tempting as it is.*

'Approve? This match was your father's idea.'

That took time to sink in.

Odaka had told her just the other night that her father would allow her to refuse any proposal she did not agree with, and yet here he was, arranging her wedding. Could she refuse? Should she?

'Lord Raelan, I appreciate your candour. The offer is indeed a most tempting one. I will think on it.'

With that she turned quickly, trying to avoid seeing his reaction, but she was not quite quick enough. Raelan's brow was furrowed, whether in anger or confusion she couldn't tell, but she was not staying to find out.

Janessa rushed from the vestibule as fast as she could without running. She passed Odaka in the corridor outside and before he could speak she raised a hand to check him. Odaka Du'ur was not put off so easily, though, and he followed her down the corridor.

'Might I ask what your majesty's answer was?'

So, Odaka had been complicit in this arrangement all along.

'No you may not,' she replied, not even attempting to hide her annoyance.

'Your father will want to know as soon as possible.'

That made her stop. She rounded on Odaka who only looked down at her impassively. 'You told me my father would allow me to make my own decision. Was that a lie?'

'Of course not. The decision is entirely down to you, though, as I told you before, there are consequences to all your decisions.'

'Yes, you've made that perfectly clear. And now the kingdom relies on my decision. Despite what my father expects, I cannot make this choice without thought.'

With that she moved on down the corridor, relieved that Odaka made no effort to follow.

She had to think. Her father would allow her to make up her own mind, but had made his own wishes perfectly clear. She could choose her own husband if she wished, but the choice should be made for the good of the Free States.

What choice was there? Tall, arrogant Raelan – or would the shorter, no less arrogant Leon fit the bill?

She clearly had no choice at all.

Once in her chamber, she stared out of the window onto the city . . . the city that was forbidden to her.

Only it wasn't.

It was forbidden to Princess Janessa Mastragall, a place she would rule over but never venture into . . . but then, had she always to be a princess?

Janessa opened the oak chest at the bottom of her bed and rummaged to the bottom. There, rolled into a tight ball, were the plain brown dress and shawl she always kept hidden. She bundled them up, hiding them beneath the skirts of her silken frock, and made her way down through the palace.

When she passed the Sentinels they stood to attention, but not one of them questioned where she was going. Why would they? Skyhelm was, after all, her home. One day it would be the place from where she governed the Free States. Why would anyone question her?

She moved down, gradually, to the kitchens, becoming more discreet as she did so. No one would wonder about her wandering the halls of the upper palace, but there was no reason for her to be down in its bowels, where the servants worked and slept. When she was a child at play, no one had questioned her when she ran about the kitchens and servants' quarters; but now a grown woman, she could not be seen mixing with the servants. But over the years Janessa had become adept at subterfuge.

In the shadows of the kitchen stores she stepped out of her silken dress and donned the drab clothes she had kept hidden in her chamber for so long. Pulling the shawl over her distinctive head of red curls, she stepped into the kitchen. Within the hubbub of cooks preparing vege-tables, meat and fowl for Skyhelm's guests, no one gave Janessa a second glance. She strolled towards the side door, picking up two empty pails, and walked out into the yard beyond.

A massive wall surrounded the palace, each of its gates guarded by Skyhelm's Sentinels, but they thought nothing of a young girl leaving the palace grounds to fetch milk for the kitchens. Getting back into the palace was never quite as easy, but leaving was always the same. It had been many days since she had done this, days since she had taken her freedom in the city, but right now this was what she needed.

With the shawl drawn over her head, she never got a second glance from the guards at the east gate as she walked right by. Once outside she placed the pails down and ran. She was free – free from the cloying opulence of the palace, free from Odaka and Raelan. Free from her duty and responsibility.

On the streets of Steelhaven she was no longer Princess Janessa.

She was no one.

Once outside the Crown District she splashed through the muck of the streets, quickly coating her shiny shoes in filth. Turning a corner she dodged a carthorse that was pulling a dray stacked high with neeps, laughing as the driver cursed her for a menace.

The sights and sounds of the city filled her head – people talking, laughing, shouting . . . living. No longer was she bound to the cloistered corridors. Out here she was unfettered, liberated from the shadow of her responsibilities.

Janessa could only envy these people, envy their freedom to choose their paths, their freedom to choose their lives and their loves.

Before long she reached her destination. It was a quiet tree-lined square, a single statue at its centre depicting Craetus, one of the ancient Sword Kings, his great battle blade held aloft.

Janessa was breathing heavily, feeling the blood coursing through her veins. With a smile on her face and her cheeks flushed, she sat on an iron bench, taking in the quiet, listening to the babble of street vendors beyond the square mixed with the tweetings of the few birds that remained in the bare branches.

As she sat she felt the first of the autumn chill, pulled the shawl tighter around her shoulders and glanced up to the parapet of Skyhelm, still visible on the distant skyline. She wondered what Odaka and Nordaine would do if they went to her chamber and found her missing. Would they question Graye? Would they think her kidnapped? Would they unleash the Sentinels to find her?

Let them panic. Let them fear for her. She needed this. She deserved this. If she was to be forced into a marriage not of her choosing, then the least they could do was allow her an afternoon's respite before . . .

He was standing behind her.

She hadn't heard him approach, but then she never did. He always came from nowhere, moving up on her like a shadow.

Janessa looked up and smiled. He did not smile back, but then he never did.

He sat beside her on the bench, and they stared at one another. As always, Janessa reached up and lightly traced the latticework of scars that marred one side of his beautiful face. At least they had not been added to since she had last seen him.

When she had first come here, when she had first stolen from the

178

palace all those years ago, running away from some long forgotten rebuke, she had come to this place. As she cried to herself, wanting nothing more than to run away from this city and her family, he had come to her, and silently comforted her. Over the years, when she was hurt or lonely, she had come here, and he would be waiting.

That first time he had come to her he had borne but a single scar on his face. Every time they met afterwards there would be more scars, more marks, but she never asked their origin and he never told.

It was enough that they were there for one another. River, he had called himself, and she thought it apt, for when he spoke in his soft voice she could picture a lonely brook that sang its own wistful tune. At first he had been reluctant to talk to her, but now it was as though he could not wait to unburden himself, as he spoke of his hopes and his dreams for freedom, for a new life – always for a new life, as though the one he had was almost too much for him to bear.

So desperate had she been to keep him, so desperate to retain her secret love, she had never told him her real name, and on seeing a bird perched in a nearby tree had told him it was Jay. She had not wanted to lie, but it had seemed apt at the time. Gods, perhaps River was not even his name, but it mattered little to her. All that mattered was that they at least had some time together.

'Hello, River,' she whispered with a smile.

'Hello, Jay.' He did not smile back, but she could see in his eyes that he was grateful she had come.

Then, beneath the shadow of an old, leafless elm, they kissed.

TWENTY-THREE

For the past few nights Rag had slept on a hard pallet bed. It weren't all that comfortable, but it was a damn sight better than sleeping on a tavern roof. She had to admit, though – the company weren't quite as good as her previous crew. Burney snored like a braying donkey and Rag found herself staring through the dark at the plaster peeling off the ceiling for hours on end. How Krupps and Steraglio managed to sleep through it she had no idea, but they were out like snuffed candles while she just got to lie there, listening to the racket.

The three men shared a room in a tiny house two doors down from The Black Hart. Krupps had said it would be best if she moved in as well, with her being one of their crew now. Rag had wondered if it was a good idea, sharing with three grown men and all. She was young, but under no illusions about what might happen to her if one of them took a fancy. Eventually though, her yearning to join the Guild had won out. If this was what it took, this was what she'd do.

Steraglio stared at her from time to time. He thought he was doing it when she wouldn't notice, but she could see him out of the corner of her eye sometimes. He scared her – not that she'd ever admit it. She tried to stay out of his way, or have one of the other blokes around. Burney was big and scary looking but gentle enough. Krupps, with his handsome face and cheeky smile, put her at ease. Quick with a wink and a grin, he'd taken to calling her 'Sweets', which Rag really liked. People had rarely made the effort to be nice to her. As time passed she found herself liking Krupps more and more.

Despite the cramped sleeping arrangements, Rag had no complaints. She was beginning to feel like part of the gang. Sometimes Krupps and

Burney would even ask her opinion on things – nothing too important, but it made her feel more like she was an equal – one of the boys.

But the best thing was that she no longer had to thieve for coppers to pay for food. The house had a pantry and Krupps made breakfast – eggs and either ham or spiced sausage – every day. With bread and cheese around noon and some kind of broth in the evening, Rag had never eaten so well. A few times she'd stuffed herself so stupid she'd nearly cried with the pain and joy of it.

She didn't forget those she'd left behind. She missed Chirpy and Migs and Tidge, even Fender if she thought about it really hard, but they were the past now. She had a new crew, a real crew, not just young lads chancing it on the street corners.

Even so, as the days went by and nothing happened, she was beginning to wonder about things. All they seemed to do was sit around and drink. Occasionally Steraglio would open a book, occasionally Krupps would disappear from the house for a while, but other than that they didn't seem to do much at all. Not that Rag was complaining. It wasn't her place. They must surely know what they were doing.

After a few days though, they were suddenly in business.

'Okay, Sweets,' Krupps said. Rag had just woken up and come down the stairs. They were all sitting there, waiting for her. 'It's time to get some work done.'

Krupps was dressed up like a dandy, in clothes Rag had never seen before. He wore a shirt with billowing sleeves, a satin waistcoat and matching britches. Over a chair was a coat made from the same material. He'd slicked back his hair with some kind of balm and he smelled almost sickly sweet. Steraglio was similarly dressed, though he still smelled of stale socks. Burney looked the same as ever, sweaty and heavy.

'Where we off?' Rag asked, picking the sleep from her eyes.

'You'll find that out soon enough,' Krupps replied. 'Now put this on.'

With that he picked up a pile of bright blue silk and threw it in her direction. It wasn't until Rag caught it and held it up she realised it was a frock.

Rag had never worn a dress before, and she was damned if she was about to start now. Especially one that would make her look like a Verdant Street whore.

'You lot must be joking if you think I'm putting this on.'

'We're not joking, Sweets. And you'll need to brush that hair of yours as well.'

She stared at them in turn. Their faces confirmed this was no joke.

Back upstairs it took an age to get the dress on but eventually she managed after she'd worked out the difference between front and back. The matching shoes, thankfully, had flat soles – no way she could have walked with the pointy heels the street girls sometimes wore. Her hair proved a challenge, knotted and tangled as it was, but she finally got a comb through it, and came back downstairs.

Krupps smiled. 'Sweets! You look—'

'Not a fucking word,' she snapped, feeling totally stupid.

'Might have to work on the manners,' said Steraglio.

'Is someone going to tell me what all this is for?' Rag gestured down at the dress, which hung off her like some gaudy sheet.

'All in good time, Sweets. For now, just get used to looking like a right little lady.'

Fuck that, she wanted to say, *and fuck this dress*, but she kept her mouth shut. She'd complained enough already.

'Right then, let's go,' said Krupps, opening the door to the house.

As Rag and Steraglio followed him out she asked if Burney was coming too.

'This needs a bit of subtlety, Sweets. Burney's no good at that so we'll be leaving him out for the moment.'

Sounded fair enough. Burney was as subtle as a warhorse.

They moved south across the city, towards its centre, and Rag soon realised where they were going. She needed to keep her mouth shut, not harass them with questions, but she couldn't stop herself.

'We're going to the Crown District,' she said finally.

'Very good,' Steraglio replied. 'But do you think you can concentrate on looking pretty in that dress and doing less talking?'

Rag wanted to tell him to fuck off, but thought better of it – Krupps wouldn't always be around to protect her. She wanted to know how they were going to get in, since the Crown District was walled off from the rest of the city, but she guessed she'd find out soon enough.

At one of the wrought iron gates that allowed entry to the district, Krupps signalled for them to stop.

'Right, let me do the talking. Once we're in, try to look as natural as possible. Like we belong.' He glanced at Rag, as though she might find that a struggle. 'Well . . . just do your best.'

With that he walked up to the gate. There were three Greencoats standing around idly, but as they approached the men stood to attention.

Rag thought the game was up then and there. How would they ever get in? This had been a stupid idea; she looked about as much a toff as she did a cow at calf.

'All right, mate?' said one of the Greencoats, reaching forward to shake Krupps by the hand.

'How've you been, Westley?' Krupps replied.

If Rag was one thing she was quick – quick to see trouble and quick to see coin. As the men shook hands, even though it happened in an instant, she saw a gold crown pass from Krupps' palm to the Greencoat's.

'Mustn't grumble, my old mate,' Westley replied, moving to one side and signalling to the other two Greencoats. The iron gate squeaked as they pulled it open, allowing entry to a part of the city Rag had never been in before. This was the Crown District, home to the wealthy and the privileged, and to more riches than Rag could possibly imagine . . . and she could imagine a lot.

Krupps grinned as he strolled in, like it was the most natural thing in the world. Rag paused on the threshold, knowing it was wrong, knowing she was forbidden from going inside. She just didn't belong in there – but a firm shove from Steraglio soon changed her mind, and she stumbled through the gate after Krupps.

Once inside, Rag could only marvel at the buildings, their clean, stone-clad fronts, their gleaming windows . . . the fact that they even had windows. Here and there the pathways were lined with trimmed grass verges decorated with flowers. Even though the blooms were losing their lustre with the approaching autumn, to Rag they still looked beautiful. Here and there stood a bush, expertly trimmed to resemble a bird or a fawn. How long had they taken to craft? And something was strange . . . It took Rag some time before she realised that this part of the city didn't stink of rotting food or steaming turds.

The streets did not teem with the great unwashed: there was hardly a soul about. Rag marvelled at so much space for so few people. Those she *did* see seemed to glide, with a grace far removed from the stomping, shifty gait of those in Dockside or Northgate. It was like these people didn't have a care in the world; wandering aimlessly in their immaculately tailored garb, smelling of perfume and exotic oils . . . and that was just the men.

'Close your mouth,' said Steraglio quietly. 'You're gawping at these people like they're wandering around naked. We're trying to fit in. You staring like that will only draw attention. We might as well have put a monkey in the dress.'

Rag rallied. They were here to do a job, and she was damned if she'd be the one to cock it up.

'Do we know where we're going?' Steraglio asked, looking more and more agitated the longer they wandered through the wide streets.

'Calm down,' Krupps replied. 'I know exactly where we're going.'

It was clear Steraglio felt as out of place as Rag. A deep frown creased his severe features and he glanced around like a pullet looking out for a fox.

Before long they came out in a wide, tree lined square. The magnificent lawn in the middle was surrounded by four rows of houses, each protected by spiked iron railings.

'There we are,' said Krupps, nodding his head to the house at the far north east of the square. 'Home of Barnus Juno. Richest spice broker in Steelhaven.'

The house rose up three storeys, but unlike similar sized buildings in other parts of the city its walls were straight, its roof tiled all neat and even.

'So what do we think?' Krupps directed his question at Steraglio.

'We think all the downstairs windows are barred,' he replied, squinting across the wide, green lawn. 'What about the back?'

'No entrance, it backs onto the opera house at the far side.'

'So we're left with the front door or the second storey.'

Krupps nodded in agreement. 'So, Sweets, which is it?'

Rag froze. This was why they'd brought her. This was her job: breaking into some spice merchant's house. But how?

'Erm . . .'

'I fucking knew it,' said Steraglio. 'This was all a waste of fucking time.'

Krupps gave him a dark look, and Steraglio backed down. He walked off across the lawn, mumbling curses to himself.

'You can get in, can't you, Sweets?' Krupps asked. This time his usual gentle tone had the slightest edge.

Rag had to blag this or come clean and tell him she had no idea how to break houses. If she came clean, that was it with the Guild. It was back to the roof of the Bull and pinching for coppers all over again.

She smiled at him, and gave him the wink he'd given her so often.

'Course I can, Sweets,' she said mockingly. She was pleased, and more than a little relieved, when her gamble paid off and Krupps smiled back at her.

'Good girl. So which is it – door or window?'

Rag looked back to the house. She had little experience picking locks. Fender had tried to show her a couple of times, but all she'd done was bend one of his picks and break the other in a padlock. After that he'd not let her near any of his gear again.

'Window will be easier,' she said, trying her best to sound like she knew what she was on about.

'Good. That's good. We know the layout, so there should be no surprises on the night. Just climb up to the first storey, slip in the window, then come down and let us in the front door. Easy as.'

'And this Barnus Juno is definitely away is he?' she said. The last thing she wanted was to break in and find some angry spice merchant waiting for her with a cleaver.

'He's in Coppergate. Won't be back for a week. There's no one inside . . . unless of course he left his dog behind.'

'Fucking what?' she said, probably a little too loudly.

Krupps laughed. 'You are so easy to dupe, Sweets. Relax, there's no dog and no merchant. Just you, us and a pile of money waiting to be taken to its new home.'

'And we know the Guild are on board with this?' More questions she knew she shouldn't be asking, but she just couldn't help herself.

'You need to learn a bit of trust,' Krupps said, laying a hand on her shoulder. 'Would we be mad enough to pull this one without the Guild's say-so? I know Burney's dumb and Steraglio's "fearless", but I'm not mad. Why would I chance bringing that down on myself?'

That made sense, she supposed. No one wanted to upset the Guild, no matter what the job paid.

'Are you two done yet?' said Steraglio, tramping his way back across the manicured lawn.

'Just about,' Krupps replied. 'We'll need an iron-crow for the window. You can handle an iron can't you?' Rag had no idea what an iron-crow was, but she nodded anyway.

'Right then, now we've got that cleared up, let's go,' said Steraglio, leading the way back towards the gate and not waiting to see if anyone followed.

Krupps and Rag moved after him, though he led them at a heady pace. It was like the place was judging them, accusing them before they'd even started, and the quicker they left it behind the better. And it was as they turned a corner, nearly at the gate, that they came to a sudden stop, almost walking straight into two sumptuously dressed ladies.

One was tall and slim, her face heavily painted but not enough to fill the scores of wrinkles that lined her flesh. Somehow the powder and paint made her look even older and more grotesque than she already was. The other was much shorter and nearly as wide as she was tall, her ample bosom almost spilling out over the top of her red frock.

Steraglio took a step sideways, frowning his annoyance, and Krupps stepped in before his accomplice could unsettle the women.

'I do apologise,' he said, affecting a haughty, yet still charming, air. 'In our haste we almost blundered into you. Do excuse us.'

The tall woman glanced down her nose in disdain, but her smaller, plumper friend had noticed Rag.

'Oh, what do we have here?' she said, her smile bloating her cheeks like a drunkard's belly. 'How delightful. And what a pretty dress. Where are you off to with your papa, my dear?'

Rag stared. The woman describing the monstrosity she was wearing as 'pretty' had her a bit confused. If she opened her mouth and spoke like the back street cutpurse she was the game was up, so she simply looked on dumbly.

'I'm afraid my daughter is simple,' said Krupps, quickly grabbing Rag by the arm. 'Never been the same since her mother's passing. Her uncle and I are—'

'How terribly tragic.' The fat woman bent down and stroked a hand through Rag's hair – thank the gods she'd combed it earlier. As she leaned over, her huge breasts almost fell out of her dress. Rag turned her head in disgust.

The second woman took a step forward, peering down her long nose. 'Yes, terribly tragic. What did you say your names were?'

'We didn't,' said Krupps with a smile.

The tall woman peered at him expectantly.

Krupps seemed stumped. For all his breezy talk it was clear he didn't know what to say next. This woman looked shrewd: saying the wrong name in the wrong place might have her screaming for the Greencoats.

Out of the corner of her eye, Rag saw Steraglio reach for something in the sleeve of his jacket. Slowly, a long silver blade appeared in his hand.

'So, your names are . . .?' the woman said, her tone becoming serious. She wouldn't be put off until this was sorted. Her fat friend stopped stroking Rag's hair and turned to the men doubtfully.

Steraglio took a single step forward.

186

'*Fuck off, you old bags!*' Rag shouted at the top of her voice.

With that she bowled past them, knocking into Steraglio and pushing him towards the gate. In that instant they were all moving, Steraglio leading the way and Krupps taking the rear as they tore across the gleaming cobbles and away. When they finally got to the gate it was still open, and they slowed to a walk before sauntering through, Krupps smiling at Westley and the other two Greencoats as he did so.

'That could have gone worse,' said Krupps cheerily, as they made their way back to the house.

Rag could only agree with him, glancing towards Steraglio, who had concealed his blade once more. It could have gone a lot bloody worse.

TWENTY-FOUR

K aira waited in her room for three days. She had been told someone
would contact her, but no one came the first night, or the second.
The landlord of the Pony and Fiddle didn't seem to mind her staying
there, he simply provided her with food and asked for nothing in return.

And so she waited.

In the meantime she busied herself by honing her body and mind, using
the scant environment offered by the room to test herself physically and
mentally. She used the bed and roof beams to sharpen her muscles: fifty
pull-ups, a hundred push-ups, two hundred sit-ups. She lifted the wooden
table on her back and squatted till her thighs burned. Then she stretched,
gripping her ankles and bending till her forehead touched her knees,
keeping her legs arrow straight and touching her palms to the floor, then
reaching each arm over one shoulder to bring her hands together behind
her back.

The need to remain strong and supple was not lost on her. This mission
would be a difficult one and Kaira had no idea when her fighting prowess
would be needed.

To strengthen her mind she simply sat and prayed. Vorena would only
watch over her if she remained resolute of thought and purpose. Nothing
must be allowed to sway her, nothing must be allowed to stand in her way.
It was not easy to keep focus in a place so alien to all she knew, and without
the constant presence of her sisters. The Shieldmaidens were an order used
to working as a single unit, and without them by her side, Kaira found it
more difficult to find the strength she would need for the task ahead.

But the undertaking had been given. It was her penance for the loss of control she had displayed. Kaira would carry out her mission, perform her duty, and let nothing stop her.

On the third day there was a knock at the door.

She opened it a crack, looking out into the gloom, expecting it to be her contact, but prepared in case it wasn't. At first all she saw was darkness, but, as her eyes adjusted to the light given off by the single candle in its wall sconce, she saw a figure standing in the gloom.

'Are you going to invite me in?' came a voice from the dark. It was a woman's voice, and young. This might have put another at her ease, but Kaira had trained girls who were young, girls who were small, and knew just how dangerous they could be.

Nevertheless, she took a step back and opened the door to the stranger, her muscles taut and ready for any attack.

The young girl entered. She was slight, a cloak covering her from head to knee, and when she drew back the hood she was smiling.

'You are well?' she asked conversationally, as if they were old friends, like this was the most ordinary thing in the world. Like Kaira's world hadn't collapsed around her and she hadn't been disgraced, forced to leave her home and compelled to perform a task for which she was wholly unsuited.

'Who are you?' said Kaira in reply, in no mood for pleasantries.

The girl smiled wider. 'I have lots of names, but you can call me Buttercup.'

Buttercup? What kind of name was that? It was something old, sentimental farmers called their prized heifers. 'Is that some kind of joke?'

The girl's smile lost some of its humour. 'You'll find I joke only on rare occasions. Now is not one of those occasions. So I'll ask again – are you well? Are you fit?'

Of course I am fit, I am a Shieldmaiden of Vorena, a defender of the weak, an instrument of righteousness honed and tempered in the flames of battle, ready to strike down the enemies of my gods and my king.

'Yes.'

'Excellent. You'll need to be where we're going. I've set up a meet, so all you need do is turn up and perhaps demonstrate some of your . . . abilities.'

Kaira was under no illusions as to what that meant. Hopefully she wouldn't have to kill anyone in the process.

'How will I know what to do once I've proved myself?'

Buttercup inclined her head, as though she were talking to a child. 'You leave that to me, pet. Try not to do too much thinking. Let's stick to what we're good at.'

Kaira clenched her fists, resisting the temptation to teach this pup some respect, but she felt she would have the chance to vent her frustrations soon enough.

'Shall we?' said the girl, gesturing to the door.

Kaira donned her cloak and followed in silence.

The journey through the streets seemed a little less grimy than it had done when Kaira first left the Temple of Autumn. The people she passed were a little less threatening, the whores a little less pitiful.

It was with a growing sense of foreboding that she realised she was getting used to the squalor, adapting to it, and that made her more fearful than anything. Within the confines of the Temple she had been shielded from this, somehow kept pure from the rotten taint of the city, but the more she walked its streets, mixed with its lost and forgotten denizens, the greater the chance that she become more like them.

Kaira gritted her teeth against the prospect. She could never allow herself to be tainted. Despite everything, she was still a Shieldmaiden, still a chosen sister of Vorena, a bright flame in the dark, a beacon for the lost. No matter how deep she trod in the mire she could never forget that.

'We're here,' Buttercup said.

They were north of a bustling meat market, the stench of which almost turned Kaira's stomach. Buttercup led them down an alley between a pair of tall, stone buildings. Two men waited at the top of a staircase. They nodded at Buttercup as she made her way down into the dark and eyed Kaira with amused suspicion as she passed them. At the bottom of the stairs Buttercup opened a rotting door and moved into a dank cellar.

The smell of damp assailed Kaira's nose and she paused to allow her eyes time to adjust to the dark. In the gloom she could see a man with his back to her, sitting at a table. A bottle of wine and a goblet rested to one side of him.

Buttercup and Kaira waited as the man gorged himself on a plate of cured meats and hard bread, occasionally dipping one or the other into his goblet.

As she waited, Kaira was aware that there were other figures in the dark, at the edges of the cellar, watching and waiting. Her every nerve was on edge, her every muscle taut and ready to strike at the first sign of danger. Something screamed in her head that this was wrong, that she was putting herself in needless danger, but she managed to quell the compulsion to flee.

She must go through with this if her mission were not to fail.

At last the man finished his meal, quaffing down what remained of his wine and wiping his mouth with a cloth. He sat back, breathing out happily, then turned to face the two women.

'Ah, Buttercup,' he breathed. 'Always a delight, my dear. And who have you brought to see us?'

'Palien, may I introduce Kaira? Former mercenary, now unfortunately unemployed.'

'Ah yes.' Palien stood, looking Kaira up and down with an appraising eye. He was a lean man, despite his obvious appetite, with a thick head of dark hair and a large moustache that curled across his top lip. His eyes were small and dark and Kaira felt uncomfortable under their gaze. 'We've heard much about you. And you certainly look the part.'

He ran finger and thumb through his moustache, weighing her up. Kaira half expected him to come and check the firmness of her haunches as he might do a thoroughbred horse.

'Do you think you can use her?' Buttercup said. Kaira hated being spoken for like a child, but she had been advised to be silent. Under the circumstances it was probably for the best.

Palien waggled his head from side to side. 'Possibly. But there's only one way to find out for sure.'

Kaira felt a sudden presence at her shoulder. She didn't have to turn her head to know it was a man . . . a big one too. He had moved in without her hearing or seeing him – that was good work. He might well be dangerous. As he raised his arm and struck down with his hand axe she realised there was no 'might' about it.

She leaned back, bending her spine impossibly far as the axe cut the air an inch from her nose. There was barely enough time to right herself and dodge back before he cut in again – three desperate swipes aimed at her head, shoulder and midriff. She evaded with three lightning-quick steps.

He was, indeed, a big one, his ugly face made uglier by the snarl on his scarred lips. His nose and teeth were smashed in, indicating he had fought plenty of opponents on the streets.

But Kaira was not of the streets.

She was a warrior born, and trained in a temple dedicated to all arts martial.

He didn't stand a chance.

As he moved forward, raising his arm high to cut down once more, Kaira stepped in and spun on her heel. She pressed in close with her back to him as his arm came down and over her shoulder. Her hands gripped him about the wrist and she wrenched down on the arm that held that wicked-looking axe, snapping it at the elbow. The axe clattered to the cellar floor as he bellowed in pain. She wrenched his broken arm around, hearing his roar grow shrill as she slammed the sole of her foot against his knee and the heel of her palm in his jaw in quick succession. He was silent as he collapsed to the ground, but another assailant was already rushing from the shadows.

This one stabbed out with his blade, aiming at her head, and Kaira backed away just far enough to avoid the keen edge but still close enough to feel it part the air in front of her. As he drew back for another strike her foot came up quick and sharp, hitting him between the legs. He gave out a yelp like a whipped bitch, dropping the blade and gripping his fruits in both hands. She grabbed a fistful of his hair and brought her knee up, smashing his nose in and whipping his head back sharply until it crashed against the ground.

Kaira turned in time to see Palien make two swift motions with his hand, signalling for two more of his men to come forward. One was small and wiry, a billhook in one hand and a crude shank in the other. The second was broader at the shoulders, gripping a dark wooden cudgel in both hands.

These men were more measured, more careful about their approach, circling her, looking for a gap in her defences.

Kaira waited. They would have to make a move eventually; it was only a matter of time. A sharp intake of breath warned of the first attack, as the one with the club rushed in, closely followed by his smaller friend.

She ducked the cudgel, spinning just in time to avoid the billhook but it still tore a slice in her tunic. With her hand flat and solid she managed to strike out, hitting the smaller man in the throat, enough to make him back off, but not quite hard enough to be fatal – Palien might not appreciate her killing his men, but she reckoned maiming might be acceptable.

The cudgel came down once more, and Kaira braced her legs, catching the wooden weapon in her hands and stopping it mid strike. Her attacker had just enough time to furrow his brow in confusion before she wrenched it from his grasp and rapped it across his head, dropping him like a sack of old spuds.

She got the cudgel up in time to stop the billhook as it cut in once more, its wielder now recovered. It struck her weapon, sending shards of splinters flying, and its sharp point lodged in the wood. The man tugged on it, trying to wrench it free, but it was stuck fast, and Kaira was not about to let go of the cudgel. With a growl of frustration he released it, relying on his crude shank, stabbing out in three swift strikes which Kaira easily avoided.

With a quick swipe she batted the shank from his hand. He opened his mouth to curse her, but she was quicker than his profanity, bringing the cudgel up, the billhook still stuck in it, and smashing him under the jaw. His mouth clamped shut, biting down hard on his tongue and sending a spray of blood from his mouth as he fell backwards and landed in a heap.

Kaira looked around for the next attacker but none came. All she received was a slow clap of the hands from Palien, who looked strangely amused at the easy besting of his men.

'An impressive display,' he said admiringly. 'You weren't lying, were you, Buttercup?'

'I never lie, Palien,' she replied, though Kaira doubted the truth of that.

'But what to do with you? You're far too pretty to act as a strongarm, though I'm sure if you turned up ready to collect a stipend from the traders we protect they would be falling over themselves to pay up. What to do, what to do?'

'I have a suggestion,' said Buttercup, moving in and almost touching Palien. He didn't seem to mind her getting so close. 'Perhaps she would be best suited to keeping Ryder in check. She could keep him alive while he finalises the deal with Bolo, and if he's failing in his duties, pissing too much of our money down the drain, she could apply some gentle persuasion to keep him on track. Ryder would be much more inclined to listen to a woman, especially one with such obvious skills.'

Palien raised an eyebrow as he thought on it. Then he nodded. 'An inspired idea. For a beauty like this Ryder will roll over and let his tummy be tickled. I remember now why I keep you around, my dear.' Buttercup smiled. 'All right, I think I can trust you to make the arrangements. And try to find something better for her to wear. She looks as if she came in with the last load of refugees.'

Kaira took all this in silence. Her blood was still pumping from the thrill of real combat, but she managed to suppress her urge to carry on, to smash Palien for his insolence, to slap Buttercup until she begged for mercy.

For now, she must bide her time.

After bidding Palien farewell, Buttercup led Kaira from the cellar, a grin on her face.

'You look pleased with yourself,' Kaira said, when they had put the building far behind them.

'Of course I'm pleased with myself. That went far better than I could have possibly planned. Well done, by the way. Your display was exemplary.'

Exemplary? Kaira took no special pleasure in such an achievement. She was a defender of the weak and helpless – despite the thrill of combat, it gave her no pleasure to inflict pain on others, but she was all too aware of what they expected of her. 'That's why I'm here, isn't it? To act the mercenary, until I must act the assassin.'

Buttercup stopped abruptly, and pulled her to one side of the street, her features darkening.

'You are here to help me find the power behind the Guild so that we might destroy it. The Guild seeks ever more wealth and power: they would enslave every innocent in the Free States if it meant achieving that goal. You are a weapon, Kaira Stormfall, a weapon that will strike down the evil that infects this city. It is what you were born for.'

'But how can this fulfil that aim? I am to act as nursemaid to a servant of this Palien. How will watching over a lowly criminal help me achieve my mission?'

Buttercup smiled once more. 'Lowly criminal? Oh, Merrick Ryder is much more than that. He has a long and intimate history with the Guild. He also has the ear of its leaders. For months I have worked with Palien, trying to get an audience with them, but to no end. Ryder was given his current task by the leaders of the Guild themselves. Should he succeed it is highly likely they will wish to congratulate him in person. And if he fails they will want to see him killed with their own eyes. If you aid him as we are planning, you will be at his shoulder when he meets them, for whatever reward they choose to give him. Then you will have your chance to strike.'

'If this Ryder is so important why does he require me? If he's so valued by the Guild's masters, he must be able to take care of himself.'

'He doesn't know he requires your aid yet, but he will. Once you have his trust you must stay by his side until the time is right.'

'And how will I gain his trust?'

Buttercup grinned, putting her arm into Kaira's like an old friend and guiding her on through the streets.

'You just leave that to me.'

TWENTY-FIVE

The Tower of Sails was an ancient structure, built from rocks hewn out of the black cliffs that ran the length of the coastline. It looked out over the great crescent shaped bay, in itself an ingenious construction, which could comfortably moor a thousand ships. Though past its heyday it was still a bustling hub for freight, sprouting myriad trade routes across the Midral Sea, with galleons, caravels, brigantines, pinnaces and more coming and going in their hundreds every day. And it was from the Tower of Sails that all this movement was plotted, controlled and docketed in intricate detail.

As a structure of such importance it was guarded day and night by the Harbourwatch, their crown and anchor livery proudly displayed on tabards covering their red lobstered plate. Their distinct halberds stood ten feet long, the blades fashioned to resemble flying sails.

No one was allowed entry to the tower unless they had the correct authorisations, lest they interfere with the inner workings of the harbour's administration. An audience with the harbourmistress herself needed to be applied for in writing, and it might take up to a tenday before the proper permissions were granted.

It took Merrick Ryder less than an hour.

'Would you care for some wine?' she asked. 'Or perhaps something a little stronger?'

The harbourmistress stood next to a polished oak cabinet housing an array of wines and spirits, some in intricately blown glass bottles, others in decanters or moulded bronze jugs.

'I'll have whatever you're having, Terese,' Merrick replied, flashing his smile at her.

Terese was approaching her middle years, older than Merrick usually liked, but still relatively attractive. Though her hair was turning grey, it hadn't lost its lustre, and her face was lined but far from wrinkled. Years presiding over Steelhaven's vast harbour from a leather-bound chair had left her with a little extra weight about her arse, but Merrick could put up with that. He'd never minded a bit of meat on a woman.

'Something stronger it is,' she said, pouring two glasses of golden liqueur from a decanter.

She walked over and handed him the glass, then sat on the edge of her huge desk. 'So, what can I do for you . . . or is there something you can do for me?'

There was a twinkle in Terese's eye, and the suggestion certainly wasn't lost on Merrick. He would have loved to show her; loved to have bent her over the desk and given her what she was asking for, but he doubted that was the way to go. Some women were all about that, all about giving themselves to the moment, but despite Terese's flirtation he doubted she was that kind. Her desk was too meticulously tidy, every ledger in date order on its proper shelf, her quills arranged in order of size by the inkwell. There were no scrolls or manuscripts strewn about, everything had a place. It told him Terese was methodical, in control, and bending her over her desk might be momentarily pleasurable, but it probably wouldn't get him what he needed.

'I'm here representing certain parties,' Merrick said after sampling the liqueur. It was hot and sweet. Whether Terese would prove similar was yet to be discerned. 'Parties who appreciate speed and efficiency. Their cargo is perishable, and they need to be in and out of port within a night. These are parties who also reward discretion. Parties who would be willing to pay generously should you be able to accommodate their needs.'

'Really?' she replied, taking a sip from her glass. When she lowered it there was a half smile on her face, but nothing else.

She's good, thought Merrick. *And clearly this isn't the first time someone's offered her a bribe.*

There were two ways to handle this. You could either try to keep talking and hope that something you said would resonate, that something you offered might sway them into accepting. Or you could keep quiet, wait for them to make the next move, give you a clue as to their price.

And everyone had a price.

Terese's office was clear of sentimentality, but the furniture was finely crafted and expensive, a tapestry hung on one wall depicting trade routes throughout the Midral Sea which must have cost a fortune, and there were two paintings by old masters even Merrick recognised, and he was certainly no connoisseur of the arts. This room was not kitted out by a harbourmaster's earnings. Terese had to have something else on the go, some other scam on the side that paid handsomely. Merrick knew if he kept quiet long enough, she would indicate just how handsomely.

'How's the drink?' she asked after the silence had seemed to go on for an age.

Her resolve was starting to crack. 'It's fine,' Merrick replied.

Another pause. More dead air in which they simply gazed at one another.

'So who are the parties you represent?' she said finally.

'Like you care?' he replied, smiling again so she could see the white of his teeth.

That got him a smile in return.

Then it was gone.

She placed her glass down on the desk beside her and fixed him with a steely glare. 'I've worked this harbour for twenty years,' she said. Suddenly Merrick felt like a child being scolded by his nursemaid. 'Many of the laws and regulations by which this harbour is run were put in place by me. One of them is the penalty for smuggling which, depending on the cargo in question, can run from a hefty fine to the loss of fingers and even to the gallows.'

This wasn't going quite as well as he had expected. Merrick leaned forward and placed his own glass down beside hers. 'I see. Then it appears we have little left to talk about.'

Her smile returned. 'So eager to see me, and yet so quick to leave? Sit down, boy, and let me tell you how it is.' She stood and walked behind her desk, easing herself into her chair so slowly the leather creaked as though it were in pain.

Down to business.

'It will cost three hundred crowns per ship. That will guarantee you a berth for one night, complete discretion, and you stay out of the docking ledger. I want the money in advance and once it's delivered you won't try to contact me again. Are we clear?'

Fucking damn right. 'As a bell, Terese,' Merrick replied, smiling his best smile.

This time she didn't return it.

'Then if there's nothing else, I'm a busy woman.'

She stared at him, but Merrick had already got the message. He couldn't leave the tower and the smell of rotting fish behind him quick enough.

Back on the streets he felt elated. His heart was pounding and he could still taste the warm liqueur on his tongue. What he needed right now was a victory drink.

But where to go?

There were a thousand drinking holes in the city, and Merrick had drunk in pretty much all of them. This called for something special though; there was nothing like celebrating with friends and he wanted somewhere familiar, somewhere he'd be welcomed. There was only one place for it . . . The Soggy Dog!

Of course the last time he'd been here, there'd been a slight incident when he was caught cheating at cards. That in itself wouldn't have been so bad if the man that caught him hadn't subsequently found out Merrick had been sleeping with his wife. But surely everyone would have forgotten about that by now . . . wouldn't they?

When he reached the door of The Soggy Dog he paused. Was it such a good idea? His hand drifted to the hilt of the sword by his side.

There was always that. The one thing he could rely on.

He opened the door, readying himself for a tirade of abuse, steeling himself for a flung stool or table or worse.

They never came.

'Ryder! It's been too long!'

Merrick looked across the tavern to see Uli the barkeep smiling at him from behind the bar. Carefully, Merrick made his way across the alehouse. He saw his old friend Olleg playing cards with Gerlin in a booth, and gave them a nod and a smile. Olleg raised one podgy hand and waved back, whereas Gerlin just scowled. Gerlin had never liked him anyway, so it was a bit much to expect a hug and a kiss from that end.

Karll was also standing at the end of the bar, giving Merrick a sideways glance as he approached. Not surprising after what his wife had done, but it wasn't all Merrick's fault.

'What'll it be, Ryder? Usual?' asked Uli.

Merrick didn't really have a usual; he drank ale, wine, spirits . . . whatever was on offer, but who was he to question his favourite barkeep?

'Absolutely,' he replied. 'And a round of drinks for all my friends.' With that he slapped a handful of coppers on the bar top. 'Keep them coming, Uli. And have one yourself.'

At the promise of free drinks, Olleg and Gerlin finished their card game and practically fell over one another in their rush to get to the bar. Olleg sported a wide grin that split his fat face. Gerlin still wore his scowl.

'Ryder, you old dog,' Olleg bellowed for the entire bar to hear. 'Where've you been hiding yourself these past few days?'

'Here and there, Olleg. You know me – places to go, people to see.'

Olleg laughed and gave him a knowing wink. Uli placed a row of tankards on the table and filled them with wine from a pewter jug.

'More like people's wives to see,' said Karll suddenly, raising his head from his drink and giving Merrick a reproachful look.

'I never meant it to go so far, old friend,' said Merrick, grasping one of the tankards and offering it to Karll. Olleg and Gerlin also took one. 'Here's to water under the bridge. We've all been friends a while now. Let's drink to the future, not dwell on the past.'

'Aye, the future,' said Olleg, raising his tankard.

Reluctantly, Gerlin and Karll raised their tankards and the four of them, along with Uli, drained them with gusto.

When they'd all slammed their tankards back on the bar, and Uli began to fill them once more, Merrick slapped Karll on the arm.

'Never mind, old mate. Have another drink.' Uli had filled the tankards by now and Merrick was quick to offer Karll another one.

'Yes, another drink,' shouted Olleg. 'I don't remember a woman I couldn't forget after a good drink.' He raised his tankard to the ceiling.

Merrick furrowed his brow trying to follow the fat gambler's logic, but it was too early in the day for any of that, and he satisfied himself by draining his tankard and demanding Uli fill it again.

Four rounds later, the room was satisfyingly hazy and the four of them were laughing together again like old times. It was good to block out the world and the Guild and mad slavers, to have a drink with friends without the threat of imminent violence.

The afternoon seemed to go by in a blur. Olleg laughed longest and loudest, but as ever became less annoying the more Merrick had to drink. They even managed to raise a smile from Karll, and it seemed Olleg had been right about the forgetting his woman thing. Gerlin tried to retain his sour expression, but Merrick managed to win him over eventually, and they were soon laughing like little boys about nothing in particular.

As the sky outside started to darken, a gaggle of drunken seamen stumbled in, doubling the number of patrons in an instant. A couple of them looked as if they were up for a bit of trouble, calling Olleg a 'fat fucker' on more than one occasion, as well as spotting Merrick for a preening fop – but he couldn't argue there. It only took two rounds of ale for them to settle in though, and in no time the whole bar was joined together in a raucous chorus of 'The Bosun's Lost his Rigging', quickly followed by a few verses of 'My Dog Digs Deep Ditches'. Olleg insisted on singing the 'put a stoat right down his britches' line louder than any of the sailors.

In all the excitement, Merrick realised he hadn't taken a piss since he'd arrived – no small feat considering the amount he'd had to drink – and stumbled out the back, still laughing at Olleg, at the sailors, at life in general.

He breathed an audible sigh as his piss broke free and pattered into the gutter. Merrick had always pissed like a horse and derived much pleasure from it – many said it was a sign of good health and who was he to argue with that? Once finished he fumbled to tie the drawstring of his breeks, glancing up at the moon, which glared back down at him, fat and blood red.

The killing moon.

'Not a good sign, is it, Ryder?' In his surprise he almost caught the end of his pecker in the knot he was tying. 'Red moon's a bad omen.'

Merrick turned, wobbling slightly, squinting to see who had been watching him through the gloom. 'Who's there?' he called. 'I warn you, I'm armed.'

'We can see that.' A figure walked out of the shadows of the alley, and Merrick felt the hairs prickle at the nape of his neck.

'Shanka! How good to see you.'

'I bet it is,' said Shanka the Lender.

His long, lank hair framed a hard, angular face that was all malice and cruelty. Why had Merrick decided to borrow money from such a man? Was he insane? But then why did anyone borrow from men like Shanka – it was desperation.

'I was going to come and see you, right after I'd—'

'Save it, Ryder. It's too late for any of that shit. You owe me, you're overdue and it's time to pay. One way or the other.'

Merrick knew without checking that the money he'd had in his coin-purse was all but gone. Not that it mattered; even before he'd bought drinks for the entire tavern he hadn't had enough to cover the debt he owed.

'Now, wait a minute, Shanka. I can pay. I'm working on a job for the Guild even as we speak.'

'Yeah, it looks like it. If you were working for the Guild you wouldn't be pissing it up in The Soggy Dog. You'd be doing your best to finish the job so they could pay you . . . and you could pay me.'

'It's the truth,' Merrick said, more desperately than he would have liked.

The shadows behind Shanka suddenly moved and two more figures stepped forward, broad, dangerous-looking bastards. Merrick eyed the door back to the tavern, but before he could even think of using it, someone walked through, someone big and burly he didn't recognise; another one of Shanka's enforcers.

'I want my money or I'll take something you won't want to lose. What'll it be?'

'You'll get your money, Shanka. It's a promise. I've just got to finish the job *uuuffff*.'

The nearest one of Shanka's men hit him in the gut. It was a solid blow, one that went from your belly right down to your toes. Merrick was winded but he managed to stay on his feet, staggering back against the wall, conscious that he was wading ankle deep through muddy piss.

There was nothing else for it. He would have to teach these fuckers a thing or two. There was no way he was letting Shanka and his thugs take liberties.

Merrick stood as straight as he could, placing a hand on the hilt of his sword, the other gripping the top of the sheath.

'I feel it only fair to warn you, Shanka, I know how to use this. Don't test me, or I'll be forced to draw steel. I was schooled in the Collegium of House Tarnath, taught the sixty-six *Principiums Martial* by Lord Macharias himself. I've killed twelve men in single combat and I'll feel no remorse when I stand over your bleeding fucking corpses. Now back off.'

Though his men looked to one another uncertainly, Shanka was distinctly underwhelmed. 'Break this cunt's legs,' he ordered.

If his men bore any doubts, Shanka dispelled them instantly with his command.

Merrick drew his sword . . . or at least the hilt of his sword. As he pulled it free the blade remained stuck in the ill-fitting sheath, leaving Merrick holding nothing but a useless hunk of metal.

Bollocks!

Shanka's men were bearing down on him now, the first one clearly fighting the urge to laugh his head off. Merrick flung the hilt, which hit the man square in the face, and then he tried his best to bravely flee. He hadn't taken three steps before another of Shanka's men hit him in the jaw.

Merrick fell against the wall, his knees giving out beneath him. Another blow to the face and he was lying on the ground, wallowing in a pool of piss and mud.

They weighed in then, sticking the boot in, punching him mercilessly. He felt one of his ribs crack, curled into a ball, but then he took one straight in the spine. Merrick yelped, trying to cover his head and his body and his back, but he simply didn't have enough arms to block the deluge of kicks and punches that were raining down. His nose burst. His lips cracked. One of his teeth came loose.

They grabbed his arms, hauled him up, and through fast swelling eyes Merrick could see Shanka leering at him from behind dark locks of lank greasy hair.

'What did I tell you, you little cu—'

A commotion behind Shanka made him turn. One of his men collapsed forward as if he'd been felled with an axe.

Merrick saw a figure in the shadows, moving fast and gracefully. Shanka's thugs dropped him to the piss-wet floor, and he could do little more than listen to the cries and squeals of men in pain, men in a panic as they were beaten, a crack of a bone breaking, the slap of a body hitting the dirt.

He must have been slipping away fast. Must have taken one too many knocks to the head, because when the commotion had stopped, and he was just about to slide into oblivion, he was sure he heard a woman speak his name.

An angel spoke his name.

TWENTY-SIX

River had studied the palace layout so diligently that the images were scrawled across his mind's eye as elaborately as they had been on the vellum scrolls the Father had given him.

He stood in the darkness of the street, waiting to go forward, but he had already done this a hundred times in his imagining, already scaled the walls, already stalked the palace corridors avoiding the Sentinels as they went about their duties.

Gaining entry to the Crown District had been easy enough; the wall that surrounded it was not high, the guards not vigilant enough to stop River as he *flowed past, silent as the night*. The sentries that roamed the palace would be a different prospect, however. Fortunate, then, that the Father of Killers had someone in the palace, someone who was happy to provide them with detailed layouts. Someone only too willing to patiently plot the movements of the palace guards as they patrolled the massive building.

Two burly sentries moved towards him along the base of the hundred foot wall that surrounded Skyhelm. They were silent, vigilant, rather than locked in conversation as the guards in the Crown District had been. But despite their watchfulness they were just men: they would not see and they would not hear.

River struck out from the dark as they passed by, his footfalls making no sound as he sprinted to the base of the wall and ran eight feet up the stone face before leaping to grasp the thick cornice that sprouted fifteen feet up its side. He pulled himself up easily, gripping the stone wall with fingers of iron, moving like a spider, keeping out of the light given off by the lanterns that ran along the wall's base.

Slowly and silently he eased his way up, keeping himself flat. He knew there would be more sentries at the summit, and were one of them to peer over the side they might well see his black shadow moving towards them like a giant insect. This was the most dangerous time, when he was the most vulnerable, but he could not rush it; he had to remain silent.

When he was almost at the top of the wall he paused and waited, listening for footfalls on the causeway above. They came, slowly but surely, as he waited in the dark.

If the Father's spy had told them true, it would be a crossbowman, lightly armoured. The man's footsteps approached inexorably, then stopped right above where River clung. His heart began to race, but he managed to quell any panic. He was River, *he flowed with the current, raced to meet the sea.* Nothing could stop him.

After a brief pause, the footsteps moved on, and River breathed out long and slow. Once their sound became more distant, he slowly heaved himself up, peering over the lip of the wall. There was no one around in either direction, so River climbed onto the walkway and slipped silently into the shadows.

Even in the dark he could make out the palace, and the grounds surrounding it. He peered through the dimness, trying to spy the sentries that stood between him and the palace. To the north was a path that led up from the main gate. It was laid with fine gravel that would make a hellish racket underfoot and quickly give away his whereabouts. To the west were Skyhelm's gardens, where the lawn would hide his footfalls, but where also patrolled a sentry and his hound. He couldn't see them yet, though the dog might well have caught his scent – a strange new smell in the grounds. But River must press on.

He moved forward, keeping his head low and slipping down the stair that led from the walkway. Most of the palace grounds were brightly lit with ornamental lanterns, but there was still enough shadow for River to conceal himself. The gardens were in darkness, and he was only too eager to reach them and bathe in the concealment they offered.

Once his feet touched the soft grass, River knelt and reached for the sack tied to his back. He loosed it, taking out the contents that slumbered there, and untied the bonds that secured their tiny feet. From a pouch at his waist he took a vial and unstoppered it. The two rabbits he had brought were drugged, but only mildly. The smelling salts in the vial were enough to wake them with a start, and each one ran off in a desperate panic, hurtling into the dark as though a fox were after them.

River watched and waited, *still as the lake in summer*. Almost imme-diately he was greeted by the sound of barking off to the left, along with the desperate shout of a sentry trying to curb his dog. As the snarling moved in one direction, River moved in the other, closing in on the palace.

Torches surrounded the base of Skyhelm, lighting up the magnificent building like a pyre. It rose up into the air, myriad windows adorning its faces, towers rising still further out from the main structure. The corridors within would be like a maze, but one River had studied intently. He knew them by heart.

An armoured sentry walked beneath a pergola at the base of the building, and River waited in the dark for him to pass before sprinting into the light. He planted a foot on one of the granite pillars that held up the structure and leapt to the roof.

His feet padded quietly across the tiled roof, making barely a sound as he reached the wall and the base of a huge window. It was open – the Father's man in the palace had done his work well.

River slid the window open a touch more, squeezing himself into the room beyond. It was huge inside, a hall clearly used for entertaining the elite of the city, but now it lay silent and in darkness.

He moved across the marble floor to the northern end of the room where stood a massive double door. As he opened it, a chink of light lanced in and he paused, eyes fast adjusting to the corridor beyond. There were no sentries and he moved out into the well-lit corridor, feeling vulnerable once again in the harsh light, but keeping his heartbeat steady with the power of his will, *a will none could withstand, like the coming of the tides.*

A staircase rose up at the end of the corridor, which would take him to the upper levels of the palace. There, he would find fewer guards. And there he would find his mark.

Before he could take two steps a voice echoed down the corridor, rooting him to the spot.

'Who goes? Stop where you are.'

An armoured figure was moving towards him from the other end of the passage. But how could this be? River had studied the plans: he knew the patrols, had learned them until he could recite them in his sleep.

Clearly the Father's man was not as proficient as they had believed.

River merely stood tall in the corridor, showing the palms of his hands, which were splayed out to either side, giving the sentry no reason to think he would resist. The armoured man had drawn his sword now, brandishing it threateningly, but they were in a tight corridor – he would not be able to make a swing.

Not that River would ever have given him the chance.

Before he could reach out with a huge gauntleted hand, River moved in, one hand pushing the sword aside, the other reaching to grab the lip of the sentry's helmet. He slammed the man's head into the wall, the resultant clang louder than River would have liked, but necessary if he was going to down him quickly. The greatsword went clattering to the floor as the man struggled desperately to grab hold of his assailant, but River was on him now, moving with speed and grace, *like the rapids flowing through the mountains*, and had his arm about the sentry's throat. The man was strong, gripping River's arm with incredible force, but he would never be able to wrestle himself free, not before he succumbed to lack of air. Steadily the strength left his limbs, and he sagged in River's arms.

With some difficulty, River managed to pull the guard into the great, dark hall, concealing him in the shadows. There was no need to kill him: he would not wake for some time.

River took the stairs three at a time, still silent as the death he had come to bring, brushing past a curtain, *like the currents past the reeds*. This time, though, he was even more vigilant. If the Father's man inside the palace had made one mistake, how many more might he have made? River could not afford to be stopped before he completed his task, could not afford to stumble into another lone sentry, or two, or three. Though he would be able to dispatch them easily enough, the alarm would most likely be raised, making it doubtful he would reach his mark before he was overwhelmed.

River stopped at the end of another passage, hearing the laughter of men through an open door. It was a ramshackle chamber that smelled strongly of male musk and pipe smoke. As he moved past, the men inside, unaware he was there, japed with one another, their faces creased in mirth.

It made River pause for a moment as he passed, remembering one of the Father's lessons.

Laughter is for the weak, he had said, with a swipe of the lash. River had flinched, his movement provoking yet another stinging lick of the scourge. *It reveals the hearts of men, and they too are weak. Your heart must be stone, like the pebble on the riverbed, unyielding, immovable.*

He had often wondered what it must be like to share such mirth with another man. River had brothers, true, but he shared no brotherhood with them. They did not laugh like others, and they shared no love.

Such things were not for him. He was not weak like other men. He was strong, *like the current after spring rains*. Not prone to the failings that afflicted the weak. It was why he could not be stopped.

Up and up he went, the pattern of the corridors vivid in his mind. He knew his way before he reached a junction, could see the route laid out, forming before him even though he had never trodden these hallways before. Here and there were patrols of guards; here and there were courtiers and serfs going about their night time business, but River was a shadow, moving about them like a hushed breeze.

The door to her chamber stood ahead of him. There was no one there to guard it, no one there to stand in his way. He grasped the handle and the door opened with merciful silence, and in a short breath he was inside, greeted by the near darkness within.

A single candle guttered by the window, spreading a soft light across the chamber. Stairs led up to a huge bed which rested on a raised dais, its four posts carved of thick oak, a canopy of woven fabric covering its top. River didn't move, allowing his eyes to adjust, allowing himself time to focus on his mark. He could hear her soft, even breath through the blackness and as he took a tentative step forward he pulled a single blade from its sheath.

Then he stopped.

A thought seemed to press in his head, a doubt he had felt before. More than once.

This girl was innocent.

But the Father of Killers had condemned her.

From what little River understood of it, this was her father's war . . . the king's war. Nothing to do with her.

But River could not disobey the Father of Killers.

She had committed no crime.

If he did not do as he was bid, he would be punished. Granted another scar to join those already displaying the shame of failure and weakness on his face.

He took another step forward, creeping silently towards her, feeling the reassurance of the blade in his hand. This was what he did. This was what he was made to do. He was River, *the unstoppable river*, who lived to carry out his Father's bidding.

But what right did he have? No matter how many times he had been reminded with the word and the lash, he still could not justify it in his head.

Another step took him up the stair to the dais on which the bed stood. Her breath was so soft, her dreams clearly untroubled. River could not remember the last time he had slept untroubled by nightmares, the last time he had not been plagued by terrors.

But to succumb to them would only show weakness, to admit to them would only bring his Father's wrath.

He was at the bedside now, and she was within arm's length. It would take only a single swift strike. One quick cut to end her life before she even had time to wake. River pressed forward as the flickering candlelight showed him her face.

A face he knew.

As his heart filled with a horror worse than a thousand night terrors, the blade slipped from his hand, clattering to the wooden floor.

It was her, the girl from the gardens. His girl: the one of a hundred secret meetings. The girl of a thousand gentle kisses.

Jay.

She woke with a sharp intake of breath, her flame red hair falling about her face. She saw him standing there, a shadow in the night, but she did not scream.

'Who are you?' she asked, after what seemed like an age. There was no fear in her voice, and River could only admire her for that.

Slowly he lowered his face so she could see his scarred features in the light.

She smiled, though uncertainly, as she fought with her lack of understanding.

'What are you doing here?' Jay rose from her bed. 'How did you get in?'

He did not answer, could not. What would he tell her – that he had been sent by the Father of Killers? That she was marked for death and he was the one to carry out the sentence? He could not tell her, and instead he stared at her, at that face, that beauty that never failed to make his heart leap.

She moved from her bed and River could only watch her as she took another candle and lit it from the last barely glowing embers of the fire in her room. As she moved back towards him, her beautiful face radiant in the light, she suddenly saw his blade, lying between them on the floor.

'What's that?' she asked, her curiosity extinguished as realisation dawned.

Still he could not speak, transfixed where he stood. His mouth worked, forming words that never came. She shook her head in disbelief. He shook his in denial. This could not be. She was the only one he had ever . . .

The door to the chamber burst open. River spun to see a young man, little older than himself, come striding in. He was tall, dark haired, walking with all the sureness of a trained warrior, his hand poised over the sword at his hip.

'Janessa, get back,' the warrior ordered, seeming unsurprised at River's presence.

'Raelan, wait,' Janessa replied, but the warrior was already advancing, his sword singing from its sheath. River was already moving, though, *flowing with the banks, coursing to the seas.*

The young warrior struck, his blow measured and precise, his arm well practised. River could have dodged it blindfolded, but he allowed it to pass him by a hair's breadth as he moved in, faster than his opponent could see. Before the man could recover his stance, River had grasped the sword at the hilt, his elbow striking up to hit jawbone.

As his enemy crashed to the ground, River twisted the weapon in his grip and raised it for a killing blow. It was heavier than he was used to, a knight's weapon, but one he could still wield. It would be a quick death.

'No!' Jay cried, covering the young warrior with her body, before River could land that final blow. He paused, holding the sword aloft until he saw the look in her eyes – the fear and hurt and defiance.

River's heart clenched in his chest. He opened his mouth to speak, but again, no words would come. With a heartbroken breath he sent the sword spinning across the room where it struck the floorboards.

The warrior was still dazed on the ground where Jay stood. Her brow was furrowed in confusion but still she took River by the hand.

'You have to run,' she said. 'Or they will kill you.'

He turned to go, moving towards the open window, but knew he could not leave without some kind of explanation. If he might never see her again he had to make it clear he would never have hurt her. He had not come to this place to kill *her*, but to kill another, a princess. Not her . . . not Jay . . . not his love.

'I—'

His words were cut short by a scything pain in his side. He staggered, his hand reaching to his hip where it came away covered in blood. The young warrior, still dazed but on his knees, was holding River's blade in his fist, now also covered in blood.

Jay looked at him, anguish writ in her eyes.

River took a step towards her. He wanted to hold her, to tell her of his regret, that he had had no choice in this, but before he could utter a word more figures burst into the room – armoured sentries, their swords drawn.

He spun on his heel, stumbling a little from the pain, but keeping his composure.

He was River.

He had no weakness, no doubt, no thought but that of escape.

In two steps he was at the window.

Another – he had leapt into the night.

TWENTY-SEVEN

'So what do I do now?' It pained her to ask such a question, Kaira was so used to a life of regimented control. This was a situation to which she was wholly unsuited.

'I suggest you start by praying he wakes up,' Buttercup replied. She was treating it like a game, despite the fact that a man might be dying.

The man she had learned was Merrick Ryder lay on her bed in the Pony and Fiddle. Kaira had done her best to treat the man's injuries – she was no battlefield chirurgeon, but she knew how to stitch and dress a wound. His head was bandaged, both his eyes beginning to swell, his nose bust, probably broken, and his lip split in three places. For the bruises on his body she could do little. If his ribs were broken he would be of little use. Kaira could only hope Merrick Ryder was tougher than he looked.

Right now he didn't look even remotely tough.

'And what if he dies? What then?'

'Then we'll find some other way to raise you through the ranks of the Guild. Ryder's not the only card in our hand.'

Kaira glanced down at Merrick, watching his chest rise and fall, his breath shallow but even. What she knew of the man painted a rather ugly picture but she couldn't help but feel some sympathy. She had been brought up in the Temple of Autumn, trained as a peerless fighter, but also a defender of the weak and helpless. She had been raised alongside the Daughters of Arlor, that order dedicated to the care of those who could not care for themselves. Their gentle and forgiving character served to assuage the martial temperament of the Shieldmaidens, and, despite

Kaira's disciplined upbringing, she could not help but feel compassion for a man beaten almost to death, despite his base, criminal nature.

Buttercup, however, had no such compassion.

'Look, I'll be back by first light. If he's dead by then we'll wait until dark, dump his body in the Storway and persuade Palien to give you another position. Until then . . . make yourself comfortable with your new friend.'

She winked and made for the door.

'You're just going to leave me here with him?' Kaira did not relish the prospect of acting as nursemaid.

'Yes I am. Don't worry, I think you'll be safe enough.' She gestured to the beaten and bandaged form lying helpless on the bed. 'Or might you find it hard to control yourself? A life cloistered in that monastery, no men around. I've heard about women like you.'

Kaira clenched her fists. Buttercup's suggestion was a quip too far, but she kept control. 'Get out,' she said.

Buttercup smiled, but left promptly all the same. Even she realised she was walking a dangerous path by provoking Kaira.

As the door slammed, Merrick gave a moan, his broken lips moving as he tried to speak. Kaira dipped a clean cloth in a bowl of cold water and placed it to his lips, squeezing a couple of drops into his mouth. It seemed to calm him.

She had wanted to intervene sooner. Wanted to take Shanka and his men before they turned Merrick's face to mush, but Buttercup had held her back. She wanted Merrick grateful, and in no condition to refuse her help, but Kaira certainly hadn't envisioned that he'd end up almost dead. As they'd begun to beat him, she had moved as quickly as she could, but it hadn't been quite quick enough. Their only link to the inner circle of the Guild was dancing on a sword edge and might fall into oblivion at any moment.

If Merrick could not help her succeed in her mission, how long might it take to be granted an audience with the powers behind the Guild? Could she be in the wilderness – separated from her sisters and all the life she knew – for months, even years? It was unthinkable.

It pained her that there was nothing she could do about it. Kaira Stormfall would have fought any man or beast in defence of the weak and to carry out the will of Vorena, but in this she felt truly powerless. Her entire future lay with a man who might die from his wounds at any second.

But it was what it was.

'Are you all right over there? You look a bit concerned about something.'

Kaira started at the weak voice. Merrick was looking at her through his blackened eyes, his cracked lips formed into a sly grin.

'No. I . . . er . . .' She realised she must have been scowling. 'You're awake.' *Of course he was awake, what a stupid thing to say.*

'Well spotted,' he replied, shifting his body, trying to sit. It only made him wince with pain.

'Don't try to move,' she said, taking a step towards him. She laid a hand on his chest to settle him back down, but he tried to push her away. Clearly a stubborn one.

'I'm fine,' he said, grimacing at the pain. Kaira helped him sit up, positioning his pillows so he was more comfortable. 'Though it does feel like someone kicked the living shit out of me.'

'They did,' she replied.

He looked at her, afresh. 'You're my angel,' he said, his grin cracking the scab that had formed on his lip, making him wince once more.

'Please don't talk,' she said, reaching for the water bowl.

'You wouldn't believe the number of people who say that to me. Even when my lips aren't smashed up like a blind cobbler's thumbs.' She offered him the sodden cloth, but he just stared at her. 'You have the most beautiful smile.'

She hadn't even realised she was smiling.

Kaira steeled herself. She was not here to make light with the man – especially a man responsible for brokering slaves.

'Be quiet and take this,' she demanded. It was a command that brooked no argument, and Merrick seemed to take the hint.

Having dabbed his bleeding lip with the cloth he regarded her again with a raised eyebrow. 'So, who are you?'

'My name is Kaira . . .' *Stormfall. Your name is Kaira Stormfall. But then . . . you are Stormfall no longer.*

'Kaira, you have my eternal thanks. Do you make a habit of rescuing vulnerable men in the street?'

'I was sent by Palien to ensure you were kept from harm.'

'And you very nearly managed it.' He grimaced as he shifted, trying to get more comfortable. Eventually he seemed to find the position that hurt least. 'I've got to say, his taste in bodyguards has vastly improved of late.'

213

'You're lucky I arrived when I did.' *Though you'd have been much luckier if Buttercup had allowed me to intervene earlier.*

'My dear, it's clear I'm lucky you arrived at all.' He smiled.

Kaira suddenly felt self-conscious, realising she was looking at him intently. She felt a sudden urge to hurt him, but also to smile back – even thank him for his compliment.

'So, Palien has sent me a bodyguard? How thoughtful.' Merrick shifted his weight, swinging his legs over the side of the bed. Kaira helped him, moving in close, and as she did so he turned his face towards hers.

That smile again. So close.

She took a step backwards.

'Would you mind bringing me a mirror, angel? I'd like to take a look at the damage.' He gestured to his battered face.

Kaira glanced about the room. She had little need for mirrors, only ever relying on them before ceremonies to ensure her regalia looked its best, polished to a reflective sheen, her sword at the proper level on her hip, her cloak draped in the correct fashion. Still, she spotted a hand mirror sitting on the shelf and passed it to Merrick. He paused for a second, as if he was uncertain he wanted to see. Then he held it up before his face, regarding himself at first with disgust, then acceptance and finally approval.

'Could be worse, I suppose.'

'It won't look so bad once you've been cleaned up,' she said. He seemed somewhat reassured. 'Can you stand up?'

'Only one way to find out, I suppose.' He placed the mirror on the bed and held his hands out for her to help him.

Kaira pulled him unsteadily to his feet. He breathed sharply through his teeth, but managed to remain standing.

'Nothing broken at least,' he said, taking a shaky step forward.

'Good,' she replied, conscious that he was still holding her hands.

He looked at her and smiled again. She wanted to smile back, but tried to resist the temptation. Kaira was not here to make friends; she was here to ensure this man lived long enough for her to finish her mission.

'You know, you have the most beautiful eyes,' he said. For all his bluster, his words sounded genuine.

It made Kaira want to hit him more than ever.

'You should lie down again and rest. Tomorrow you continue with your task.' She wrested her hands from his and he sank back to the bed with a soft moan.

'Not one for conversation, are you?'

'I speak when it's necessary,' she replied. 'Not just to fill the air with noise.'

'Suit yourself. Just trying to be friendly.' He adjusted his head on the pillows with a sigh.

Kaira felt a twinge of guilt. Perhaps he *was* just being friendly. Perhaps he *did* think she had beautiful . . .

He is a villain, a trader in human misery, and as soon as you have eliminated the heads of the Guild you might well have to do the same to him.

The room felt stuffy. The smell of blood and sweat, though not unfamiliar to Kaira, became stifling. When Merrick closed his eyes she stepped out into the corridor, taking a deep breath. The air was not much better, but at least she wasn't sharing it with a man she might have to kill.

When she eventually stepped back inside, Merrick was snoring loudly. Kaira waited in the chair for morning.

It was long after dawn when Buttercup arrived, but Merrick was still sleeping. Thankfully his snoring had ceased as the first light began to creep through the chamber's single window.

'Still alive then,' said Buttercup, as Merrick stirred, then opened his eyes.

'Another angel,' he said with a smile. 'Must be my lucky day. Any chance one of you could run along and find me a cup of wine?'

'For now, your drinking days are over. Look at the mess it's got you in.' Buttercup looked him up and down with a shake of her head. 'From now on it's water or nothing.'

'Water?' Buttercup might just have suggested he drink his own urine. 'Are you trying to poison me, woman? Everyone knows what comes down the Storway isn't fit for dogs or peasants.'

'Get used to it. And get up; you've lain there long enough. You're not being paid to loaf around in bed. There are things that require your attention.'

Scowling, but not complaining, Merrick sat up gingerly, then pulled himself to his feet. Kaira noted he was much steadier than the night before. Had he been feigning or was he just healing fast? Time would tell.

'Just for the record,' he said, vainly trying to dust down his filthy, blood-smeared clothing, 'I'm not being paid at all. Apparently my debts with Shanka were going to be settled, but if last night was anything to go by it's not happened, has it?'

'That's in hand,' Buttercup replied.

'In hand?' Merrick looked incredulous. 'In hand? Look at my fucking face.' He offered up his pulped visage.

Buttercup was unmoved. 'And it would be much, much worse without our help. Stop moaning like an old washerwoman. Put your boots on.'

Merrick grumbled but began fumbling with his boots.

Buttercup turned to Kaira. 'See he gets cleaned up, then stay with him . . . at all times! Don't even let him use the privy alone.'

Merrick appeared taken with that, but a stern look from Kaira made him shrug and turn back to the boots.

'Now, if you're both clear on what's expected of you, I have business elsewhere.' She paused on the threshold. 'And see if you can find him a decent blade. That last one wasn't up to much. We wouldn't want our legendary swordsman left holding a useless weapon, would we?'

She winked at Merrick then left. He threw her an obscene gesture – once she was gone.

'I'm starting to dislike that woman,' he said. 'There's something about her that I just don't trust.'

You don't know the half of it.

'Where are we bound next?' asked Kaira, keen to change the subject.

'I have to get cleaned up, obviously. Find a decent change of clothes. Then there's a lovely tavern in Dockside I was thinking of dropping in on. And you're welcome to join me. It never hurts to have a beautiful companion on your arm whilst frequenting a favourite drinking haunt.'

'But Buttercup said—'

'Buttercup can kiss my arse . . . if you'll pardon the phrase. With what I've been through in the past few days I deserve a drink at the very least.'

'Have you not had enough to drink recently?'

He frowned at her. 'What? Are you thinking of joining the Daughters or something? Live a little. Let your hair down.' He glanced at her short cropped hair. 'You know what I mean.'

'You have a task and it is my job to ensure you complete it. There will be no diversion. No drinking, no alehouses. Nothing must distract you.'

He looked quizzical. 'Nothing? Are you sure about that?'

'Yes, I am.'

'And just how are you going to—'

She struck out, grabbing his hair in one hand and pressing hard against the yellowing bruise on one of his eyes. Merrick yowled like a wounded alley cat, reaching up to stop her, but she slapped his hands away.

216

'All right! All right!' he yelled. 'You win!' He fell back on the bed, his hand covering his eye. 'There's no need for more violence.'

'Good. Then we understand one another?'

'I understand that my angel's turned into a maniac. I'm starting to realise why Palien hired you.' He gave her a wounded look. Then fingered the bandage around his head.

'It's time we left,' Kaira said. She had made her point, and had shown she knew how to handle Merrick from now on.

Obediently he stood up then walked to the door, finally managing to pull the bloodstained dressing clear and throwing it to the ground.

'You're buying me a new sword,' he said petulantly as he left the chamber before her.

As Kaira turned and locked the door, she couldn't suppress a grin.

TWENTY-EIGHT

The palace of Skyhelm was in upheaval. From two floors above, Janessa could hear Garret barking at his men. Odaka's bass voice also rumbled along the corridors, frequently clearing them of servants and handmaids even before he appeared.

Janessa sat in her chamber, the governess at her side. Graye stood in one corner of the room, her face anguished. Though the floor had been cleaned of blood, some still stained the rug that covered most of the chamber. Janessa could only stare at that stain, a reminder that River had been badly wounded.

River, who had come to *slay* her as she slept.

Where Raelan was she didn't know; the young lord had been carried off by a contingent of his father's bodyguard.

He had saved her life. Or had he? Had she really been in mortal danger? Would River really have murdered her? He had spoken so tenderly to her only the other day. Opened his heart to her. Had it been a ruse, something planned all along? But why had he not killed her when they had first met? It would have been so easy to take her life unobserved at their meeting place. Surely much easier than breaking into Skyhelm.

Yes, he had told her of his life: of abuse, of hardship and being forced to do things increasingly alien to his nature. But never for a moment could she have imagined this – imagined he was . . . what? A killer? An assassin?

Of course she had wondered at his scars, those marks of maltreatment, but she had never thought . . .

Perhaps she had always been in danger. Certainly Garret was assuming

218

she still was. He had doubled the number of Sentinels on every post, set about castigating the knights on duty, screaming at them like a madman as he admonished them for their lack of vigilance.

And what would her father do when he found out? The king was battling to save the Free States. But if he knew that his daughter was in danger from assassins, he would almost certainly abandon the defence of his kingdom, if only for a while, and ride back to protect her himself.

She could not impose such a choice on him. He must be allowed to focus on protecting his people.

Janessa stood up, making Governess Nordaine, who had wearily succumbed to sleep, stir from her slumber.

'I must speak to Odaka,' Janessa said.

Graye looked shocked. 'We must stay here for now. We can't go—'

'I can do what I like, Graye.'

She hadn't meant to snap; Graye was only thinking of her safety, but she couldn't allow word of this to reach her father before he faced the Khurtas in battle. Nothing must distract him now.

'Graye is right,' said Nordaine groggily. 'We must stay here.' But Janessa was already making her way to the door.

She hurried down the corridors of Skyhelm, nightgown flowing, her hair a mess, calling out that she must speak to Odaka. The two Sentinels who had been assigned to her struggled to keep up. Janessa knew she might appear hysterical, treading the corridors of the palace like some wild banshee, but she didn't care.

No one dared to stop her, the palace servants moving from her path, Nordaine and Graye following behind but not daring to restrain her.

Janessa reached the lower corridors, guided by Odaka's voice to a chamber door. There she stopped to dismiss Nordaine and Graye.

'You can go now,' she told them.

'What do you mean?' Graye asked.

'I have to do this alone. I am a girl no longer, Graye. I will be queen one day, and you will not always be at my shoulder in case I should stumble.'

Governess Nordaine made to speak, but Janessa held up a hand to stay her, surprised when it worked.

The women left Janessa at the door.

Steeling herself for the confrontation with Odaka, Janessa opened the door, but before she could tell the regent of her wishes, that her father not be told of the attempt on her life, she stopped in her tracks.

Odaka was not alone. Baroness Isabelle Magrida looked with slight amusement towards Janessa as she stormed in. Her son Leon complemented his mother's gesture as a sly smile crept up one side of his mouth.

'Majesty,' said Odaka, bowing as she entered.

The baroness inclined her head with a curtsy and Leon granted her a slight bow, as though the effort were almost too great.

Janessa regarded the three of them for a moment, unsure of how to proceed. She wanted to tell Odaka that what had happened in the palace must be kept a secret, at least for now, but not in front of the baroness or her son. It did not concern them, and it was certain they lacked discretion.

It was Odaka who broke the silence first. 'I was just reassuring our guests,' he said. 'Skyhelm is secure, the most secure place in the city.'

Isabelle seemed unconvinced. 'And yet an assassin was allowed to breach its defences, regent. If it had not been for Lord Raelan, the princess would have been murdered. Had my own son been chambered closer, the assassin would now be dead, instead of escaped into the night.' She turned to Janessa, affecting a look of sympathy. 'And how are you, my dear? You need to rest in bed after such an ordeal.' *My dear?* Janessa winced. 'If there is anything my son or I can do for you, please do not hesitate to ask.'

And what would you do, Baroness? Don some armour, grab a halberd and stand at my door of an evening?

'I am most grateful for your concern,' Janessa said, affecting a smile almost as insincere as that of the baroness. 'But I can assure you I am quite well. If that is all, there are matters I must now discuss with the regent.'

Isabelle's expression curdled briefly, but her mask was back up in an instant. 'Of course, my dear.' *My dear again? I am "majesty" to the likes of you!* 'Come, Leon. We will away to our chambers and rest . . . if we can.'

They bowed and left.

Janessa immediately turned to Odaka.

'Has word of tonight's events been sent to my father yet?' she asked.

Odaka frowned, shaking his head. 'We have been ensuring the palace was secure, my lady.'

'Good. My father is not to know about this until the trouble in the north is concluded.'

Trouble? Janessa realised she had made it sound as though her father were settling some minor diplomatic dispute, not fighting a war for the very survival of the realm and the lives of his subjects.

'But your father must be told. Amon Tugha has struck within the capital, within his palace, and against his daughter. The Elharim has made his intentions clear – he will show no mercy, not stop until the king and the Mastragall line is eradicated. I cannot keep that from him.'

'You can and will, Odaka. This must not reach my father's ears. He must not be distracted at this crucial time.' Again, she had not meant to sound so forceful, even dictatorial, but it was almost becoming second nature.

Odaka said nothing. Janessa wondered whether she had overstepped the mark, but remembered his words: *And I live to obey.*

'Your father will find out about this eventually. When he learns I have kept it from him—'

'At *my* command. You have kept it from him on *my* order. My father must also learn that if I am to rule one day, I must be allowed to make decisions. If he hears of this would-be assassin he will send men back to the city to protect me, men who need to be fighting under my father's banner. The news will burden him unnecessarily. I cannot allow that. I *will* not allow that.'

Odaka finally nodded. 'As you wish, my lady. I will see to it that no word is sent until after the armies of the Free States have faced the Khurtic horde.'

Janessa felt calm. In control. She almost thanked Odaka, but managed to stop herself.

'Has anyone been hurt? Other than Lord Raelan, I mean?'

'One of the palace sentries was injured, but he will live. Unless Garret throttles him for his failure. Other than that, only Lord Raelan encountered the assassin.'

'And how is he? Does he recover?'

As though on cue, the door to the chamber opened. Two Sentinels entered and behind them strode Lord Raelan, flanked by his own bodyguard: two of Valdor's notorious Border Wolves. These grizzled men from the north were sticking close to their young ward.

All three took to the knee before Janessa and bowed their heads.

'Your majesty,' said Raelan. 'I heard you were here. It gladdens me to see you safe.'

Something about him had changed, something that made Janessa somehow pleased to see him, and glad that he seemed unharmed.

'Please, Lord Raelan, stand.' He and his men obeyed, and she saw the yellowing bruise on his jaw where he had been struck by River. 'You are well, I hope?'

'I am, my lady. And all the better to see you safe.'

She examined his face with concern. 'Your wounds . . .'

'It is nothing. I've had worse in the training yard. I am only sorry that I allowed your assassin to escape. Would that I had been able to capture him.'

'Yes . . . it is regrettable he escaped. It seems the Elharim's influence has reached Steelhaven already.'

'But you are safe now, my lady. I vow to protect you. My wolves and I will be your guard night and day.'

Janessa felt Odaka shuffle uncomfortably at the suggestion the Sentinels could not protect their princess but he remained silent.

'I am flattered that you see it as your duty to protect me, but I assure you, Lord Raelan, it isn't necessary. I am quite safe. The guard has been doubled and my door is watched over day and night. An army of assassins could not reach me now.'

'Very well, my lady. But please know I am your servant. An attack on you is an attack on everything I hold dear.'

Janessa smiled. 'You flatter me with your devotion, Lord Raelan.'

Raelan stepped forward, looking somewhat uncomfortable. He lowered his voice so only she could hear.

'You should know, my lady, that my devotion to you is unswerving. I would do anything for you. Go to any lengths to protect you. Give my life even.'

Janessa was taken aback. Where was such an outpouring of emotion when he had proposed? Did he mean this, or was he just play acting, trying to win her over that she might ultimately gift him the throne?

'I . . . I appreciate your words, Lord Raelan. And do not doubt that I am still considering your . . . proposal.' The word almost stuck in her throat.

He shook his head. 'Please, my lady . . . Janessa. My concern, my fear for you, is real. It would destroy me to think anyone might harm you.'

Raelan was gazing at her ardently, his voice no longer lowered. He didn't give a damn if his profession of love was heard by everyone present, even his grim bodyguard.

Janessa reeled. Did he really love her? Was this baring of his soul what she had looked for?

It was overwhelming. She felt uncertain before all those eyes, awaiting her response. Should she accept his proposal of marriage now, in front of Odaka and Raelan's own men?

'Thank you,' was all she could manage to say.

Janessa glanced down, realising she was still in her nightgown. She managed to twitch out an awkward smile from one corner of her mouth, spun on her heel and aimed for the door.

Her head was ablaze with frantic thought as she rushed back to her bedchamber. She willed back tears, wishing now that her father *was* here. He would know what to do, he would tell her what to do.

But then he had already told her – his wishes were that she should marry Raelan.

A Sentinel stood at her chamber door.

'I have been sent to be the guard within your room, majesty. On the orders of the regent.'

She turned on him, her anxiety fuelling her rage like a spark to a fire. 'Am I expected to be watched while I sleep?' she bellowed, glaring up at the armoured man.

He made some uncertain noises, clearly at a loss for what to do. The knight could neither refuse the orders of the regent nor ignore the anger of his princess. Janessa felt guilty. This man had done her no wrong; her outburst had been unacceptable.

'Oh, just stay out here,' she cried, pushing open the door to the bedchamber and slamming it behind her.

The tears came then. Janessa managed to stifle the sobs, to preserve her dignity. One day she would have to rule this land, this city, and a weak queen would be worse than no queen at all.

And then she sensed something lurking in the shadows at the far corner of the room. Though almost imperceptible in the gloom, she could tell the figure was shivering in the dark.

Janessa might have screamed, might have fled back through the door, but she didn't. Somehow she knew . . .

He moved into the light, hood drawn back, his face now visible in the candlelight – that scarred yet beautiful face.

Janessa rushed to him as he stumbled forward, and she managed to support him in her arms. She felt the feverish heat of his body, the clamminess of his skin, the thin film of sweat that covered him. He clutched his side where his clothing was crimson-stained. His hands were covered in congealed blood.

With some effort, Janessa moved him to her bed, where he fell back, gritting his teeth but making no sound.

'We have to stop the bleeding,' she said, gathering a fistful of linen sheets and vainly trying to staunch the blood oozing from his side.

She was weeping – but he was smiling.

He raised a hand to her face to let a tear trickle onto his bloodstained finger.

She opened her mouth to speak, but before she could utter a word the door to her chamber opened.

'I know you said you wanted to be alone, but I couldn't sleep. Garret's all but screaming the place down,' said Graye as she walked in. 'I'm glad I'm not one—'

She stopped, staring at them both on the bed, the colour draining from her face.

Janessa sprinted across the room, slamming the door shut before Graye could think to run out. She placed a hand over Graye's mouth before she could cry out in alarm.

Janessa could see the fear in her friend's eyes.

'You have to trust me, Graye. You have to trust me as you never have before.' Graye's eyes flitted to the man lying on the bed. 'He is my friend, Graye – you have to believe me. He would never hurt me. He couldn't.' Janessa knew how hard this must be to believe. 'If I move my hand will you cry out?' Graye hesitated then shook her head.

Janessa removed her hand.

'What in the hells is going on?' Graye said in a hoarse whisper.

'I don't have time to explain right now, Graye. All I can tell you is that he's wounded and I have to stop the bleeding. Will you help me?'

Graye looked over to the man lying on the bed, clutching the crimson sheet to his side, his breath laboured.

'Of course,' she replied.

TWENTY-NINE

She came for him before dawn, awakening him as the grey light of an autumn day began to filter through the shutters. This time she didn't speak, but Waylian knew what to do.

Silently he donned his robe, not even bothering to splash water on his face, before following her down the winding staircase to the base of the Tower.

Part of him was thankful no one else had yet risen. For the past few days he'd been too ashamed to show his face in the communal areas, far too embarrassed to see another soul. He could feel them laughing behind his back, pointing their fingers and whispering to one another.

'There goes the idiot from the refectory.'

'That's the one who screams out random profanities.'

'Yes, I hear he tugs himself to sleep every night too, then cries into his pillow after.'

Waylian could do without the ridicule. He had enough to deal with already, feeling so out of place here now. The books he read made no more sense, the lessons he attended were no more enlightening and it was only a matter of time before he was dismissed from the Tower altogether.

Then at least he would be able to return home.

There would be a certain shame in that, of course, but Waylian didn't care. He could weather comments about his failure: they would die off soon enough. Then he could become a scribe or scholar of some kind, and settle into a life outside the realms of magick.

He was damned sure he wouldn't miss it.

His mistress was waiting for him as he made his way down the stairs.

Mercifully there was no disdain in her eyes on this particular morning. She might still resemble a leering gargoyle, lacking emotion, still look fearsome, but Waylian didn't feel any particular hostility was being directed at him. She was just indifferent to him.

Gelredida was through the great double doors before he reached the bottom of the stairs, and Waylian was at pains to keep up with her. Not that it mattered. He must be her silent shadow. Why she even wanted him along was a mystery: it wasn't as though he could contribute any great insight into things, though he knew by now what kind of things they were heading off to investigate.

This was the third night she had summoned him. The first had been to investigate the hideous, eviscerated corpse that had caused him to evacuate his guts all over the floor. The second was just after he had managed to humiliate himself in front of Gerdy and Bram and the rest of the students. She had come for him that night, waking him from his embarrassed dreams and leading him through the streets to another house surrounded by Greencoats. This time there had been no crowd, no cloying mass of humanity trying to get a sight of the carnage. That murder had been just as grotesque as the first, the body of the man just as badly butchered, the symbols daubed on the walls even more obscene to look upon, though Waylian had just as little understanding of their significance. That time, though, he had managed to hold his evening meal down, despite its insistence on rising towards his mouth.

Now, as he followed Gelredida through the shabby streets, he was more sanguine about what he might see. He guessed one mutilated body was much the same as any other. Tonight's murder would probably hold few surprises for him.

Waylian took little notice of their route. The streets all looked the same to him: ramshackle houses built too close together, squatting in muddy streets with muddier beggars pleading for coin.

He had expected the Greencoats to be waiting for his mistress as they had been previously, so it came as something of a surprise when she stopped and knocked on the unguarded front door of a huge stone building, its windows long since boarded over.

After some time a shutter in the door opened. There was no exchange of words, but whoever lurked inside must have recognised Gelredida, since the door quickly opened and Waylian's mistress walked in.

He had never seen the interior of a whorehouse before, but still, this was not what he would have expected. The door opened on a wide room, with several sofas scattered about. Scantily clad girls of various shapes and sizes sat around, some looking bored, others fearful, one openly weeping. This one was being comforted by a whore with a bosom larger than Waylian had ever seen.

It almost made him resentful being so close to these women. He had heard of whores and the men that took solace in their company, of course, but he had never been so close to one. Being in their presence made him feel grimy, as if he might fall victim to some disease just by being in the same room.

Magistra Gelredida was greeted by an ageing woman. Her face was heavily wrinkled and looked grotesque, being as gaudily painted as those of the other whores. She might possibly have been desirable once, it was hard to tell now, age and a livid scar beside her left eye having long since kissed goodbye to her beauty.

'You've told no one?' Gelredida asked.

The whore raised one painted eyebrow. 'What do you think?' she replied.

'And these?' The Red Witch gestured to the score of girls in their various states of undress.

'We both know what'll assure their silence.'

Gelredida produced a pouch from out of nowhere, and Waylian heard the telltale chink of coins as she placed it in the hand of the brothel-mistress.

'She's upstairs,' said the old whore. 'The door's open. The smell should guide you right enough.'

With that she was off into another room hidden by a thick curtain.

Gelredida took the stairs, and Waylian was quick to follow, having no desire to be left alone with these women of the night.

'Why are there no Greencoats here, Magistra?' he asked as they reached the first floor landing.

'It's the way I want it,' Gelredida replied. 'This way we might investigate the scene untroubled and word of this can be kept to a minimum.'

'But how can you guarantee the silence of those . . . women?'

Gelredida stopped and turned, regarding Waylian with a wry smile.

'All men are braggarts by nature, and women of means are most often gossips and rumourmongers. Whores, however, learn to keep their peace . . . if the price is right. I would sooner trust the discretion of a whore than of anyone else in this city.'

She made her way along the corridor. Waylian followed, and, as the sound of sobbing from downstairs receded, a familiar smell began to assail his nostrils. The stink of rot, of carcasses, wafted down the corridor as though they were about to enter a butcher's shop. Waylian braced himself for what he was about to see as Gelredida turned through an open door.

There were candles, black-stemmed with glowing red flames, as before. The walls bore their familiar dark sigils – but Waylian's attention went immediately to the corpse. This time, instead of being splayed on the ground, the body of this unfortunate whore was nailed to the ceiling, her entrails dangling down to caress the floor like the branches of a willow tree. How the killer had managed to nail her there without alerting the rest of the brothel's occupants he had no idea. But then they weren't dealing with any ordinary killer. This was a rogue caster, a foul magicker of the most despicable kind. Who knew what fell tricks he had used to accomplish his ghastly deed.

As Waylian regarded her, staring blankly from milk-white eyes, he suddenly felt a pang of shame. Downstairs he had considered those women whores. He had thought them base and unworthy of his compassion. But this was just a girl, not much older than he was. A girl who might have had dreams, might have aspired to something more than spreading her legs for coin, but now those dreams were slain along with her. And slain in the most obscene manner.

'We should get her down,' he said, as Gelredida busied herself examining the walls.

'She can stay where she is for the moment. I doubt she's late for any appointments.'

Waylian felt anger well up from his belly. The humiliation of the last few days, coupled with his current shame, seemed to boil up within him.

'We need to get her down!' he cried, too loud.

Gelredida rounded on him, her face creased in annoyance. He braced himself for the tirade, for the abuse and the ridicule, but it never came. Her features softened and she slowly nodded.

'Very well. Use that.' She gestured to a chair in one corner before turning back to the wall and studying the sigils closely, though not close enough to touch them.

Waylian grabbed the chair and dragged it through the pool of blood, the legs making a trail along the floorboards, until it was positioned beneath the girl. He climbed on it, grasping a nail that secured one of her feet to the ceiling. Congealed blood on the head of the nail made his fingers slippery and he couldn't get proper purchase. After pulling his robe over his hand Waylian managed to get a grip on the nail and he tugged.

It finally came away in a shower of plaster and the girl's leg dropped, dangling uselessly. He used the same technique on the other leg, and her body slumped, hanging from her arms. Thankfully, Waylian had prepared himself, and he managed to take the girl's weight, her entrails still dangling, soaking his robe in blood. He didn't care about that. He just wanted her down off that ceiling.

A week ago this would have made him sick to his stomach, but recent events had hardened him. Waylian felt like a boy no longer.

Her exsanguinated body was light as a child's doll, and even Waylian, weakling that he was, could take her weight. Finally, he managed to remove the nails securing her hands, and she flopped over his shoulder like an old, empty sack. He climbed off the chair and laid her out on the floor. As he knelt beside her he tried to close her eyes but try as he might, he couldn't seem to get them to shut all the way. She still looked out from half-closed lids, almost as though she were pretending to sleep but still peeking. The splaying of her entrails and the pallid white tinge to her flesh, however, made it obvious she was not.

A sharp intake of breath from his mistress made Waylian glance her way. She had thrown back her hood now, and was standing some paces away from the wall, as though suddenly understanding the symbols daubed there.

'It cannot be,' she whispered. 'Madness. Only a fool would . . .'

Waylian moved to her side. He regarded the sigils but they only made him feel nauseous. Even though he had no understanding of what they meant, he could sense they were forbidden – writings that should be seen by no mortal eye.

'What we have here, Waylian, is a ritual of the most diabolical origin.' *Waylian? She called me Waylian.* 'I did not recognise it with the first murder. I did not think it possible with the second, but this poor girl has proved beyond doubt what our foe is up to.'

Waylian could only turn his eyes away from the wall before the bile rising in his throat threatened to make him puke. As he did he saw two burly men at the door.

'Ah,' said Gelredida, 'you're here. As you can see, it's something of a mess.' She gestured to the corpse. 'I'm sure you know what to do.' She flung a bag of coins to one of the men, and Waylian began to wonder just how much money she had inside that robe of hers.

As the men pulled out a pile of hempen sacks and some rope, one of them asked, 'The Storway?'

'Yes,' Gelredida replied. 'And don't weight the body down this time, otherwise it'll never reach the sea. We don't want her bobbing up in the harbour.'

Waylian was suddenly horrified. 'You can't just—'

His mistress fixed him with a stern look.

The men went about their business, wrapping the body in the sacks and securing them tight with the rope.

'No, this isn't right,' Waylian said as one of them hoisted the body onto his shoulder. This had been a human being, a girl with a life and feelings. She couldn't just be discarded like so much sewage. 'She should be buried.' Gelredida was annoyed but Waylian didn't care any more. 'You can't. This is wrong.'

He stared at her, trying his best to hold her gaze. She stared back, her eyes boring into him, assessing him as though he were being tested in the classroom. But for the second time she acquiesced to his demands, producing another two crowns from inside her robes.

'Very well.' She flung the coins on the ground. 'You look like resourceful gentlemen, and that should ensure you get the body out of the city un-noticed. See that she's buried on Dancer's Hill. No need to mark the grave.'

When neither of them complained, Gelredida walked from the room.

As Waylian followed her he was suddenly aware of the blood covering his robe, the blood of a girl he'd never met and whose name he didn't know.

Gelredida made her way down the stairs and towards the door, but Waylian paused, turning to the weeping girl.

'What was her name?' he asked, as gently as he could manage.

The girl looked up at him, her painted face smeared and runny with tears. 'What do you care?' she asked.

'Just tell me,' he demanded, his voice less gentle.

'Kaylee,' said the girl, before burying her head in her neighbour's shoulder.

Waylian nodded his thanks and quickly followed his mistress out into the night.

It was some time before he realised Gelredida was not headed back to the Tower of Magisters. Even though his sense of direction was awful he knew they were heading away from the great building.

They came to the end of an alleyway, which opened up to a wide, paved clearing spreading to left and right. Through the gloom, Waylian could see a spiked fence stretching out in both directions. As they drew closer he saw that beyond the fence was a knoll, on which stood a dark and brooding edifice, all crumbling domes and broken spires.

'What is this, Magistra?' he asked as they neared the fence, which Waylian could now see was wrought in brass, each stanchion etched with tiny, indecipherable symbols.

Gelredida did not answer, but continued walking along the perimeter, never taking her eyes from the dark monument that squatted ominously at the top of the hill.

Eventually they reached a gate. It was embossed with a grotesque frieze wrought from the same brass as the fence. Rendered in eerie detail were scenes of horror: men, women and children being torn apart by ghastly, emaciated creatures, all talons and fangs and naked fury. Waylian was repulsed by the scene but strangely couldn't drag his eyes away from it.

In the centre of the gate was a square block of metal, its surface covered with symbols similar to those on the fence stanchions. Gelredida took a deep breath then leaned in close, whispering to the block as though she were confiding in a lover.

The wave of nausea that engulfed Waylian was similar to that he had felt when looking at the daubed sigils at the scenes of the recent murders. He raised a hand to his face in time to staunch a drop of blood as it seeped from his nostril.

Before he could cry out in alarm, the gate moved. The characters depicted on the brass frieze shifted mechanically, some throwing up their arms, other widening their gaping mouths in some macabre mockery of a puppet show. All at once the figures drew back, somehow opening the brass gate and leaving the pathway clear to the imposing monument.

Waylian followed his mistress as she made her way up the hill. Though the feeling of nausea relented, it was replaced with an overwhelming sense of dread, as though they were trespassing on unholy ground and at any moment the guardians of this place might leap forth and inflict their punishment on transgressors.

By the time they reached the monument, Waylian was all but terrified out of his wits.

Gelredida stopped before an entrance to the monolith, which looked to have had a huge stone block jammed into it.

'The Chapel of Ghouls,' she breathed. 'You've heard of it?'

'Yes, Magistra,' he replied.

'Of course you have; even the lowliest street urchin has heard of it. For almost seven centuries this tomb has sat in the middle of the city, like a canker at its heart. Over the years people have made up their own tales about this place, much of it myth and rumour. Tales that go back the seven centuries since they were trapped here.'

'The ghouls?'

'Yes, of course the ghouls. They ran rife throughout the provinces, threatening to turn it into a land of the dead. It took the Wyvern Guard to finally lure them here with the help of the Crucible of Magisters. This was the only ground on which they could be stopped. By the time they had finally bound the creatures to this place there was almost nothing left of either order.'

'But what does this have to do with—'

'Someone is trying to enact a ritual. An ancient and forbidden rite that will bring these monsters back to run rampant. I didn't want to believe it before, but now it's time to face the truth.'

'But why? Why would someone want to release these creatures?'

Gelredida shook her head. 'Madness. Hubris. Insane curiosity. The motive does not matter. The fact that someone is trying is all that matters. Someone is trying to become the Maleficar Necrus.'

'Can we stop them?' His voice quailed, but he was not ashamed of his fear.

'We have to, Waylian. If these creatures are unleashed on the city they will leave nothing alive.'

He could see fear in Gelredida's eyes and he had to admit, *that* unnerved him more than anything else.

His mistress placed a hand on the huge stone slab that covered the entrance as though she were feeling for something. Once satisfied, she nodded. 'The wards are still in place. They have not been weakened, yet. There is still time.'

With that she turned from the monument, and Waylian followed as she made her way back down the path and out through the gate. He barely heard its grinding and squeaking as the ancient brass portal closed behind them – all he could think was if these ghouls could strike terror in the Red Witch, they must be truly deserving of fear.

THIRTY

At night the Crown District was aflame with dancing lights. The lamplighters didn't just ignite torches in their stanchions, but also thousands of tiny candles that sat within the intricately laid out flowerbeds and lined the mosaic pathways. The various ponds and miniature waterways that criss-crossed the district were likewise illuminated by thousands of floating candleholders, each bearing a bright flame.

Rag was amazed at the sight, imagining herself as a bird looking down on the scene, which must have rivalled the starry night sky for its majesty. It was an all too brief diversion, though, as she walked across the polished cobbles with her crew. Krupps was unusually silent, stern even, as they again headed for the merchant's house. Steraglio was his usual dark and brooding self and Burney strolled along without a care in the world. Rag brought up the rear, wondering again what she had got herself into.

She was at the back of the group and could turn around and be gone before any of them even noticed she was missing. Would it be so bad going back to the roof of the Bull? No Guild, no crew, no pot to piss in? She knew Chirpy, Migs and Tidge would be glad to see her. Fender would take the piss for fucking up her big chance, but she guessed she could live with that.

It had all seemed so easy when they'd been talking about it, before any actual robbing, but now she was racked with doubt. What if they got caught? What if someone or, gods forbid, something was in the house?

Rag shook her head, clearing out the doubt. This was what she wanted, what she'd yearned for – a way into the Guild – and now she had it within her grasp, there was no way she was going to balls it up.

The merchant's house was in sight now, and Rag's stomach felt like it was trying to digest half a brick. Krupps and the others were relying on her to get them in. She'd told them she was a housebreaker. She clearly weren't no housebreaker, but she'd best learn quick. The other day Steraglio had been ready to knife those two old bags, and Rag knew he'd have no qualms about knifing her good and proper if she couldn't come up with the goods.

As they got near to the house, Steraglio and Burney broke away. Without a word they snuffed out every candle and lantern that lined the way, plunging the immediate area into darkness, while Krupps and Rag moved up to the spiked iron railing that surrounded the house.

'This is it then, Sweets. You ready?'

No, I'm shitting myself.

Rag nodded.

'Okay then, take this.' He opened his coat and pulled out what she'd learned was an iron-crow. It was a rod of metal, almost two foot long, tapered flat and bent at the end for levering things open. In this case the upstairs window.

She took it from him, hooking it in her belt, and Krupps gave her a wink and a smile, then turned towards the spiked railing and grabbed hold, bracing himself against it. Rag climbed up onto his back, planted a foot on his shoulder and kicked off, jumping over the spikes at the top of the fence and landing deftly on the other side.

She wasted no time; it wouldn't do for the rest of them to have got over the railing only to find her still at the front door wondering how in the hells she was going to get up to the first floor.

The side of the house was lined with prominent stonework and it weren't nothing for Rag to get her fingers in between the stone, finding purchase in the crumbling mortar and climbing up the side easy as pie. She reached the first floor in no time, growing ever more confident with the ease she was moving. Stepping out to the sill of the window she allowed herself a glance down.

That was a mistake!

She wouldn't normally mind – she was used to running on rooftops – but it was seeing the spiked railings waiting for her at the bottom that gave her the fear. It was so bad she missed her footing on the sill, a tiny slip that would have meant nothing on the ground, but here a good dozen feet up might have been fatal. She panicked, gripping the window jamb and the brickwork so as it nearly broke her fingernails off. She felt a tug at her belt, looking down in time to see the iron-crow come loose and go sailing down towards the ground. It bounced off the paving with an almighty clang.

Rag hung there for some moments. Waiting for someone to come out and see what the racket was all about. In the shadows below she could see the lads, frozen in place, all watching for sign of movement – the same as her – but it never came.

Come on, Rag, hold it together. Just open the friggin' window and climb in.

Gingerly she reached out, feeling down to the bottom of the window, praying and praying that it would be open and she wouldn't need the iron. She pulled, feeling the window give a little, and allowed herself a smile. *Easy as cutting a dead man's purse.* Another tug and the window slid up wide enough for her to get in. Rag eased herself over, holding on to the frame and sliding her legs then the rest of her body through the gap.

And she was in.

It was dark inside, darker than night – took time for her eyes to adjust. Even after waiting what seemed an age she still couldn't see more than a few feet ahead. *It ain't gonna get any better just sitting here.*

She began to move, looking for the door. As she did, she kept quiet as death, questions of all sorts starting to go through her head. What if the merchant was here? What if he *did* have a dog? A fucking big dog with fucking big teeth?

She reached the door, opened it a bit and waited, listening for any hint of man or beast. When there was nothing, she made her way down the stairs as quick as she could, and turned the handle of the door.

Only it didn't open.

Looking closer she saw there was a big deadlock keyhole staring at her like a big laughing mouth. *What were you expecting?* Through the stained glass in the door she could see the other three had made it over the railing now and were waiting on this side. Waiting for her to let them in.

Desperately Rag looked around for a key. There was a chest of drawers and she rifled through it, pushing aside papers, a spyglass, a letter opener, some big wooden blocks for fuck knew what, and all manner of shit besides, but no key. Two pairs of boots sat in the hall and she turned them upside down, getting more desperate with every breath, but still no key. If she had to look through the whole bloody house she could be here all night. That would go down real well with the blokes sat outside like bloody lemons.

She stood in the hall, feeling the panic rise, feeling the tears welling up. Then she saw it, all shiny and silver, hanging on a hook on the wall by its chain.

Bloody key!

Rag almost snapped that chain as she grabbed it off the hook, jamming it into the lock and hoping on hope it was the right fit. When the deadbolt turned she let out the breath she'd been holding for the gods knew how long.

Krupps pushed his way in the door almost before she'd had time to open it. 'Nice one, Sweets,' he said as he quickly moved past her, closely followed by Burney.

'Trying to wake the whole fucking neighbourhood?' said Steraglio, brandishing the iron-crow she'd dropped, before following the other two up the staircase and leaving her to shut the door behind them.

As she followed she could hear them going to work, shifting furniture, sifting through drawers.

'I thought you said it would be here,' said Krupps, his voice a harsh whisper in the dark.

'It fucking should be,' Steraglio replied. 'Coles told me it was under the merchant's bed.'

'There's nothing under there but a bloody bedpan. Now where is it, you fucking dolt?'

Rag paused at the top of the stairs, having no desire to get between the two men while they squabbled.

'Mind your fucking mouth,' said Steraglio, and she could see through a chink in the door he had stopped his frantic search and was staring at Krupps.

'Or what?' Krupps replied. He too had stopped his search, his right hand creeping towards the inside of his coat.

'Oi, lads!' Burney's voice seemed way too loud in the dark house, but Rag was relieved when she heard it. 'This what you're looking for?'

Both Steraglio and Krupps rushed to the room Burney was searching in.

'Yes,' said Krupps. 'Nice one, Burney. At least there's one person I can rely on.' Rag moved to the doorway of the room, and saw the three of them standing over a huge chest. 'Right, cop hold, Burney, and we'll get the fuck out of here.'

Burney bent down, managing to get his arms around the chest, but when he tried to lift it, it wouldn't budge. Krupps and Steraglio looked on, their expressions turning from relief to concern as Burney huffed and puffed, pushing and pulling the casket with all his quite considerable might, but the thing simply would not move.

'Is this thing nailed down?' Burney said finally, as he collapsed on top of it.

'Fuck,' said Steraglio, stomping off to one corner of the room, seething with anger.

'This has got to be a joke,' said Krupps. 'Coles is having a laugh! "One casket," he said. "Just grab it and leave," he said.'

Rag had no idea who this 'Coles' was, but she guessed he would be in for a right kicking when Krupps got his hands on him.

A sound from downstairs diverted Rag's attention from the squabbling men. She turned, taking a step down then stopping dead.

The door handle was turning.

'Someone's here!' she whispered. It was still loud enough to silence the lads.

As she stood frozen to the staircase, the door opened and a man strolled in. He held a lantern in one hand, which shed a stark light on the walls, and he walked across the entrance hall until he saw her standing there, and froze in his tracks.

Rag and the man stared at one another. In the lantern light she could see he wore a fine hand-stitched jacket, a wide sash holding in his generous girth and pantaloons tight to his flabby thighs, as was the style in the richer parts of the city.

He held her gaze, then slowly smiled. 'What have we here?' he asked, his voice deep and rich. 'Find anything interesting, my dear?'

She opened her mouth to answer, but before she had a chance, Krupps and Steraglio erupted from the shadows, grabbing hold of the man. There must have been another staircase elsewhere in the house and they had managed to sneak down and come at the merchant from a room off to one side.

'As a matter of fact,' said Krupps, 'we *have* found something.'

Before the man could speak they bundled him off into the side room they had leapt from. He dropped the lantern to the floor where it started to burn the intricately woven carpet and Rag moved forward, picking it up and stamping out the meagre flames.

She could hear them in the next room, shouting and knocking over

237

furniture as the merchant noisily protested. There was a sound that could only have been a punch followed by a pained cry.

This was all going wrong – they said no one would be hurt.

Rag moved to the entrance to the room, her lantern illuminating it, and she saw they were tying the man to a chair with some rope. Burney was with them now, standing over him menacingly.

'Barnus Juno, I'm guessing?' Krupps said. There was a level of threat in his voice Rag had never heard before. It frightened her.

'Who are you? What do you want?' Barnus asked, clearly terrified.

'I think you know what we want. Now where's the fucking key to that chest?'

Barnus glanced at each of the three men in turn, but found no hope there. Each looked as ruthless as the next: Burney with his brawn, Steraglio with his drawn blade and Krupps with his calm menace.

'I don't have it,' Barnus replied.

Even Rag could tell he was lying.

Krupps gave Burney a nod, and the big man put a fist in Barnus' gut, then one to his jaw.

'Careful,' said Krupps. 'We need him able to speak.'

Barnus spat blood and what might have been a tooth. 'I promise you, I don't have it.' Burney hit him again and he gave a low groan, followed by a strangled sob.

Rag wanted to run in between them, to tell them to stop, to leave the poor bastard alone and get out as quick as they could before they went too far.

She didn't move, though. She knew it would be stupid to get in the way. It had been stupid to come here . . . to trust these men. They weren't the crew she thought they were. They'd lied to her: there wasn't supposed to be anyone here. No one was supposed to get hurt, but here they were, beating this poor bloke to shit.

Before they could hit him again there was an insistent rapping at the door, and everyone stopped.

'Barnus? Are you in there?' It was a woman's voice, high pitched, haughty.

Barnus opened his mouth in warning but Burney clapped a hand over it before he could make a sound. Krupps and Steraglio swiftly crept past Rag, moving to either side of the door, ducking low so they couldn't be seen through its stained glass arch.

'I heard a noise, Barnus! Are you home?'

The handle to the door turned, and Krupps clamped a hand over it. With his other hand he reached into his jacket and pulled out a blade, more cleaver than knife, whilst the woman on the other side struggled to open the door. Steraglio licked his lips, brandishing his own blade, as though willing the woman to enter so he could stick her with it.

This was too much! They were gonna kill that merchant and now they were gonna kill some stupid old woman. Something had to be done.

Rag meowed loudly.

Why she did it she couldn't say – it didn't even sound much like a fucking cat, more like someone had stood on a rusty nail, but it was all she could think of at short notice.

The woman's face appeared at the glass and she peered inside, but clearly it was too dark for her to see.

With a quick grumble about being woken in the dead of night, she walked away.

Krupps let out an audible sigh. 'Right.' He walked into the room where Barnus was still tied up, Burney's hand still over his mouth. 'No more titting about. Tell us where the key is, or my friend here's gonna cut out your eye.'

Barnus sat there in total panic.

'Right, you little shit,' said Steraglio, reaching forward with his blade.

'Wait! Wait!' Barnus squealed. 'It's in the main bedchamber! Under the mattress.'

Krupps looked at Burney and Steraglio unbelievingly. 'Did neither of you two think of checking under the mattress?'

With that, all three moved off as one in their haste to find the key and open the chest. Rag stood rooted to the spot, watching as they almost fell over one another in their eagerness to rush up the stairs.

Slowly she looked back at Barnus. His eyes were wide with fear, blood trickling from his mouth. He stared at her pleadingly.

Rag checked out the staircase the lads had used. She knew full well they'd probably kill the merchant. None of them was wearing a mask, and even in the gloom she was pretty sure Barnus would remember the faces of the four ruffians who had terrorised him. The lads wouldn't leave a witness for the Greencoats.

She moved to the chair, desperately fumbling with the rope that tied the merchant, listening all the while to the sound of furniture being moved and footsteps clapping along the floorboards upstairs. Finally she teased the rope free and stood back.

Barnus flashed a smile of thanks . . . then backhanded her across the face, knocking her back on her arse and smacking her head.

She was dazed, couldn't get up, but she could still see him fumbling for something in his desk drawer. That something glinted in the candle-light; it could only be a blade.

'I'll teach you bastards to steal from Barnus Juno,' he said, his eyes wide with animal fury.

Someone was coming down the stairs now, and the merchant darted into concealment.

Rag was too stunned to speak.

Burney walked in, his brow creased with consternation.

'It's the wrong key, you fuc—'

He cried out in pain as Barnus buried the blade in his upper arm. Before Barnus could withdraw and stab again, Burney reeled back, taking the blade with him.

'You fuckers! Do you know who I am?' Barnus screeched, leaping forward, his hands like claws, but Burney was able to fend him off with a swipe of his other arm. He pulled the blade clear, but the bloodied weapon fell to the floor as Barnus came at him again. What the merchant was trying to achieve, Rag had no idea, but he was clearly no match for the big bastard he was attacking.

As Burney pushed him backwards, Krupps and Steraglio hurried in.

'What the fuck?' said Krupps, staggering as Barnus landed a blow against his jaw.

Steraglio was not about to suffer the same punishment and drew his knife, just as Rag managed to find her feet.

She tried to shout *no* or *stop* or something, but found no words. Steraglio had stabbed Barnus three times – in the chest, abdomen and thigh – before the merchant even knew he'd been struck.

Then it was like a pack of dogs taking down a bear – the first one had drawn blood and the rest knew their prey was on its way out. Burney struck next, smashing his fist into the merchant's neck. Krupps, fast recovered from his crack to the jaw, drew his own blade, and soon all three of them were attacking in a frenzy, stabbing, punching and kicking Barnus to the ground. The merchant's squeals of agony were masked by the three robbers' cries of hate.

Rag watched helplessly as they made a bloody mess of the man they'd come to rob.

240

When it was over and Barnus had stopped moving, Krupps gave her a look. His eyes were accusing enough; he didn't need to say the words.

'Let's get the fuck out of here,' he said, moving towards the door.

All three of them bundled out of the house. Rag only paused for a second to glance down at Barnus, his fine clothes soaked in dark blood. Then she followed them.

The gate stood wide. Barnus must have left it open when he came home. With nothing to stop them, they were off into the night.

As she ran, Rag realised there would be payback for this.

She wanted to flee from these men and what they'd done, to escape the inevitable retribution that would soon be pursuing them, but where would she go? Who would take her in now?

She could go straight to the Greencoats, but why would they believe her? How could she explain she hadn't meant any harm – that no one was supposed to get hurt?

So she followed the three men, knowing full well she was just as guilty of the murder as those who'd done the deed.

THIRTY-ONE

They came in like the tide, only difference was they didn't look like they'd be going back out any time soon. Thousands streamed into the Town, a seething mass of pitiful men, women and children, carrying what little they had with them in carts and on the backs of livestock.

Nobul and the rest of the Greencoats had watched them from Saviour's Bridge, moving like a mass of slurry into the makeshift homes they would be forced to occupy for as long as it took King Cael to stick it to the Khurtas. He'd wondered at the time whether it was wise to let them in unsupervised, with no one to tell them where to go or which hovel they should settle in, but Kilgar had thought it made sense.

'If they're gonna kill each other,' he'd said, staring down with that one eye, 'no use us getting in the way.'

Nobul could kind of see where he was coming from. Then again, if there had been someone down there, an authority figure or two, filtering the crowds to the quietest areas, surely it would have made things easier. Might even have saved some lives.

As it was, the refugees had been left to their own devices. The way into the Old City was left open and in they flooded. Of course it had been carnage. Everyone wanted the best plots closest to the Storway so they could flush their shit straight into the sea. As was always the way, it was the strongest, roughest and meanest who got to keep them.

The Greencoats had done a sweep through in the days afterwards when everything had calmed down. They'd found thirteen bodies, two

242

of them children from the same family, their mother raped and butchered.

Nobul had wanted to get angry at that, wanted to vent his ire and go hunting for the culprits – but what was the use? There were far too many candidates and no one brave enough to point him at the right ones.

It was not long after that they started getting reports of people going missing.

At first it had been in ones and twos, then the first family had disappeared and the Greencoats had been forced to take notice.

No one seemed to have a clue. It was like they'd been spirited away by the Lord of Crows himself. There were no signs of a struggle, no screams, it was almost as if they'd upped sticks and run – just taken themselves off to Arlor knew where.

The Greencoats had to look like they were doing something, though, if only to avert a panic. It wouldn't do for hysteria to grip the Town; several thousand refugees going wild and taking the law into their own hands. Thirteen murders in one night was bad enough. The last thing they wanted was a massacre.

The Greencoats had to spread themselves thin, so it was patrols of two. Each pair would pick a street and randomly kick in doors, search houses, make arrests – though that rarely happened, as they simply didn't have room in the city gaols. That way everyone could see they were acting on the reports, doing something to help, squeezing out the criminal element.

In reality, Nobul knew it was a waste of time. There were too many criminals to count, and even the normal folk – the farmers and traders and craftsmen – were turning to thieving and mugging and cheating just to feed themselves and their families.

So it was with a heavy sense of reluctance Nobul walked into the Town with Denny at his side. The lad had shown he wasn't much in a fight, but he'd certainly proved himself loyal, and there wasn't another in Amber Watch whom Nobul would rather have had watching his back. Besides, over the past few days of kicking in doors the worst they'd had was an irate mother screaming at them to bring an apothecary for her sick baby. They'd done their best to calm her down but without success. In the end they'd both backed off and left her. Nobul had felt a touch guilty, but she wasn't the only woman with a sick child, and the Daughters of Arlor were doing their best to tend the sick and starving. What could the Greencoats do anyway?

'What do you think it is then?' Denny asked as they made their way down a dilapidated street.

'What do I think what is?' Nobul replied, trying his best not to step in the crap that littered their path. It seemed the only thing that had changed on these streets before they'd cleared them out was that most of the dog shit was now replaced by that of humans.

'Where these missing people are going.'

Nobul shrugged his big shoulders. 'Fucked if I know. One thing I'm sure of is that turning over these hovels ain't gonna help us find the answer.'

'I agree with that, all right,' Denny said. He'd been extremely vocal over the past few days, offering his opinion on why they should be looking for real criminals and not phantoms in the night. It had done him no good, and Kilgar had merely reminded him of the virtues of obeying orders without question, since it would save him a fat lip. That had finally shut Denny up.

'Want to know what I think?'

'Not really,' said Nobul, feeling no guilt at Denny's immediate look of disappointment. As much as Denny made him smile sometimes, there was a time and a place for his madcap theories.

They moved further down the street, and Denny turned to Nobul with a look of resignation on his face. 'What about this one?' He pointed to a door he'd picked at random.

'It's as good as any,' Nobul replied. 'You first.'

'Why me? It's always me. Right, we're tossing for it.' Denny fished for a coin.

'Tails,' Nobul said, as Denny sent the coin spinning through the air. He caught it, slapped it on the back of his hand, then sneaked a peek.

'Balls,' he said.

Nobul allowed himself a smile.

Denny braced his hands to either side of the door and kicked out. There was a splintering of wood, but it didn't give all the way. A second kick and the door burst inwards. Denny rushed inside, Nobul at his back, weapon drawn.

'No one move, in the name of King Cael,' shouted Denny.

Nobul could see there was only one man in the hovel. His lean features looked fearful and he glanced towards a short knife on his table, but clearly thought better of reaching for it.

The place reeked, a stale mouldering stench, and Nobul wondered how this man had managed to manifest such a stink in the short time he'd been here. He gave the room a cursory glance. Nothing seemed untoward, but the man glanced around desperately, like a cornered animal.

'Name?' demanded Denny.

'P— Pardo,' the man replied. 'Ivaar Pardo of Briar Lock.'

'Dreldun, eh? Long walk from the north.'

'Where else was I supposed to go?'

Denny nodded his agreement. 'Just you is it, Ivaar?'

'Yes. No family to speak of.'

No family, or none to speak of?

'Do you know why we're here, Ivaar?' Nobul had to admit that, though Denny was shit in a fight, he could certainly sound authoritative when he wanted to.

'Er . . . I guess it's because of the missing folk?'

'The missing folk, that's right, Ivaar. What do you know about it?'

Ivaar glanced at Nobul, then back at Denny, like he was a hare trying to work out which hound was going to rip his throat out first. 'I don't know nothing. Honest I don't.'

Denny let that one hang there. Sometimes it was best to say nothing, and let them stew in it. On occasion they'd wonder what you knew, wonder if you knew something they weren't telling, and then tell you anyway. Ivaar didn't say a word.

Finally, Denny nodded. 'Fair enough. If we turned this place over, Ivaar, would we find anything we shouldn't?'

'No, sir. Nothing here.'

'Good. I hate wasting my time, Ivaar.' Nobul could tell Denny was almost done, but though he didn't like spending much time in these hovels, something was niggling at him. Maybe it was that smell, or the guilty look Ivaar had put on as soon as he realised who they were.

'Wait a minute,' he said, as Denny turned to leave. He walked to a chest in the corner over which two flies buzzed incessantly. 'What's in here?' he said, flipping the lid open with his foot.

'It's mine!' Ivaar cried, as Nobul revealed what lay in the chest.

It was full of food. Some of it rotting, most of it well past ripe, but food nonetheless. Bread, hard sausage, dried meats, a bag of spuds more eyes than potato, apples more shrivelled than an old man's ball sack, and a pig's head with eyes still intact.

'It's mine,' Ivaar cried again, moving towards the chest, but Denny pushed him back.

'How long you had this lot?' he asked, wrinkling his nose at the sudden stench that pervaded the tiny room.

'Got nothing to do with you! It's all mine!'

'It's all fucking rotten. You could have fed three families on this.'

'It's mine.'

Denny backhanded Ivaar across the face. He staggered back, tears welling in his eyes. Nobul saw Ivaar eye the knife that sat on his table again, so he stared, holding him with that gaze of cold, dead steel, and gradually the man relented, even taking a step away.

'So what we gonna do now?' asked Denny, scrunching his nose up as he looked in the chest.

'Not much we can do,' Nobul replied. 'We can't start handing it out – it'll just make people sick.'

Denny turned back to Ivaar. 'People are starving and you've let this all go rotten. I've half a mind to make you eat the lot, right here and now.'

Ivaar looked fearful, a tear breaking over his eyelid and running down his cheek.

'Won't do any good now,' said Nobul. 'Come on, I've had enough of this stink.'

He walked out into the open air, Denny close behind.

'We should have given him a beating,' Denny said as they walked back towards the city.

Nobul just shook his head. 'What for? Teach him a lesson? Poor bloke's got enough to contend with. We might all have before long.'

'What's that supposed to mean?'

'It means we might have several thousand angry fucking Khurtas knocking on our door in a few weeks. And what are we doing about it?'

'Nah, the king's taking them on at Kelbur Fenn. Should be any day now – could even be today. Once he's given them a kicking things'll get back to normal.'

'Don't be too sure about that. Doesn't matter how many knights and archers and foot you've got, something can always turn a battle against you.'

Nobul could see Denny wanted to argue, but they both knew who had the most experience of war.

'This is pointless,' said Denny after they'd made their way along the street for a while. 'Let's go back to the barracks. I could murder a drink.'

On any other day, Nobul would have told him 'no'. On any other day he would have carried out his duty, not for fear of what Kilgar might do, but because that was what kept him busy, kept his mind occupied. Today, though, it all just felt like shit, this place and its stink and the piteous faces of everyone living here. If you could call it living.

He nodded, and Denny smiled. Obviously he hadn't been expecting Nobul to agree.

'So where do you think they are? The missing refugees?' Denny asked as they made their way back over Saviour's Bridge. Nobul had to admire his persistence.

'Don't know,' he replied. 'But I'm pretty sure kicking in slum doorways ain't gonna find us the culprits.'

'Where would you start then?'

'Where d'you think? If the Guild doesn't know what's going on then nobody does. It's them needs their doors kicking in.'

'Good luck with that,' Denny grinned. 'But make sure you let me know the day you decide to take on those mad bastards, and I'll make sure I'm on a different watch.'

The boy had a point. The Guild had eyes and ears everywhere, and they greased plenty of palms in the Greencoats. It was a dangerous line of inquiry, and would most likely get whichever nosy bastard decided to investigate a quick knife between the shoulder blades.

They walked on, and Nobul could tell Denny was just dying for him to ask.

'Go on then, what's your theory?'

Denny's grin widened. 'Funny you should ask. You know these murders?' *Who didn't?* 'It's all linked. The murders we've seen, those poor mutilated fuckers all over the city – they're just the start. Practice, if you will. Whatever mad bastard is doing that is the one what spirited off the refugees.'

Nobul raised an eyebrow. 'And how have they managed that?'

'They're a caster, ain't they? It's all magick.' Denny wiggled his fingers in front of him as though conjuring something out of thin air. Nobul knew full well Denny could barely manage to conjure piss from his cock without help, so magick would have been more than a tall order.

'Right,' said Nobul, managing a smile. He'd smiled a few times recently, and mostly it had been at things Denny said.

'You mark me. When it all comes out in the wash, you'll see those two things are linked. I'm telling you.'

The barracks were almost in sight, when Denny spied two Greencoats ahead, leaning idly against a rough wooden shack.

'There's Platt and Firby,' he said, lifting his hand up to wave, but they hadn't seen him before two figures emerged from the passing crowd and grasped the Greencoats' attention.

Something about the pair gave Nobul pause. He couldn't say what it was, just a feeling in his gut, but it was enough to make him stop Denny before he could call out, pulling him to one side of the street to watch.

One of the newcomers was a man, lean, just over average height, with a mop of brown hair. The way he held himself Nobul could tell he displayed confidence. Whether that meant he was a fighter or a bluffer was impossible to tell, but either way he carried a sword at his side. He smiled at the two Greencoats, chatting with an easy familiarity, and it was clear he liked to talk. Even from this distance, though, Nobul could see a mass of bruises on his face. Clearly someone hadn't liked what he had to say recently.

The second was a woman, tall, statuesque even. She held her head down, as though trying to blend in, but with her cropped blonde hair and striking features that wasn't easy. Despite her attempts to look insignificant, it was obvious she was thickly muscled about the shoulders, slim in the waist – a warrior's frame.

Something was odd about the pair of them, and Nobul knew it.

'Friends of yours?' he asked Denny, keeping his eyes on the four of them. The handsome one with the bruised face made a joke and the Greencoats laughed, but not the woman.

'Platt and Firby? Yeah, known 'em for ages. Firby's being tipped for serjeant before long. Why, what's up?'

Nobul didn't answer. Something most definitely *was* up, and if he waited long enough . . . there – a purse passed from the dandy's hand to one of the Greencoats while they were all still laughing.

'See that?' Nobul said, almost ready to walk over there and ask what the fuck they were up to.

'See what?' said Denny.

'Bribe money.'

'What the fuck do you care? Lots of the fellas do it.'

Nobul was suddenly angry. Lots of fellas did do it, but that didn't make it right. The Greencoats being so easy to buy off was why the Guild was rife in this city – because they were allowed to be. That was why he'd been forced to pay protection money for years – because there was no one he could turn to. That's why there were people going missing – because the Greencoats were too scared or their palms too well greased to investigate who was really involved. That's why his boy had died . . .

No, that wasn't why his boy had died, was it? His boy had died because Nobul was a cold, hard, bullying bastard.

'Yeah. Lots of fellas do it,' Nobul said, feeling his anger die.

He watched as they finished their conversation, and the man bid his goodbyes to the two Greencoats. He and his woman disappeared into the crowd, and for a minute Nobul considered following them. He took a step forward, but there was a sudden wail, a cry that rose over the hubbub of the street.

Denny turned. 'What the fu—'

He was cut off by another cry, this time from somewhere else.

Like it was infectious, like a plague carried on the wind, the cries went from mouth to mouth and a panic gripped the streets. A woman ran past clutching her child's hand. A man pushed his cart full of oysters, spilling his load and not caring a jot. Some old man dropped to his knees sobbing his eyes out.

Nobul moved forward into the crowd, demanding to know what was wrong, but people were just pushing past, gripped by fear. Finally he grabbed a passer-by, a woman of middling years with tears in her eyes.

'What's going on?' he demanded.

She looked up at him as though in a daze. 'We've lost,' she gasped. 'The Khurtas have beat them.'

Nobul stared at her in disbelief, then, feeling her squirming in his grip, he let her go.

Then he heard it – a mournful cry rising over the blather and noise.

'The king is dead!' someone cried. 'They've murdered King Cael!'

Nobul looked at Denny.

Neither of them knew what to say.

THIRTY-TWO

It felt comfortable on his hip; the best blade he'd owned since . . . well, forever. It had been a bargain too. He and Kaira had bought it from a stall in a Northgate market, and as Merrick had tested its weight and run his finger along the keen edge he could only wonder what some scabby street trader was doing with such superior steel. The vendor obviously had no idea what he possessed, because he'd sold it for a pittance. Apparently the stallholder's entire batch of weapons had come from an old burned-out forge, the owner having vanished. Someone had missed out on a lot of coin, but that wasn't Merrick's problem. He had a sword worthy of him now – that was all that mattered. If Shanka and his thugs, or any other bastard for that matter, wanted to take him on they'd better know how to fight or would find themselves stuck with three foot of folded steel.

And that wasn't the only ace up his sleeve.

Kaira was beautiful, he had to give her that. She could do with a bit of rouge on her cheeks and lips, perhaps some kohl around the eyes, but she was still better looking than most of the ladies Merrick was used to consorting with. And in addition to her looks she could clearly handle herself in a fight. She was almost as tall as he was, the muscles beneath her tunic taut and hard. Broad in the shoulder and keen of eye, she went about her duty of guarding him with a vigilance that made him feel . . . safe? Safer than he'd felt in a long time anyway, at least as long as he'd been in debt to Shanka.

Now all he had to do was get a smile out of her, and who knew where that might lead. It wasn't easy though; she was a solemn one and no mistake. News about the king certainly hadn't made that any better.

Merrick didn't waste his time fawning over the Mastragalls, but neither did he despise them like some. He knew the necessity for a country to be ruled by a strong hand, and he of all people couldn't begrudge someone a little bit of privilege – he'd had enough of his own before he'd pissed it all away. Kaira was taking it hard. She'd received the news of Cael's murder with a stiff lip and a firm jaw when the hysteria had first hit the streets, but he could tell she was struggling with it.

Well, he guessed some people were just unfailingly patriotic.

The pair made their way through the streets, her at his shoulder, his ever-present guardian. Everyone they passed was subdued; there was something in the air, some sense of anticipation that before long something was going to happen; and nothing good.

No announcement had yet been made by the street criers, but Merrick knew it was coming. Having defeated their armies at Kelbur Fenn there would be nothing to stop the Khurtas sweeping through the Free States. Rumour was rife and panic would soon follow. The best they could hope for was that the Khurtas would pillage enough to be satisfied, then piss off back where they came from. Deep down, Merrick knew the chances of that were slim, but he couldn't really bring himself to care.

He was finished with all this now, his part over with. As soon as he'd said his goodbyes and all debts were cleared, he'd be out of this shit tip faster than coin from a gambler's purse.

'Where are we going now?' Kaira asked.

Merrick hadn't been expecting questions – she'd not asked anything of him so far – and he was almost caught off guard.

'Sorry, is there somewhere else you need to be?'

She didn't answer, just shook her head, which only made him feel bad.

'If you must know, we're off to see Palien. My part's all done; people have been paid off, everyone's ready to move. I can tell him the whys and wherefores and be on my merry way. Don't worry, we won't be long. Then I can take you to that waterfront bar, as promised.' *May as well have one last drink before I leave all this behind.*

More silence. He'd tried to tempt her more than once with the promise of fine wine and finer company, but it was clear she wasn't interested. Merrick found that most annoying.

'Then we're almost done?'

'Seriously, do you have other plans? Is Palien not paying you enough? Have you got more lucrative prospects elsewhere?'

She shook her head again. 'I'm just keen for this to be over.'

251

He glanced at her, but could read little on that strong face of hers. 'If it makes you feel better, that makes two of us.'

'You have doubts about this?'

'Doubts? Who said anything about doubts? I just want this to be finished so I can go back to my life. You've got no idea how much I'm being inconvenienced.'

'So all you care about is—'

'What do you want to know, Kaira?' He was beginning to prefer it when she was silent. 'Is all I care about money? Yes, I guess it is. Do I feel guilty about . . .'

He stopped. It wouldn't do to be talking about this in the street but she'd prodded him in the wrong place.

Was he proud of himself? Of course he fucking wasn't, but what could he do? If he hadn't done this, and to the best of his capability, he'd be rotting in a ditch somewhere. Kaira probably didn't appreciate that, but he didn't have to explain it to her. She was his strongarm, she wasn't being paid to know the ins and outs, she was being paid to keep him alive long enough to see a boatload of slaves off across the deep blue.

'Perhaps we should talk about this later,' he found himself saying.

Did he want to talk about it later? He'd thought he didn't want to talk about it any time. Talking about it made it real, made him actually think about what he had done, what he was condemning those poor wretches to, and that couldn't be good. Could it?

They walked the rest of the way in silence, Merrick trying his best not to contemplate the consequences of his actions, both for him and for those whose lives he was brokering. When they got to the house where Palien was holed up, all he cared about was getting this business concluded and getting out alive.

The pair of them were ushered up three flights of stairs, to find Palien dining on a sunlit terrace.

'I hope it's good news, Ryder,' Palien said as he ate. Eating, always eating. How did he manage to stay lean as a starving wolf . . . and twice as vicious?

'Of course it's good news,' Merrick replied with a smile. It wouldn't do to look frightened in front of this evil bastard. 'The Harbour Tower is yours. Half the Greencoats who will be on duty are also paid off. We won't get anywhere with the Sentinels, but that's not really a concern, is it? We're not taking anyone from the palace.'

Palien nodded as he ate, his lips curling up with satisfaction.

'Excellent,' he said through half-chewed steak. 'And with old man Cael gone to the Lord of Crows it'll be that much easier, now that the city is in mourning. They'll all be too preoccupied with their own woes to notice a few missing peasants.'

'We don't know he's dead,' Kaira said. Her voice was so forceful and determined it stopped Palien mid chew.

Merrick felt the sudden tension in the air, heard Palien's men shuffling in discomfort. It was never a good idea to speak unless spoken to in situations like this, but obviously no one had told Kaira that.

'I guess what she means is, you need to stay on your guard, at least until this is all finished,' Merrick said as quickly as he could. 'You shouldn't rely on anything until the boat's loaded and you're in the clear.'

Palien slowly nodded, but he didn't take his eyes off Kaira. 'I guess you're right. I'm starting to see why they hired you, Ryder.'

'It's not just because of my winning smile.' Best to try to make light of this, before Kaira got them both gutted. 'So, if that's our business concluded, I'll be off. I assume my debts will all be—'

'What the fuck are you talking about?' Palien was looking straight at him now.

'Er . . . my part in this . . . is over now?'

Palien smiled, but there was no humour in it. In fact it was the most evil thing Merrick had ever seen.

'Don't be fucking stupid, Ryder. You still need to see the merchandise on its way and collect the payment. What made you think we were finished with you yet?'

The fact that I've seen this deal through from start to finish despite considerable risk to my person. 'Well . . . I . . .'

Palien nodded to one of his men, and Merrick suddenly felt hands grasp his jerkin. He barely had time to protest, time to glance at Kaira who stood there watching as he was dragged to the edge of the roof and dangled over it, the tips of his toes seeking to find purchase.

'You keep wriggling, don't you, Ryder?' Palien said, turning his attention back to his meal. 'Like a worm on a hook. Always looking for your escape route, always looking to see if you can jump off the horse before it gets to the finish. *Well you can't!*' He screamed those last words so loud Merrick thought his ears would pop. 'This does not end for you until we fucking say it does. Is that clear enough?'

'Yes,' he said, as bravely as he could. Glancing down he saw the ground three storeys below, and wondered if the mud was wet and sloppy enough to cushion the fall.

Somehow he doubted it.

'Good. Then I trust I can leave you to make the final preparations. Will you need any more hands to help you collect the payment?'

Merrick shook his head. The fewer of Palien's thugs that were involved with the money, the less chance they'd have of a double cross. And the chances of that were already pretty high. 'We can handle that. Bolo's well aware of the consequences should he decide to fuck us around.'

'Excellent.' Palien signalled for the thug to pull him back to safety. 'On your way then.' With that he went back to his meal.

Merrick wasn't about to hang around for anyone else to show him the sights and headed for the stairs as quick as he could manage without running like a little girl from a spider.

Once they were out on the street he could hardly hold his anger.

'What the fuck was that? "We don't know he's dead." You don't contradict Palien like that. Are you trying to get us both killed?'

'I couldn't stop myself. That man has—'

'That man has the power to see us both dead and disappeared. If he wants to pleasure himself over a painting of our poor dead queen then wipe his cock on your tunic, he can do it, and you should keep your mouth shut while he does.'

Her brow furrowed, and for a second Merrick wondered if he'd gone a bit far, until she nodded. He knew he was probably taking it out on her because he'd thought he was out, free of all this shit, and now it was damn clear he wasn't.

'I think I know how you feel about this. I feel the same, but we've got to get used to the people we're in bed with.'

'I'm not—'

'It's a turn of phrase, Kaira. It means shut the fuck up and survive another day.' She just gave him a blank look. 'Arlor's Blood! This is like talking to a child.'

He walked off, too frustrated to speak, needing time to himself for once, but there was no chance he would get it. Her long stride easily matched his own and she clearly couldn't take a hint.

Time for a drink, and no amount of whining or bullying from his blonde-haired, blue-eyed conscience was going to stop him.

As Merrick walked into the alehouse he half expected her to grab his arm and pull him clear, but she didn't; she just followed him inside.

'Wine,' he ordered at the bar. As the landlord poured him a goblet Merrick told him to leave the bottle. To his surprise, Kaira asked for a second goblet.

'What's got into you? Think you can stomach some wine now?'

'I'm finding in recent days I can stomach many things I thought I couldn't.'

Was that a dig? Did she mean him?

Oh, who cared?

'To getting through this,' he said, raising his goblet. She just stared at him until he signalled for her to do the same. He clinked his goblet against hers and quaffed the lot down. She looked at him, then at her full cup with some trepidation before draining it in one. Merrick was already refilling the goblets as she winced at the taste. He had to admit, it wasn't the best vintage, but he hadn't thought it anywhere near that bad.

'Did you mean what you said?' she asked, after they'd drained two more cups. 'About feeling the same?'

'Feeling the same? About what we're doing? I guess so. Why, how do you feel?'

She thought long and hard before answering. 'As if I'm being used. As if I'm some kind of tool someone else is using to keep their hands clean. And the more they use me, the filthier I become.'

For a woman who didn't say much, this Kaira certainly did plenty of thinking.

'That's a . . . very good way of putting it. But it's best not to think like that. It'll only lead to doubt. Doubt will lead to hesitation and that will get you killed. Or worse: it'll get *me* killed.'

'We all die, Merrick Ryder.'

'Fuck, woman, enough with the philosophy. We've got a job to do. Pissing and moaning won't get it done for us. I don't know why you're crying about it so much anyway. Surely you can walk away from this any time you like. Me, I'm tied to this by the balls.'

She shook her head. 'I too am tied to this.' *But not by your balls, I hope.* 'And I must see it through to the end.'

'Well then,' Merrick raised his glass again, 'here's to happy endings.' They clinked glasses and downed their wine once more. 'Now, speaking of happy endings, I have to go and pee.'

He gave her his best smile, then walked out the back to drain his bladder, hoping on hope Kaira didn't take Buttercup's earlier advice and follow him to the privy.

THIRTY-THREE

S he watched him go, and it wasn't until he had exited the door at
the rear of the alehouse that she realised she was smiling.

What was it about him she found so fascinating? It wasn't as if
she had never come into contact with men before. She knew many men
– merchants who traded at the temple, soldiers who came to train with
the Shieldmaidens, the poor and the old and the sick who came for
succour from the Daughters.

But she had never met a man like Merrick Ryder. Yes, she had met
handsome men, most of them arrogant souls who knew how good
looking they were and would play on it for the rewards it could bring.
Ryder was not *just* one of those men though; there was something troubling him within, something more to him than just an easy word and an
easy smile. Every now and then there would be something in his eyes
– a far-off look as though he were haunted by the past . . . or perhaps
by his current deeds, Kaira could not tell which.

Either way, she was determined not to fall prey to his charm. Yes, he
had offered regret at what he had to do, and it was likely his claims were
genuine, but the day was soon coming when she might well have to end
his life. Were she to concentrate too much on his more attractive qualities
it might make that task so much more difficult.

She glanced around the alehouse, trying to distract her thoughts from
how this might end. The place was busy, mostly with men and serving
maids, a hum of conversation filling the room. She could hear much of
it; mundane talk and speculation, some of it lascivious, some of it
panicked speculation on the future of the city.

She desperately wanted to be back in the Temple of Autumn. They would be making their preparations even now, readying themselves for war. If indeed the king had been defeated there must be a counterattack before the Khurtas could move into the Free States. Who better than the Shieldmaidens to lead such an attack, to strike forward into the heart of the enemy and stop their advance?

Would it have been better for her if she had been allowed to go to the front when she had requested it? She might have met her end at Kelbur Fenn with the rest of the army, but surely it would have been a better fate than the one she had to look forward to now – condemned to the squalor of the city, tasked with an impossible mission.

But she had to see this through. For better or for worse, this was her fate, and she would face it as a true sister of Vorena should.

Kaira raised the goblet to her lips, tasting the bitter, vinegary concoction that passed for wine in this place. In the Temple of Autumn they would drink on ceremonial occasions or at feast times, and wine of superior vintage, not like this filth. It was yet another reminder of what she was missing, of what she had thrown away when she had made the High Abbot pay for his affront.

Still, Kaira found it difficult to admonish herself about that. Yes, she had all but ruined her future and brought shame on herself, but oh, how that man had deserved his punishment.

She sighed and stared at the goblet of wine. Despite its sour flavour it must have been strong. Kaira felt a sluggishness in the head, her sharp edge gone. What was she doing, here in this place? Mixing with these lost souls, drinking this muck?

For a terrifying moment she saw what her future might be. What if she should never satisfy the Exarch and the Matron Mother? What if she should never be allowed to reclaim her place within the Temple of Autumn? Would she be condemned to a life of squalor in this city? Forced to live alongside the feckless and wanton of Steelhaven for the rest of her days? Made to rely on the same pointless distractions of wine and lust and . . .

Kaira stopped herself.

Lust indeed. What was she even thinking?

'Something on your mind?'

She looked up to see Merrick standing there, smiling at her as if he knew her thoughts.

'No.'

'All right, don't worry yourself, I was only asking. I'm sure it was nothing that bad.'

If only you knew.

They had another drink. This one was easier to get down, smooth almost, and Kaira was beginning to feel comfortable for the first time since she'd left the temple. Part of that worried her, but another part simply didn't care.

'I think you should tell me more about yourself, Kaira. If we're stuck in this for the duration, we should at least get to know one another.'

She thought desperately. Should she make something up? Should she just tell him the truth? *No, the truth would not do.* Kaira cursed herself and her luck. She hadn't envisioned this, and Buttercup certainly hadn't warned her that there might be some kind of interrogation, that she might need to cover her tracks with subterfuge.

'I'm . . . well . . . there's nothing to tell really.'

'Nothing to tell? You're a woman, yet you fight like a man. The only women I've ever seen do that are the Shieldmaidens . . .'

Kaira felt panic rising within her as he trailed off. She hadn't said a thing and yet already he had discovered her. What if he delved deeper? What if he worked out why she was using him?

'I was disgraced,' she said, knowing no way to speak but with the truth. 'I struck the High Abbot and was dismissed from the order.'

Merrick smiled. 'You struck the High Abbot? Ha! I love it. You're a dark horse, Kaira. The more I learn, the more I like you.'

'And what about you?' she asked, desperate to steer the conversation away from herself.

'Me? There's not much to know,' he replied. 'But since you asked.' He smiled at her, then glanced past her shoulder. 'Barkeep! Another one of these!'

Kaira looked down, shocked to see they had drunk the entire bottle between them. Almost instantly both their goblets were filled anew, and Merrick was raising his to his lips. When he had quaffed down the goblet he stood theatrically, as though he were about to take to the stage.

'I know it might surprise you to learn, since you've only seen me at my worst, that I was raised of noble stock. My father was a captain in the Sentinels of Skyhelm, my mother the third daughter of a Braegan earl or baron, I forget which; he was dead before I was born. Anyway, I was raised for greatness, trained in the sword and the horse, educated by the greatest of tutors and taught all the manners befitting a man of my birth.'

At first Kaira was unsure whether or not he was jesting; he spoke every word with a wry smile, but there was something about his manner, the way he spoke, that made them believable.

'I know what you're thinking,' he continued. 'How on earth did he fall so low? It's a sad tale, and I'm sure you won't be interested in all the details, but it begins with my father, the great and honourable Tannick Ryder, abandoning my mother when I was still but a boy.' The wry smile was gone now, and Kaira could almost taste the bitterness of his words. 'Just upped and left one night, without a word. We knew he hadn't been kidnapped or murdered, because he was seen riding out of the Lych Gate on his horse. Left his sword and armour behind too, so wherever he was going it wasn't into battle. Never to be heard from again. It broke my mother's heart.'

He stopped, as though the thought of his mother's loss brought him pain. Kaira reached over to place a hand on his, but he moved it before she could touch him.

'I'm sorry,' she said.

'Oh, don't feel sorry for me. I haven't even got to the shit part yet. The part where my mother is carried off by the Sweet Canker and poor little Merrick's left behind to manage the estate. Poor little Merrick with no parents to guide him, a fancy for the ladies and a fondness for the gambling tables. Three years I managed to hold on to that fortune. Three years before I had to sell the house and lands, along with my father's sword and armour. It was surprising how little they went for . . . or at least how little I sold them for, but that's the thing when you're young and drunk and desperate; you just don't realise the value of things.'

It was clear he was realising the value of things now.

He raised the goblet to his lips again, pausing as he did so, as though the wine was the root of all his problems – before succumbing to its temptation and taking a long sip.

Kaira felt a pang of guilt at his words. She was using him, this man who had lost everything, but she couldn't bring herself to pity him. Merrick had been the cause of his own problems – given everything, only to squander it needlessly. It was easy to put that down to the folly of youth, but there were plenty of others who had suffered more at the hands of the Sweet Canker. There were others who were suffering now, who had never got to experience the privilege brought by luck of birth.

Merrick was a product of his own folly, but it was clear there was good in him.

'Your past is behind you now. Perhaps there is hope for your future?' she said, after taking a sip from her goblet.

He smiled at that. 'Damn right there's hope. As soon as I've finished with this crappy business, all debts will be paid off. Then I'm free to leave this place and its shitty streets behind me.'

For all he had suffered, Merrick seemed to have learned nothing. All he thought about was himself, caring not a bit for those who would pay for his future with their liberty.

'But what of those who will be sold into bondage? Is it right that their suffering should benefit you?'

He raised an eyebrow. 'Are you preaching at me now, sister? I know you were a Shieldmaiden, beholden to your temple, but all that's gone now. You kind of blew that away when you gave the High Abbot a kicking. Save your sermons. I don't need them.'

'But there is—'

'Enough!' He slammed his goblet down on the bar. Several patrons nearby stopped their conversations, looking on at the promise of violence. 'I don't have a choice in this. And neither do you. You can't go back to your temple any more than I can go back to my . . .'

He stopped, as though he realised he had lost control and was speaking too loud. In an instant the smile was back on his face.

'Look, maybe delving into one another's past was a poor idea. You're right: it should be the future we think about.' He moved closer to her. She could smell him; a deep musk, as though he had bathed in exotic oils. Mixed with the wine she'd drunk it almost made her head spin. 'Those years you were locked away in that temple – they're behind you now. You can do anything you like, go anywhere you want, be with anyone you desire.'

Merrick grinned, raising an eyebrow and moving closer so she could almost feel his breath on her face. She had never been this close to a man other than in combat, but still she didn't push him away. She wasn't even sure she wanted to.

'What say we get ourselves a room?'

He ran his fingertips down her arm and into her open hand. She could feel his touch teasing her palm.

Kaira gripped Merrick's hand, squeezing it so that at first he thought she might be reciprocating his approach. Her grip tightened, and Merrick's expression soon turned from one of smug confidence to consternation as his knuckles cracked and ground together.

He managed to let out a sigh of pain before she planted her free hand firmly in the middle of his chest, knocking him off balance and sending him sprawling to the floor.

There were shouts of laughter, along with cheers of approval, from several of the alehouse's other patrons, but Kaira ignored them as she turned and marched out of the door.

She rushed through streets still busy in the gathering dusk. As she made her way from the alehouse, the freshness of the air seemed to make her head spin. She stumbled into a man, who cursed her. Rather than admonish him for his rudeness Kaira broke into a run, straining for breath, feeling trapped in these oppressive streets, the buildings on either side bearing down as if they might fall in on her at any moment.

How long she ran for she couldn't tell, but when she eventually reached the harbour she stopped. The air was no sweeter here, the smell of horse dung and urine replaced with fish and the salt sea.

Suddenly her stomach began roiling like the sea before her and she bent over and retched. Her vomit was the colour of the wine she'd consumed, only it tasted even worse on the way out.

She had been stupid to allow herself to get drunk, to allow herself to listen to that man, but she had been drawn in by his sorry tale, by the past that haunted him. Despite all his protestation to the contrary, he was still a loathsome maggot. Any potential he might have had for living a virtuous life was gone now. She knew it.

He was nothing to her.

With one sleeve she wiped tears from her eyes and a stream of bile from her lips then looked out to the sea, to the endless dark ocean, and wished as she'd never wished before that she could simply sail off and leave all this behind her.

A group of sailors were loading the last of their cargo down on the dock, and Kaira was suddenly envious of them. They would be setting sail soon, as free as the wind at their backs. How they must feel, with nothing to confine them but the waves and the distant horizon.

The temptation to join them was almost overwhelming, until her eyes fell on a child, sitting in the shadows some feet away. Kaira couldn't tell whether it was boy or girl, the face was so filthy and hair so unkempt.

This made her check her fanciful thoughts of flight; made her remember her duty.

This was why she had to stay. This was why she had to fight, to protect children like this, the vulnerable, who could not protect themselves.

Kaira stood to her full height, feeling renewed vigour in her limbs, and a strengthening of her will. She would carry out her mission and destroy the power behind the Guild, even if it meant Merrick's death.

Even if it meant her own death.

Nothing would stop her.

THIRTY-FOUR

The floor was covered with chequered tiles of dark mahogany and light oak. They were waxed and polished to such a sheen that Waylian's sandals squeaked as he walked across them. Adorning the walls were thick woven tapestries depicting scenes from history – the Windhammer's crafting of the nine swords, King Darnaith's victory over the Golgarthans, the Argent Fleet setting sail on its Fourth Glorious Crusade.

These tapestries rose up twenty feet high to meet a ceiling intricately painted with depictions of gods from all over the known world: Jarl the Healer and the Hollow Man, worshipped by druids and hedge witches across the Free States; Helion and the Moonsyr, observed by the Elharim of the far-off Riverlands; Ancient Gorm and Kaga the Creator from the grasslands of Equ'un; Tzargor Ungoth and Skargan Bonestrife from the snowy wastes of Golgartha; all spinning around one another as though part of the same divine constellation.

Simply looking at it made Waylian dizzy, and this was just the ante-chamber. Beyond the massive brass doors that stood opposite, vigilantly guarded by four Raven Knights, was the Crucible Chamber. The prospect of stepping over that hallowed threshold filled him with dread, even with Magistra Gelredida at his side. It was the seat of power within the Tower of Magisters, where sat the ruling council, the five most powerful casters in the Free States, and by definition the world. Waylian had never felt so small and unworthy in his life.

Two of the Raven Knights marched forward to where the pair of them stood. Waylian almost took a step back as they approached; so imposing were they in their armour of black, their beaked greathelms peering down from atop their massive frames.

Gelredida casually held out her hands and one of the knights slid an iron bracelet over each of her wrists. Waylian watched agog as the bracelets suddenly tightened of their own accord, the intricate gilding on each manacle suddenly moving and twisting as they shrank to fit her delicate wrists. Without a word the Raven Knights returned to their positions at the door.

'They are to counteract my powers,' Gelredida said, answering Waylian's unspoken question. 'Magick may not be used within the Crucible Chamber. All those who enter must wear these so that, whatever their allegiance, they may not use their talent on others.'

'The council do not trust one another?' It seemed madness that such a measure should be enforced.

'The Crucible of Magisters has not always had such a civilised and unified membership. We have not always lived in such an enlightened age, and there was a time when these bonds would have saved lives. It is an antiquated convention, but some traditions are hard to break.'

She spoke the words in such a way that Waylian wondered if she meant there was still a thick seam of discord running through the council after so many centuries of strife and misrule. He guessed he would just have to wait and see.

'As an apprentice will I be allowed in the chamber?'

'Now that I am . . . helpless, I am permitted someone to accompany me. A bodyguard, if you will.' She didn't even try to disguise the irony in her words. 'Besides, this experience will be good for you.'

'And I don't have to wear any manacles? What if I—'

'If you what? Suddenly manifest a modicum of talent with one of the Arts? Please, Grimm, try not to make me laugh. This is an occasion that requires solemnity, not hilarity.' Gelredida didn't look as if she was going to laugh any time soon. 'If any apprentice was strong enough in the Arts to be a danger, it would be the first time in a thousand years.'

Two of the Raven Knights grabbed the thick brass rings bolted to the centre of the huge doors and pulled. There had been no fanfare, no banging of gongs, but on some kind of silent signal, the knights were given their orders and Gelredida granted her audience.

Waylian felt his heart pounding in his chest as the Crucible Chamber was revealed. The Magistra walked forward and Waylian followed, marvelling at the vast chamber that sat almost at the summit of the Tower of Magisters.

It was a wide semicircle surrounded by a gallery carved from solid stone, as though the tower itself was a kind of vast, solid monolith hewn from a natural rock formation. Waylian had seen the lower levels. He knew they were crafted from wood and stone, so how this solid room had been built so high up, he could only guess at.

Friezes and intricate sigils were carved into the rock. Everywhere he looked Waylian could only wonder at the craftsmanship. Gargoyles leered at him from every shadowy corner, seemingly trying to tear themselves from the solid rock, but as he entered, his attention was inextricably drawn to the five pulpits that stood at the centre of the room.

The five Archmasters sat behind their pulpits with expressions of haughty indifference. When he had first been inducted into the Tower as an apprentice over a year ago Waylian had seen them at the inaugural ceremony and listened to them give speeches on the differing Arts. Their names were legend – indelibly etched on his consciousness. Each of them represented a different discipline of magick – one of the five Primary Arts – and they were unrivalled masters: casters with no peer in all the far-off continents of the world.

To the far left sat Hoylen Crabbe, Master Invoker and Keeper of the Books. He was a thin man with black hair set in a severe widow's peak, his dark robes studded with ancient sigils, which naturally Waylian didn't recognise. Though he only looked in his mid-forties, Waylian knew that a man of such power had to be much older.

Next to him was Crannock Marghil, Master Channeller and Keeper of the Keys. Unlike Crabbe, Crannock looked every one of his eighty-odd years, his hair thin and wispy, his liver-spotted flesh almost translucent. He wore thick eyeglasses and his shoulders barely supported the red and blue robe that hung from them. It was said the Channeller's Art was the most dangerous of the five, and it was clear Crannock had paid dearly for his talent.

In the centre sat Drennan Folds, Master Summoner and Keeper of the Scrolls. He was a heavy-set man, with grey hair still thick about his scalp and sideburns which ran all the way down his face to almost meet at his chin. His brow was creased in a perpetual furrow and his brown robes looked all but starched to his broad frame. He bore an ugly scar from forehead to cheek, which bisected his eye, the injury having turned it a milky colour in contrast to the other, which was ice blue. Clearly

Drennan had paid his own price for his Art, and Waylian almost shuddered at the thought of what foul creature he must have summoned to give him such a mark.

At Drennan's left hand was Nero Laius, Master Diviner and Keeper of the Ravens. He was short in comparison to his peers, with a curly mop of grey hair and an almost kindly look to him. Waylian knew it would not do to underestimate such a man though – none of the Archmasters had reached their position without dirtying their hands to some extent.

Finally, on the far right sat Lucen Kalvor, Master Alchemist and Keeper of the Instruments. He looked even younger than Hoylen Crabbe and was the newest of the Archmasters after his predecessor, and Lucen's previous tutor, had been found dead in his chambers. No one had been able to discover the old man's cause of death, and it was a seldom spoken rumour that Lucen had topped his tutor to usurp his position. If there were any truth to it, none accused the handsome young Archmaster and he was shown due deference, either out of fear or the respect that his position demanded.

These five watched as Gelredida and Waylian approached. Even though their eyes were focused on his mistress, Waylian couldn't help but feel intimidated.

'Magistra Gelredida,' said Nero Laius with a smile. 'A rare pleasure to see you in these chambers.' Waylian couldn't work out whether or not he was being genuine.

'A pleasure? I am sure, Archmaster Laius,' Gelredida replied. 'My heart beats that much faster now that I stand before the Crucible.'

That, on the other hand, even Waylian knew, smacked of insincerity. Nevertheless, Archmaster Laius kept the smile on his lips.

'Enough with the pleasantries.' Drennan Folds' scowl deepened, his milky-white eye seeming to darken slightly with his displeasure. 'We have matters that require our attention. Why have you requested an audience?'

Gelredida offered Folds a wry look, her weathered features regarding him with barely shadowed amusement.

Folds seemed to recede a little, and it was clear there was much history between these two. Waylian dare not even speculate as to the nature of it.

'I take it you are all aware of the murders taking place in the city? Mutilated corpses? Forbidden ciphers?'

'We are.' This was Crannock Marghil, his voice as thin and weak as the flesh that covered his ancient bones. 'A terrible business, we all agree. But we are led to believe it is nothing but the work of a rogue caster. Certainly nothing that should concern the Crucible.'

'I'm afraid, Archmaster Marghil, it is exactly the kind of thing that should concern you.'

'Come, come, Magistra,' said Archmaster Laius. 'I'm sure someone of your boundless ability and vigilance can manage to track down one lone murderer.'

Gelredida smiled back. 'I agree. But this is no ordinary murderer. This is a singularly cunning and dangerous killer, who could put us all in danger.'

Drennan Folds barked with laughter. 'And what could be so dangerous about him that he could frighten our own Red Witch?'

Waylian felt the hairs on his neck prickle. He had heard Bram call her that several times, but only when he was sure she was out of earshot. For someone to call her that to her face . . .

Gelredida regarded Archmaster Folds, unruffled by his attempt to provoke her. 'Because, Drennan, they are attempting to use the Ninth Art.'

The Archmasters fell silent.

The Ninth Art. Waylian had only heard about it in stories. He'd certainly never studied it in a book. It was said to be the one Art that was forbidden – five were known to the Caste, three were lost, leaving only one. And what a horror that last one was.

Legend told it was abuse of the Ninth Art that had unleashed the Hells on Earth; that had opened the gates to the underworld and released a daemonic horde onto the lands of men, and that only by Arlor's might was total destruction averted.

If someone was dabbling in the Ninth Art, they were either insane or drenched in more evil than Waylian could ever comprehend. Whichever it was, they had to be stopped.

Until now he hadn't appreciated just how important it had been to catch their quarry. Before, he had just thought the culprit a rogue caster, a sadist . . . a killer.

Now it was clear the one they were after was much, much more.

'What proof do you have?' asked Crannock Marghil, once Gelredida's words had sunk in.

'I have studied the sigils daubed at the site of each murder. Whoever the killer is, they have learned well their ancient lore and the path of the Gate Walker.'

'But the closest Waystone is . . .'

'Yes, the Chapel of Ghouls.'

Drennan Folds sat forward, peering at Gelredida with his one good eye. 'So why hasn't the gate been opened? If this is the Maleficar Necrus returned, why is the city not plagued by daemons?'

'I am unsure. The caster might not be proficient enough with their wards. Perhaps they might not have managed to find a sacrifice strong enough to complete the ritual. They might just be biding their time.'

'A lot of "mights", Magistra. How are we to work with "mights"?'

'You can at least help me find this killer. Nero could have his diviners search for signs. We could—'

'There is little aid the diviners could give. If this rogue caster is using the Ninth Art the sacrifice needed to find him would be—'

'Would be worth it!'

Gelredida was clearly losing patience.

'Magistra.' It was Hoylen Crabbe, who hadn't spoken till now. His voice was deep and rich, and Waylian felt some kind of hypnotic lull, as though drawn to Crabbe like a bee to honey. 'Our king is dead. We have enemies at our doorstep. The Crucible has much to consider, much planning for the protection of our city, and you bring us this? There could never be a rogue caster powerful enough to master the Ninth Art. Only an Archmaster could—'

'If the Chapel of Ghouls is opened there won't be a city left to protect,' said Gelredida. 'There won't be anything left.'

'We are more than confident in your abilities, Magistra. You will find this killer; of that we are sure.' Crabbe smiled, and it seemed there was no more to say. The decision was made and even Gelredida could do nothing to sway it.

The doors behind them suddenly opened, and Waylian thought it might be a sign for them to leave, but Gelredida stood her ground, looking up at each of them with stern defiance.

'We have other petitioners to see, Magistra,' said Master Folds, indicating towards the brass doors.

'I think perhaps Magistra Gelredida might stay to witness this,' said Crabbe. 'Then she can see first hand just what we are up against. Perhaps her opinion might be of value. She is, after all, concerned for the well-being of our city.'

'Preposterous,' barked Folds. 'She is not a member of the Crucible.'

Crannock Marghil raised a withered hand to curb Master Folds' ire. 'Perhaps just this once, Drennan, we might dispense with protocol?'

Drennan Folds clearly wanted her gone, but he reluctantly deferred to his fellow Archmasters. Gelredida bowed briefly, then moved to one side of the chamber, seeming to blend into the shadows.

Waylian looked to the open doorway. He didn't quite know what he expected to enter though those brass doors – but it certainly wasn't what came strolling in.

Flanked by two Raven Knights came a portly, dark-skinned man, perhaps from Dravhistan or Kajrapur, if the headwrap he wore was any indication. He was dressed in flowing blue robes tied at the waist by a red sash and he clutched a shoulder bag close to his side. His smile was wide as he entered and he walked to the centre of the chamber, touching a finger to forehead then lips before bowing theatrically in front of the five Archmasters.

'Greetings, O great and powerful lords of the Crucible. My name is Massoum Am Kalhed Las Fahir Am Jadar Abbasi, and I bring salutations from the Prince of the Riverlands.'

'We know who you are,' said Drennan Folds, his voice dripping with contempt. 'And we know why you're here. You have come to make a traitor's bargain. Do you think us betrayers? Do you think us fools who would turn our backs on our own kind?'

Abbasi's smile wavered just slightly. 'Humility and inadequacy forbid me from attempting to discern what men as great and powerful as you might think, my lord. I am but a humble messenger, here to make an offer on behalf of the Elharim you know as Amon Tugha.'

Waylian felt his mouth suddenly go dry. This was the herald of Amon Tugha himself. The man who had invaded the Free States. The warrior who had slain their king.

'Speak then,' said Master Folds. 'And be gone from this place while you're still able.'

The foreigner smiled nervously, bowed once more and reached into the bag at his side. The Archmasters shifted slightly as he did so, clearly afraid of what he might produce, especially since they were all wearing the iron manacles that meant their magick was useless should it be a weapon. But Abbasi simply pulled out an old ragged doll and placed it on the ground. He reached into his bag a further four times, pulling out another four dolls and placing them on the floor in front of him.

Waylian almost let out a sigh, but the Archmasters did not share his relief.

As Abbasi sat the final doll on the ground, Master Folds shot to his feet. 'What is the meaning of this?' His milky eye looked as if it might pop out of its socket.

Massoum Abbasi stepped back, holding his hands up as though unsure of what he had done to cause such offence.

'Apologies, masters. I did not mean to cause you alarm.'

'Then you clearly have no idea of what these represent,' said old Crannock Marghil, looking mournfully at the small dolls.

Waylian had no idea either. They were crudely made rag dolls, like any pauper's child might own. Each was dressed in a different colour, with differing hair styles, some grey, some dark, one wispy and . . . as he looked . . . Waylian couldn't help but think they reminded him of . . .

'My lords,' said Abbasi. 'I am aware of what these represent . . . as are you. But the Prince of the Riverlands does not show this as a sign of his intent, merely as a show of the power available to him. A power he vows not to use in return for your . . . inaction.' The Archmasters shifted uncomfortably but none of them spoke. 'Now your king is dead and your armies routed, there will be no one to stand against the horde that sweeps towards your city. But fear not. Amon Tugha is generous, and those who refuse to stand against him will be not only spared, but also rewarded.'

Waylian felt anger well up inside. Who did this messenger think he was, to offer such a bargain? To think they might betray their city, their people, for the mercy of a foreign invader?

But the Archmasters still did not move and gave no reply.

It was as much their cowardice as the messenger's arrogance that filled Waylian with a sudden fury. He couldn't stop himself from wanting to take a step forward, opening his mouth to shout at this cur, and telling him the Crucible would not just stand by and allow this foreigner to insult them in their own hallowed chamber.

He felt a hand grip his arm so tightly he almost cried out. It was clear the Red Witch was also moved to anger, but she was wise enough not to speak. As her fingers dug into the flesh of his arm, Waylian decided it was best he follow her example.

Crannock Marghil finally nodded his ancient head. 'Your message is delivered. Return to your Elharim master and tell him we will think on it.'

Massoum Abbasi bowed, touching his forehead and lips one last time. 'That is all he asks, O great master.'

270

With that he backed away from the five pulpits and retreated from the chamber, followed by the Raven Knights, and leaving the five rag dolls behind.

Gelredida strode forward, careful not to step near the dolls. 'It is clear you all have much to discuss,' she said.

'And it's clear you have much to do,' said Master Folds, obviously disturbed by what had occurred. Waylian had no idea of the dolls' significance, but felt it must have been grave indeed.

Gelredida inclined her head then turned to leave. Waylian followed her out of the huge brass doors, daring a single glance back as they were closed behind him. If the Archmasters had much to discuss they were in no hurry to begin; and, as the door slammed shut, each of them looked solemn in his own way, his mouth closed, eyes fixed on the dolls that bore such a striking resemblance to each of the five men.

'You are not to speak of what you have witnessed here today,' said the Magistra after the manacles had been removed from her wrists and they made their way down the huge winding staircase that ran the entire height of the Tower.

'I don't understand any of it, anyway.'

She stopped before him, turning to look him in the eye. He could see her assessing him, as though she were weighing up the value of explaining things to such a useless apprentice.

'There is a high price to pay for the use of magick, Waylian. It is a price you may one day have to pay, if you ever manifest any talent. The Archmasters are fearful old men, and Amon Tugha has just exploited that fear. Those dolls represent the magicks of the old days, of the wytch-workers and the shamans of the northern lands. Each of the Archmasters is now marked, cursed with old magicks that will exact a heavy cost in the countering. But Amon Tugha has made it clear there will be no price to pay if they sit on their behinds and do nothing.'

'And is that why they would not offer you any more aid in capturing the rogue? Because of what it would cost?'

Gelredida smiled at him. It was a small gesture, but one Waylian had never received before, and it took him aback.

'You are learning, Waylian. We might make an apprentice of you yet.' With that she turned and made her way down the stairs. 'That will be all for today. I think you've earned some respite from my company.'

It was a respite Waylian would gladly have accepted on any other day, but he had to admit: the old bird was starting to grow on him.

Nevertheless, he wasn't one to pass up a free afternoon, so as soon as she headed off to her chambers, Waylian could barely stop himself sprinting for his own.

When he finally reached them, almost breathless from his run and grateful he hadn't bumped into any of the other apprentices, he stopped suddenly. The door to his chamber was ajar, and there was the faintest flicker of candlelight from within.

Waylian gingerly pushed his door open, wondering what would be waiting to greet him. What he saw inside was beyond anything he could have imagined.

On his bed, laid out as though ready for her funeral, was the naked form of Gerdy. Her hair had been splayed out on his pillow, her flesh smooth and soft in the winking light. Beside her, smiling from ear to ear, stood Rembram Thule.

'Ta da!' he said, gesturing to Gerdy's supine body as if he'd just conjured her from thin air.

Waylian quickly entered the room and slammed the door behind him before anyone else saw what Bram had brought him.

'What the fuck is this?' he asked, his voice shriller than he'd have liked, but under the circumstances it was probably appropriate.

'I've brought you a gift, Grimm,' replied Bram. 'It's what you wanted, isn't it?'

'Yes . . . no . . . well, not like this. What have you done to her?'

Bram stepped forward and tousled Gerdy's hair. 'Oh, just a couple of drops of mugwort infused with tangleroot. Elementary stuff, Grimm. Even you could manage it.'

'You've drugged her?'

Bram frowned. 'How else was I supposed to get her here?'

Waylian could only look down at Gerdy in dismay. 'But . . . what am I supposed to do with her now?'

'Anything you want, Grimm. That's kind of the idea.' He gave a suggestive wink. 'Anyway, I'm guessing you don't want an audience, so I'll see you later.' As Waylian stared at Gerdy on his bed, Bram sidled past and opened the door, pausing for a moment. 'Do let me know how you get on, won't you?' And with another wink, he was gone, closing the door behind him.

Waylian stared after him, suddenly not wanting to look at the naked girl on his bed.

What in the hells was Bram thinking?

And what was he supposed to do now?

He supposed he could wait for her to wake up, then try to explain what had happened. But then, Bram wasn't here. There was no one to back up his story. If Gerdy woke up naked in a strange room she was likely to scream the place down. Waylian was damned if he was going to hang around for that.

Half-heartedly he grabbed a spare blanket and flung it over Gerdy in a limp gesture to spare her modesty. Then, without a glance back, he ran out the door and fled down the corridor.

He could only hope she'd wake up, wonder how in the hells she'd got there and just go back to her own chamber.

With any luck she wouldn't wake up yelling for the Raven Knights that she'd been drugged by some raper. And who would they all point the finger at then?

Yes, Waylian Grimm, that's who.

As he ran down the corridor, he'd never wished for the quiet boredom of his hometown of Groffham quite so much.

THIRTY-FIVE

The Promenade of Kings was lined with more people than Nobul had ever seen in one place. There were thousands: men and women, children and elders. Rich standing next to poor, warriors next to priests. But despite that mass of people, the air was eerily silent.

Even the dark clouds billowing overhead seemed to be waiting – observing the vigil kept within the city, waiting until the old man had been brought by before unleashing their deluge on the filthy streets below.

Nobul was part of the Greencoat detail posted to control the crowd, but he couldn't see as how they'd be needed. There might be plenty of tears, but Nobul couldn't see any sign that there'd be trouble.

They were all there, standing in a row: Kilgar and Denny, Anton, Dustin, Edric, Hake. Hells, even Bilgot was there, waiting in solemn silence, all the piss and bluster gone out of him. It was like there was something in the air, something that had leeched the spirit from every man, woman and dog in the streets.

But it wasn't every day a city buried its king.

There was a murmur from the crowd. Heads turned, necks stretching to see what was going on. From the front, Nobul could see that the main gate to the promenade had been opened. It wouldn't be long now.

'This is a shit business,' Denny murmured beside him. 'What the fuck are we gonna do now?'

'Well,' Nobul said, trying his best to keep his voice down. 'We're gonna stand right here and be all upstanding and respectful as they bring the king past.'

'That's not what I meant.'

No, Nobul knew exactly what Denny meant, but he didn't have an answer for him. What were they going to do now they had no king? Cael Mastragall had been the Uniter. He'd brought the Free States together, taken warring provinces and made them a kingdom. Who was going to hold that together now – his daughter? A girl barely old enough to marry? Nobul doubted she'd be much in the way of a strong ruler. Not with the devious bastards that ruled the other provinces vying for their slice of power. She'd be lucky to survive the year.

That wasn't Nobul's problem. What he was more concerned with was what the Khurtas might do next. Was he worried though? Did he even give a shit if they came right up to the walls, banging their war drums?

Did he fuck.

It might be his chance to get back to the old days. There'd be no choice then. Yes, he'd most likely get himself killed this time, but what a death he'd have. And he'd make sure he took plenty of those savage bastards with him.

He could see the procession now – armoured knights on two massive destriers leading the way, followed by a palanquin. Nobul couldn't quite see yet, but he guessed the king was laid out on it, most likely clutching his sword to his chest like every king before him.

The promenade was lined with statues of old kings dead and gone, watching as the latest of their number was carried past. There were too many to count, the promenade leading off further than the eye could see. How many of them had been carried along displayed in all their glory like Cael?

It was a better send off than Nobul would ever get, but then again – dead was dead. He glanced at the crowd, looking at their mournful faces, and wondered if they even knew why they were weeping. Were they sorry for the king they loved, or sorry for themselves – under threat from a foreign horde and with no one left to lead them against it?

King Cael had certainly been loved, but Nobul couldn't help but wonder if the old man truly deserved it. Nobul had served under him on campaign, seen first hand how ruthless the old bastard could be. At Bakhaus Gate they'd managed to win because they were as much afraid of the king and his strict discipline as they were of the enemy. Nobul had seen one man flogged to death for thieving. He could barely bring himself to remember what they'd done to the two lads caught raping.

It came with the territory, though. Cael had to be a ruthless bastard. Without him the Aeslanti would have run rampant and turned the Free

States into a slave nation. As much as Nobul had hated him at the time, he knew they had much to thank Cael for.

'Here he comes,' said Denny out of the side of his mouth.

Kilgar leaned over. 'Another word from you and there'll be a boot up your arse, boy.'

Denny clamped his jaw shut.

Nobul watched as those white destriers got closer. The Knights of the Blood astride them had done their best to polish their armour and barding, but there was no mistaking men fresh from battle. The red tabards they wore were ripped and bloodstained, the matching flags tattered and torn. One of them had a dented greathelm, the other looked like someone had taken to his spaulder and vambrace with a hammer.

People were weeping openly now, young girls and old men joined in grief. Nobul had to admit it moved him a bit, but he had no tears left. He hadn't shed any for his son, and he wasn't about to shed any for an old bastard he'd never even spoke to.

'Steady, lads,' said Kilgar, and Nobul wondered if there was about to be trouble when he noticed Hake and Anton. Both of them were weeping like girls. Well, let them have their grief. Nobul had done plenty of weeping in his time, though none of it recent. He'd wept for dead friends, for a dead wife; hells, he'd even wept for himself from time to time. If a man wanted to cry then let him. Anyone who'd ever seen battle knew there was no great shame in it.

The knights had passed them now, their horses shying and skittish, surrounded as they were by the huge crowd. Nobul could see the palanquin and the men that carried it. The knights on horseback had looked battered, but these men looked as though they had been to the hells and back. It wasn't just the dishevelled state of their armour; Nobul could easily recognise the faces of men haunted by war.

But then who better to carry their king to his final interment? Who better than men who had fought beside him, suffered with him, bled with him. If Nobul was ever to be conveyed to his final rest he would hope it would be by men such as this.

As for the king, he looked more magnificent than ever, lying in his shining armour of office, the ancient sword, the fabled Helsbayn, clutched to his body, his steel crown firmly affixed to his head.

Suddenly one of the soldiers stumbled, fatigue taking his legs away, and he almost fell. The palanquin tipped, the king's body almost toppling off as the crowd breathed out in horror. Before he could think, Nobul was moving, striding forward to take the palanquin's weight from the man and righting it once more.

For a moment Nobul locked eyes with the young soldier and he saw something there he hadn't seen for a long time. It was emptiness, a void that only the true horror of battle could bring, and they shared that look for just an instant.

Nobul nodded to him, taking the weight of the palanquin on his shoulder and allowing the man some respite. He deserved more, but it was all Nobul could give him. Before he knew it they were moving on once more, the relentless momentum of the procession urging the palanquin onwards. Nobul had no time to think, he just moved on, taking the weight on his shoulder and carrying the king to his final resting place, whether he was worthy of the honour or not.

Honour? Was it an honour to carry such a man? Nobul knew he wasn't in a position to judge anyone. The deeds he'd done in his life were no better or worse than those of King Cael Mastragall. As for being worthy? He'd served under Cael's command back in the day. Nobul reckoned he was as worthy as any.

As they moved forward, Nobul could smell the other men, their stink permeating the air. Any man who'd spent weeks on campaign started to smell all kinds of awful, but there was another smell beneath the dirt and grime and sweat. It was the stink of rot, of festering wounds gone too long untended, the hollow, putrid stench of teeth gone too long uncared for and feet with too many open sores.

It brought back memories Nobul would rather have left forgot. On the way back from Bakhaus Gate as many men had died from the cold and hunger as had died in battle and he'd almost been one of them. He knew what these men were going through, and it filled him with deep sadness. It wasn't the death of the king people should have been mourning; it was the thousands of others left by the roadside to go unburied. It was the young lads, shivering in their own shit and crying for their mothers. Bright-faced young men who'd marched off to war with the promise of victory and glory only to find their end in a lonely field, far from home.

But then life wasn't ever fair, was it?

The vast Sepulchre of Crowns came into view up ahead. Nobul could see the huge building just past the destriers trotting in front of him. It was an ancient mausoleum, housing the coffins of a hundred dead kings and queens. Since half the kings had worshipped the Old Gods and the other half Arlor and Vorena, it wasn't seen as right that the funeral rites for Steelhaven's rulers should take place in the Temple of Autumn. So the Sepulchre of Crowns was where they were all laid to rest, under the watchful eye of gods old and new. Nobul wondered whether Arlor and the Lord of Crows were even now arguing over who got to take the old bastard to the hells.

A vast stairway led up to the doors of the Sepulchre, and the lads carrying the front of the palanquin lowered it so as the king didn't slide right off the back. In front, the horses took the stairs like they were practised, their footing sure on the wide stone steps. Nobul began to feel the strain as they made their way up, but if none of these lads was about to complain then he wasn't neither. Waiting at the top were representatives from the Temple of Autumn: Shieldmaidens bearing their weapons and arms proudly, alongside white-clad priestesses whose heads were shrouded in respect. They led the way through vast double doors rising almost twenty feet.

Inside, the Sepulchre of Crowns was a magnificent sight. Vast columns rose up to a massive glass ceiling, covered in multicoloured panes that painted everything inside with a differing hue. Lining the walls were friezes hewn from marble and statues depicting every king and queen of Steelhaven, marking their final resting place. For a second Nobul almost forgot the reason he was there, almost forgot the burden he still carried on his shoulder.

As they reached the altar at the end of the long paved aisle, Nobul and the bearers heaved the palanquin from their shoulders, and laid their king before it. Nobul became aware of the rest of the congregation, 'the great and the good' of the Free States, and suddenly felt out of place.

The dark-skinned regent, Odaka Du'ur, looked on, his face a stern mask. He had been the king's adviser; they had shed blood together. Nobul knew well how that could bond one man to another. Beside Odaka Du'ur stood many others, dressed in their robes of state; most of them Nobul wouldn't have recognised if he fell over them in the street. Only one stood out, and this despite her diminutive size and the modest black gown she wore.

Princess Janessa held herself erect with a grim expression that sat oddly on her pretty face. Nobul could see she was holding back tears, trying to do her duty as she watched them present her father.

Nobul suddenly felt guilty for all the things he'd thought about the old man. Yes he'd been a bastard and sent many a man to his grave, but who could say Nobul Jacks would have done any different if he'd been in Cael's boots?

He began to feel he'd outstayed his welcome. People were here to mourn, to show their respects and send their king off to the hells or the Halls of Arlor or whatever it was they believed. Nobul was only here because he'd wanted to help some poor lad. Nobul shifted to the back of the Sepulchre, and before they could close the massive doors, he managed to slip outside.

Once the doors had slammed shut behind him, he could only feel relief, sucking in a big gulp of air as the first of the rainfall spattered down around him.

A while later, when the men and women of King Cael's court had listened to the words of priests and mumbled their prayers, it was the turn of the common folk to say their goodbyes to their king. None of them seemed to mind queuing in the rain, and most of them were drenched by the time they got to enter the Sepulchre.

Nobul stood alongside the rest of the lads, watching as the king's subjects filed past to see him in state, to lay a flower or two and shed a tear over him. It seemed the whole city had been moved to grief, but Nobul didn't feel like joining in. If the Khurtas came there'd be plenty of tears to shed soon enough. Wasn't worth shedding them now over one old man.

'Makes you think, doesn't it?' said Denny.

'What does?' Nobul replied.

'All these people come to cry over one man. Makes you wonder what it might be like when you die.'

'Not really.'

'I mean, my old ma will probably come, if I die first. I haven't got no kids, no wife. What if I never get married? I don't fancy dying alone.'

'We all die alone, Denny. Ain't no one can do it for you.'

They stood for a while longer. As the day wore on the crowd thinned. Once the streets were nearly empty there was no need for Amber Watch to be standing around any longer.

As they made their way back to the barracks, Denny walked beside Nobul, and it was obvious something was troubling him.

'You're a veteran of Bakhaus Gate. You've killed people before, haven't you?' he said finally.

Nobul felt a stiffness in his neck. It was a question that he was not going to answer. If he told Denny 'no' it'd be an obvious lie, and if he said 'yes' it would only lead to more unwanted questions.

'*I* killed someone once,' Denny said, before Nobul could think of a reply. 'Weren't no criminal neither, just a bystander in the wrong place at the wrong time.'

Now *that* Nobul had not been expecting.

He looked at Denny, and he could tell the lad was uncomfortable.

'It were an accident . . . Kilgar and the lads know, but I haven't told no one else. You won't tell no one, will you, Lincon?'

Nobul shook his head. He'd killed enough times, and spoken to enough men who'd killed, to know what a bastard it could be to live with. Some handled it better than others, but he imagined Denny of all people wasn't suited to it.

'Thanks. I know I can rely on you, mate. I trust you.'

'We've all done things we're not proud of, lad,' Nobul said. Gods knew he was testament to that.

'Yeah . . . It lives with you though, doesn't it? Stays with you. Nights are the worst.' *Isn't that the truth.* 'I can still see him lying there, eyes all dead and glassy, covered in blood. I shot him, see. We was trying to catch a killer, thought we had him too, cornered on a rooftop, and then all the hells happened at once. My crossbow just went off, and when it had all calmed down there was this lad, lying on the roof, stuck with the bolt and bleeding to death.'

Nobul clenched his fists.

Denny had been the one that killed his fucking boy.

'Anyway, I should shut up. Best not to dwell on things.'

With that Denny walked on, locked in his own thoughts.

Nobul's fists were clenched so tight his nails almost broke the skin, but he just watched as Denny walked away. Watched as the bloke that killed his boy showed his back to him.

And Nobul didn't do a thing.

THIRTY-SIX

They spoke at length of the peril the Free States faced.

Odaka, Garret and Durket listened intently to General Hawke's recounting of the Battle of Kelbur Fenn, to how the enemy had come at them in a massive wave, a single horde of screaming, painted warriors. At first these were easily cut down by the Knights of the Blood, but they were just bait – warriors sacrificed by Amon Tugha to lure the armies of the Free States into a trap.

The Khurtas were a rabble, a horde of savage killers, but it seemed the Elharim warlord had turned them into something more. While the king's knights ploughed through their ranks on the field, thousands more were silently moving beyond the valley of Kelbur Fenn to flank the waiting armies of the Free States. They unleashed their beasts of war: fell hounds and armoured bears, quickly following with spear and axe to sack the supply wagons and hack down the reserve forces.

At the front, the Khurtas had been routed, or so it seemed, and the Knights of the Blood gave chase. What awaited them beyond the valley was no broken horde though, but the Elharim's artillery – his war machines and his archers, waiting for the knights to ride within range. They were cut down almost to a man, and by the time the king led the few survivors back to his own lines, all he found was a decimated wagon train and his reserve levies slaughtered.

It was later, as they counted their dead, that they discovered the king had been murdered. No one saw the assassin and no mark was left on his body, but he was found in his tent, his sacred sword still sheathed at his side, his eyes shut as though he merely rested.

All this Janessa listened to without saying a word. She took little notice of General Hawke's tales of war or even his account of her father's assassination. Even when he went on to tell of the relentless horde's movements, how they had passed Coppergate, all but ignoring the city and moving into Braega, she had barely registered his words. The men recognised her grief, and carried on their meeting as though she were not there, talking of troop movements, bolstering defences, auxiliary levies, mercenary companies, and a score of other things.

Janessa was glad of their consideration, but it was not just grief that occupied her mind. It was not just the fact that her father had been killed, his body brought back on a plain wooden pallet, unadorned and inglorious, that concerned her. It wasn't even that she was now burdened with the responsibility of governing the Free States and seeing to the well-being of its peoples. She knew it was this that should have been foremost in her thoughts; that there were thousands relying on her and her council to make the right decision, to protect and defend them.

And yet, to her shame, all Janessa could think of was River.

'. . . and we must speak to the Banker's League,' Odaka said.

It was as though his words suddenly brought her back to the meeting, the faces of the other men suddenly coming into sharp focus. Why this comment meant anything more to her than anything else that had been said she did not know, but there was something in it, something in Odaka's tone, that made her think this was the most important thing of all.

'Why is that?' she asked.

The men all turned to her, as though noticing her for the first time. Odaka looked to Chancellor Durket, whose face contorted with a sickly smile before he began speaking.

'Majesty, the conflicts your father has been involved in over the years, the strife that has afflicted the Free States, has taken a devastating toll on the Crown coffers. We are already indebted to the Banker's League for just over ten million crowns. If we are to face the Khurtas and see them struck from our lands we will need further funds to pay for troops, equipment, supplies.'

Janessa had been little involved with the running of her father's kingdom, but even she knew the Banker's League was a consortium headed by rich and powerful figures from several foreign countries. Without their aid the Free States would be at the mercy of its enemies.

'So what should we do?'

Durket looked to Odaka, who offered little help, forcing him to continue. 'We have set up a meeting with one of their representatives. I'm sure we will be able to come to a mutually beneficial arrangement.'

'I will speak with him.' She'd said it before she'd even thought about the words.

'Majesty?' Durket's eyes seemed to bulge. 'I think it best if I . . .'

'I said I will speak with him, Chancellor.'

Durket nodded, but Odaka took up where Durket had left off.

'I understand your eagerness to take up your father's mantle, but perhaps we should begin with other, less testing, matters of state. The Banker's League can be . . . tricky, at best.'

'I will soon be responsible for *all* matters of state. My father did not hide behind his council, and neither will I.' She stood, hoping it might give her a modicum of authority, but feared it made her look more like a petulant child. 'General Hawke, we will discuss later what supplies our armies need to face the enemy. Chancellor, I will need to see all ledgers relating to the Crown's expenditure. Odaka, you will make the arrangements for my coronation immediately. Our people cannot be left without a monarch, especially with the enemy at our gates.'

Each of the men nodded at her demands and Janessa, for the first time ever, almost felt up to her task. Her fists were clenched, if only to stop them shaking, but it still felt good. She felt in command.

Nevertheless, she had to leave before she crumbled. Before the veneer of control sloughed off and revealed what lay beneath – that she was scared and in pain.

'If that will be all, gentlemen?'

She rose to leave, and the four men stood and bowed their heads as she passed.

The corridors of Skyhelm housed more Sentinels than Janessa had ever seen. Some of her father's Knights of the Blood also stood vigil taking some respite before their return to the war in the north, though Janessa guessed they were no longer her father's – they were now hers.

As surrounded as she was by men who would gladly give their lives for her, Janessa still felt vulnerable. She made her way to her chamber as fast as she could. When she reached it she took from her gown the only key that would open her door, and unlocked it.

It was dark inside, as it always was. Years ago, in a different life, Janessa had hated it when her room was plunged into darkness. Now she didn't care, for she knew *he* would be waiting in the shadow.

She locked the door behind her and, within a moment, felt his breath on her neck, his arms moving to envelop her. She closed her eyes and let herself succumb to him.

Over the past days he had stayed in her chamber and she had nursed him back to health. During that time she had told him everything, as he had told her his own fears and dreams days before in the tiny square. They had found solace in one another, a union of thought and spirit. Raelan and Leon and thoughts of any other suitor were forgotten. Only one man owned her heart.

She wanted him more than anything, wanted to feel his kiss, his arms around her, the weight of him on her. Yet she had resisted, as had he. Now though, after her father's funeral, after endless council meetings, she was tired; she could resist no longer and she would not allow River to either.

They fell on the bed, and he kissed her lips. She kissed him back greedily, sharing his breath, running her fingers over his back, feeling the scars and the taut muscle beneath. One hand ran down his hard chest, brushing over the bandage that protected the now healed wound at his side. There was a livid scar – just one more to join his score of others. As her hand moved down towards his groin he stopped her.

'We should not,' he said, words she had heard him say so many times, but she was in no mood to stop now. She would be queen soon enough, servant and master to thousands, responsible for the lives and souls of her subjects. Surely she deserved this . . . this one respite from duty and obligation?

'We should,' she replied, moving her hand further down.

He was strong enough to stop her if he truly wished, but it was clear his desire was as deep as hers and he allowed her to fumble at the drawstring of his trews as he kissed her neck, her breath coming in rapid gasps.

Frantically she pulled up her skirts then pulled him inside her, their lips locked together, her tongue darting forward. She gasped as he pushed inside, her mouth still locked to his, losing herself in the sensation and taste of him.

River began to move his hips, at first slowly then more urgently. For a moment she stopped kissing him and opened her eyes to look at his face, seeing he was already watching her. She wanted to say something, but nothing seemed appropriate. Before she knew it her eyes were closed once more, and she had grasped the hard flesh of his buttocks, pulling him deeper inside her, faster, until with a final chorused gasp it was over.

She let out a long breath, revelling in the feeling as River clung on to her. Slowly he raised his head and she could see tears in his eyes. For days they had confided in one another, and Janessa knew those tears were a bitter mix of joy and regret. She knew they would taste much the same as her own, and she kissed them away, feeling their saltiness on her lips and reassuring him with her smile.

Later, as she lay in his arms, surrounded by the dark and the sounds of the night outside, she felt more at peace than she ever had before. The pain of her father's loss, the threat to the Free States, her responsibilities as ruler all seemed to fade.

'I wish it could be like this forever,' she whispered.

'Then we should leave this place,' he replied.

Somehow she'd known he would say those words before he even spoke them.

'We can't,' she said. *But you can; you can do anything you wish.* 'I am to be queen. I cannot abandon my people.' *Your people? They are your father's people; you did not ask for this. Run away, run far from this place and never come back.*

'Then I will stay by your side, to protect you.'

She smiled at that. At his naïveté. At his stubborn sense of loyalty. 'You cannot.'

And in an instant it was clear that she would have to make a choice between the Steel Crown and her lover. She would never be able to have both.

'I will not leave you. The Father of Killers has vowed to take you, and he will not stop until his task is done. Your guards cannot protect you. These walls cannot protect you. Only I can protect you. We must leave this place . . . together.'

And as quick as that her choice was made. He had made the decision for her, the one she wanted, and with it he had freed her of any burden.

'But where would we go?'

'Far away, over the seas if we have to, where no one knows us.'

'But . . .'

She stopped. Janessa could think of no further excuses. There was no reason she should not run away with River and leave this place behind her. She had not asked for this responsibility, to be married off for political prudence, to be forced to rule a nation and its people simply by chance of birth. She could not cope with this. She was not strong enough. Steelhaven and the Free States would be better off without her. A man like Odaka would make a far better ruler.

Why couldn't she just live like other women? Why couldn't she choose her own husband and have all the things other people could: a family, a home, the chance to grow old with the one she loved?

And she *could* have those things; it was all so easy.

Just take River's hand and run away.

'Yes,' she said. 'Yes, we'll do it.'

For the first time since she had met him, she saw River smile. It was a good smile, a kind smile. She knew that she had made the right choice.

'Then we should not tarry,' River said. 'The Father of Killers will not wait long. It's been many days. Even now he may have sent one of my brothers. We must go immediately.'

'We'll need food and clothes for the journey,' she said. 'I can get those. Then we can be away.' Just saying the words thrilled her.

She kissed him for a long time before rising from the bed and donning her gown. As she left the chamber and moved down the corridor to find the supplies they would need, her stomach was turning cartwheels.

Everything about this was wrong. Her head told her she was betraying her people, Odaka, even the memory of her father, but at the same time her heart told her this was the right thing to do, and her heart was winning over her head . . . it always had.

For a time she had been a slave to duty, forced to do what she thought was right, but she had always been the wild wolf of the family.

Now was not the time to be caged.

As she reached the end of the corridor, two Sentinels moved forward to accompany her, but she dismissed them with a gesture. On the way down to the kitchens she saw many more men watching the palace than usual. It would be difficult for her and River to get out of Skyhelm unseen, but she had done it many times before, and if River had managed to make his way in without being spotted, she was damn sure he could get out again.

The lower levels of the palace were in darkness, but Janessa needed no light to find her way. The air smelled of cooked meats and vegetables from the night's supper and she suddenly wondered if she'd been missed at the grand dinner table.

It didn't matter now. She would be missed soon enough. Perhaps the mystery surrounding her disappearance would baffle historians for years to come.

Janessa was creeping along in the dark, her hand teasing the wall beside her, when she saw a dull light ahead. It was strange for anyone to be here in the kitchens at this hour, and she stood in the dark, wondering who it might be and whether she should proceed. But then how could she let anything stop her now? She could not wait.

Before she could move forward once again she heard a sound from around the corner. It was a gasp, a laboured pant – and Janessa knew what it was. Even had she not experienced such pleasures herself so recently she would have known the sound of lovers locked in passion.

It grew louder, pealing out in the dark as the lovemaking grew more insistent. The sound of a table scraping on the tiled stone floor accompanied the rhythmic gasps. Janessa would have left, not wanting to intrude on such an intimate act, until she heard the words.

'Come on, fuck me!'

It wasn't the words themselves that made her stop in her tracks, but the fact she recognised the voice.

But no, it couldn't be. She almost dismissed it, until she heard the man.

'Shhh. You'll wake the servants.'

No! No, it couldn't be him too.

'Just shut up and fuck me, my lord!'

Gods, it *was* her!

Janessa couldn't resist going forward, peering round the corner, and there she was, lying on the table on which the kitchen staff prepared meals, her legs wrapped around Lord Raelan Logar as he thrust inside her again and again.

Graye.

Her friend Graye.

Janessa stood and watched as the man who had professed his love and proposed marriage to her rutted with the girl who had been her closest confidante for most of her life.

Just then Graye opened her eyes and saw Janessa standing there. She didn't speak, but looked horrified, grabbing Raelan and shaking him.

'What is it? Oh . . .' he said, as he too saw Janessa standing in the candlelight. For several awkward moments they stood watching one another until Raelan plucked up the courage to speak.

'Janessa . . . majesty . . . I can explain,' he said as he fumbled his erection back into his trews.

'Really?' answered Janessa. 'I assume this means you've reconsidered your offer of marriage, Lord Raelan?' She couldn't bring herself to be furious, gods knew she had been with her own lover just moments before, but she was enjoying seeing Raelan squirm.

'Er . . .'

'And you!' Janessa looked at Graye, whose face was almost mournful. 'Were you going to let me marry a man you'd already . . . is that my gown?'

Graye tugged at the dress she was half wearing, trying her best to cover her modesty.

'You're welcome to each other,' Janessa said finally, turning to leave.

'Janessa, wait,' begged Raelan, but she was in no mood to listen. She didn't get far, though.

'Yes,' said a voice from the dark. 'Please wait, your majesty.'

The voice was deep and filled with malice. Like Janessa, Raelan and Graye turned as a hulking figure moved from the surrounding shadow.

He was tall, bare chested, his shoulders thick and powerful – and covered in scars. His face bore not an ounce of kindness and thick black brows furrowed in a scowl beneath cropped, black hair.

'Who are you? What do you want?' Raelan demanded, moving forward. He reached for the sword that wasn't at his side.

'Who am I?' said the man. 'I am Mountain, and I bring the sky to thunder and the earth to quake. Why am I here?' He looked at Janessa, and his eyes were like a wolf's. 'I am here at the behest of my father. I have come for you.'

As he looked at Janessa she suddenly knew true horror for the first time in her life. In this man's eyes there was no compassion, and she knew there would be no mercy.

'Never!' bellowed Raelan, rushing forward. Even without a weapon, and after all he had done, he was still willing to defend her. Though Janessa could admire him for that, against this man he was no match.

The assassin moved with frightening speed for someone of such size, easily avoiding Raelan's clumsy attack. Before the young lord could throw another punch, this man, this Mountain had struck him three times in the throat, his hands slamming into Raelan like iron hammers.

Raelan fell silently, landing heavily on the floor.

Graye screamed at the top of her lungs as Janessa stood frozen, looking on in blind terror.

How could this be happening? How could he have got in here, found her here? And where was . . .

Mountain moved fast as a serpent, grasping Graye and taking her up in his hands as though she were nothing more than a rag doll. Those massive hands twisted, snapping her neck and silencing her scream. Dropping Graye's lifeless body to the floor, the monster moved on Janessa. 'Now, your majesty,' he said, taking a step towards her and smiling without any hint of humour. 'My father will have your heart.'

THIRTY-SEVEN

For the first time she had not locked the door behind her. River had not, at first, taken it as an omen, but as time drew on he began to grow more and more uneasy.

Why had he let her go? And alone?

He donned his tunic, moving towards the door, but quickly slipped into the shadows of the room as he heard voices approaching from the other side of it, voices he did not recognise.

River watched from the dark as the door opened and someone entered.

'Told you she weren't here.' It was a woman, elevated in years.

'We'd best be quick; it's been days since this room's been turned over.' A second woman, this one much younger.

'Right, you do the linen. I'll give it a quick dust. And light some candles. I can't see a bloomin' thing in here.'

They both entered, one bearing a candle, the other carrying a bucket and a pile of bedding over one shoulder.

His heart began to beat faster. River knew he could not be discovered here, and if they were to illuminate the room even he would not be able to hide from them.

The door began to swing shut and he made his move, slipping through the shadows and making it through the door with barely more noise than a breath of air. As it slammed behind him, he heard one of the women say, 'What was that?' but he was already gone.

What now? He couldn't stay in the corridor and wait for them to come out again, but neither could he go roaming the palace, waiting to be spotted by the guards.

He had to find Jay.

River knew the layout of the palace. If she wanted supplies for their journey, surely she would make for the kitchen, but how to get there? Trying to make his way through the palace was folly. There were twice as many sentries as there had been when he first came to this place, and little chance he could avoid them a second time.

He moved to one of the windows, peering out at the sheer drop, before moving up onto the sill and easing himself out. A few nights ago, escaping through the window of Jay's chamber, he had clung there as the palace guard searched for him in vain. Now his wound was all but healed and he felt as strong as ever – navigating the sheer walls would hold no challenge for him.

There was a side door to the kitchens. If he could make it down quickly he could soon be with Jay. They could take what they needed and leave this place tonight. His heart soared at the prospect, spurring him to move faster down the side of the building.

River paused near the base of the northernmost tower, his eyes scanning for sentries on the path that led around the base of Skyhelm. No one appeared.

With trepidation, he climbed down, expecting at any moment a sentry to appear around a corner, but nothing.

A feeling of unease crept up on him as he made his way towards the side door. It soon turned to fear as he saw the bodies lying there, armour crumpled, limbs splayed unnaturally.

River broke into a run, panic rising within him. As he entered the dark passage leading to the kitchens, he heard a scream – a woman. River felt sick. He was scared as he'd never been before. Not for himself – but for Jay . . .

He sped towards the end of the corridor, racing forward, not caring if anyone was lying in wait. There was a voice he recognised – a deep and sonorous tone.

With a roar he burst into the room, in time to see Mountain bearing down on Jay. She was paralysed with fear. There were corpses on the floor.

Mountain turned to block River's attack, turning the lightning-fast strike aside and countering with a head butt. It rocked River back and he fell hard against a table.

'You? We thought you were dead,' said the giant, his brow furrowed in confusion.

'I will not allow you to harm her,' River replied, still reeling from the blow.

Mountain launched himself forward, reaching out with massive hands.

'Run!' screamed River, just as Mountain's hands clamped around his throat. Fingers squeezed tight, blocking River's airways, and he looked into his brother's eyes, seeing only malice there.

'What has happened to you, River?' said his brother. 'What has this witch done to you that you would betray our Father?'

River could feel his vision blurring as Mountain closed his grip. There was nothing he could do against such strength; nothing that could stop his brother's wrath. The end would be inevitable, and all his talent, all his deadly skill, could not stop it. Still, he could not bring himself to have regrets, could not bring himself to feel sorrow for sacrificing the Father's love. For a few stolen moments with Jay he would have sacrificed the world.

Mountain screamed, snarling as he arched his back and dropped River to the ground. The giant spun, and River could see he was clawing at his shoulder blade from which protruded a kitchen knife. Blood was seeping from the wound. Jay stood defiant as Mountain approached her. River sprang forward to kick Mountain in the back of the legs, knocking them out from under him. He kept moving, rolling to his feet and grasping Jay by the arms.

'I told you to run,' he said.

'I won't leave you,' she replied, looking at Mountain, who was rising to his feet.

'You have to go. I cannot fight him while protecting you.' He thrust her towards the door, then turned again to face Mountain.

His brother looked down at him, showing yellow teeth in a grimace as he reached behind and finally pulled the knife from his back. With a flick of his wrist he threw it at River, who deftly avoided it.

Mountain was a formidable sight, a devastating weapon. The Father had said this mission was beyond him, requiring subtlety and stealth. Clearly, since River had failed to kill Jay, the Father of Killers had changed his mind. Now he had decided power and strength were exactly what was required.

River reclined into a defensive stance, preparing himself to face his brother, when there came a commotion from behind.

Armoured guards clattered into the room, their swords already drawn, their purpose obvious.

'Protect the princess!' bellowed one, pulling Jay behind him. Though she protested she could not resist. River was relieved: she was safe. Somewhere else in the palace a bell was ringing, reaching even into the bowels of Skyhelm, alerting everyone to danger.

River knew he had to escape. If they caught him he would be questioned, and Jay would undoubtedly reveal the nature of their relationship just to protect him. He could not allow her to do that. Not for him.

Mountain rushed ahead of him. River followed, with the armoured guards clattering in pursuit. His brother smashed his foot against the door, sending the deadbolt and shards of splinters flying into the night and they hurtled on until their way was blocked by half a dozen newly alerted sentries. They were gripping fearsome halberds and they quickly surrounded the pair.

Mountain smiled. 'Are you ready to fight, brother?'

River did not answer. He had no desire to harm these men; they were only doing their duty.

But his brother cared little about those he killed.

As the first guard charged in, his halberd sweeping down in an arc, Mountain moved with terrifying speed. He caught the descending haft, halting it in midair. The two of them stood for a moment as the sentry vainly tried to wrench the weapon from the giant's grip. With a scything blow of his hand, Mountain smashed the haft asunder then swept the blade down in a devastating arc that all but took the sentry's head off. The body toppled to one side. Mountain launched what remained of the weapon at another charging sentry, and took him full in the faceplate of his helm, knocking him off his feet.

River knew these men would all meet their deaths, but he was too busy avoiding the swords of his own opponents to intervene. Blades seemed to sweep in from every angle, and it was all he could do to dodge them or slap them aside. He could feel the wound in his side, so recently healed, pulling and stretching, the knitted flesh threatening to split as he twisted to avoid being stuck like a pig.

As soon as a gap opened he was away, over the corpses, once more on Mountain's trail. He could see the hulking form of his brother running up a staircase towards the parapet of the palace wall, taking the steps four at a time. He followed Mountain up the stairway, arriving at the top to see to see his brother standing on the battlement, watching him with a smile. A taunting gesture that asked whether River was brave enough to follow him.

As Mountain leapt out into the blackness of the night, River did not pause. Planting his foot on one of the merlons he followed his brother, leaping into the void – only empty air between him and the ground a hundred feet below.

River heard the sound of smashing slate. Then a roof came at him out of the dark at frightening speed, his feet hitting the tiles, feeling them splinter beneath him. He just had time to notice the massive hole his brother had made in the roof before he toppled back towards the edge.

River grabbed wildly at some guttering, but it cracked and gave way, and he was falling again. His ribs smacked against something that briefly halted his descent before he landed heavily on the cobbles.

He couldn't get his breath and foundered there a while, desperately trying to heave in a lungful of air.

A scream, a woman's voice, and River barely had time to raise himself to a crouch before a huge wooden table came crashing through the window of the house. Mountain quickly followed it, his body battered and gashed from his fall. Yet he grinned as he bore down on River, who now rose with the strength of desperation.

Mountain swung in with two quick blows that River avoided. As he dodged aside he found his feet crunching on smashed glass and he deftly stooped, picking up a shard in his bare palm. The glass cut into his flesh, but rather a weapon that shed his blood than face Mountain unarmed.

His brother came in again, one mighty fist threatening to take River's head off; but the two of them had fought many times before under the watchful eye of their Father. They had tested one another at length, and River knew that for all his strength, Mountain could never match him for speed.

River ducked, slashing twice with the glass shard, opening Mountain up across the abdomen in two matching red stripes. His brother grunted away the pain, clenching his fists and striking in again with a roar.

When they had been younger, boys barely grown, Mountain had once taken River in those meaty arms and beaten him until his eyes bled. River had known then that Mountain might one day end him and had vowed he would never be defeated by him again. Tonight he would honour that vow.

River twisted away from those lethal fists, using the momentum of his turn to power his strike. He planted the glass at the base of Mountain's neck, snapping off the end only when it was far enough into the muscle and sinew.

His brother roared in agony, his fingers slick with blood, vainly trying to pull the glass from his neck.

As they both stood, heaving in gulps of air, River saw a glint of fear in his brother's eyes, something he had never seen before. It filled him with satisfaction.

Without a word, Mountain turned and ran with surprising speed.

For an instant River almost considered letting him go, letting him return to their father with news that River lived and had betrayed him for the love of a woman.

But he knew he could not.

His father would not stop, and once Mountain's wounds were healed he would be dispatched once more to kill Jay, and perhaps he would not be sent alone.

River easily followed his quarry; Mountain was leaving a trail of devastation, smashing people aside and crashing through abandoned boxes, lugs and handcarts.

They crossed an empty square, and River saw a bridge up ahead. He leapt up, planting his foot on a vendor's dray to propel himself, then higher onto an outhouse roof. Up he climbed until he was at the first storey as his brother, now staggering, passed below him.

River leapt like a cat, dropping on his quarry from height. His brother collapsed beneath his attack, but came up fighting. River ducked a blow, planting his foot into the side of Mountain's knee. He batted his brother's grasping hand aside and punched forward, hitting that big thick neck with a fist powered by fury.

Mountain fell backwards, his head hitting the hard stone of the bridge as he collapsed to the ground. He was struggling, desperately clutching his throat, and River watched him wallowing in defeat, realising his father had to be sent a message.

Somewhere in the distance River could hear the sound of the militia shouting in pursuit.

Let them come . . . they would be too late, as they always were.

As his brother desperately tried to crawl away, River wrapped an arm around his neck, squeezing for all his might. Mountain's grip was strong as he tried to pull himself free, but he would never be strong enough.

Steadily Mountain grew weaker, his grip slackening until lack of air caused his legs to buckle. Once his brother had sagged in his arms, River wrenched his neck sideways, giving a furious cry as the neck cracked.

He looked down at the lifeless body without pity or remorse.

When the militiamen reached the bridge, they would find nothing there but the broken corpse of a mutilated giant.

River would be gone.

THIRTY-EIGHT

T here'd been little said once they returned to their house near The
Black Hart. They'd killed some fella in the richest district of
Steelhaven and didn't have a pot of piss to show for it. What were
they supposed to say?

Steraglio brooded in a corner. Every now and then he'd give Rag a
dirty look; some of the dirtiest looks she'd ever seen, and they spoke all
sorts of nasty. It was clear he blamed her for the robbery going tits up
and she was sure he'd have shown her just how pissed off he was if
Krupps hadn't been around – though she weren't Krupps' favourite
person either. He hadn't spoke a word to her since they'd got back, not
even looked in her direction.

Not that she minded. That night had shown her a side of him she
hadn't known about, didn't like, and she was sure as shit didn't want to
see again. But then they'd all three of them been in on it, stabbing and
kicking and punching the poor bastard till he was nothing more than a
sack of bloody meat on the floor. Even Burney – big, dumb, brain-like-
a-fried-egg Burney – had joined in when the killing started.

Rag wanted nothing more than to get out, to leave this place behind
her, but she hadn't. She'd stayed and suffered the shitty atmosphere and
the shittier looks. Where would she have gone, anyway? Sitting in a house
full of bloody awful tension, but with a roof over your head and food
in your belly, was better than sitting in the rain with no roof and no
food. Besides, there was still the question of the Guild. She hadn't asked
where they were on that: whether or not she still had a chance. She'd
have to ask sooner or later. That was the whole reason she'd gone through

with this in the first place. She wasn't going anywhere until she'd at least managed to find out where she stood.

'Who wants supper?' Burney said, as they all sat around the small downstairs room.

'How can you think of food at a time like this?' Steraglio replied.

'A time like what? Besides, doesn't matter what sort of time it is, we've got to eat.'

'Doesn't matter what time . . . ? I'll tell you what time it is: it's time we were thinking about getting the fuck away from here. If the Greencoats don't catch up with us then the Guild soon will. Too many people know it was us that did the job, so they'll know it was us did the fucking murdering. When they find out where we live, they'll come round here and hang us – *if* we're lucky.'

The Guild? Why would the Guild come round? They'd already told her the Guild had sanctioned this. They *had* sanctioned this, hadn't they?

'How would anyone know where we are?' Burney said, his brow creasing in confusion.

'Because – you fucking idiot – people do. Coles was our man on the inside, gave us the job in the first place. He knows where we live. Westley – our Greencoated friend who works the gate to the Crown District – he knows our names and where we live. Everyone that goes in the Hart, they all know where we live too. But then it's not easy for us to be discreet when we've got a big lumbering fuckwit like you in our crew!'

Burney's brow furrowed even more. 'Bollocks! It weren't my fault everything went to shit. I wasn't the one what untied him. And I got cut.' He pointed to the crude bandage on his upper arm still stained with blood.

'No, it wasn't you that untied him, was it.' Steraglio looked at Rag, almost unable to contain himself.

'All right, that's enough,' said Krupps.

Steraglio and Burney obviously wanted to continue their row but thought better of it. Krupps had settled into a black mood since the robbery. They clearly feared to provoke him.

It made Rag nervous. She'd thought Krupps wasn't so bad. She'd thought he had a sweet spot for her too, which always helped. Now she didn't know what to think.

'Going on about it isn't going to change anything. This whole thing's gone to shit – but there's always a way out.' Krupps went back to staring at the ceiling, his handsome features framed by what little light was coming in through the window.

Rag suddenly felt she had to get out. What was she doing here anyway? There was nothing she could do to contribute, and she'd been cooped up inside since the failed robbery . . . if you could call it a robbery. If she slipped out, disappeared for a while, would any of them notice? Steraglio probably would; he'd have no one to glare at.

While the other lads sat in silence, Rag slipped towards the door. Just a few hours out in the fresh air. Then she'd come back and Krupps would have a plan.

She stopped when someone on the other side of the door knocked three times in quick succession.

They all looked up, held like rats in the beam of a lantern. Burney looked at Steraglio, Steraglio looked at Krupps and Krupps looked to the door.

No one looked at Rag.

Krupps nodded at Burney to answer it, and Rag saw Steraglio going for his knife. As the big fella went to the door, Krupps eyed the room for possible ways of escape. Rag suddenly felt ill and frightened. She wanted to be out the window and over the roof, but something made her stay. It was like her shoes were nailed to the floor, rooting her to the spot.

'Who is it?' Burney asked, his hand hovering near the door's deadbolt.

'It's Coles,' said a voice from the other side.

The lads seemed to relax a bit, so Rag did likewise.

Burney slid back the deadbolts at the top and bottom of the door and pulled it open.

Coles came flying into the room, knocking Burney backwards and over a chair. He was followed through the door by three . . . no, four of the biggest blokes Rag had ever seen. One of them set about Burney before he could get back up, smacking him again and again with a club covered in metal studs. Another went for Steraglio, who dropped his knife and held up his hands in surrender. It didn't stop him taking a mighty whack to the arm and squealing like a girl.

Krupps just backed away, all slow and steady, affecting a smile. 'What can we do for you, lads?' he said, as the big blokes bore down on him.

One of them looked around the room impassively, his face lumpy and scarred like it had been whacked in by a woodsman's axe.

'Someone wants a word with you lot. I think you know what for.'

None of them protested.

'It weren't my fault, lads,' said Coles, rising to his feet. He was a thin bloke, teeth all crooked and brown, his thinning hair lank and swept across his head in greasy clumps. 'They knew who'd done it straight away. I swear I didn't tell them nothing.'

'Other than where to find us,' said Krupps, but he didn't look angry, and Rag reckoned he'd have done the same in Coles' shoes.

'Right, let's go then,' said the biggest thug.

Two of them picked up Burney, whose head was bleeding freely. As Steraglio and Krupps were hustled to the door Rag tried to meld into the corner, hoping in the confusion they might miss her.

Unfortunately, they didn't.

A gesture with the big, studded club indicated that she should follow.

They were led through the streets. Weren't no Greencoats this end of the city. Never around when they could be of use. The four of them, along with Coles, were ushered along, wrangled like livestock through the shadowy alleyways.

Several times Rag thought about doing a runner and not stopping till she was back at the Bull. What had she been thinking leaving her boys behind? Who did she think she was trying to get into the Guild, trying to make it big? She was a small-time picker off the streets. She should have known her place, should have kept her nose out. Now she was in shit deeper than she'd ever been, and with the Guild there weren't no getting out of it, at least not with all the fingers and toes you started with.

They got to a doorway leading into a big old warehouse. More fellas waited for them, their faces mysterious and frightening in the uncertain light of lanterns and candles. On a crate in the centre sat a bloke smaller than the rest, mop of curly hair on his head, picking at his fingernails with a little knife. The five of them were all lined up in front of him, Burney now swaying dumbly as his head bled, Coles looking all nervous and fidgety.

The curly-haired fella looked up and smiled, like they was all there for a party, like he was dead pleased to see everyone.

'Hello there,' he said, white teeth shining in the lantern light. 'Glad you could all make it.' One of the thugs closed the big door behind them, and Rag began to feel like she couldn't breathe, like all the air had left the room. 'Do any of you know who I am?'

Coles looked along the line, then tentatively put his hand up. 'Erm, yes, sir. I do, sir. You're Mister Friedrik, sir.'

'Indeed I am,' said Friedrik, looking pleased that someone recognised him. 'I'm Mister Friedrik. And you're Coles, I know that. So who are the rest of you?' He looked along the line expectantly.

The lads told him their names: Steraglio, Burney, Krupps; then it came to Rag. She looked up at the man, trying her hardest to hold back the tears. Should she play on that maybe? Should she hope he wouldn't hurt a little girl, especially one that was blubbing her eyes out?

No. Even though Rag was scared to death she wouldn't do that. She weren't no coward . . .

'Rag,' she whispered. Either Friedrik had excellent hearing, or he didn't care what her name was.

'So, I guess you all know why you're here?'

There was a pause as the five of them waited to see who'd be the first to speak. It was Coles that broke the silence, and not in a good way.

'It wasn't me, Mister Friedrik,' he said, dropping to his knees. 'I never wanted to. It was his idea.' He gestured along the line at no one in particular. 'They said they'd kill me unless I went along with it. I've got two kids, Mister Friedrik. Only bairns, they rely on me. Their mother's sick. I had no choice. Please, Mister Friedrik . . .'

As Coles carried on with his begging, Friedrik glanced wearily to one of his men. The big bastard walked forward and smashed Coles over the head with that studded club. Rag could hear the crunch as it split his skull open, and he fell forward. She glanced to where Coles lay, a bloody mess, his eyes staring blankly. As much as she'd wanted him to shut up, she had to admit that had been a harsh way to do it.

'Now,' Friedrik continued as though nothing had happened. 'This is all very vexing for me.' He heaved himself off the box and began to pace in front of them. 'I'm as eager to encourage business ventures as the next man. I don't mind a bit of healthy competition. If someone wants to make a name for themselves then I say "good luck" to them. But you see, we had an arrangement with poor old Barnus. You could even say we were friends. So when someone comes in and shits all over the deals I've made, I have to make an example. I'm sure you understand.' The lads nodded, but Rag was too scared to move. 'Now, I'm nothing if not a reasonable man, so here's the deal: I'm always looking for new blood. You've shown yourselves to be a bunch of forward-thinking go-getters. Shit, you must all have balls of steel to have done what you did without permission from me. So I'm willing to make a vacancy available in my organisation. Only one, though. So whichever one of you can bring me the heads of the other three gets to join my club. Feel free to start any time.'

Rag hadn't quite registered what had been said before Burney took a step forward. 'You can fuck off,' he shouted, blood streaming down his face, and looking thoroughly dazed. 'If you think we'll just—'

He didn't get to finish his sentence. Steraglio pulled a knife from his sleeve and stuck it into his neck. As he drew it out a stream of blood shot from Burney's throat. He had enough time to clap a hand to the spurting hole before he collapsed with a bubbling grunt.

Steraglio turned, but Krupps was already moving, grabbing the wrist that held the knife and punching forward. They both went over, Steraglio pulling Krupps on top of him. Everyone just watched them.

The pair of them rolled around on the filthy floor, all the while that knife held desperately between them. Krupps got in a head butt, Steraglio bit into Krupps' arm, and they both moaned and groaned and whined as they scratched and clawed at each other on the warehouse floor. It was vicious, like two wild dogs scrapping over a bone, and Rag felt herself growing sicker every moment.

Krupps' strength eventually won out. He managed to roll Steraglio on his back, both hands on the knife, twisting it to point down at Steraglio's throat. And now it moved so slowly, closer and closer, and Rag could see the panic in Steraglio's eyes.

'Wait,' he said, his voice high and desperate. 'Krupps, wait. Please, just fucking wait.'

Krupps didn't. He pushed and pushed and the knife finally pierced Steraglio's neck. Rag could see the blood, a trickle at first as Steraglio began to gag, then a flood from his neck and from his mouth as, with a final effort, Krupps shoved the knife in all the way to the hilt.

Steraglio continued to struggle, spitting blood as it bubbled out through his mouth, but Krupps just kept the knife there, waiting for his 'friend' to die. When he'd finally stopped moving, Krupps pulled out the knife and struggled to his feet, breathing hard. He looked at Friedrik, who stared back, unmoved.

'As I said, there's only one vacancy.'

Friedrik didn't look her way, but Rag knew what he meant.

She backed away as Krupps turned towards her. He was still breathing hard, but his face was determined. All they'd been through, all his kind words and playful winks, meant absolutely nothing.

He was going to kill her.

302

She turned and ran, getting to the door before anyone else could move. As she grabbed the handle Rag hoped against hope no one had locked it, feeling blind relief when it opened. The waning light of evening lanced in, filling her with hope as she sped out into the alleyway and ran for her life.

She splashed through a puddle, almost falling, a glance over her shoulder revealing Krupps on her heels. His face didn't look angry though; he wasn't raging or slavering at the mouth. He was calm, almost businesslike – as though chasing down girls and murdering them were a daily pastime. It made him even more terrifying.

The alley turned one way, then another. She needed to find another living soul, anyone. An 'innocent' girl, chased by a knife-wielding maniac. It would take one heartless bastard not to help her.

Another bend in the alley and she almost ran straight into a wall.

Fucking dead end!

She looked round desperately, seeing a rotted plank of wood and picking it up. Krupps was on the way, she could hear his footfalls splashing through the puddles. As he turned the corner she swung at him, the wood hitting his face, shattering into rotten splinters and sending him sprawling.

The knife spun away into the dirt and she went for it, reaching out, feeling her heart racing, her fingers ready to close around the hilt. But Krupps' fingers closed around her ankle first.

She was pulled off her feet, splashing into the wet. The knife was there, so close, but she couldn't reach it. Krupps pulled her to him, moving on top of her, crushing her under his weight. He planted a fist in her face, the shock of it knocking out her breath and any words that she might have said. Another punch and she'd gone dizzy, the alleyway spinning, Krupps' face moving in circles.

'Sorry, Sweets,' he said, that handsome face looking down at her with no emotion. 'I didn't want it to end like this.' He reached past her, picking up the knife, mud-smeared but still keen.

Rag wanted to say something, wanted to beg for her life like Coles had done, but it hadn't done him no good, and it wouldn't do her none neither. She could only hope it wouldn't hurt too much.

A flash of green.

Krupps looked up, and she could see those impassive features turn to panic. Something hit him. Hit him hard enough that he fell off her, splashing into a puddle.

There was a commotion, and blokes in green all over them. One of them was going at Krupps like he was born for it, hitting him, smashing him, fist pumping up and down like he wasn't ever going to stop.

Someone put his arms round her and lifted her up. Her head was still spinning and all of a sudden she got groggier, like she was tired out. Her clothes were wet and something was dribbling down her face.

'You're okay,' said a deep voice. 'You're safe now.'

Rag couldn't place the fella, but she was sure she'd seen him before. And even though she couldn't remember where she knew him from, when he said she was safe, she knew he meant it.

THIRTY-NINE

He was drunk again, but that was nothing out of the ordinary. As Merrick staggered down the street he almost slipped on the oily cobbles. He'd barely had a chance to curse the whalers and their carelessness before he threw up on the dock. Someone, most likely some hairy-arsed sailor, was laughing at him as he heaved, but Merrick paid him no heed.

He felt a lot better when he'd finished, though his head still spun. He looked around with a satisfied grin, pleased to see the looks of disgust on the faces of passers-by. As he wiped his mouth he looked out over the dock. The sun was shining and it was a mild afternoon for the time of year. Sooner or later, most likely sooner, it would start to get cold, the harsh sea winds blowing up from the Midral and whipping through Steelhaven's streets like a howling devil. It was nothing compared to what was coming from the north though, but with any luck he'd be leagues across the sea by the time the Khurtas arrived. If they even got here.

There'd been rumours they were heading straight for the city. Merrick thought it unlikely – there were hundreds of miles between Steelhaven and the horde. They'd hopefully likely get bored with raping and pillaging and fuck off back to where they came from before the week was out. Still, better safe than sorry. No point hanging around and waiting to be gutted by some savage when he could be sailing off to sunnier climes. He looked good with a tan, and the exotic ladies of Jal Nassan would most likely go wild for a handsome, foreign stranger with tales of . . . well, whatever he decided to make up.

The prospect of freedom made him more eager than ever to have this

305

whole foul business concluded. He could leave this stinking city and its Guild behind him. And he could leave that mad bitch Kaira behind him too – that would be a blessing in itself.

What had got into her head anyway? He'd only touched her hand, only moved in like he had a thousand times before with a thousand other women. Merrick was no stranger to being rebuffed, no stranger to a slapped face, but there was no need for her to flatten him in the middle of the bar and make him look a prize cock.

Clearly she was frustrated – most likely all those years stuck in the Temple of Autumn with no men to unleash her pent-up desires on.

So far he'd managed to avoid her, but he knew sooner or later they'd have to meet up. His business with Bolo was almost concluded, and he wanted her by his side for that one last meeting in case things turned to shit. If Bolo tried to pull a fast one, Merrick was quite happy to unleash Kaira and all her pent-up aggression on him. It would be like throwing a terrier into a nest of rats – just sit back and watch the carnage.

The thought brought a grin to his face.

He walked down to the harbour and fished in his pocket, feeling the satisfaction as his hand closed around the pewter flask. It was cool in his hand, almost inviting, as he unscrewed the cap and placed it to his lips. Despite the cold of the flask, the liquor was warm and sweet in his mouth and he swilled the last of the vomit from his teeth before swallowing it down. Never failed to settle a poorly stomach.

With one hand on the pommel of his sword and the other grasping his flask, Merrick swaggered down towards the vast crescent-shaped bay. All was well; he had nothing to worry about. Just broker the sale of the merchandise and all debts paid. Then he was free to roam the high seas until doomsday.

The bay was busy. Either people were taking the threat from the north seriously and clearing out by sea, or it was a particularly good time for commerce. The wood and stone jetties were abuzz with dockworkers and seamen, foreign merchants and brokers. It was clear business was not halted by the threat of war. Indeed, it was clear business thrived on war, and sea-trade best of all.

Perhaps that was something he should branch into. Once this was all over he could start his own business trading throughout the Midral Sea. He could buy his own little merchantman, nothing too extravagant, at least not to start. Another swig from his flask and Merrick had almost convinced himself he was ready to be a merchant baron, master of the high seas, favoured by lords and kings in ten nations.

What was there to stop him?

As he strolled along the harbour, his dreams of future riches stirred up by the sea breeze, he saw someone who caught his eye. The man wasn't from Steelhaven, that much was clear, but he wasn't out of place amongst the flood of overseas traders. What made him stand out to Merrick was that he'd seen him somewhere before.

Moored at the jetty was a caravel, its crew hard at work with sail and rope. If Merrick had any aspiration for a life at sea, he should really work out what all those ropes and pulleys did. Or maybe he'd just pay someone else to do all that – that's what sailors were for, anyway. Why have a dog and bark yourself?

The man was obviously waiting to board his ship and Merrick made his way closer, racking his brain all the while until, when he was within arm's length of him, he remembered. This was the exotic foreigner who had sought an audience with Palien days earlier. Whatever business they'd had was clearly concluded, and the man now awaited his boat home. By the way he gripped his shoulder bag and stared pensively out to sea, it was a journey that couldn't come soon enough.

Merrick should have left things there, should have let the man go about his business, but he'd always been a nosy bastard. It had got him into trouble so often – why break old habits now?

'A beautiful day,' Merrick said.

The man turned, looking surprised but instantly hiding it behind a smile.

Shrewd. Merrick recognised a man used to masking his true feelings.

'Indeed it is,' replied the foreigner. 'I am sad to be leaving this place. Your city is truly beautiful, er . . .'

'Ryder. Merrick Ryder,' Merrick replied, believing none of the man's assessment of his city. A dumb, blind, noseless crone could tell the place was a dump.

'Greetings, Ryder. I am Massoum Am Kalhed Las Fahir Am Jadar Abbasi, a poor spice trader come to Steelhaven to broker trade.'

Poor spice trader – that was a new one.

'And has your visit been as lucrative as you'd hoped?'

'Indeed it has, Ryder. Indeed it has. But alas I must now return home, for all journeys have their end.'

'Yes they do.' Merrick couldn't have agreed more. The journey he was on right now couldn't end soon enough. 'But at least you got to meet some interesting people?'

Massoum smiled. 'Your city overflows with interesting people. A fascinating blend. If only I could stay longer to experience more. A man could swim forever in this city's sea of culture.'

All right, enough of the horseshit.

'I'll grant you, this city has its share of culture, but let's not pretend it also hasn't got its share of scum.'

Massoum nodded knowingly.

'You are an astute fellow. Of course you're right, but is that not true of every city in all the world?'

'This one more than most.' Though Merrick hadn't been to most cities in the Free States, let alone the world, he had a pretty good idea that this was among the worst. 'And forgive me, but you don't seem the kind of man who'd do well in a place like this for very long. It's obvious you're not here for the culture. Or for the spice trade.'

Massoum inclined his head. 'I see there is little point trying to hide the truth from you, my friend. Let's just say I am a messenger. Now that my messages are delivered it is time for me to leave this place.'

'And not a moment too soon, I'll wager.' Massoum had no answer to that, so Merrick continued. 'So, your messages, were they from the mouths of rich and powerful men? Or are you simply here bandying words for merchants and sailors?'

'I am nothing if not discreet, my friend. Whether I convey the words of kings or beggars I am bound by the laws of my trade never to discuss my employers' business but with those I am paid to contact.'

'I see. But tell me one thing – are you happy working for the men you convey these words for?'

Merrick didn't know why he'd asked that. Was it that pang of guilt crawling up his back again? Was he really interested in what this foreigner had to say? Was he looking for some kind of justification? Or would he find some kind of kinship with this stranger?

'*Happy* does not come into it, my friend. Whether my work is for tyrant or saint, it matters not. Their words would still be passed on, even if I were not the one doing it.'

And there it was, the justification he'd been fishing for.

'So even though we work for tyrants, it doesn't mean we're . . .'

'Tyrants ourselves? Capable of unspeakable evil? Is the shore evil for the ships it wrecks? Is the wolf evil for the lambs it slaughters?'

'But we're not wolves, we're men. We have a choice.'

Massoum nodded at his words. 'Of course you are right. But should the wolf choose to spare the lamb, there are always other wolves.'

Merrick took another swig from his flask. This conversation wasn't going at all how he'd expected. All he'd wanted to do was find out what this bastard was doing here, not have a discussion on the rights and wrongs of what he was doing.

'There are always wolves,' said Merrick. 'But then for every wolf there's a shepherd.'

Where the fuck did that come from?

'Indeed. And so there is the choice, my friend. The wolf or the shepherd. It is the moral choice every man must one day make. I have found it pays more to take the wolf's path. Although doubtless the shepherd sleeps sounder in his bed.'

'Doubtless he does,' said Merrick, with another swig from his flask.

There was a shout from aboard the caravel signalling that they were ready to go. Massoum turned to Merrick and bowed, touching a hand to forehead and lips.

'It has been a pleasure talking with you,' he said. 'But I must leave. May the Desert Wind guide your path, Merrick Ryder.'

'Aye, and yours,' Merrick replied with a nod.

As Massoum boarded the ship Merrick lifted the flask to his lips once more, only to find it was empty.

The mooring ropes were untied and the caravel's sails unfurled. It began to move slowly until a sudden gust caught the bright yellow canvas and pushed it away from the bay.

Massoum gave a wave from the deck. 'Remember, my friend, the shepherd or the wolf. It is a simple choice.'

Merrick could only nod as he watched the ship move off. Then he turned back to the city.

Shepherd or fucking wolf, indeed. What a load of shit. He had no say about what he was. Choose the wolf and have it on your conscience forever, or choose the shepherd and have your balls cut off.

Not really a choice at all.

But then he'd never been very good about making the right decision.

FORTY

She had been looking at the body since the dawn light began to filter through the windows' stained glass. Janessa had dismissed everyone else from the chapel and, thinking her grief stricken, the Sentinels had dutifully obeyed. It wasn't grief though: Raelan had proved his professed love was false and she'd be a liar if she claimed to have felt anything for him. But there was still an empty feeling in her stomach, a dark pit of hurt.

Was it guilt she felt? Some responsibility for his death?

Raelan had tried to defend her, and paid for that bravery with his life, but had he and Graye not been rutting like a pair of stray dogs he would have been safely elsewhere.

Graye. The mere thought of her was enough to bring tears. Poor Graye. Though she and Raelan had betrayed her, they hadn't deserved to die. Janessa herself had been about to turn her back on the crown, on her people, all for the love of one man.

Her friend's body had been sent from the city, back north to Braega where she would be buried on her ancestral lands alongside her parents. Janessa would never see her again, and she was finding that hard.

Raelan's body lay in the small chapel, wrapped in black velvet. He would be buried on Dancer's Hill, which would be the wish of his father. In the north they still worshipped the Old Gods, with Arlor and Vorena shown only cursory respect. They would never get the body to Valdor before it started to decay, and Duke Bannon Logar was still fighting a rearguard action to the north. He could hardly leave the armies of the Free States, even to see his son buried. Word had been sent to him and

Janessa could only imagine his woe after losing his dear friend the king and then his son in only a matter of days.

For now, Raelan would lie here alone in the dark, and until someone came for him Janessa was determined to stay by his side.

The door opened behind her, the light from outside lancing into the chapel and shedding harsh light on the shrouded corpse.

'I gave instructions to be left alone,' said Janessa.

'I understand, majesty, but I must speak with you.'

Janessa turned to see Odaka closing the door to the chapel. He looked grave, his face drawn, eyes red as though he hadn't slept for days.

She knew what Odaka had come to talk about. The question of marriage, a political arrangement, was still hanging over her, hanging over the Free States. She remembered the pact she had made with River and how close they had come to leaving this all behind. Could she still do that? Would he even come back for her?

'This most recent attempt on your life only hastens the need for you to form an alliance. If anything happens to you before we can make such an accord the Free States will be thrown into chaos. We cannot allow that, especially not with invaders on our doorstep.'

'I know what is at stake, Odaka.'

But did she? Did she really appreciate everything that might be lost? Janessa certainly hadn't appreciated it when she'd been with River. When she had fallen into his arms and all she'd wanted was to run away and leave this place behind.

'You need to make a choice, my lady. I know it is a difficult one, but . . .'

'But it has to be made, I know.' She turned to him, seeing his face, his serious manner, and knew the burden he was carrying. He held her kingdom on his shoulders while all she thought about was herself.

She looked down at his hand. In the dim half-light she couldn't see the scar on his palm but she knew it was there. Her father had borne one just the same. In the old days, when she was just a child, the two men had sealed their bond in blood before they fought the Aeslanti. It was said Odaka Du'ur led a tribe fifty thousand strong, but had turned his back on all that power to serve King Cael. Janessa didn't know if she believed all the tales, but she believed Odaka had been loyal to her father, as much as he was now loyal to her.

'And what a choice I have,' she said. 'Do I choose Lord Leon, who is to all evidence slovenly and selfish? Or perhaps Lord Bartolomeo who, much like his father, is already rumoured to have fathered a score of bastards?

There's always Duke Vargus of Stelmorn, though he's well into his eighties and has fathered no children despite the seven wives he's outlived. Or perhaps Lord Cadran of Braega? I hear he's almost seven now. I'm sure he'll make a great statesman once he's fully mastered his letters.'

'I understand your reluctance, my lady. Nevertheless, we have to move quickly. I have already made arrangements for you to be escorted to a safe place outside the city. From there we can conduct a marriage and—'

'No, I won't leave.' The thought of going anywhere without River filled her with dread. But River was gone to the gods knew where. The body of the giant assassin had been found at the Aldwark Bridge but of her lover there had been no sign. She was determined to stay in the city until she knew his fate.

'Your noble gesture is admirable, but your safety is my first concern.'

Noble gesture? Did Odaka think she was staying out of some kind of loyalty to her city, to her people? His assumption only shamed her. She was staying out of love for a man who would have taken her away from her people. Taken her far from a city that could soon be razed to the ground.

'Noble gesture or not, Odaka, I cannot leave. My place is here.' As she said the words she began to believe them, began to convince herself she was acting out of duty, but it still couldn't dispel the thought of River and what he meant to her.

'But it is obvious we cannot protect you here. The palace is not safe.'

'The city is not safe, Odaka. Everyone in it is at risk. Why not their queen also?'

Their queen? It was the first time she had said the word. The first time she had thought seriously about taking on that mantle. The mere thought of it weighed heavy on her shoulders.

Odaka was about to argue when the door to the chapel opened. Two grizzled warriors entered and Janessa recognised them as Lord Raelan's bodyguard, the Border Wolves of Valdor. They each knelt before her and bowed their heads.

'We have come for the prince,' said one. It was curious they should call him that, but then it was the tradition in Valdor to call their young lordlings princes. It had, after all, once been a kingdom in its own right.

'Of course. You are taking him to be buried now?'

'Yes, your majesty. There's no point in waiting on it.'

Janessa nodded. 'Then I will accompany you.'

The men looked at one another, shifting uncomfortably.

'It is too dangerous for you to leave the palace, my lady,' said Odaka.

'And besides, Lord Raelan is to have a pagan burial. It would not do for the future queen of Steelhaven to be seen attending a pagan ceremony. You will soon be defender of the city's faith, Arlor's earthly hand. It is against protocol.'

'To the hells with protocol, Odaka!' she snapped, looking at Raelan's body. Despite his betrayal she still respected him.

The Border Wolves stood awaiting their instructions, and Janessa could only feel sympathy for them – they had let their ward be murdered. She could only imagine what punishment awaited them back in Valdor . . . what shame.

'Very well,' she said. 'Take him.'

With another bow, the warriors lifted the pallet on which Raelan lay and carried it from the chamber.

When they had left, Odaka turned back to her. 'My lady, I am sorry, but—'

'I know what needs to be done,' she snapped. 'Now more than ever.'

She pushed past Odaka and walked from the chapel. Two Sentinels were immediately in step, clanking along beside her.

Janessa had no idea where she was going. Skyhelm was huge, with many rooms, but none of them held any allure for her. As she passed her father's throne room, though, she stopped.

It was a massive chamber made of bare stone. Since the reign of King Godrik the Mourner the chamber had been stark and grey, displaying no flags or trophies. Where a king held his court there could be no distractions, no opulence.

Janessa paused on the threshold, looking across the vast hall to the throne. Like the rest of the room it was hewn from bare stone, cold and impartial, as should be a king's judgements. Or a queen's.

She walked into the hall, her Sentinels following her every step as she made her way towards the throne. Some day soon she would have to sit on that seat and rule a nation. Or she could marry and hand the responsibility over. Oh that the choice were that easy.

As a child she had played in this place, hiding behind the stone columns, climbing into the huge stone chair. Of course it had been forbidden, but the young Janessa, the flame-haired wolf, hadn't cared.

Now that it might be her duty to sit on that throne, it scared her for the first time.

'Magnificent, isn't it?'

Janessa turned at the voice but not before the Sentinels, who spun round noisily, hands quick to grasp their swords.

Baroness Isabelle stood in the archway that led to the hall, a guileless smile on her face. She strolled across the threshold. 'Please, don't be alarmed: I am quite harmless.'

The Sentinels seemed to relax a touch, but Janessa wasn't sure just how harmless this woman really was. Nevertheless, she gave them a nod and they moved their hands from their swords.

'I have not yet had a chance to offer my condolences,' said Isabelle. 'Your father was a great king, and Lord Raelan would have made a worthy successor.'

'I appreciate the sentiment,' said Janessa.

'You should know I share your sadness. My husband was so recently butchered by the very horde that threatens our lands. I know how hard it can be, especially when our duty weighs as heavy as our grief. But we must think to the future.' *Ah, here it comes.* 'The people need something to rally to. They need someone to follow. A ruler who deserves their fealty. Who deserves to sit upon that seat.' She gestured to the stone chair.

'Of course,' Janessa replied. 'And I will give them that.'

'*You* will? You think you can give the Free States, and all its people, stability? We face destruction. A merciless enemy. You think you can face it down all alone? You are but a girl, untried and untested.'

'I am stronger than I look.'

Isabelle smiled. 'You will need to be.'

This was starting to grate. Janessa had allowed this woman to speak her mind, but it was clear what she wanted. Leon was the only feasible candidate, and his mother could smell the power, could taste it – of that there was no doubt.

Isabelle moved in close. 'I know you have men around you. Men you think you can trust. But whom can you really rely on? A queen needs a husband. Someone to keep her safe. Your life has already been threatened twice. If you married, the alliance would double the strength of this palace, this city. Eyes are already looking towards Steelhaven from the other provinces. A display of strength is needed. An alliance that will fortify the Free States—'

'Yes, I have heard all this before,' Janessa snapped. It stopped Isabelle in her tracks, but the woman's expression did not falter. 'And now one suitor is gone he must be replaced. You are here to tell me Leon is the best choice?'

'He is the only choice,' said Isabelle. 'Not a perfect choice, I'll admit. I am his mother, but even I know the boy has faults. He was indulged, spoiled, but you are a clever girl. You can bring him to heel.'

What was she? A trainer of hounds now? She did not want a man that needed training, she wanted . . .

. . . she wanted River.

'And is Leon so easy to manipulate?'

Isabelle raised an eyebrow. 'He requires some work, that is all. That is not to say he doesn't have his virtues.'

'I'm sure. I will think on it, my lady.'

'Think fast. The Free States face destruction and you must marry. The choice is clear. Do not wait too long, or your wedding day might be amidst the rubble of this city.'

Without waiting for a reply, Isabelle turned and strode from the throne room. Janessa watched her go, thinking about her words and their implications.

To save her city, her country, she would have to wed to form a strong and lasting alliance. And there was only one suitable choice – Leon Magrida.

The thought repulsed her. She had so recently been in River's arms. A man she loved and who loved her in return without question or demand. She would never have the same with Leon. She had considered marrying Raelan, but then the young lord of Valdor had been a strong and capable man.

Leon was as far from that as one could get.

The throne room and all it represented suddenly felt oppressive. Janessa had to get out. She walked from the chamber closely followed by her Sentinels. She would have preferred solitude, preferred to run far from here, but the days when that might be possible were gone.

As Janessa made her way through the palace she recognised there would be no such thing as solitude ever again. She worked her way up through the stairways, increasing her pace as she did so, feeling the walls moving in, feeling her breath coming in short gasps. Her Sentinels were diligent in their duty, following close, not letting her out of their sight.

When she finally reached the summit of the tower to look out over the city, they were not far behind.

Janessa placed a hand on the parapet, staring out to the north. She could not see Dancer's Hill but knew that some time soon Raelan would be buried there.

Now there was only Leon Magrida.

If a man like Raelan had betrayed her, what depths might Leon be capable of sinking to? How could she marry such a man – even for the good of her people? And when she was in love with someone else?

315

Again she stared out across the rooftops of the city. Was River somewhere out there waiting for her? Was he dead? Had he decided to escape the city without her?

Exhausted and confused, doubt began to creep into her mind about any man, any suitor. Any lover.

Whom could she trust? Whose advice could she take?

Even Graye had betrayed her in the end, a friend she had confided in for most of her life. And Odaka had been her father's man, not hers. Could she really trust him?

'Bring me the regent,' she said to one of her guards, who bowed dutifully and left to carry out her order.

As she surveyed her city, waiting for Odaka, she became more resolute. This was her city, her people. There was only one person she could trust in all the world. Only one person she had ever really needed.

When finally Odaka arrived, bowing before her, she had made up her mind completely.

'You will advance the preparations for my coronation,' she said, continuing before Odaka had time to argue. 'I will not be leaving the city. I will stay with the people of Steelhaven and face what they face. Suffer what they suffer. There will be no marriage. No alliance. My father united the Free States and I will secure that union, but not at the behest of a king. I will be queen of this city and rule it as my father would have.'

Odaka only stared at her.

For fleeting moments she wondered what he might say, almost wanting him to argue, to talk her down, but he did not.

'As you command, majesty,' he said finally. Bowing low and turning to leave.

And as he did so, Janessa could have sworn she saw him smile.

FORTY-ONE

He was holding her down, his weight crushing her, squeezing the air from her lungs. She could smell his breath on her face, hot and sickly like meat left out in the sun. As he fumbled between her legs she wanted to scream, wanted to lash out, but she couldn't move. It wasn't fear that paralysed her, just a deadness in her limbs. Her eyes were wide, she could see his face leering down, his tongue stuck out like a slug, swollen and wet. He grabbed the inside of her thigh and squeezed. It was just to inflict pain, just to hurt her. Tears were coming now, flooding out across her face, but it didn't stop him. His breath was getting more fevered, more ragged, and he was moving between her legs, his body heaving and writhing for position. As she moved her head, frantic and desperate, she finally managed to shake off the hand that clamped her mouth shut, but the scream wouldn't come, lost in her throat as he . . .

Rag opened her eyes, heart pounding.

She could still smell him, still see him on top of her, but it was only a ghost.

A dead man?

The room was small but airy. A window was open somewhere: she could feel the breeze as it cooled the place; and a bird chirruped nearby.

Rag raised a hand to her face, wincing as she touched her eye, feeling the sting of her swollen flesh. Maybe raising her head would be a good idea, give her a look at her surroundings, see what was what. As she lifted it off the pillow, the room spun, her head feeling like a barrel of oil on top of her shoulders.

All right, maybe not such a good idea after all.

Where was she anyway? Some kind of infirmary? Someone's home?

It wouldn't do to give in to blind panic at a time like this, but Rag was most definitely on the brink. She knew she had to move, had to get out of here and quick. If she remembered right, Krupps had taken a right beating and it was the Greencoats what gave it. If they'd questioned him, he might well have told them everything; about the murder and the part Rag had played in it. She wasn't about to hang around: a trip to the gallows weren't inviting.

She willed herself to move, raising her head once more, feeling the room spin again but ignoring it. It was only dizziness – it couldn't hurt her . . . but it appeared it was going to make her throw up.

The desire to lie back down was almost overwhelming but Rag fought it – fought it like she'd fought Krupps in that back alley, all desperate and like her life depended on it. This time, though, she managed to win out, holding down the sick.

There was a door – she could see it sitting there all spinny and blurry in her vision. All she had to do was get up, start walking and she'd be out before anyone knew it.

Rag braced her hands on the edge of the bed and pushed off, ready to land deftly and get the hells out of here. As her feet touched the floor her knees gave way, collapsing beneath her like dried twigs. She clawed at the sheets, gritting her teeth against the nausea and the dizziness and trying her hardest to get up but it was too hard, just too hard.

Tears began to well in her eyes.

No bloody tears, she thought. *How am I ever going to get into the Guild if I cry like a baby every time something goes wrong?*

The door opened with a creak and a young lad walked in. He was blonde and fresh faced, with a jug in his hand, probably water, probably for her, and he looked at her floundering there for a second. It was clear he had no idea what to do, and Rag didn't really have advice for him, so she couldn't really complain that he was just standing there, looking at her hanging from the bed sheets.

Without a word to her he ran off. She could hear him calling for someone at the top of his voice, telling whoever it was that the girl was awake.

That was it then: all over. They'd come back now and put her to the question and as soon as she could walk, which didn't feel like it would be any time soon, they'd give her a short rope and a long drop.

Footsteps, quick and heavy – here it came. As he walked in she recognised him straight away, despite the blur of her vision. When he'd picked her up back in the alley she thought she knew his face. Now that she could see him proper, Rag was sure she knew who it was.

He was a big bastard: thick neck, short hair, face that had seen plenty of action. No wonder Markus had been so frightened of him. Rag barely knew the bloke and she was already scared.

When he picked her up, though, when he helped her off the floor and placed her back on the bed he was almost gentle, those eyes that could have looked so hard if he'd wanted only seemed to look concerned. It reminded her of when she'd seen him on Dancer's Hill putting Markus in the ground. He hadn't seemed so fierce then neither.

'You shouldn't try to move,' he said in a deep voice that could so easily have sounded menacing if he'd chose. 'You've taken a bit of a beating.'

Rag appreciated his concern, but the fact she was still in trouble certainly wasn't lost on her. Any moment now it would start. *How did you know Krupps? Were you with him that night? Did you join in the stabbing and the butchering too?*

She braced herself for it, knew it was coming.

The young lad walked in behind him and the big fella turned around. 'You just left her lying on the floor?'

The lad looked up like he had no idea what his own name was. 'I didn't know what to do. I'm not surgeon trained.'

'For fuck's sake, Denny.' The big bloke turned back to her then, lifting a hand to her cheek as though checking it for fever. 'My name's Lincon,' he said, all soft like. 'What's yours?'

'Rag.' She was caught so off guard she'd said it before she could stop herself. Until she'd tried to speak, Rag hadn't realised how weak she was, how parched.

'Go get some water,' said Lincon, over one shoulder, and it was enough to send the young lad, Denny, scuttling off to fetch it. 'You're safe now, Rag. No one's gonna hurt you.'

Rag didn't know this bloke other than what she'd gathered from Markus. By all accounts he'd been a cold, hard bastard who'd treated that lad like shit, but when he told her she was safe, that no one was gonna hurt her again, she trusted his word like she'd never trusted no one.

Weren't they going to question her? Hadn't Krupps told them everything by now?

'Where's . . . ?' She could barely bring herself to say his name. What he'd done . . . what he'd tried to do. 'Where's . . . ?'

'Don't you worry yourself about that no more,' Lincon said. 'He won't hurt you again. He won't hurt no one again; the serjeant's seen to that all right.'

'He's . . . ?'

'As a doornail, love.'

Denny came in with the water and Lincon held up a cup for him to pour. Then he cradled Rag's pounding head and lifted the cup to her lips.

As she drank, she could only look into his face, seeing those cold, steel eyes. She'd thought he was a monster, but he was giving her water, caring for her like she was his own.

No one had ever cared for Rag when she was sick before. She'd always been the one to act mother, always taken care of Chirpy, Migs and Tidge when they'd caught a fever or got a cut or a graze. It made her nervous, made her wary, but still she let him hold her head up and pour that drink right into her mouth. When the cup was empty he laid her head back down on the pillow.

'Where is he now?' she asked. Now she had some wet on her lips it was easier to speak.

'As I said, he's dead, love. You don't need to worry.'

'No, I mean his body. Where's his body?'

Lincon looked around uncertain, like he didn't really know how to answer.

'Until someone comes to take him off for a burial he's . . . erm . . . in our cellar. It's cool down there, see.'

Rag closed her eyes. Nothing else to say. That was all she needed for now. Lincon sat with her for a while longer, at least as long as it took her to fall asleep.

When she woke later it was dark. What moonlight there was in the room showed she was alone again, and this time Rag knew she had to get up, had to use her legs no matter what.

She sat up in the dark and, holding her breath, slid off the bed and placed a foot on the floor, only breathing out when she managed to put some weight on it without collapsing. Both feet and she realised she could stand, a little shaky but not as bad as she had been.

Somewhere along the line she'd lost her shoes, but that was the least of her worries. Her head throbbed and in the dark she was going to struggle to find Krupps' body.

Rag opened the door to the room and peered out. The corridor beyond was just as dark as her room. It was like this place was deserted. Typical Greencoats – never around when something was going on.

She stepped out, closing the door behind her, and moved along the corridor. It wasn't long before she heard the sound of someone snoring. As she got closer she saw it was the young lad who'd come into her room earlier, Denny was it? He was slumped in a chair, arms folded, and at his side was sheathed a short blade.

Just what she needed.

Her eyes flitted from Denny's face to the sword handle as she reached out, willing him to stay asleep. She grasped the handle, pulling it upwards, feeling it slide easy in the sheath, blowing out one long breath as the blade came free. Denny snored on as he was disarmed, and Rag allowed herself a smile as she tucked the blade under her arm and padded away down the corridor. He'd most likely be in the shit later for losing it, but right now Rag's need was the greater.

'We're not taking him!' The voice bellowed from a room to Rag's left, and she barely had time to slam herself against the wall, hugging the shadows for dear life, as a door opened, illuminating the corridor. A tall man in a robe walked out, followed by a grizzled brute with one eye and half an arm. They was both clearly pissed off about something.

'You're the District Sexton; it's your fucking job! What am I supposed to do with him?' growled the one-eyed man.

'Burn him in the courtyard for all I care, but unless you can afford the fee the city graveyards are full. And as I've said, the fee's gone up.'

'Since when?' He was clearly growing angrier.

'Since the recent influx of refugees from the four corners of the Free States. Most of them won't last the winter. Not to mention the bodies that'll be coming in from the north soon enough. The burial yards are full as it is. If you can't afford it, you'll just have to dump him in the Storway. Either way – you killed him, so he's your responsibility.'

With that the robed man stomped off.

'Twat,' mumbled the grizzled brute, as he set off in the opposite direction.

Neither of them even noticed Rag was there.

Before the door could swing fully closed after them, she moved forward, jamming her arm inside. Once she'd slipped through the gap, Rag squinted against the lantern light that illuminated the room, until her eyes adjusted. Her heart began to beat a little faster as she spotted the dark passage leading downwards.

She picked up the lantern off the table and stepped down towards the cellar. It smelled stale, and she wrinkled her nose against it, but considering there was a dead body down there, at least it didn't stink of rot.

Or she hoped there was a dead body down here. If not she was in deep shit.

The lantern did its job piercing the darkness as she reached the bottom of the stairs, but it didn't stop the ominous feeling in her stomach. The walls were covered in damp, and somewhere she could have sworn she heard a rat squeak.

This all paled when she saw that in the centre of the cellar, lying on a wooden table, was a body. She couldn't see its face – someone had draped a brown woollen blanket over him – but Rag knew who it was, lying there in the dark and the cold.

Her courage almost gave out right then. She almost dropped the blade and turned and ran back up the stairs.

Almost.

Weren't no one going to do this for her. Weren't no one ever going to do anything for her again. This was her chance. Her one last chance.

She sat the lantern to one side and walked forward. Any moment she expected the body to move, to sit up and throw the sheet aside and look at her and say, 'All right, Sweets? Shall we carry on where we left off?' And then he'd take her by the throat and squeeze and squeeze and squeeze.

But Krupps didn't do that, because he weren't there no more. There was a body all right, but it weren't him. Krupps was gone now, off to wherever bastards went when they died.

All that was left was meat on a slab.

With that in mind, Rag reached out and grabbed the edge of the sheet. No point in doing it slow, prolonging the act, and she pulled it aside, showing Krupps to the world. Or at least what was left of him.

She hadn't been far wrong about meat on a slab. Those Greencoats had done a job on him all right. His face was a mess of blood, the flesh all blue and black beneath, his mouth hung slack and she could see the teeth within smashed and ruined. Weren't nothing of his eyes but swollen lumps.

Rag looked at him for a while, wondering how she felt about this. He'd tried to do her in, right enough, but she still couldn't bring herself to hate him totally for it. If she'd had the guts and the strength, wouldn't she have done the same to him?

Right now, though, she didn't feel nothing for him. And for what she was about to do Rag reckoned that was just about the right way to feel.

The blade suddenly felt heavy in her hand, but she lifted it anyway, pausing to take a breath before sinking it into his neck as he lay there. Krupps didn't make no sound or protest as she went at it, carving him up like a hunk of meat. The going was tough even though the blade was keen all right, but she guessed cutting a head off weren't no easy thing. There was less blood than she'd expected, and she reckoned that was a blessing – she still wasn't good with blood. As she continued, Rag resorted to using the blade like a saw, heaving back and forth like cutting through a log, and it seemed to be the best way. There was bone and gristle in the middle – that was the hardest to get through – but when that was done, the rest was easy.

Once she'd sawed right the way through that neck to the table beneath, Krupps' head moved all of a sudden. Rag stepped back, just watching as it rolled right off the table and hit the cellar floor with a thud. She stared at it, wondering what to do next, feeling the weight of the knife in her hand, strangely tempted to start carving other bits off him, but there weren't no time for that.

Rag grabbed the brown blanket he'd been laid under and rolled the head inside, wrapping it up tight. A bloodstain appeared in the wool, but there weren't nothing she could do about that now. Besides, it was dark and with any luck no one would even notice.

Leaving the blade behind, she grabbed the lantern and made her way back up the stairs, only too glad to be leaving the cellar behind her. Someone was going to get a big surprise when they went down there later, and she almost laughed as she imagined them shitting themselves in fright at finding a decapitated body.

Once at the top she ditched the lantern and opened the door to the corridor beyond. It was still dark and quiet, no sign of anyone, and Rag slipped out, letting the door close behind her.

She had no idea where she was, or how to get out, but it wouldn't do to stand around and wait for someone to give her directions. She padded along quiet as the grave, her bare feet making barely a sound as she worked her way around the building, into a wide courtyard. There was still no Greencoat in sight as she hurried across the yard, spurred on by her fear and her excitement, her bruised face and fuddled head all but forgotten.

The yard led out onto the street, a quiet street she didn't recognise, but it didn't matter. She was out now, and she had her prize and it would all be worth it.

As she ran, with the filth of the streets squelching beneath the soles of her feet, she got to thinking that all her troubles were almost finished.

FORTY-TWO

Waylian had heard nothing.

Gerdy had seemingly returned to her own chamber without raising any alarms. If she knew whose room she had awoken in she didn't care – or at least not enough to notify anyone important. Later, when he'd come back to his room and found it empty, relief washed over him like the evening tide.

He'd not seen Gerdy since, which was a blessing he could not stop giving thanks for. As for Rembram Thule – he could rot in the hells.

For a long time he'd tried to work out why Bram had done it. Waylian thought he was a friend, but what kind of bastard drugged someone and left them in a friend's bedchamber?

Surely that wasn't normal?

As he sat and stewed about it, Waylian realised he couldn't bear to be in his room any more, and so he grabbed one of the thick tomes he'd been given by the Magistra and fled.

When he finally reached the top of the tower he remembered it had been here that he and Bram had looked out over the city. Now it seemed even when Waylian tried to find some semblance of solitude, Bram was there to ruin it for him. Nevertheless, there was nowhere else he could go, nowhere else he could be guaranteed privacy.

He sat in the shadow of the parapet and opened his book. *The Invoker's Art* by Samael Hayn. Another great masterwork no doubt. How could he ever hold himself back from delving into this rich opus of knowledge?

Quite easily, he reckoned.

Waylian read for some time. None of the words sank in. Even the introduction was dry as a desert and twice as endless, more interested in the author's notably dull life than in introducing the subject in question. It was so bloody pointless.

He clenched his teeth against the pain of it, the humiliation of it. This book was just the final straw. Yet it was useless to blame anything, anyone but himself; it was his own fault. He'd decided to come here, he'd decided to pack his bags and leave everyone behind and come to the big city. It was his arrogance and pride and ambition that had led him to this. It was nobody else's fault everything had turned to shit.

With a snarl he flung the book over the side of the tower, hearing its pages flap desperately for a second before it soared off on the wind. Someone, somewhere, would probably find it, most likely quite battered and missing some pages – and they were bloody well welcome. Waylian could only hope they made more sense out of it than he ever would.

He put his head in his hands. When he looked up his vision was blurred with tears. Waylian hadn't wanted to cry and he'd managed to stop himself so far, but a sob followed the tears, and was itself followed by a flood as he broke down on that roof. He hated it here. He wanted to go home, back to his mother, back to his brother and his bloody dog. And he hated that dog. It had snarled whenever he came near and had even tried to bite him once. It hadn't drugged anyone and left them in his room though, so it was one up on Bram ruddy Thule.

In that moment it all came out, all Waylian's misery and self-loathing and regret, as he poured out his tears on that lonely roof, overlooking a city he hardly knew, miles away from home. And never mind his loneliness and his uselessness – there was an invading army on its way to the city gates, and a rogue magicker on the loose within its walls.

What in the hells was he even doing here?

It was clear then what he had to do. There was no point waiting to be dismissed, waiting for the inevitable. Waiting for an army of savages to descend and cut him and everyone else in the city to offal. He had no friends here, he had no life here and he didn't want the title of Magister enough to suffer all this.

It was time to go.

He opened his eyes and made to stand when he saw her there, watching him. Magistra Gelredida stood on the stairway that led up to the tower summit, her face an emotionless mask.

This was all he bloody needed. Though it didn't matter now what she said or how she said it. He was going. She could ridicule him all she wanted. It wouldn't make any difference.

Even so, he wiped the tears away with the sleeve of his robe, sniffing up the snot that had gathered in his nostrils.

'Is everything all right?' she asked.

Like you bloody care.

'Yes, I'm fine,' he answered, using the parapet to help him gain his feet.

'You don't look fine.' *Here we go, let the ridicule commence. She could do her worst, it didn't matter a shit now.* 'Is there something you wish to talk about?'

Was this a trick?

'I . . . er . . . it's nothing, Magistra.'

It was nothing. It was all for nothing.

'It doesn't look like nothing to me, Waylian. People don't burst into floods of tears for no good reason. Or are you prone to outbursts of unbridled emotion?'

Here we go. 'No, Magistra. I've just . . .' *Oh, what did it matter now?* 'I've just had enough. I'm failing in my studies, I'm not making any friends and I'm missing my family. I think I'd like to leave the Tower and return home. I think that's for the best.'

She studied him, looking deep into his eyes as though searching for something. 'Best for whom, Waylian?'

'Best for . . .' *For me! For you! For everyone!* 'Best for . . . It's just best if I go now, before I'm dismissed.'

'I see.' She nodded, considering his words. 'So you're giving in? Throwing away any potential future you might have here to go back to your ordinary, provincial life?'

'I'm not . . .'

But then he was, wasn't he.

He was giving in, he was running away. What choice did he have? 'Yes, I guess I am. But it's only a matter of time before I'm dismissed. This way I'm not wasting any more of anyone's time. Especially yours.'

Gelredida sighed, then looked out across the city. 'That's a shame, Waylian. I had high hopes for you.'

'I'm sorry, Magistra?'

She looked at him with an expression that could only have been sympathy. 'Come now, Waylian. I know I've been a little hard on you, but it was only for your own good. Some students require nurture. Others, a boot in the arse. It's always been clear which one you've needed. Do you think I'd have spent so much time on you if there was no potential?'

'I . . . Potential? But I'm completely out of my depth.'

'You're an apprentice, Waylian. A neophyte. Do you expect to be calling down thunderstorms and turning iron to gold in your first year? It takes some people decades to learn their first geas. Loyalty is as much a virtue for apprentices as anything. And it is clear you are loyal, Waylian.'

'So I'm not going to be dismissed?'

That raised a smile. Only a small trace of a smile that looked like it might split the skin at the corners of her mouth, but it was, for only the second time, a definite smile.

'Of course not, Waylian. Good apprentices are hard to find, and I'm not in the habit of taking on a new one every tenday. It's bad enough I have to put up with you.'

The smile was gone now, and Waylian was unsure if she was joking. Not that it mattered. She'd said he wasn't useless, or at least implied it. That was good enough for now.

He stood tall, ready to begin his work anew. Magistra Gelredida thought he had potential, and that was all the affirmation he needed.

'Shall we continue with our lessons then, Magistra?'

'We shall. Since those fools in the Crucible Chamber have decided to sit on their hands, it may well be up to the two of us to save this city. It looks like we have a lot of work to do.'

Had anyone else said that to him, Waylian might have found it frightening, but beside his mistress he suddenly felt as if he could accomplish anything, even hold back the Khurtic hordes. Who knew? Maybe he'd be the one to take the head of Amon Tugha and present it to the . . . well, whoever ended up ruling this place. The queen, he supposed.

'Have you never thought of sitting on the council, Magistra?' he asked as they made their way towards the stairs. 'You never wanted to become an Archmaster?'

'The traditions of the Crucible Chamber go back centuries. Each of the Primary Arts is represented by one man, and one man only. None of those who represent their Art can show any of the talents of the others. I am doubly blessed and cursed, in that I have more than one talent at my disposal, but it also means I am tainted in the eyes of the council. I can never be an Archmaster.'

'It seems an outdated tradition. Surely the Archmasters should be picked for their wisdom and power.'

That seemed to amuse Gelredida.

'Ah, you have much to learn of tradition, Waylian. Many of our customs hark back to the days of the Sword Kings and the War of the Red Snows. They are traditions that have kept us safe, but also kept us from progressing our Art. That is why three of the Arts have been lost over the years. But our traditions are there to protect us. Much of our knowledge and lore was taken from ancient tribes whose ambition and lust for power far exceeded their ability to control it. Our traditions keep us safe from such lusts.'

It reminded Waylian of what he and Bram had talked about days before, of the ancient histories of war and blood. 'I've read about those first days of the Caste. What was it . . . *they took our words of power with hearts of dark stone?*'

Gelredida stopped in her tracks and turned to look at him.

'What did you say?'

She asked the question as though he'd just called her a wrinkled old prune. Waylian suddenly blanched. Perhaps he was being too familiar; perhaps he'd overstepped the mark.

'Er . . . it was just something I heard . . .'

'Say it again,' she snarled, reaching forward to grasp his robe.

'*They took our words of power . . . with hearts of dark stone.*'

'Black stone! Hearts of black stone! Where did you read those words?'

'I . . . I didn't read them, someone told them to me.'

'Who? Who told them to you?'

Waylian's mind was reeling. Gelredida was furious, her ire aimed directly at him. The change from just moments ago was enough to almost loosen his bowels. He thought for a moment of lying to save his friend, but what in the hells did he owe Bram?

'It was Rembram Thule. We were just talking about—'

'Where is he? Where is he right now?'

'I— I'm not sure . . . he could be in his chambers or the refectory . . .'

Gelredida grasped him firmly by the arm and led him down from the tower roof. He clattered after her down the stone staircase, at pains to keep up.

They sped to the apprentice chambers but Bram was not there. Neither was he in the refectory, and Waylian was beginning to worry for the lad's safety, such was the Magistra's growing ire. Other apprentices could only watch in surprise, moving out of their path as she dragged Waylian through the corridors. Clearly they thought he had done something to offend his mistress, but then they already considered him a moron, so it mattered little what they thought.

'He's not here, Waylian. Where is he? We must find him.'

She was holding both his arms now, staring into his eyes as if the roof might fall in and the tower collapse about their ears. Her nails dug into his flesh and Waylian began to get a dread sense of foreboding.

'I don't know where he is. I don't understand. What could he have done?'

'Those words. I know you didn't read them in any book and I know you don't speak the tongue they were originally uttered in. In every place we've found a body, a mutilated corpse, there have been sigils on the walls, signs and ciphers in ancient tongues long dead. And on the wall of each place we've been to was written "*they took our words of power with hearts of black stone*". It's an ancient curse, left by the shamans of the north. Part of a vow made after the War of the Red Snows. Only a few people know that language. Only a very few.'

'But Bram's just an apprentice.'

'That's why we have to find him. He has no idea what he might unleash. No idea what he might bring down on this city, so *think*, Waylian. Where could he be?'

It was impossible. Where could he be? There were very few places left to look. He definitely wouldn't be in the library; that was a certainty. Perhaps . . .

'Gerdy! He was . . . friendly with a girl called Gerdy.'

Gelredida pulled him back towards the apprentice chambers, scattering several students who dared get in her way. They eventually found Gerdy's door nestled within the heart of the female chambers. Without knocking, the Magistra turned the handle and strode inside.

There was no Gerdy, but the room was in disarray, as though someone had fought hard against an intruder.

The Red Witch let go of him now. She moved with a speed that belied her years as she made her way up through the tower.

'Where are we going, Magistra?' Waylian asked. 'How will we find them? If they're not in the tower they could be anywhere in the city by now.'

'There is only one way of finding them. And I will not be refused this time.'

She mumbled as much to herself as Waylian, as though asserting in her own mind what she would do before she did it.

They came to an opulent corridor, all polished wooden panelling and grim portraits of ancient magisters. Gelredida picked a door, again not pausing to knock. Waylian could do nothing but follow, even though he felt every inch the trespasser.

Despite her abrupt entrance, Gelredida was greeted with a smile from the room's occupant. Waylian recognised Archmaster Nero Laius from their meeting in the Crucible Hall as he looked up from beneath his mop of curly grey hair.

'Magistra. To what do I owe this pleasure?' he said.

'Let's dispense with the pleasantries,' Gelredida replied. She loomed over Nero, though he looked anything but intimidated. 'I need you to find someone, and I'm not in the mood to be turned down.'

Nero's smile wavered. He glanced to Waylian, who could only look back with equal helplessness. 'Since you've asked so nicely, how could I possibly refuse?'

FORTY-THREE

They were in rows, mouths gagged, hands bound with rope rather than chain lest they make a clangour in the night as they were herded aboard ship. Women and their children were kept together; it made them panic less. Men were kept where the slavers could concentrate their best guards to quell any sign of dissent, should someone be stupid enough to try to make a break for it. Merrick had already watched them beat one man almost to death. He still lay in one corner of the room, not moving. Maybe he was dead already, maybe he would live. It was hard to tell.

What do you care; you're the wolf, remember? The wolf gets paid, the shepherd gets to sleep at night. You can't have both.

He looked up to a gantry that ran the length of one wall. Bolo was there watching, surrounded by his men. It was clear he was enjoying himself, sipping wine, eating grapes and laughing hard.

'How much longer?' asked Kaira. She'd stood beside him in silence most of the evening, watching, waiting. Her eyes were fixed on the piteous crowd, starved and beaten and waiting for the inevitable. Merrick had thought she might burst into tears at one point, but the implacable warrior had defied his expectations. Now she just looked furious. He could only hope he didn't end up the target of her ire.

'Won't be long now,' he said. 'We have a short window of opportunity on the dock at ten bells. Then they'll take these people across and load them aboard.'

'And we have to stay and watch?' She looked at him, anger in her eyes, her jaw locked. It was clear she was struggling to hold it in. Merrick had to admit, that scared him a bit.

'I suppose we could ask for payment now. Then we can be on our way.'

'And then we hand the money over? Will we be rewarded by the men who run the Guild?'

'There's every chance of that, I guess. But I wouldn't be so eager to meet them if I were you. It's not always a good sign.' *Sometimes it's a sign you're about to have something chopped off.*

'I'm not. I'm just eager for this business to be over.'

Her fists were clenched, the muscles in her arms and shoulders bunched.

'All right.' Merrick held up his hands, trying his best to calm her. He wasn't about to touch her, though. He'd learned his lesson there all right. 'We'll go ask Bolo for the payment. Then we can get the fuck out of here.'

As they made their way up to the gantry, Kaira didn't take her eyes off the crowd as they were being prepared for their journey. Merrick could see them being poked and prodded as if they were being got ready for market, and he knew that *he* had done this. *He* had made this possible; this whole affair was on *his* shoulders.

It wasn't him though; it was those he worked for. He was just an employee. *And whether you work for tyrant or saint, it matters not.* And if not Merrick then some other poor bastard forced to do the work of the Guild.

It wasn't his fault.

Better the wolf than the shepherd.

Bolo's guards moved to block the pair as they neared the top of the gantry, but with a gesture of his arm the pirate lord waved them aside. He smiled as Merrick drew closer, as if they were old friends, business partners meeting to chat about old times.

Merrick could only smile back. *Better the wolf.*

'My friend,' said Bolo. 'It is pleasing to see you, but alas our business is almost concluded.'

'And everything's on track?' asked Merrick, keen to have this finished with.

'Of course. Everything is moving as planned. But you look agitated. Does something trouble you?'

'Me?' *Better the wolf, don't forget that.* 'I'm fine. Not too sure about this lot.' He gestured to the rows of bedraggled slaves.

'Please, do not concern yourself. They are on their way to a better place. A better future. Were they to remain here they would only be condemned to a life of poverty, and possibly be slaughtered at the hands of the Elharim warlord. It is better this way. Better for them, anyway.'

And better for your coffers, no doubt. 'Is that how you persuaded them all to come so quietly? Persuaded them they were off to a better life?'

Bolo's smile spread across his face. 'Food and shelter where there is none is a temptation most cannot resist. When a man's family is starving and you offer him bread he will follow you anywhere.'

'Even into slavery?' *Careful, Ryder.*

'I think we have very different definitions of slavery. These people will be cared for by the rich and privileged of four continents . . . most of them, anyway.'

What about the ones that end up in the whorehouses and fighting pits?

'I'm sure they'll thank you when they get to wherever they're going.' He looked to the guards surrounding them, then at Kaira, whose hate-filled eyes were fixed on Bolo – giving her the look of a rabid dog.

Perhaps it was time to go.

'If we're concluded here, we'll take the final payment and be on our way. If it please you?'

Bolo leaned against the railing and smiled. 'Yes. It pleases me, my friend.' With his foot he flipped open the lid of a casket that sat next to him. 'You will find this concludes our business.'

Merrick looked down at all that money glimmering in its box. What he could do with all that. The places he could go. The things he could buy.

Then he looked to the crowd below.

Better the wolf. Better the fucking wolf. Don't even think about it!

He took a step forward, a step towards the money, but then stopped.

But you're no wolf. You never were. Not that you're a shepherd either, Merrick Ryder. You're nothing but a coward. You were a coward when you squandered your parents' fortune. You were a coward when you got in hock to the Guild.

You're a fucking coward now!

A face glanced up from the crowd, young, innocent. Well, not for long.

Take the money, coward!

'Is something amiss?' Bolo asked.

Take the money and leave! Leave all this shit behind like you've left everything else, every other responsibility you ever had.

'I'm no coward,' whispered Merrick.

Bolo frowned. 'What ails you, my friend? Here is the payment you have asked for. Now take it and go about your business.'

Merrick looked at Bolo, then over the gantry to the scores of men, women and children awaiting their fate.

'I . . . I can't . . .' he whispered.

Coward!

'You can't what?' asked Bolo, clearly growing impatient. 'The money is here. Take it now or leave empty handed. This is your choice.'

'I . . . I'm . . .' *I'm the shepherd . . . please tell me I'm the shepherd.*

'What?' Bolo was getting agitated, his fingers drumming against the jewelled hilt of his cutlass. 'What is wrong with you?'

He stared, his handsome brow furrowing. Merrick could see it now, see the man standing before him, the man he could one day become. All he had to do was take the money and be on his way to a new life with limitless potential. All he had to do was abandon the innocents who stood below, silently awaiting their fate.

'I am the shepherd,' said Merrick, spitting the words through gritted teeth as his hand moved to his hip. 'And *you're* the wolf.' Fingers closed around the hilt of his sword, pulling it free of its sheath faster than Bolo's guards could move, faster than Bolo's hand could grasp his jewelled cutlass.

The slaver's eyes went wide as he realised what was happening, that he would never unsheathe his weapon in time. Bolo opened his mouth to speak, but the sword pierced his throat before any words could reach it.

Two guards stepped forward, too late to save their paymaster but more than willing to avenge him. Merrick spun, his blade flashing through the air with a hum, opening the neck of one. He managed to duck the clumsy blow of the second bodyguard, thrusting his sword without thought into the man's chest.

As the pair fell to the ground, Merrick took a step back, glancing at Bolo who desperately clawed at his throat, trying in vain to stem the blood that flowed free from his wound. He was trying to speak, but Merrick had heard enough words from him. He watched while Bolo slowly drowned in his own blood, drinking in the sight, feeding on it, savouring it like a fine wine.

There were five men left, along with Kaira, all standing staring at him in disbelief, but in a moment they had gathered their wits, reaching for their weapons. Down below, over the gantry, Merrick could hear someone shout a warning cry as they saw what was happening up above them.

Merrick looked to Bolo's five bodyguards and smiled.

'You've all got one chance to live,' he said, flicking blood from the end of his sword, revelling in its balance and the feel of the grip in his palm. It had been so long, so many years since he'd felt such a thrill. He had missed it. 'I was taught in the Collegium of House Tarnath, trained in the sixty-six *Principiums Martial* by Lord Macharias himself. I've killed twelve men . . . er . . .' He looked down at the three corpses before him. 'Actually, that's fifteen men in single combat, and I'm in just the mood to add some more. You can run and live, or stay and die. What's it to be?'

The five men looked uncertain at first, and Merrick wasn't sure what they'd do. Kaira just stood and watched. Whether she would help him or throw in her lot with the slavers, he didn't know.

He'd find out soon enough.

The giant took a step forward. Merrick remembered his name was Lago, Bolo's scarred and fearsome second in command. He stared down mournfully at his dead master, now crumpled with a gorget of his own blood. When he looked up at Merrick, his face contorted in rage. 'You have murdered Bolo Pavitas, Slavelord of the Four Seas, and Prince of Keidro Bay. High Admiral of the Silken Fleet and—'

'Fucking hells!' Merrick shouted. 'Can we just get on with it?'

Lago bellowed, raising his falchion high. He was ferocious, a hulking mound of muscle, bearing down with his huge, razor-sharp blade. Merrick could only imagine the fear he instilled in his slaves, the terror they must have felt when caught in the eye of his furious storm.

It meant nothing.

He moved in, offering himself as an easy target before stepping swiftly to one side. Lago's blade came crashing down, smashing into the gantry and sending splinters flying just as Merrick's sword pierced below his armpit, driving in almost to the hilt. The massive slaver didn't even have a chance to cry out before he collapsed in a vast heap.

There was no time to gloat, though. On seeing Lago charge in, the other four steeled themselves, racing forward as one.

But Merrick had trained in the blade yards of the Collegium, facing half a dozen swordsmen at once, taking beating after beating with their training swords. The *Principiums Martial* were hard learned and long remembered, but Merrick had mastered them all before he was fourteen.

His blade moved as though it were possessed, seeking its targets with a hunger, showing no mercy as it pierced flesh, sending gouts of blood and severed limbs flying. Within three breaths Merrick was standing amidst nothing but corpses.

He breathed hard. Though he moved with grace and speed as he slew, it had been a long time since he'd drilled his body, and it wasn't used to such exertion.

Kaira looked at him as he leaned back, stretching the crick from his spine. More slavers were running up the stairs to the gantry, and it wouldn't be long before he was facing a dozen bloodthirsty thugs.

'Are you with me?' he asked.

Because if you're not there's every chance I'm a fucking dead man.

Kaira looked at him for endless moments as the screaming horde drew closer. Then, just as he thought he might have to flee, she smiled. Like a lioness on the hunt she stooped with elegant grace, picked up a sword dropped by one of the dead slavers and turned to face the mass of ruffians charging up the stairs.

The first of them came up screaming from below. Whether he was confident of victory when he saw he was facing a woman Merrick couldn't tell, but he certainly looked as if he regretted his actions as Kaira spun her weapon with practised ease and hacked off his arm at the shoulder.

'Vorena!' she screamed, leaping high and landing among the rest of the charging mob. Two were knocked back down the stairs by the strength of her attack, others taken off guard, doing their best to avoid this mad woman who had jumped into their midst.

Merrick moved forward to lend his own blade to the fray, but he was suddenly struck with awe as he watched Kaira's display of power. Her blade was undaunted by the flesh it carved, her face a mask of steely concentration, showing no anger, only studied and disciplined focus.

Within moments men were screaming for mercy, others fleeing for their lives in the face of the onslaught, but Kaira was not to be thwarted. She leapt over the rail of the stairway, her sword slashing through the bonds that held the first batch of slaves.

'Run,' she yelled at them; a group of men whose sudden freedom seemed to instil strength in their limbs. 'Or take your vengeance.' Kaira lifted her blade, pointing to the remaining slavers who were now desperate to escape this place.

Merrick allowed himself a smile as he saw them choose vengeance.

It was the choice he'd have made had he been in their place.

What he saw then was brutal and bloody, but he forced himself to keep looking. This was partly his fault anyway; he should at least watch while these men were torn apart with bare hands or strangled with ropes. It was only right.

When the bloodletting was done, and the remaining slaves released from their bonds, Merrick continued to watch for a while as fathers were reunited with wives and children. Kaira did her best to tend any wounded, accepting the gushing thanks of the thronging crowd, and he couldn't help but feel envious. But she'd played no part in their internment – she deserved their thanks.

He on the other hand . . .

Despite the warmth of the sight, though, Merrick couldn't help but taste the bitterness of it. His troubles had been all but over – but now he had made more trouble for himself than he would ever escape. He had killed Bolo and betrayed the Guild, and they would never forgive him for that.

But then he remembered Bolo's casket . . .

The slaver's body was surrounded by the corpses of his men. The casket lay on its side, its precious contents spilled out at the dead slaver's feet.

Merrick knelt down, righting the copper-bound box and sweeping up a handful of coins. There was blood mixed in with the gold, sticky and black in his palm. But what did it matter; coin was coin. It could be washed . . . and spent.

He threw the coins in the casket and scooped up another handful. This time the blood ran through his fingers and when he tried to fling the gold in the box it stuck to his palm.

'You think that will save you?'

Merrick looked up to see Kaira standing next to him.

'I think it will help,' he replied. 'You want half, I'm happy to split it. The gods know we've earned it.'

Kaira shook her head and her look of disappointment almost hurt. Almost.

'There are others more deserving,' she said.

'What others . . . ?' Merrick glanced down at the dishevelled mass. 'Wait . . . oh no! You can't seriously think . . .'

That's it, keep the money. It's not like you've ever done the right thing in your life anyway.

He glanced down again at the families. At the pitiful faces.

Fuck!

He stood, pointing to the casket like he was accusing it . . . of what he didn't know. 'All right then, take it. I hope it makes you happy.'

Kaira picked up the box and closed the lid. 'Trust me – it wouldn't have made you happy,' she replied, turning and making her way down the stairway to hand out the coin.

No, it might not have made me happy. But it might have kept me alive. For a while at least.

And he stayed long enough to watch, as the coin . . . his coin . . . was given away without a second thought.

FORTY-FOUR

He watched from the rooftops, lurking as close as he dared. He monitored the movements of armoured men, of sentries, of the militia in their green jackets patrolling the streets. Had there been a way in, he would have taken it; had there been a way to climb the wall without being seen, he would have used it. For a day and a night he watched and waited, but the palace was secure against him now; there was no way through.

She was in there somewhere; River could feel it. He yearned for her, pined for her so intensely it was like a knife in his gut. If he watched for long enough, surely he might catch sight of her, one fleeting glimpse to still his heart as it beat against his chest, *like the waves against the rocks.*

Jay did not come, though, protected as she was by her armoured guards, kept cloistered within the palace walls like a bird safe in its cage.

But those guards and sentries could not protect her forever – a thousand, thousand men could not keep her safe. If the Father of Killers put his mark on her they would never keep her from him.

Only River could keep her safe.

Only River.

As time wore on though, he knew that waiting for the inevitable would never keep her from harm's way . . . from his Father's wrath. He had to act, had to take the fight to those that would seek to kill her. By waiting in the shadows he could not protect her and he knew, with sudden and clear clarity, what he had to do.

If there were another way he would have taken it, but the longer he tarried here, watching from afar, the longer the Father of Killers had to make his plans.

The way was clear. River would have to kill his Father.

As dusk leeched the light from the sky, he made his way across the city's rooftops, his feet sure on the slate tiles as he went. Usually he felt free, felt alive on the hunt, but this time River's heart was heavy. Even though he knew it must be done, it weighed on him that he was about to face his Father. This was the man who had raised him, nurtured him, taught him to survive, and now he was to suffer the greatest betrayal a son could inflict.

And how would he defeat him? The Father of Killers was the consummate assassin, the deadliest man River had ever known. He had no weakness, no flaw in his armour. For every attack River had, his Father had a counter. River could not say the same on his side.

They had fought one another countless times over the years, and River had not once bested his Father in combat. But he had to do something and it must be now. He would not wait, *for the River waits for nothing and no one.*

Lights flickered in the distance, marking his route, and River's eyes were keen, tempered in the darkness of subterranean tunnels and beneath black starless skies. The rooftops were his playground and he could have made his way blindfold had he wanted to. It was this superior sense that alerted him to someone on his trail. It was the faintest of notions – shadows in his periphery, but it was enough.

There were only two men left alive who could track him as he made his way across the city. River's heart beat all the faster at the prospect it might be his Father.

As he leapt a ten-foot gap and landed silently on a flat rooftop, he rolled, turning as he tumbled and coming up to face his hunter. He fully expected his Father, expected a quick death, for he had no weapons, but it was not the Father of Killers who came after him.

Forest waited in the shadows for several moments before revealing himself. With a sure step he moved from the darkness, his feline grace almost mesmerising. River had always admired Forest, his older brother, sometimes a companion, sometimes a mentor, always a danger.

As River waited, Forest smiled.

'Our Father is disappointed in you,' he said, pacing, moving like a cat on the prowl.

River had no answer to that. His guilt bore down heavily on him, his betrayal like an iron weight about his neck.

'Though brutal and stupid, Mountain was still his son. Father wept for a night and a day at his loss. He knew it was you that killed him – there was no other that could have bested him. Other than me.'

'Have you come to fight me, brother?' River asked, his every sinew tensed, his eyes scanning, waiting for Forest to strike, swift and true as only he could.

But Forest just laughed. 'No, I have not come to fight you, River. Our Father has already lost one son. He has no wish to lose another.'

'So he has sent you to bring me home? I tell you now, I will not go other than with murder in my heart.'

Forest showed just a sliver of emotion. River's suggestion that he would do harm to their Father was clearly crossing a line.

'He does not want you home. You have turned your back on him, and in turn he has turned his on you. You should die for this, River. I urged him to let me kill you, but he refused my request. Instead, he offers you mercy. More than you deserve.'

For a fleeting moment River felt relief, but he knew mercy was different from forgiveness.

'Mercy? The Father of Killers offers mercy? No, I do not believe you, brother.'

'Do not be so quick to judge. His mercy does not come without a price, River. You should know that.'

'And what would he have me do?'

Forest smiled anew. 'He would have you perform one last task for him. Leave the city and travel over the seas. Certain men in a place known as Keidro Bay have been marked, and you will see them to their rest. Do this and you will live. That is the mercy our Father offers.'

No, he could never . . . 'Leave the city? And leave Jay with no one to protect her? You think me a fool? You would have me gift you her life?'

Suddenly the smile was gone from Forest's face. 'What has she done to you, brother? What has she poisoned you with that you would spit in our Father's face?'

'She has shown me . . .' *Love.* 'She has shown me there is another path than that of the killer. She has shown me that we are not born to this, Forest. We are men like any other. We don't have to—'

'Enough!' Forest spat. 'Don't try and infect me with the same poison she has poured in your ear. We are sons to the Father of Killers. We are the weapons in his hands. The swift blades in the night. Not born to

341

this? Perhaps you weren't, but then you were always weak. This is what I am, and no one will ever turn me from it.'

It was clear he could never talk Forest round. His brother's devotion was too strong.

'I will not do it. Go and tell our Father that. Tell him that I would rather die.'

Forest looked down, his head nodding. When he looked back up, the smile had returned to his face.

'My Father predicted this might be your reaction. And so he is willing to bargain.'

Bargain? River thought this a curious choice of words. The Father of Killers was uncompromising, single minded in purpose. He made no bargains. When his mind was made up there was no changing it.

'What do you mean? The Father—'

'The Father offers you one chance, River. You are his son. He has no wish to end your life. It is a chance, brother, one you should take.'

'And what is the nature of this bargain?'

'If you do this one last thing for him, if you kill a mere five men of his choosing, he vows to spare your . . . what should we call her? Your lover? But know that you can never return. Come back to the city and the bargain is annulled. The life of your princess forfeit.'

'He offers to make a pact? We both know the Father makes no pacts.'

'On this occasion he is willing to break with tradition. It is a generous offer. I would take it were I in your . . . predicament.' With that, Forest flung something towards River, who caught it deftly. 'This should seal your passage on a ship to Keidro Bay. There you will be given the names of the men you are to visit – five Lords of the Serpent Road. Evil men, pirates and slavers all, each more than deserving of death. Take it and go, brother. Do this thing and she will be safe. That is the word of our Father.'

River glanced into his palm, seeing the purse of coins.

'Just like that? I go, and she will be spared?'

'Just like that, brother,' Forest replied. 'But don't tarry too long. Our Father is not a patient man.'

He backed away, keeping his eyes on River. Now more than ever there was little trust between them. Had the roles been reversed, River would not have shown his back either.

Forest reached the edge of the flat roof, then stepped back into oblivion, dropping from the edge like a stone.

As soon as he was gone, River turned and ran, taking the rooftops as fast as his legs would carry him, determined to put as much distance between himself and Forest as he could. Though their parlay had been without incident, he knew how unpredictable his brother could be.

As River ran he was more vigilant than ever, waiting for the strike to come from the growing dark. But that strike never came, and when he found himself at the city's southernmost rooftop overlooking the docks, he finally stopped.

River realised he had been running in a daze, no rhyme or reason to his direction, but it had brought him here.

To a place from which he might flee the city.

He turned back, looking out across Steelhaven's rooftops towards the palace in the distance. Towards his love.

Could he trust the Father of Killers? Would Jay be safe if he kept his part of the bargain? His Father had certainly never given him any reason to doubt his word.

But how could he go without first speaking to Jay? She would never know what had become of him. She might think he had abandoned her.

If he stayed, if he tried to complete his vow to murder the Father, he would surely be killed, and Jay left with no protector. But if the Father kept his word, and there was no reason to think he would not, she would be spared death at his hands. All River had to do was leave.

Surely it was the only way.

He climbed down from the rooftops, bracing himself against the tight walls of an alleyway as he eased himself to the ground, then walked out into the dockside, making his way down to the crescent bay.

It was hard to believe he could do this, could run away and leave her, and more than once he stopped, turning back to the city, feeling the pull of it.

But he had no choice.

Gripping the bag of coins tightly in his hand, River ran down to the dock. Countless ships were moored, and it did not take him long to find one bound for Keidro Bay. As he approached it, he saw the name emblazoned on the side, painted in stark white against the black bow – *The Maiden's Saviour.*

River almost laughed. Was this some kind of portent? And if so, was it telling him he was doing the right thing, or that he should turn back?

Without thinking on it, he walked up the gangplank and was quickly confronted by a grizzled sailor, his head covered by a bandanna, the tattoos on his thick arms still visible in the waning light.

'Not a passenger ship,' he said simply, regarding River with cold eyes.

'Not even for this?' River replied, tossing him the bag of coins.

The man weighed it in his fist. 'You must be desperate or rich to pay so much for passage to Keidro. What is it? You got business with the Lords of the Serpent Road?' He laughed at his joke then, and busied himself on deck, leaving River alone.

Whether these men, these pirate lords, were as evil as Forest had said, River did not know, but that would not stop him. Better for them they did not know River was coming.

Coming with only murder in his heart.

FORTY-FIVE

The brass gates to the Chapel of Ghouls lay open. Waylian stood outside them beside the Magistra and two Raven Knights. Despite their presence this place still filled him with dread.

'Should we wait for the Greencoats, Magistra?' he asked, looking sideways at the two dark-armoured warriors. They were imposing, their beaked helms hiding their faces, but Waylian wasn't sure they would be enough to stand against a man schooled in the Ninth Art.

'There is no time,' said Gelredida, moving forward across the threshold, the Raven Knights at her shoulder. 'You are free to wait here if you wish.'

Those words were a challenge, and Waylian knew it. Of all the tasks she had given him over the months, Waylian knew this one was the most significant.

Would it win him her respect?

There was no way to tell, but refuse and he would most definitely lose it, of that he was certain.

Reluctantly, Waylian followed.

Archmaster Laius had directed them to this place, and as they entered, Waylian began to wish the old diviner had been less proficient. It had taken him no time at all to scry his astrolabe and rummage in chicken gizzards before he'd specified the Chapel of Ghouls. To Waylian, Laius's divination had looked almost comical, as he went about his business like some sort of street charlatan, but Gelredida trusted his assessment without question, castigating herself for her stupidity, and had immediately rushed here after demanding the service of the first Raven Knights she saw.

345

So it had brought them to this – this eerie monolith in the north of the city.

Waylian tried to stay as close as he could to the Raven Knights as they made their way up towards the Chapel itself, spears held out in front of them. The place gave him an uncontrollable sense of foreboding, elevating his fear, but he knew he couldn't turn back. The Magistra was relying on him. Hopefully she just wanted moral support, because he doubted he'd be any good if this came to violence.

The four of them moved up to the stone building, to the entryway that had previously been blocked by a massive stone, only to find it lying beside the Chapel, crushed and broken as though a giant had smashed it asunder with an enormous warhammer.

Waylian stared into the black entrance, into the abyss, the fear clasping his heart like the gripping of an armoured fist. Magistra Gelredida suddenly grasped his robe, holding her hand up for silence. At first Waylian could hear nothing, just wrinkled his nose against the strange smell, but soon he heard it: a low chant, words repeated over and over again in a language he had no comprehension of.

And then the Magistra was moving, her urgency clear. The two knights clattered after her as she rushed through the entrance and Waylian could do nothing but follow.

They hurried along a dark corridor, coming out into a gigantic atrium. It was impossibly large. From the outside, the Chapel of Ghouls was a towering monolith, but it could in no way house an interior so massive. It made Waylian's head spin with its vast basalt walls intricately carved with sigils and friezes, each as grotesque as those depicted on the gates outside.

Several flights of stairs, each carved into the rock, twisted and wound their way upwards to a platform high above. Gelredida did not pause, mounting the stairs followed by her knights. Waylian barely had time to catch his breath, barely had time to marvel at the Chapel's interior, barely had time to register his panic before following them.

The stairs came out onto a platform high above the Chapel. Windows carved in the rock let in the night air and a stiff breeze threatened to throw Waylian over the edge and to the ground fifty feet below. However, what he saw on the platform made him forget the imminent danger of falling. The floor of the high dais was covered in black sigils, pictograms daubed and etched into the stonework. Something dark and foul was smeared all around, some kind of black gore that stank like death.

Rembram Thule was at the platform's centre, chanting his foul incantation. He did not stop as the four of them appeared. He was too enrapt in his ritual, too focused on the object of his rite . . . Gerdy.

She was staked out, her eyes glazed and staring, her mouth gagged tight with a knotted rope. Waylian saw she was naked, and thought for a moment he should do something to cover her modesty as he had done some nights before, but right now that was the least of her worries. Her main worry was the dagger in Bram's hand.

As he saw what was happening, one of the Raven Knights bellowed, charging forward with his spear held out menacingly. Gelredida shouted something Waylian didn't hear, a warning that was lost above the knight's battle cry – a battle cry that only served to alert Bram to their presence.

The boy looked up, but Waylian could see he was a boy no longer. His eyes were dark rimmed and there was no colour in them, the irises now two jet pools of black hatred. As the knight charged, Bram stood fast, a mirthless smile spreading across his lips, a black mist already emanating from his clenched fists. What dark magicks he was conjuring, Waylian could not comprehend, but he knew they were steeped in evil.

Rembram's smiling lips twisted into a silent incantation as he thrust out his fists. The Raven Knight suddenly stiffened in his charge and Waylian could hear a sickening crack from within his armour, as though every bone in his body had suddenly snapped as one. Without a sound the knight crumpled to the ground.

The second knight was more wary, circling round to the right as Gelredida held a hand up.

'You have to stop this, boy. You have no idea what you're doing.'

Bram only grinned. 'I know exactly what I'm doing, you old witch. I'm going to watch this place fall. I am the bringer of oblivion. The Maleficar Necrus.'

With that he raised the knife high over Gerdy's supine body.

Waylian screamed wordlessly, a cry of fear and pain and regret.

Gelredida stepped forward, already uttering something from deep in her throat, fingers twisting into some intricate formation.

The remaining Raven Knight stepped in, raising his spear high, his arm poised to bring it down in a death blow.

As Bram's knife thrust towards Gerdy, Gelredida unleashed her magicks in a flurry of purple light. Waylian could feel it sucking the energy from the atmosphere, from the stone of the rooftop, and it took his breath with it, as though it had reached into his chest and stolen the very air from his lungs.

It shot towards Bram, and Waylian watched as it travelled, leaving a contrail of enervating mist in its wake. The energy turned in the air as it reached Bram, seemingly drawn to the knife he gripped in his fist and drove down through the air towards Gerdy's bare chest. Before the dagger could pierce her flesh it was consumed by the purple light, but this did not stop Bram's strike. The dagger, now wreathed in magick, plunged into her body, right up to the hilt.

Waylian saw with horror the wound instantly turn black. Bram wrenched the dagger free in a flurry of black mist, just as the Raven Knight's spear came down to impale him.

With preternatural speed, Bram moved, twisting aside and slicing the haft of the spear in two with the dagger. The Raven Knight barely had time to register his weapon was sundered before Bram screamed in his face. It was a fell voice: a daemonic cry that almost burst Waylian's eardrums, and its power was enough to send the knight hurtling back over the edge of the platform.

'What have you done?' Gelredida cried, moving forward.

Waylian could see the wound on Gerdy's chest spreading, turning her flesh dark and necrotic, branching out like a spider web, following an arterial path like a black flood through her veins.

'You know exactly what I've done,' Bram replied, a self-satisfied smile creeping across his lips as if he'd just beaten someone at cards rather than murdered a girl in cold blood.

Gelredida pulled something from her robe and flung it while Bram was still talking. It burst as it flew through the air, spreading spore-like dust all over the boy's head. He reeled back, dropping the dagger and yelping like a beaten hound.

Gelredida rushed forward to Gerdy's body. 'Waylian,' she barked. 'You have to help me.'

Bram's face began to burn, coming up in livid welts, and he stumbled back, clawing at the skin.

Gelredida knelt beside Gerdy, laying her hands on the black flesh of her chest.

'What do you want me to do?' said Waylian, unable to take his eyes off the dead girl.

Gelredida looked up, her eyes burning into him, into his very soul.

'Kill him!' she growled.

Waylian looked at Bram, who seemed to be recovering from the poisonous dust. His face was burned, his flesh peeling in places, but he was regaining some control. He stared at Waylian, then at Gelredida, seeing the Magistra lay her hands on Gerdy's chest and begin to absorb the blackness from her body, leeching the darkness from her veins. Gelredida's hands were already turning as black as the dead flesh on Gerdy's chest.

'No,' screamed Bram. 'You won't. You can't stop it!'

He rushed forward, but Waylian was already moving to intercept him. He didn't know where his courage came from, whether he was more scared of what Gelredida would do if he didn't act, or whether he knew Bram's ritual had to be stopped at all costs. Either way he leapt forward, bowling into Bram before he could speak any more foul incantations.

They went down in a heap, rolling across the platform. When they came to rest, by some miracle Waylian was on top of Bram, hands clenched around his throat. Bram only smiled as Waylian did his best to choke the life from him.

Then he gripped Waylian's belly.

It was like being stuck with hot pokers. Waylian held on for as long as he could, but the pain was too intense. He screamed in defiance, trying desperately to throttle Bram, seeing the spittle rise from his mouth, but it was no good. White hot pain was searing through his innards, and he had to pull away, to wrench himself free of Bram's grip.

He fell back, suppressing a scream of agony, and as he writhed on the ground Bram looked down at him, his face a mask of contempt.

'How does it feel to know you're going to die, Grimm?' said Bram, the black of his eyes spreading, covering what little white was left in them. His hands twisted into claws, the fingertips turning black and sharp like a hawk's talons.

This was it. This was how it was going to end.

Something hit Bram hard on the head, sending dust flying as it bounced away. Waylian looked up to see two more figures on the platform – Greencoats, one big and hulking, the other young and fearful looking – but then Waylian could hardly blame him for that.

He tried to stand, but could only flail uselessly on the ground as the two men circled Bram, who was still reeling from a rock to the head.

'Go on then,' said the smaller Greencoat.

'*You* fucking go on then,' said his tough-looking friend, eyeing Bram's claws warily.

Before either of them could act, Bram raised himself up to full height, lifting his arms above his head and screaming to the heavens before smashing them into the ground at his feet.

Waylian had enough time to register the deafening sound of the impact, before madness ensued. Cracks appeared in the platform, spreading from where Bram's fists had struck. The dais began to split, each crack widening. In a sudden conflagration of flying bricks and dust, the floor collapsed beneath them. All Waylian could hear was a cacophony, all he could see was a grey mess of rubble as he fell towards the floor of the chapel fifty feet below.

Something hit him in the face, then something struck him in the back, knocking the wind from his lungs. It took him a moment to realise he had come to rest, a pile of fallen rock sticking in his back every which way.

As the grey haze of dust began to subside he tried to move, first his arms then his legs, relief washing over him as he found that, somehow, the only injuries he had suffered were a few cuts and bruises. Even the searing pain in his gut was subsiding, and he tried to rise, keen to fill his lungs with air again.

Before he could pull himself to his feet, something smashed into his chest, knocking him back to the ground. He opened his eyes, crusty with blood and dust, and could see the malevolent face of Rembram Thule glaring down.

'You've ruined everything!' he said, his words carefully measured as though he were suppressing his rage. Waylian could only hope he'd keep suppressing it long enough for help to arrive. 'This was to be my moment of glory. My apotheosis. And you've fucked it up!'

His rage wasn't suppressed any more. Those claws were growing again, his fingers enlarging into grotesque talons like black crab pincers, nebulous streams of black mist seeping from them.

'Bram . . . wait,' was all Waylian could manage.

Pitiful, even for him.

Bram only smiled. 'The wait is over, Grimm. Time for you to go.' He reached back, ready to strike with one black-clawed hand.

This wasn't fair. This wasn't supposed to be happening. Waylian hadn't even wanted to be here. Why hadn't he stayed at home? Why hadn't he become a scribe like his uncle, or even a farmer? Nothing bad ever happened to farmers.

Waylian's rage burned within him. The injustice, the humiliation, stoked a fire in his chest. He could feel it filling him with strength, filling him with . . . power.

In that instant he spoke a word. Afterwards he would have no idea what that word was or what it meant, but it was enough. Words of power generally were.

As he spat the word from his lips, the weight was lifted from his chest. Bram was smashed backwards against the wall, shattering one of the grotesque friezes to dust and raining more rubble onto the ground.

When Waylian finally had the strength to stand he saw Bram's body stretched in the dirt. And all he could do was stare.

Had that really come from him? That power? That magick?

It looked like it had . . . and there'd been no one around to see it.

Somewhere in the Chapel of Ghouls, Waylian could hear someone calling for help.

FORTY-SIX

'It's too quiet.'

It was the fourth or fifth time Denny had said that. The lad was right of course: it *was* too quiet, and Nobul should have been all the warier for it.

He wasn't. He wasn't wary because all he could do was look at the back of Denny's head as they did their rounds through the lamp-lit streets and think about smashing it in with his fists.

You killed my son, you little cunt, and I should stove your fucking head in.

But he didn't. He didn't say a word, but he thought about it. Thought about it a lot.

Denny had picked up on it, of course; Nobul had never been one to hide his feelings and anyone with eyes could see he was brooding over something. When the lad had asked what the matter was, Nobul had just shrugged. That had been enough for Denny; he wasn't particularly inquisitive, or very bright for that matter, and when Nobul shrugged that was the end of it.

As they walked the streets the feeling only got worse. Nobul found himself gripping the sword at his side, wanting to pull it out, wanting to use it, to stab Denny right there in the street, to scream at him that he was a murdering shit – that he'd killed a defenceless boy and he had to suffer for it.

The only thing that stopped him was the knowledge it was an accident. A stupid mistake, made by a stupid bastard. Denny had said he regretted it, and Nobul had no reason to think he was lying. That was the only thing that had kept the lad alive – the fact that Denny was sorry. If he'd made light of it, made a joke . . . well, Nobul had killed men for less.

'I'm bored,' said Denny, like the child he was. 'We should head towards Eastgate. See if there's any action down there.' *Why would we go looking for trouble?* 'Nights are getting colder. It don't do to be wandering around in the cold.' *It's better than lying in the ground, dead as a doorpost.* 'There must be something going on somewhere.' *Shut up, just shut your . . .*

There was movement ahead. Nobul could see figures through the dark, hear armoured men moving along the street.

'What's th—'

'Quiet!' said Nobul, sick of Denny's constant wittering.

The figures were moving fast, and Nobul had to make a quick choice: ignore it or investigate. If only to give Denny something to occupy him, he picked the latter.

The group ahead moved with surprising speed considering some were wearing heavy armour. Nobul quickened his pace, trying to get a better idea of what he was dealing with.

A patch of light gave him the chance to get a better look.

There were four of them, two in dark armour – Raven Knights from the Tower – and two in robes, who could only have been magisters. What in the hells were they doing out at this hour, and moving with such urgency?

'What do you think?' Denny whispered. 'There's something going on, isn't there?'

Yes, it was obvious something was going on, but Nobul had no idea what. If it was the affairs of magickers then he could quite happily have left them to it, but there was something in their gait, their urgency. Something was happening.

'Should we follow them, Lincon? What should we do?'

Denny certainly wasn't helping him think. That was probably why, despite every instinct telling him to leave them to it, Nobul carried on after them.

As he followed he could see the foursome making their way towards the centre of Northgate, and Nobul knew exactly what was there – hells, everyone knew exactly what was there – the Chapel of Ghouls. The thought of where this group was heading began to worry him. Members of the Caste on their way to the Chapel could not be good.

It was with rising panic Nobul saw all four go through the open gateway, a gateway that had never been opened for as long as he could remember. Despite his fear, Nobul crossed the street after them, pausing at the gate.

Denny looked at him quizzically, grasping his sword in hand. 'Are we going in?'

Nobul stared after the group, hearing the Raven Knights in their armour making a racket as they moved towards the chapel. If they needed help surely it was the Greencoats' duty to give it. He was a protector of the city now, and if the legends about the chapel were right, they'd need all the help they could get.

With Denny at his side, Nobul crossed the threshold, following the cobbled path that ran up the knoll towards the Chapel of Ghouls. He fully expected to find the foursome standing outside it, wondering how in the hells to get in, but when he saw the massive stone door lying smashed on the ground and the entrance open he stopped again, apprehension winning out over sense of duty.

'What do we do, Lincon?' Denny asked, clearly just as spooked.

'I'm fucking thinking!' he snarled.

He hadn't meant to lash out, but Denny was doing his head in, always asking questions, always on the want. Couldn't he think for himself?

Nobul stared into the dark. He should go in after them, they might need help, they certainly looked like they were ready for trouble – Raven Knights never left the Tower of magistrates unless something was up. But something was holding him back, a dark and dirty feeling in the pit of his stomach.

It was no good, he couldn't just hang around outside all night waiting for someone to come out. With a nod to Denny he rushed inside.

They came out in a massive chamber – bigger than the Sepulchre of Crowns – and the pair of them stared in awe. Not for long, though. A shout from above pulled them both from their reverie. Nobul couldn't make out the words, but they were loud and they were angry. Denny looked just about ready to piss himself, and Nobul was almost ready to join him. This was magister business, and it was never going to be pretty work. Surely they were better left to it. Either that or he and Denny should go and get help. From the shouting above it looked like it was all kicking off.

He turned to Denny, nodding his head, his mind made up.

'All right. You go and—'

Something smashed into the ground right next to them, missing Denny by less than a yard. The lad yelped in fright, and Nobul was right ready to drop his sword and scarper.

354

It was a crumpled body, one of the Raven Knights, his limbs skewed all funny, his helmet dented in on one side, something dark and nasty seeping out of the gaps like oil.

'Fucking hells,' said Denny, staring at the body.

Whatever was up there had just killed one of the feared Raven Knights. Fucking hells was probably just about the right assessment.

Nobul stopped thinking. There was no time to go and get help now; there was just them. Whatever was going off could be all over soon and who knew how bad it would be if they did nothing. Grabbing Denny by the shoulder, Nobul bolted towards a flight of stairs that led up to the roof.

He took the staircase as quick as he could, and he was pleased that Denny, despite his obvious fears, was right behind him. As they climbed, there was a strange smell, almost overpowering them with the stink of something dead, something rotting.

Denny cursed, slowing his pace and shielding his nose and mouth in the crook of his elbow, but Nobul would not stop. His blood was up now with the prospect of violence, of murder.

Was this what he wanted? Had this been what he'd been needing all this time since Markus had died? Something to fight? Something to kill?

He'd find out soon enough.

Denny slipped behind him, cursing again, but Nobul carried on, seeing the platform above. He could hear more shouts of desperation, screams of horror, and he knew he was needed. There was also something in the atmosphere, a metallic feeling like the air before a storm, but Nobul knew this was nothing to do with the weather. He had seen magickers in action before, experienced their fell work. He knew this could only be the cloying effect of sorcery.

Nobul burst out onto the platform to a scene of chaos.

The other Raven Knight lay slumped in a heap of black armour, and Nobul didn't have to look twice to know he was a goner. A grey-haired witch was doing some kind of hoodoo on a naked girl who didn't look like she was going to be up and about any time soon.

Then there was a lad lying on the ground, didn't look much older than Markus, and standing over him . . .

Nobul almost ran away right then at witnessing that thing standing there.

It was another boy, but not like any Nobul had ever seen. His eyes were black pits in his head and his hands . . . those fucking hands . . . sharp like an eagle's talons, growing longer with every moment.

Denny almost fell right back down the staircase as he came to stand beside Nobul.

'How does it feel to know you're going to die, Grimm?' said the twisted, daemonic travesty of a boy. It was clear he was evil, and though Nobul had no idea what was going on, he was sure as shit he wasn't going to stand around and let someone be torn apart by some daemonic bastard.

Nobul picked up a chunk of rock lying loose on the ground and flung it as hard as he could. The missile smacked the black-eyed lad right on the head and, as he staggered back, Nobul and Denny moved forward, brandishing their swords. Before they could attack though, those dark eyes turned on them, furious intent written in their black depths.

'Go on then,' said Denny, urging Nobul on.

'*You* fucking go on then!' he replied, not wanting to get close enough to have a piece taken out of him by those claws.

The devil boy heaved in a breath, and for a second Nobul thought he was about to charge. He had no idea what he'd do – shit himself? run like fuck? – but no attack came. Instead, the lad lifted himself up full, raising those black claws high above his head before smashing them down.

Nobul was hit by whatever it was had been unleashed. He felt himself knocked off his feet, heard a din like thunder and took shards of stone and dust in the face.

When he came round, half the platform was missing, just smashed in, a big hole where it had been. He was the only one still on it, clinging to what remained, his green jacket now grey with the dust that hung around in a huge cloud.

'Lincon!'

He heard the shout, but at first couldn't work out where it was coming from.

'Lincon, help!'

He stood gingerly, looking around in a daze, then glanced over the torn lip of the platform.

There was Denny, clinging on to a bit of masonry, dangling fifty feet above the floor of the Chapel.

'Lincon, I can't get up,' he said, tears welling in his eyes, voice all desperate.

Nobul made to reach down, to grab Denny's wrist and pull him up to safety, when he stopped.

In that instant he wondered if Markus had tears in his eyes when he'd been bleeding to death on that roof. Wondered whether he'd had time to cry out, all desperate like.

'Lincon?' said Denny. 'Lincon, help me. I'm slipping.'

He could see Denny's grip was loosening. It would have been so easy to reach out and . . .

Save the bastard that killed your son? Is that what you're made of now, Nobul Jacks? You used to be feared. You used to have men shitting in their britches and now you're going to show mercy?

Nobul turned. He could hear Denny crying out, could hear him panicking as he hung there, the desperation in his voice.

Fuck him.

Nobul moved towards the stairway, ready to walk away, ready to leave that bastard to his fate.

You're a hard one and no mistake, Nobul Jacks. Tough as they come and twice as evil. Leave a lad hanging like that, leave him alone in his last moments. Yeah, you're the toughest. No wonder you had such a reputation.

No! That wasn't him! He wasn't . . . evil.

He turned, scrabbling his way back up to the platform, lurching over the edge, ready to grab Denny and pull him back up.

But Denny wasn't there.

Nobul could just see him through the dust, laid out on his back on the floor far below.

Bloody Denny! The lad hadn't made a fucking sound. Hadn't cried out. Hadn't let him know he was falling.

Nobul raced down the stairs.

Stupid boy. What was he doing on that roof in the first place? He should have been at home where he was safe.

There was blind panic inside him now, knotting his stomach as he stumbled to the bottom. When he got there he saw the young lad in robes was helping the old woman to her feet.

Nobul ignored them. Denny was lying in the rubble, not moving, but his eyes were open, looking up like he was enjoying the clouds going by.

But there weren't no clouds to see.

Nobul knelt beside him.

'You're all right, lad,' he said. 'You're gonna be all right. Nobul's here.'

A sob escaped him. He hadn't sobbed for years, and something in him tried to hold it back, but that just made it worse.

'I'm sorry. I shouldn't have left you. You shouldn't have been alone.' The words were strangled, throttled by anger.

Anger at the world.

Anger at himself.

'I didn't mean it. I didn't mean anything I said.' He grabbed the boy now, pulling him into a tight embrace, squeezing him hard, not ever wanting to let go. 'But it'll all be fine. It'll all be okay, you'll see. We'll go back home and see your mam and we'll all be together. It'll be just like it was.'

He couldn't hold it in any more. All the pain and all the grief, held inside by so much rage and loathing. It all came out then, and Nobul Jacks didn't care if anyone saw.

And in the Chapel of Ghouls he held the boy close and wept till he was dry.

FORTY-SEVEN

The vast stone stairway that led up to the Temple of Autumn was flanked on either side by towering granite braziers. They were constantly lit, day and night, there to guide the beggars and the sick to the great temple gates that they might be given succour.

Kaira was thankful that there were no such almsmen here tonight. Thankful that there was no one here to bear witness to her slinking back into the temple like a thief.

Where else would she go, though? She had failed in her mission. After slaughtering the slavers and freeing those in bondage, there was no way she would be received back into the Guild.

She was most likely marked for death, but had no fear of that. Something else troubled her.

All her life she had been drilled in piety, duty, honour. In recent days she had learned that even the basest person could learn to do the right thing. Merrick had thrown off his ignoble past, had acted heroically, and Kaira had helped prompt this. Was it right, then, that she should turn her back on him, on others like him in the city, and return to the Temple of Autumn?

She made her way up the stairs, seeing the gate come into view before her, its outline seeming ominous in the flickering light. As though she were expected, the gate opened at her approach, revealing the great courtyard within.

Kaira had been anticipating no reception, had wanted no greeting, but there were figures awaiting her: Shieldmaidens in armour, standing in disciplined ranks.

So this was how it would be. She was to be publicly admonished.

359

She had at least been allowed to leave the Temple in furtive shame, but now on her return she was to be rebuked before her sisters.

For a fleeting moment she thought about going back down the stairs, of turning her back on the temple forever. But Kaira Stormfall had not been bred to turn and run. She had been bred to face adversity head on, to take the fight to her enemies.

Kaira steeled herself and strode through the gates.

The Exalted stood front and centre, flanked by her Shieldmaidens. Kaira could see Samina, her sister in all but blood, at the front of that rank, her features impassive, her body as a statue, bearing shield and spear in the image of Vorena, whose likeness looked down on them all.

Kaira glanced up at that statue a hundred feet above them and wondered if she had truly shamed Vorena's name. Despite the failure of her mission it didn't feel as though she had. It felt as though she had fought to the end, despite the odds being stacked against her. Surely no more could be asked of any Shieldmaiden?

She stopped before the Exalted, whose face was encased in a full helm, her body garbed in golden plate and her seven-foot spear gripped in a gauntleted fist.

There was no need for Kaira to kneel: she was a Shieldmaiden no longer; and so she simply stood and waited.

And then the Exalted proffered her a nod. It was a simple gesture, almost casual, but heavy with import. It meant some kind of acceptance; it meant she was not an outcast, a pariah.

The Exalted stepped aside, and the ranks of Shieldmaidens behind her moved without a word, forming a corridor for Kaira to walk through. She took a step forward, looking at Samina, who smiled beneath her halfhelm and offered that same nod of acceptance. As Kaira made her way along the corridor of Shieldmaidens each one acknowledged her similarly, each one honouring her.

This was the last thing Kaira had expected. For a fleeting moment she allowed herself hope, to think that perhaps she might be accepted back into the fold, that her name, her warrior's name, might be returned to her.

Kaira could now see Daedla waiting for her at the temple door. The feeling of elation she had permitted herself suddenly disappeared like a feather on the wind.

'Greetings, Kaira,' said the stooped priestess.

Kaira was quick to notice Daedla had left out her ceremonial title. It was not to be returned to her after all.

'Daedla,' Kaira acknowledged with a nod.

'The Matron Mother awaits you.'

Daedla turned and entered the temple, and Kaira followed.

As they made their way through the corridors and anterooms, Kaira realised she had not missed this place. She had grown used to the city streets of Steelhaven, and despite its scum and its filth, had felt a freedom she'd never experienced here. Her birthplace felt cold, sterile and unlived in. Did she even belong in the Temple of Autumn any more?

The Matron Mother was waiting in her chamber, her head, as always, bowed over her desk, feather quill scratching at a piece of vellum parchment.

Kaira walked forward and stood to attention. It seemed the proper thing to do.

When the Matron Mother had finished she placed her quill in its pot and sprinkled a fine cloud of pounce over the script. Then she looked up, her features inscrutable.

Kaira waited. There was no indignity that could be worse than had already been inflicted.

'Please, sit,' said the Matron Mother, gesturing to the rigid wooden chair opposite her own.

As Kaira eased herself into the seat, she felt oppressed by the place – the rigidity, the discipline, the weight of duty. Out in the city, even with the importance of her mission affecting her every action, Kaira had never felt such pressure. Only in this place, within these walls, did she feel this way . . . like a child.

'Your mission,' said the Matron Mother, reclining in her seat. 'It was a success?'

Kaira found it curious that she would ask such a question. By now she must know the outcome. Buttercup would have told her of the Guild's fury, of the slavers' massacre, of the freed slaves. What need for such a question?

'You know it was not,' Kaira replied, in no mood for games. 'I failed. The Guild will by now know I was a spy. And even if they don't suspect me as an agent of the Temple of Autumn, they will still wish me dead after what I did at the docks.'

The Matron Mother nodded. 'Of course, but was it a success?'

Kaira felt anger rising; she had not returned to be mocked, to be scorned by this old woman. She almost stood to rail in anger at the ceiling, but she managed to hold the fury in.

'I saved scores of people,' she said, not trying to hide her annoyance. 'But for my actions they would have been condemned to lives in bondage. Families would have been split asunder. Children would have been . . .'

Kaira stopped. She didn't want to go any further; the thought of what might have happened to those innocents overwhelmed her.

Besides, she realised, she had raised her voice in the presence of the Matron Mother. Even though she was no longer a Shieldmaiden, this shamed her into silence.

The Matron Mother gave her an appraising look. Then she nodded. 'So it was indeed a success.'

'What?' Kaira struggled to understand the Matron Mother's reaction. 'That was not my mission. My mission was to infiltrate the Guild and eliminate its leaders. I failed in that.'

'But you succeeded elsewhere. As you say, scores were freed from bondage. The wicked were punished for their sins. You have acted as the spear hand of Vorena, and for that you must be rewarded.'

'I don't understand.'

The Matron Mother smiled. 'No, my child. But then you do not have to understand. Merely obey.'

Kaira suddenly felt a stab of shame, but that was what this old woman did to her – shamed her, belittled her. All Kaira had ever done was serve this place, all she had ever done was carry out the bidding of others, and how had she been rewarded?

'You have done well, Kaira Stormfall. And so we shall return things to as they were before your . . . indiscretion.'

For a moment Kaira thought she had misheard.

'My standing as a Shieldmaiden?'

'Will be returned to you with full honours.'

Kaira felt dizzy, nausea almost overwhelming her. For a brief moment, a frivolous moment, Kaira almost accepted, almost laughed with joy – but then she looked around the bare room, its austerity, its cloistered confines.

'No,' she said.

The Matron Mother looked confused. 'What do you mean, "no"?'

It was madness. What was she doing? She was being given everything she wanted, everything she had yearned for, and was now turning her back on it. But something inside told her this was the right thing to do. Something inside knew that deep within this temple beat a corrupted heart. If the High Abbot's behaviour hadn't told her that so many days ago, then the Matron Mother's arrogance certainly did now.

'I am yours to use no longer.' Kaira stood, towering over the old woman. 'I will serve you no longer. I am a servant of Vorena, but I can enact her will without this temple, and without you.'

The Matron Mother shook her head in disbelief. 'We live to serve,' she said. '*You* live to serve, Kaira Stormfall. Would you so readily turn your back on your home . . . your sisters?'

The feeling of sickness did not dissipate, but Kaira's head was suddenly clear. She was not turning her back on her sisters, but opening her arms to the city. There was nothing left for her here. She could never go back to how things were.

'I cannot ignore the plight of this city. Or its people. And that is why I must refuse you.'

With that she turned, not waiting to be dismissed, and made her way out of the temple.

Kaira had thought her name and position were all she'd wanted. Thought they were something to be proud of, but it had all been hollow. She would praise Arlor, be an example of Vorena's might, but not by serving under this authority. An authority that would use her in its games; make her believe she was deserving of shame.

As she made her way out into the courtyard her sisters still awaited her. Perhaps they had been expecting her back in her armour of office, perhaps they had thought she would be accompanied by the Matron Mother, but when Kaira appeared alone in her drab attire they looked to one another questioningly.

Kaira strode across the courtyard, past the Exalted who took a step towards her, but stopped when Kaira gave her no acknowledgment. Past Samina, who looked on with sorrow at her sister.

She was done with this place, done with its cloistral ways. There were those who needed her in the city, and she would offer them that help on her own terms.

And as she made her way down the wide stone stairs, flanked by the beacon flames on either side, she realised exactly who would need her help first.

FORTY-EIGHT

He would have taken a ship, would have fled far across the oceans where no one would ever find him, but he had no coin for passage. Of course he'd had plenty of coin right there in his hands. More than he could have ever spent, at least this year, but *someone* had given all that away. Merrick couldn't even begin to express how fucking annoying that was, how much that fact vexed him. So instead of trying to find the words he was trying to hide himself inside a bottle of dubious spirits. The barkeep had told him where it was from and what it was called, but Merrick didn't care. He just wanted to get blind drunk, and from the taste of whatever was in the bottle, that wouldn't take very long.

Of course, he could have left the city northwards, but where would he have gone? There was a marauding army on its way south, refugees wandering the provinces, and he had no friends anywhere but here. Not that he had many friends here, either.

Well . . . *any* friends for that matter.

Even if he'd had friends, how would they have hidden him from the long arm of the Guild? He could have gone anywhere in the Free States, visited any of its cities and towns and backwaters, and it still wouldn't have been far enough.

And so Merrick sat in a dockside alehouse, trying his best to persuade himself that the stink of fish and sweaty sailors wasn't giving him a headache.

As he tried to drink away the inevitable, the door to the alehouse opened as it had done a dozen times already, and he stiffened as he had done on each of those dozen occasions. It was just another seaman, though, skin tanned, arms painted in faded tattoos. It wasn't one of the Guild's assassins come to cut his throat and watch him choke on his own blood.

There was still time to run, time to make his break, but nowhere would be far enough. It was just a matter of time. Why not waste the last moments he had left on foreign spirits . . . at least for as long as he could afford them.

He fished in his purse and pulled the remaining coins from within, opening his fist and letting them drop onto the table in front of him.

Six coppers. Wouldn't last long, but then he didn't have long left. What would that get him, maybe another two bottles? It would be enough to make him pass out, that was for sure. With any luck he'd never wake up again, and then he could avoid the whole messy event of drowning in his own blood.

The door opened again, and he looked up, not even bothering to reach for the sword at his side. It had served him well against Bolo and his men, but it would do him no good now. Sure, he could kill any lone assassin sent to do him mischief, but this was the Guild; there were always more assassins. Eventually they'd send one good enough to do the job right.

A young lad walked in, wooden tray in hand, selling cockles in vinegar.

Merrick let out a long breath. It had all seemed so right in that warehouse, sword in hand, remembering the old days. It had all come back to him so easily: parry, riposte, thrust, guard. Move with your opponent, not against him. Strike first, strike fast, strike hard, strike last.

And then there'd been that speech . . . what had he said?

'I am the shepherd,' he whispered under his breath.

What a load of shit. I am dog meat, more like.

Merrick took another sip from the glass, draining the rest of the peaty-tasting spirit. It made him grimace – cheap crap, lacking the smooth edge of the more expensive liquor he was used to. It was doing the trick, though, sending him blurry round the edges. He almost didn't care about what was going to happen.

Almost.

'Cockles, mister?'

The young lad made him jump, appearing out of nowhere with his tray. Merrick could smell fish and wondered if it was the cockles or the boy who stank the most. He looked down at the grim selection, and it did nothing to stir his appetite.

'No thanks,' he said, then noticed the little lad eyeing his remaining coins on the table. *Well . . . why not?* 'Want to earn yourself one of those?'

The lad looked at him warily, as if this was some trick, and then nodded.

Merrick slid five of the coppers to one side, leaving one in the centre of the table. 'If you can grab it before me, you can have it. If you're too slow I get a pot of cockles for free.'

There was a short pause as the boy considered the offer. He must have been able to tell Merrick was drunk and fancied his chances, because he gave a sharp nod and put his wooden tray on the floor.

'Right,' said Merrick, flexing his fingers. 'On the count of—'

Before he had time to begin his count, the lad's hand shot out and swiped the coin off the table.

Merrick looked at the empty spot for a brief moment, before he started to laugh.

He couldn't really argue with that, could he?

'Is giving money away becoming a habit, Ryder? Perhaps there's hope for you after all.'

Merrick almost jumped out of his skin. He hadn't heard her enter the tavern, and she'd managed to walk right up to him without him even noticing.

Kaira nodded at the boy to be on his way, and he quickly picked up his tray of cockles and scampered off before anyone could take his winnings from him. When he'd gone she sat in the seat opposite Merrick, and he looked her over for a second: those broad shoulders, that chiselled look to her attractive face. Despite everything, despite her having condemned him to certain doom, he couldn't help but admire her.

'Come to gloat, have you?' he asked. *What other reason could there be?*

'You don't know me very well at all, do you, Merrick?'

'I know you well enough.'

But did he? Fact was he hadn't known her even slightly. Hadn't known how she could fight. Hadn't known the goodness in her heart. Merrick had been ready to run with that money and leave those people destitute. Setting them free was enough. Not for her. She simply gave the money away without a second thought for the consequences. Deep down Merrick knew it had been the right thing to do, but the side of him that wanted to stay alive couldn't help but think he'd made a shit choice.

'There's the rest of my fortune,' he said with a smile, waving at the five coppers left on the table. 'Feel free to help yourself. I'm sure there's someone more deserving. I'm going to be pigswill before the day's out, anyway. May as well take it and be off.'

'I am in as much danger as you, Merrick.'

That made him laugh out loud, long and disdainful. 'Don't talk rot. Just go back to your temple. They'll take you in, that's what they do. They're hardly going to see you out on the street when there are killers on your trail.'

Now it was Kaira's turn to laugh. 'I have already returned to my temple. And I have left that place behind me. So you see, Merrick, we are in this mess together now.'

As much as he resented her for giving away his money, the prospect of having her watching his back did appeal.

'What do you mean, left it behind?'

'There is nothing there for me now. It is not the place I thought it was.'

'Really? So now you think we're kindred souls, cast out amongst the rabble with only each other for protection? Are you mad? People are coming to kill us. Hard bastards, without mercy. People who will take great pleasure in watching us suffer before we die.'

'Then perhaps we should kill them first.'

There was steel in her voice, and in her eyes. For a moment Merrick liked the idea – the prospect of sticking it to the Guild before they stuck it to him was like sweet wine on his lips. He knew it was stupid. They'd get you eventually. There was no way this would end well for either of them.

'We'd need an army,' he said

'No,' said Kaira. 'The Guild does not have an army. We would only need the right warriors to stand by our side. Warriors as feared and determined as the Guild itself.'

'But there aren't . . .'

He'd been about to say there was no one as feared as the Guild. No one as powerful and ruthless. Certainly no one that he knew of.

But actually, there was . . .

'Come with me.' Merrick rose unsteadily to his feet, leaving the five copper pennies on the table and staggering from the tavern as fast as he could with Kaira at his heels.

He made his way through the streets, keeping a wary eye out for someone, anyone, who might come at him from the crowds. It would only take one man with a knife and that would be the end of it.

That couldn't happen now, not when he was so close.

Only when he reached the Crown District did he allow himself to relax. Only when he saw the palace barracks up ahead, did he begin to breathe that bit more easily.

Garret was sitting at the same table he'd been at last time. Sipping tea in the middle of the drill yard as if he didn't have a care in the world. One of the Sentinels told the captain he had company, and he turned around to see Merrick and Kaira waiting there breathlessly.

'Didn't expect to see you so soon, Ryder,' he said.

'I didn't expect to be back so soon,' Merrick replied, slipping into the chair opposite him. Kaira stood to one side as though she were a guard on duty. Merrick only hoped Garret would be impressed by that.

The captain took a sip from his porcelain cup with the blue bird painted on the side, then said, 'Have you reconsidered my offer?'

Right to business. Merrick liked this already. 'I have. I think it's about time I took on some responsibility.'

Garret smirked humourlessly. 'You'll have that all right. King Cael gone to the Halls of Arlor, assassins trying to murder the princess, Khurtas heading for the city. We're up against it and no mistake. The Sentinels will be called upon to defend the city walls and everyone in it over the coming weeks. Chances are we'll lose more than a few. Maybe worse than that. You ready to face your end head on, lad?'

It was better than the alternative. At least in the Sentinels he'd have a fighting chance. Up against the Guild he had no chance at all.

'I'm ready. If you'll have me.'

Garret's humourless smirk turned to a genuine smile. 'You know I will, lad. I owe your father that. But what about your friend?'

Merrick glanced to Kaira, who still hadn't moved. 'Oh, she can handle herself. I can vouch for her.'

Garret thought on that. 'I'm sure you can, but I'll need a better demonstration than your word, young Merrick. It wouldn't be the first time you'd tried to fool me, would it?'

Merrick had to admit, it wouldn't. 'Feel free to try her out. I'd wager her sword arm against any of your men. Even give you two to one.'

'Two to one? I'll take those odds.' Garret turned to the two Sentinels standing watch from the archway. 'Waldin! Statton! Practice swords!'

As his men gathered their wooden weapons, Garret picked up his dainty table and moved it to one side of the drill yard. His men returned quickly bearing their wooden wasters, with a spare for Kaira.

Merrick nodded at her as she took up her sword and was pleased when she offered him a wink back.

'Begin when you're ready,' said Garret, as his men took up a defensive stance. Kaira just stood and waited for their attack. 'Waldin and Statton are two of my best,' he whispered to Merrick. 'This'll be easy money, lad.'

'Aye, easy money,' Merrick replied.

Damn right it would be.

FORTY-NINE

Rag's feet were like two lumps of meat on the end of her ankles. She'd been walking round for a day and a night but all these streets looked the same, all these warehouses had the same brickwork and slate roofs and big wooden doors. It was like she'd been walking round in circles.

When first she ran from the Greencoats' barracks she'd been elated, couldn't wait to get back to that bloke from the Guild and show him what she'd got. Now she just wanted shut of it in case the Greencoats caught up with her.

She was too stubborn to just ditch it. Rag hadn't been through all this to throw everything away now. She was gonna hold on to that head until she found the right place or the Greencoats caught her, and that was just the way of it.

Rag had always been good at hiding in plain sight. She could probably have walked right up to the palace wearing King Cael's rotting head as a hat and no one would have noticed, so wandering the streets with a bundle under her arm hadn't garnered much attention. For the first time in a while, Rag was glad that no one gave a damn about her.

She was about ready to sit down and give up, walking down one abandoned road for what she thought must have been the umpteenth time, when she realised one of the vast wooden doors was ajar.

Rag glanced up and down the street, sure it was familiar. Dusk was fast approaching and even if this was the spot, would there be anyone still inside?

There was only one way to find out.

Rag peered in, pressing her face to the darkness. She couldn't see more than two feet in front of her, but there was a sound coming from inside, a soft purring sound like the biggest cat she'd ever come across had fallen asleep.

This weren't no time for trepidation. If she was gonna get what she wanted, if this was all gonna be worth the pain and hassle and blood and gore, she'd have to walk in like she meant it. No pissing about.

She grabbed the door and pulled it to one side. It protested noisily, rusty hinges squealing as its big bulk moved aside, shedding light on the interior of the warehouse and the dusty floorboards within.

Bloodstains on the wood, smear marks where someone had been dragged off.

This was the place, all right.

Rag stepped inside, following the telltale sound of snoring until she found him. He was lying on his back, hands crossed over his fat gut, leg dangling idly over the side of an old wooden crate. She didn't recognise him as one of the thugs from the other night, but she had to take a chance. He had to be one of the Guild's men. Why would he be here otherwise? He didn't look like a vagabond sleeping rough; his clothes were too clean and it didn't look like he'd skipped any meals recently.

Now, what was that bloke's name? It had been mentioned more than once the other night but she'd been so scared she'd hardly taken any notice.

'I want to see Friedrik!' she demanded, her voice echoing through the abandoned warehouse.

The man on the crate sat up like he'd been stabbed in the arse, hand reaching instinctively to the dagger at his belt.

'What? Who the fuck are you?'

They stared at one another, he with a bewildered expression, her forcing a look of determination onto her face.

'I said, "I want to see Friedrik." You're one of his boys, ain't you?'

The man nodded. Then shook his head. Then just looked confused.

'What do you want with Friedrik?' he asked, still sitting on the crate, obviously not feeling in the slightest bit threatened, even though if she'd felt like it she could have slit his throat while he slept.

'I was here the other night, remember? I have what he asked for.'

Recognition slowly dawned on the bloke's face, then he smiled. 'You're that little thief what helped kill the merchant. You best be off, lass. If Friedrik catches you he'll cut your ears off for the laughs.'

371

'We had a deal,' she said. 'I've come to claim on it.'

'Look, girl.' He was serious now, like Rag was starting to get on his nerves. 'Piss off. I'm not summoning Friedrik here for some urchin who's got too big for her boots.' He glanced down at Rag's bare feet. 'And you haven't even got any fucking boots. On your way, I've got sleep to catch up on.'

With that he lay back down on the crate.

Rag had just about had her fill of talking.

She walked forward, unwrapping Krupps' head from the blanket that was now mostly congealed to the dead flesh. With that, she plonked it on the fella's lap.

'What the fu . . .' he managed to say, before he saw the beaten and mashed face of Krupps staring up from his crotch and his words turned into a scream. With the back of his hand he swiped the head off him like it was about to bite his cock off.

'Hells, what are you doing?'

'I told you,' said Rag, keeping her calm as best she could. 'Me and Friedrik had a deal. Now go and bloody get him.'

He looked down at that head, which stared up blankly from battered eyelids, then back at Rag. Without a word he lowered himself down from the crate, careful to avoid the head like it was a snarling dog, not taking his eyes off it as he walked past, then rushed from the warehouse.

Rag had no idea if he was coming back, but she thought it was probably best to wait. What else could she do?

She picked up Krupps and placed him gently on top of the crate, then sat down next to him, feeling the fatigue of the past few days begin to settle on her like a sack of turnips.

As she waited she thought about her roof at the Bull. About Chirpy and Migs and Tidge. Even Fender. And she thought about Markus – about how if he hadn't ended up dead she probably wouldn't have been here, sitting on a crate in a dark warehouse with a severed head, waiting for a crime lord to come and see her.

The thought made her snigger, all alone in the dark.

'Who'd have thought it, eh?' she asked.

Krupps didn't answer. He was starting to whiff a bit, and was getting interest from a few flies, but it wasn't the worst thing she'd had to put up with over the past few days, so she didn't hold it against him none.

'They say talking to yourself is the first sign of madness.'

Rag almost screamed, but managed to hold it in as the curly-haired man she knew as Friedrik entered the warehouse. He was flanked by two burly-looking thugs. The man she'd found dozing on the crate skulked behind them, as though he was scared of something.

Friedrik looked at her, then the head, then back at her again. 'Apparently we had a deal? Remind me again?'

Rag eased herself off the crate. She knew this was an important moment – one of those times that shapes how the rest of your life's gonna turn out – so she fixed him with her best stare.

'You said if one of us brought you the heads of the others we could join the Guild.'

Friedrik gave her a sideways glance. 'Is that what I said? Are you sure?' He looked to the men at either side of him. One Rag recognised as the man who'd killed Coles with a cudgel.

They both just shrugged.

'No, I don't remember saying that,' said Friedrik.

Rag felt panic grip her stomach. It wasn't like she hadn't been swindled before, hadn't been treated like a prat, but this was just a piss-take too far.

'Yes, you fucking did! You said it right here, not more than two days since.' She instantly wondered if she'd gone too far.

When Friedrik smiled, she relaxed a bit, but then a smile from the bastard who ran the Guild could mean anything.

It might mean he was gonna cut her tongue out.

He strolled forward, looking at Krupps' head. 'Mmm, now you mention it, I do remember saying something like that. Don't remember this fellow, though, but then he's clearly not as handsome as he once was. What do you reckon, lads?' His thugs laughed; a forced laugh at a shit joke. 'Yes, I may have opened a vacancy, but obviously I wanted a new recruit who could work for me, hurt for me . . . kill for me. Is that you, little girl?'

Rag thought on it. A killer she weren't, but then she'd had to do a lot these past few days she thought she weren't suited to.

'I'm a pincher,' she said.

'Ah, a pickpocket. I've got plenty of those. What would I need another for?'

'Because I'm the best there is.'

Friedrik laughed at that. His men laughed at it too.

'A bold claim, little girl. How are you going to prove it?'

She could feel herself getting angry now and did her best to swallow

373

it back down. It weren't the first time she'd been duped. It weren't even the first time she'd been laughed at, but now this bastard was just taking liberties. Rag didn't make claims lightly. She was the best – better than anyone this bastard had ever seen.

'That bloke there,' she said, gesturing over her shoulder at the one she'd found sleeping earlier. 'Tell him to pull his knife.'

Friedrik frowned. 'Tell him to what?'

'Pull his knife. Tell him.'

Friedrik glanced towards the man and shrugged. 'Go on then.'

Rag kept her eyes fixed on Friedrik but she could hear the man fumbling at his belt, could almost feel his panic and his embarrassment as he went for his knife, only to find it wasn't there.

'Ain't got it, has he?' she said, reaching round to the back of her britches. ''Cos I pinched it from him earlier, right in front of his fucking eyes!'

With that she darted forward, knife in hand. She'd never been any good with blades – they'd only got her in trouble before, but this wasn't like any of those times. This was for a game with the big boys, and if it took pulling a blade, then a blade was what she'd pull.

She leapt straight at Friedrik, that knife shooting forward, and she saw his face light up with panic. He tried backing off but he wasn't quick enough and she was on him like a tomcat on a rat. He staggered back under her weight as she pressed the knife to his throat.

Behind she could hear his minders rushing forward, but they wouldn't be quick enough.

'Tell 'em to fuck off, or I'll cut you open!'

In a panic Friedrik held up his arms. 'Fuck off!' he yelped at his men.

And there they were: her with a knife to his throat, and his men just looking on, not a clue what to do.

'So,' Rag said, suddenly feeling like the deck was stacked in her favour. 'About that vacancy you were gonna open in your club.'

'Yes, that vacancy. I think I remember now. A slot's just opened right up.' He was trying his best to smile, but the knife at his throat made it that much harder.

'So we've got a deal?'

'Yes. Shit yes, we've got a deal.'

Slowly she let him go. He was the ace in her deck, and removing that knife from his throat would be giving it away. It was a big chance she was taking, but sooner or later she was gonna have to trust him to keep his word.

When he was loose she could tell his men wanted to move forward, wanted to do her harm for laying a hand on him, but Friedrik just shook his head.

'Well, little girl. Looks like you've earned yourself a seat at the grown up table.'

She nodded, but didn't allow herself a smile. At least not yet.

'My name's Rag,' she said.

Friedrik looked at her and smiled. Then held out his hand.

'Welcome to the Guild, Rag.'

FIFTY

There was something different about his reflection. Was it the lines under his eyes? The cuts and bruises that marred his face and head? Did he look older somehow?

Waylian couldn't quite put his finger on it, but whatever external changes had been wrought by his experience it was nothing to the feeling inside. He'd thrown up a stream of black bile for almost a whole night and his guts felt like someone was twisting them in a mangle. Add to that the vile taste in his mouth, along with the throbbing in his jaw, and it seemed this magick business was clearly more trouble than it was worth.

He leaned in closer to the mirror, pulling the bruise-darkened flesh down below his right eye. The bloodshot veins that had stood out red and livid the day before were receding slightly. That was some small comfort at least.

Whether the mess of his face was down to that stone platform almost collapsing on him or something more sinister he couldn't tell. He knew there were consequences to tapping the Veil; all magickers had to suffer the consequences of their power, but he hadn't been expecting anything like this.

The throbbing in his jaw began to intensify, and Waylian probed with his tongue, feeling one of his back teeth. It moved as his tongue touched it, loosening the tooth in the gum, and he suddenly tasted blood.

As he stared at his reflection in the mirror he reached into his mouth, gripping the tooth tight in finger and thumb.

It came away far too easily.

There was no pain, but he felt a dull ache of loss as he dropped it into the bowl of water in front of him. He watched as the tooth sank to the bottom of the bowl and came to rest with a clink, a crimson trail effervescing in its wake.

At this rate, by the time he graduated to the Caste he'd be all gums, like some old crone.

The door to his chamber opened and in she walked. He was clearly getting used to it: he didn't jump or squeal and she hadn't even caught him playing with himself this time.

'Waylian. I need you.'

Of course she did. Obviously there was some menial work to do.

'Yes, Magistra. Be with you at once.'

He expected her to go at that point, and later to find her waiting impatiently for him at the end of some corridor, but instead she entered his room and closed the door behind her.

Suddenly he felt naked and vulnerable. He was stripped to the waist, but it was more than that. This was intimacy he hadn't bargained on.

'How are you?'

What? She'd never asked him that before. How in the hells was he supposed to answer that kind of question?

'I'm fine, Magistra.'

She glanced into the bowl where his tooth lay in the pale red water.

'Clearly you're not.'

'It's nothing. Just a . . .' *Just my bloody tooth fallen out of my head, that's all.*

'I can give you a poultice for that. The sick feeling will recede in time too. You've done very well, Waylian. You should be proud; you've shown great promise. I knew I was right about you.'

He just nodded. He'd never been good at handling praise, and coming from Gelredida it was a strange thing indeed.

The Magistra leaned in close, almost conspiratorially as though she felt awkward saying the words. 'She did not suffer, you know.'

That one came out of the blue.

Of course, he knew who she was referring to. Gerdy had died in the Chapel of Ghouls. Butchered like a piece of meat. Waylian had done his best to put it from his mind, but all he had done was lie awake at night, picturing that scene: Bram with the knife, the black wound spreading across her chest.

'I know, Magistra. It's just that . . . I don't know. I wish we could have . . .'

'Done something more? We did everything we could. You should feel no culpability. You acted with bravery. We did everything we could to save that girl. One man was responsible for her death and he has been punished, and a terrible disaster averted. For that you should be proud.'

'Yes, Magistra.'

Though he heard her words and appreciated them, he couldn't help but feel some of this had been his fault. Rembram had been his friend, and yet he hadn't seen through his façade. He hadn't spotted the signs. If he'd done that sooner, perhaps Gerdy would have lived.

'I think it best if we do not mention the manifestation of your abilities just yet, either. I may need you beside me in the coming months, and if it is known you have shown some talent you might be . . . hobbled.'

What?

'Hobbled, Magistra?'

'Yes. So let's keep this just between us.'

'As you wish, Magistra.' Though what she meant by 'hobbled' he had no idea, and wasn't too sure he wanted to find out.

'Very good. Meet me at the Crucible Chamber when you're ready.'

With that Gelredida left and, *gods*, was that another smile she gave him as she went? No, it couldn't have been. Who was he trying to fool?

He rinsed his mouth and spat out a gob of blood. Then donned his brown robe.

As Waylian made his way through the corridors, he found the sense of shame he'd felt in previous days was gone. The other students, whose gaze he had tried to avoid and whose whispered judgement he had feared, seemed to regard him in a different light. Respect, was it? Could there even be a degree of awe?

It was clear news travelled fast in the halls of the Tower.

Magistra Gelredida was waiting for him as promised in the ante-chamber to the Crucible Chamber. When he approached she gave him no scornful look, no silent rebuke. She merely strode towards the great brass doors, the iron bracelets already secured to her wrists, as the Raven Knights opened them to reveal the Archmasters waiting behind their pulpits.

As he and his mistress made their way to stand before the greatest magickers in the land, Waylian experienced little trepidation. When last he was here he had felt out of his depth, as though floundering in treacherous waters, but now he felt amongst his peers – his equals.

It was a shame they didn't feel the same.

At first nobody spoke, but it was clear Drennan Folds was waiting to pounce, winding himself up to launch his attack. His eyes – one white, one ice blue – peered down with unconcealed fury.

'Magick!' he bellowed when he could contain himself no longer. 'On the city streets! The gates to the Chapel of Ghouls left open! Our own Raven Knights murdered. You have much to answer for, Gelredida.'

She met his bluster with disdain. 'It's not like you weren't warned, Folds. All of you were warned and no one helped. Well, almost no one. If it were not for the aid of Archmaster Laius the city would by now be infested with . . . I hate to think on it.'

'You were party to this, Nero?' Folds turned his anger on the man to his left. 'You assisted in this madness?'

Laius could only shrug his assent.

'Archmaster Laius saw the good sense of aiding me,' said Gelredida. 'And I left him little choice. If you must rail at someone, Drennan, rail at me.'

Drennan Folds turned back to her, his face red with rage. '*Rail* at you? We should punish you severely. Practising magick on the streets like a common hedge witch. You should be—'

'Be careful, Drennan,' she said. 'Just be careful.'

Waylian expected that comment to enrage the Archmaster further, but Gelredida's veiled threat served to take some of the wind from his sails.

Hoylen Crabbe leaned forward. 'I think Archmaster Folds is merely showing his frustration. These are testing times for us all, Magistra. I'm sure we will need to take this matter no further. Despite the reckless manner in which it was done, a potential catastrophe has been averted, after all.'

Drennan Folds looked furious at that, but he held his tongue.

'And what of the catastrophe to come?' Gelredida asked. 'What has the Crucible decided regarding Amon Tugha's impending invasion?'

It seemed none of them wanted to give an answer. It was down to the venerable figure of Crannock Marghil to reply.

'We cannot act against the Elharim. The power needed to withstand that invading army would come at too high a price. We all know the cost of Bakhaus Gate; a debt so large cannot be paid again.'

Bakhaus Gate? What did this have to do with Bakhaus Gate? What cost?

Gelredida took a step forward. Waylian could see the frustration in her face, her jaw working hard as her teeth ground together.

'It has never been proved that the Sweet Canker was our price for

Bakhaus Gate. There is no way we can know that. And if we do not act on this, the Free States will suffer more than a mere plague. We will suffer annihilation.'

'We don't know that,' said Lucen Kalvor, his sharp features looking more imperious than usual. 'The Khurtas might be pillaging the north, but they are led by an Elharim. The people of the Riverlands are civilised. They can be bargained with. This Amon Tugha would not set the Free States afire just to watch it burn. It is clear he wants something more than to simply raze the city to the ground.'

'And if you grant him too much credit?' Gelredida asked. 'If you are over optimistic about his motives? What then?'

'The decision has been made,' said Crannock. 'We cannot do anything.'

Gelredida balled her fists. 'Cannot or will not? You are all fools! Blind fools!' she bellowed. Waylian almost took a step back, such was her fury.

None of the Archmasters dared to speak after that.

The Magistra turned and left them behind their pulpits, and Waylian was quick to follow. He could hear his mistress muttering and cursing under her breath even as the Raven Knights removed the iron bracelets from her wrists, even as she made her way back through the corridors of the Tower.

He had so many questions, particularly about what they had meant when talking of Bakhaus Gate and the Sweet Canker and how those two things were linked, but despite his desire for answers, it was clear the Magistra was in no mood to enlighten him.

When she reached the staircase that led up to her private chamber, Waylian paused. It was her inner sanctum. Clearly she needed to be alone with her thoughts.

'Grimm, with me!' she ordered as she climbed the spiral stairs.

With not a little trepidation he followed her. She had been alone in his chamber and now he was to be alone in hers. These were uncharted waters, and Waylian could only see choppy seas ahead.

He wasn't sure what he'd been expecting when he entered, but it certainly hadn't been such a plain and austere room. When he'd first come to the Tower, rumours of what the Red Witch kept in her chambers were rife. Familiars and homunculi were said to dwell in the rafters, taunting the caged boggits and hobs that lined the walls. Potions were said to bubble in their cauldrons day and night, waiting to be bottled in myriad vials and secreted on spider-webbed shelves.

The truth was very different.

Gelredida's chamber was large and spacious, illuminated by a single round window. The furniture was crafted from a light wood, most likely elm, rather than the brooding dark oak found in the rest of the Tower. There was also a pleasant smell of lavender pervading the air.

Waylian had little time to admire the décor though, as Gelredida grasped a piece of parchment from a shelf and sat at her desk. As she continued to chunter to herself about 'idiots' and 'short-sighted fools' she went to work on the parchment with quill and ink. Waylian couldn't see what she was writing but her delicate script was a wonder to behold. For the first time he noticed she was wearing cloth gloves that matched the colour of her robes and he found it curious, since she'd never worn gloves before.

'Can you ride, Waylian?' she asked, not taking her eyes from the parchment.

'Erm . . .'

'You can or you can't. Which is it?'

It was true he'd ridden a horse to Steelhaven from Ankavern, but it had been the first time, and one of the least pleasant experiences of his short life.

'Yes, Magistra.'

'Good. Gather what clothing you have suitable for the road. You're going on a trip.'

'Where are we going, Magistra?'

'I said *you're* going on a trip. I have things that require my attention here.'

Gelredida finished the letter with a flourish and stood, moving to a tall shelf. She knelt beside it, fishing at the bottom until a secret compartment popped open with a quiet click. Inside were wax and seal, and Gelredida proceeded to melt the edge of the black stick of wax on the fat, white candle that burned on her desk.

'Roll the letter,' she ordered, and Waylian obeyed, rolling the parchment as tightly as he could.

With one hand she sealed the letter shut with a blob of wax, then pressed the bronze seal down into it with the other.

With that done she fixed him with a grave expression. There was no admonishment there; her look was stern, but Waylian could sense no anger.

'You will take this to Silverwall. There is a small academy there, mostly scribes and artisans. There you will find a tutor named Crozius Bowe.

Show him this.' She brandished the sealed parchment. 'He will tell you where to go next.'

Waylian glanced down at the letter and at the seal pressed into the wax. It was in the shape of a wyvern rising, wings open, head rearing and ready to strike.

'Magistra, I don't understand.'

'This city needs aid, Waylian. You are to deliver a message of entreaty to the only people we can rely on to deliver that aid.'

'But what if they don't come?'

She smiled, her eyes gazing towards her single, round window.

'They will come, Waylian. They always do. Now, are you ready for your journey?'

'Yes, Magistra,' he said.

Waylian wasn't ready, though. He felt scared and useless and ill prepared.

But he supposed only time would tell just how ill prepared he really was.

FIFTY-ONE

There had been one hundred and twenty-six coronations in Steelhaven's history. Governess Nordaine had tutored Janessa in the significant kings and queens of old, from the days of the Sword Kings, when the Teutonians had been but a few disparate warring tribes, right up to the establishment of the Free States. Of course, until her father had united the provinces and the city states as one nation there had still been wars and pretenders to the Teutonian throne, but the city of Steelhaven had always had a ruling monarch – a king or queen who presided over the city and its people.

Now it was Janessa's turn. Soon, she would become Queen of Steelhaven and the Free States, but right now all she wanted to do was stop shaking.

She wore a fabulous gown too, as gowns went. The Governess had helped her select the fabrics, one from each of the provinces – satin from Braega, silk from Dreldun, lace from Stelmorn, linen from Ankavern and fur from Valdor. There were also brooches sewn into the cloth from each of the city states – copper bracelets on the sleeves, iron lining the girdle, silver leaf in the skirts and steel chains about the neck. Despite the mish-mash of colour and cloth it was still a beautiful design.

Nordaine fussed with the hem, as she had done a dozen times already. Janessa guessed it was more from nerves than a need to make the gown more presentable. She had fussed so much that whatever she was trying to adjust would be fixed by now or never at all.

'Enough,' Janessa said, instantly regretting it as she was forced to clamp her mouth shut lest the bile rise up from her throat.

Nordaine stopped her fussing and took a step back. Janessa could see tears in the governess's eyes and felt instant regret. She had behaved badly towards this woman, who had been like a mother to her, teaching her the proper etiquette and trying to educate her in the ways of state. Now those lessons were over and Nordaine could teach her nothing more. From now, Janessa had to learn her own lessons, make her own mistakes.

She took Nordaine's hand, and they looked at one another. The governess would have spoken, but only a single sob came out. Before Janessa could say any words of comfort, Odaka entered the vestibule.

He no longer wore the robes she was so used to seeing him in. Now he wore slate grey armour, a helm held in the crook of his arm, a curved sword at his side.

'Your grace,' he said, his features grim and unyielding as they always were. 'They are ready.'

Janessa nodded, giving her governess one last glance before walking towards the door. Two Sentinels were waiting for her, Garret himself standing further on at the archway to the great hall. He offered Janessa a reassuring smile as she left the vestibule, but it did nothing to calm her nerves.

The knights surrounded her as she came out into the King's Hall. When last she'd been here it was empty, but now the vast space was filled with people of rank from the Free States.

Janessa could see all eyes turn towards her as she made her way through the crowd. Duke Guido Kreeler of Ankavern was the first to offer her a bow as she entered. His son Bartolomeo was absent, clearly not interested in the coronation now she had declared her intention to take the crown without need of a husband.

Young Lord Cadran of Braega was next, smiling his innocent smile, surrounded by his aunts known as the Black Roses: a gaggle of haughty-looking women who coveted the boy's power and smothered him with their insincere affections.

There were the Lord Governors Tyran and Argus of Silverwall and Coppergate, standing beside one another as their city states did, no doubt using this rare meeting to plot their plots and fuel their greed.

And then there was the Baroness Isabelle and her son Leon. Of course they bowed in deference, but Leon barely made an attempt to hide the look of scorn on his face. Clearly the Magridas did not take well to being spurned.

Janessa focused ahead, not deigning to acknowledge any of them. Garret led the way and she was surrounded by her Sentinels, yet she did not feel entirely safe. She was exposed, under the scrutiny of strangers and a slave to events beyond her control. Everything she had strived to resist had come about, and there was no way back. The image of River's face, that scarred beautiful face, briefly appeared in her mind's eye but she quickly shut it out. If she thought of him, of the life they'd promised one another and would now never have, she would burst into tears. There were many gathered here who would love to see that, and there was no way she would grant them the satisfaction.

At the stone throne stood the High Abbot and the Matron Mother – the holy representatives of Arlor and Vorena. It was they who would preside over the ceremony. They who would crown her queen and defender of Arlor's faith.

As she neared the throne, the Sentinels ahead of her stopped, turning to face one another and creating a corridor of steel for her to march through. Janessa paused at the edge of it. She knew that once she walked through that guard of honour there would be no turning back: she would have to forget her past, forget her former lover. From this day on, what she would cherish would be the Free States and its people.

She glanced back for a moment. She knew she should have retained her regal air, but she couldn't help herself.

Odaka was standing behind her, blocking her escape and the way to freedom.

Did she want to take it, anyway? Did she want to run? She had almost run only days before, when River had offered her a way out.

Odaka looked at her impassively, but despite the emotionless look on his face Janessa felt that if she decided to change her mind, to turn and flee the great hall, he would do nothing to stop her.

Just the thought of that was enough to give her strength. To know that she really did have a choice made her decision that much simpler.

Janessa turned and walked the rest of the way to the throne, mounting the stairs to stand before the High Abbot and the Matron Mother. They in turn took a step towards her, he holding the sword of office, the Helsbayn, and she the crown her father had worn for thirty-two years.

Janessa knelt before the High Abbot, bowing her head as Odaka and Nordaine had instructed her.

'Janessa of the Mastragalls,' spoke the High Abbot, his voice loud and clear in the packed chamber. 'You are here to claim the crown of Steelhaven. To take your place on the throne of the Free States, to rule its lands and its people?'

'I am,' she replied, trying to express some degree of authority.

'You will be the embodiment of Arlor?' said the Matron Mother. 'Be his divine hand on earth, defend his faith and speak his word for as long as you have breath with which to utter it?'

'I will,' she said.

'You promise to keep the Crown's Peace, keeping safe the people and their lands and properties, seeking to start no wars, invade no principalities and usurp no titles under pain of Arlor's divine retribution?'

'I do,' she said.

The Matron Mother placed the steel crown on Janessa's head, its edge cold against her skin. 'Then I give you the crown, that you might rule your kingdom,' she said.

'I give you the sword, that you might defend it,' said the High Abbot, offering the sword as he and the Matron Mother both knelt before her.

Janessa stood, taking Helsbayn from his hands. It was heavy in her grip, its hilt worked with intricate gilding, the blade acid-etched with ancient runes from the days of the Sword Kings. The last time she had seen it, it had been in her father's hands as he lay on the altar awaiting interment. The memory snapped at her with cold teeth, but she bit back. This was no time to think on such things. No time to brood on the past.

This was the day she would start her reign.

She turned and held the sword aloft, seeing all eyes upon her, eyes of scorn, eyes of admiration, eyes of doubt.

Garret turned to that crowd, his Sentinels doing likewise, and bellowed, 'Queen Janessa Mastragall, Sovereign of Steelhaven and the Free States, Protector of Teutonia and Keeper of the Faith of Arlor.'

As one the assembled crowd bent its knee, repeating Garret's words in a solemn mantra. Janessa thought that many of them would find those words bitter to the taste, but that only made it that much sweeter for her.

She had done it; she had claimed her father's seat, and none of them would take it from her now. At least not while she still breathed.

As she watched them, kneeling there before her, she knew this wasn't enough. Suddenly seeing these so-called nobles in supplication was empty and hollow. She was cloistered in here, kept away from her people . . . the people that mattered.

Due to the threats to her life, Odaka had deemed it prudent to keep the ceremony within the bounds of the palace, but tradition dictated the kings and queens of Steelhaven should be received by the city's people upon their coronation.

Safety be damned. This was not just her day, not just the day for her noble subjects to receive her. She had to be seen, had to show the city that she was there for them, there to serve them unto death.

'Odaka,' she said, clutching that heavy sword to her side. 'I will see my people now.'

He frowned, a glimmer of concern flashing across his grim features, only to disappear beneath a veneer of obedience.

'As you command, my queen.'

He bowed and Janessa almost smiled at that. 'My queen.' It sounded good to her, as if she had always been waiting to hear those words.

Odaka led the Sentinels from the hall. Janessa did not even deign to look at the nobles, still on their knees, as she left the throne room. And leave it she did, a different woman from the one who had entered. She had walked into the great hall a timid girl, but left it a grown woman, and a queen to boot.

As she neared the front of the palace she could hear the crowd. They had been allowed into the Crown District, its gates flung open so that they might honour the queen's coronation.

The city had gathered to mourn her father, coming in their droves for his funeral. The sheer multitude of that thronging crowd had done nothing to prepare her for this.

Odaka flung open the doors to the front balcony of the palace which overlooked Skyhelm's grounds and the Crown District. Beyond the great steel gates they had come, rich and poor alike, beggar and merchant, soldier and serf.

All come to see her crowned.

And as she appeared, even from such a distance, the crowd acknowledged her. It was a cheer that went up over the city, shrouding it under a cloak of noise, filling her with pride and a sense of the task ahead.

As the deafening noise rang out over Steelhaven, Janessa Mastragall, Queen of Steelhaven and the Free States, only hoped the warlord Amon Tugha could hear it.

If he was coming to her city with murder in his heart then it was only fitting he should know what was waiting for him.

EPILOGUE

The town burned.

Azreal had no idea what they had called it before the flames took, licking at the buildings with rapacious greed. He was only glad he had come late enough to miss the screams of innocents as they were beaten, violated and put to the sword . . . in whatever order the Khurtas thought best.

Through eyes of gold he watched as the savages danced in the firelight. He did not begrudge them their pleasures for they lived such short lives, but he did not have to stay and watch, and he certainly would never have joined them in their sport.

Unlike Endellion, his sister in service to their master.

She was most likely down there now, already slaked of her thirst for cruelty, indulging her other lusts. The thought of it amused Azreal, but also made him envious of her. He wondered if their master would tolerate him if he decided to satisfy his own desires so often, and with such wanton callousness. It was doubtful, but then Endellion was so very beautiful, it was difficult to refuse her anything, as Azreal had discovered on many occasions.

He moved through the camp unseen. Past the fires as they burned, past the crude hide tents, past the pennants and banners won from the enemy as they fluttered wretchedly – the torn and blackened symbols of a nation on the brink of destruction.

The Teutonians would do well to surrender now and spare themselves the suffering to come, but Azreal knew they would not. They would fight on until the end, throwing their lives away needlessly as nations always did. Since the days of the first great conquerors there had always been those that would stand against them, occasionally victoriously, oftentimes ruinously.

Azreal had no doubt that on this occasion all that awaited the Free States was its ultimate doom.

Making his way past these strangers in this foreign land, Azreal only felt a yearning for home. The Riverlands were weeks to the north, with league upon league of blasted country between him and the verdant fields and waterways. The prospect of the journey filled him with dread, but he would gladly have made it in bare feet had his master willed it. Amon Tugha had other ideas though, and Azreal wondered if he would ever see the beauty of his homeland again.

At the centre of the camp was Amon Tugha's command tent. It was unadorned, a construction of wood and animal pelts with no banner or pennants of allegiance. Azreal's master held no allegiance; the outcast prince followed no crown or code but his own. The only flags that he took into battle were those he had won, those he had earned with blood and steel.

Of course the tent was guarded, though his master needed no bodyguard. Despite the sentries, Azreal slipped in without a sound, unseen by either of the guards posted at the entrance.

Inside there was welcome warmth, as Azreal's master held court. Braziers were lit, their yellow glow permeating the air, leaving enough shadows in the recesses of the vast tent for those who did not want to be seen.

And Azreal rarely wanted to be seen.

He paused for a second, observing his master's court. The Elharim prince sat on his wooden seat, a chair carved from the thrones of defeated chieftains. There had been nine tribes of the Khurtas, tribes in a perpetual state of war until the coming of Amon Tugha. He had united them – united them in blood and slaughter, challenging their war masters and their battle lords to mortal combat, and defeating them all. Those that had survived stood beside him now. Wolkan Brude, hulking, bearded savage that he was. Brulmak Tarr, a man who had mutilated his own body so far beyond recognition it was doubtful any wound inflicted on him could make his features worse. Stirgor Cairnmaker – dark, brooding and deadly, a peerless warrior who had almost been a match for Amon Tugha . . . almost.

Of the six other war chiefs there was nothing but blackened bones and ash, their tribes subsumed into one vast army. An army that now marched south to victory.

At the prince's feet sat two massive warhounds, gifts from his new tribe, vicious beasts as loyal to their master as Azreal was. They would fight for him, die for him, each attacking with a monster's strength and a warrior's cunning.

Azreal watched all this from the dark and no one was the wiser to his presence.

No one but his master.

'Step forward, Azreal, my brother.'

Silence filled the tent at Amon Tugha's words.

As Azreal walked from the dark, all eyes turned to him. When he appeared one of the hounds – Astur or Sul, Azreal could not tell which – lifted a lip in snarling challenge. A raised hand from Amon Tugha silenced his pet.

'My prince,' said Azreal, dropping to one knee and bowing his head.

He could feel the disquiet amongst his master's Khurtic generals. They thought the Elharim supernatural creatures, able to come and go at will, able to kill with nothing but a word. It was true the Elharim lived centuries longer than the lower races, but there was nothing supernatural about them. They simply took advantage of their longer lifespan to learn their craft, to hone their talents beyond the ken of the Khurtas, the Teutonians or any other tribe that chose to face them. Let these barbarians think them immortal. Let them show the deference owed the Elharim for their ancient sacrifice.

As Azreal rose he saw Amon Tugha smile.

His master was a peerless specimen. A prince of the Riverlands, cast out by his own mother, a warrior queen, lest he challenge his eldest brother for power of dominion. Yet with all his shame, all his dishonour, Azreal would still have followed his prince to the gates of the Abyss.

Amon Tugha was not his master's real name, it was a name given him by the Khurtas, one they could speak and understand and, most importantly, one they could follow. Azreal and his sister Endellion were the only ones who knew his true name, but they had been forbidden to speak it. Their master no longer bore the title given by his homeland. Those so-called nobles of the Riverlands had turned their backs to him, and he in turn had vowed to show them the folly of that decision.

When standing, Amon Tugha was almost seven feet, his naked torso marked with the ritual scarification and scorching that signified his rank.

His hair was blond and cropped to his temples; his eyes burned with flecks of gold. Despite all of Azreal's skill, despite all his talent and prowess, he knew he could never compete with the awesome strength of his master. To try would mean his end.

'What news, Azreal?' said Amon Tugha. 'Has the herald earned his pay?'

'He has, my prince, and he has now returned across the seas to his home.'

'And what of the city?'

'The magisters of Steelhaven are cowed within their tower. They will show us no resistance. The Guild has, as yet, given no answer. I believe they are still awaiting your arrival, but I would expect them to submit to your offer as soon as your warhost is in sight of Steelhaven's gates.' He paused, choosing his next words carefully. Though Amon Tugha was not so wasteful as to punish a messenger, Azreal still feared his wrath. 'The slaves intended for your allies at Keidro Bay were lost.'

'How?'

'They were freed by a renegade, my prince, but fear not. The Father of Killers was informed and has dispatched one of his sons to bring the pirate lords to heel. I am assured they will still aid us when the time comes.'

'And what of our brother? How does he fare?'

'The Father of Killers has received your instruction, but has not yet managed to fulfil his obligation. He still has an eye close to the queen. I am sure he will strike again soon.'

This last news seemed to trouble the prince and his brow furrowed as he brooded. Azreal could see it made the Khurtic generals nervous.

'This is not enough,' Amon Tugha said. 'I need her dead. Once their queen has fallen the rest will crumble around her and the city will be mine. But there is more than one way to reach her.'

Amon Tugha glanced to the shadows of the tent, to the Khurtic shaman who sat in silence consulting his knucklebones. The prince's dark mood slowly eased.

'What now, my lord?' Azreal was keen to have his instructions and be away from here. Though it shamed him, he could not shake the fact that this place, these people, disturbed him.

'Now you go and wash the stink of the streets from your body,' said Amon Tugha. 'And then we will make our way south where my city awaits.'

This brought murmurs of assent from the Khurtas, Brulmak Tarr loudest of all.

'As you wish.' And with that, Azreal left the tent.

Once outside he took a deep breath of the night air. He would have followed Amon Tugha across all the lands and seas of the world, such was his love for his prince, but he could not help but feel this was all folly.

His master was a brave man, and it was an injustice that his name and position had been destroyed, and for nothing, but this was no way to regain glory. To take the lands of another nation, to reduce its capital to ruin and slay its queen was no way to prove your worth to a land that had rejected you.

But where Amon Tugha led, Azreal would follow.

And he would bring his hordes with him.

And they would not stop until Steelhaven had fallen.

ACKNOWLEDGEMENTS

First and foremost I need to thank my agent, industry legend John Jarrold, who took me on after reading a part manuscript and showed a lot of faith where others might not.

Thanks to Gareth Hanrahan, Matt Keefe and Gav Thorpe for their various critiques and help with the manuscript, it's all the better for your input.

I should also mention the team at Headline: Patrick Insole for making the cover look sexy, my copyeditor and proofreader for making the words sexy, and Caitlin Raynor and Ben Willis for telling everyone how sexy it is.

And last, but by no means least, my editor, John Wordsworth. Remember, if I go down, you're going with me!